A WICKED PURCHASE . . .

When, at the height of the Peninsular War, she is offered on the auction block by her blackhearted husband, lovely Rachel Brady fears the worst. To her great relief, she is purchased by Lord Jacob Forrester, a rugged English officer whose life she once saved. She becomes Jake's right hand on the bloody campaign trail . . . and when fiery passion flares, his mistress. . . .

. . . COSTS A GENTLEMAN HIS HEART

Back in London, where propriety rules, Jake is faced with the incontestable impropriety of his relationship with Rachel. To save her from the scathing tongues of the gossipy *ton,* he casts her aside—never dreaming a stunning revelation will foil his plans to reclaim her with a proper offer. Now Jake must vie with viscounts and barons for the hand of a woman he once bought in a tavern . . . and convince a reluctant lady that his love is true . . . and truly forever. . . .

D1022694

Books by Wilma Counts

WILLED TO WED

MY LADY GOVERNESS

THE WILLFUL MISS WINTHROP

THE WAGERED WIFE

THE TROUBLE WITH HARRIET

MISS RICHARDSON COMES OF AGE

RULES OF MARRIAGE

Published by Zebra Books

RULES OF MARRIAGE

Wilma Counts

ZEBRA BOOKS
Kensington Publishing Corp.

http://www.kensingtonbooks.com

ZEBRA BOOKS are published by

Kensington Publishing Corp.
850 Third Avenue
New York, NY 10022

Copyright © 2002 by J. Wilma Counts

All rights reserved. No part of this book may be reproduced in any form or by any means without the prior written consent of the Publisher, excepting brief quotes used in reviews.

If you purchased this book without a cover you should be aware that this book is stolen property. It was reported as "unsold and destroyed" to the Publisher and neither the Author nor the Publisher has received any payment for this "stripped book."

All Kensington titles, imprints, and distributed lines are available at special quantity discounts for bulk purchases for sales promotion, premiums, fund-raising, educational or institutional use.

Special book excerpts or customized printings can also be created to fit specific needs. For details, write or phone the office of the Kensington Special Sales Manager: Kensington Publishing Corp., 850 Third Avenue, New York, NY 10022. Attn. Special Sales Department, Phone: 1-800-221-2647.

Zebra and the Z logo Reg. U.S. Pat. & TM Off.

First Printing: May 2002
10 9 8 7 6 5 4 3 2 1

Printed in the United States of America

This book is dedicated to the memory of
Winifred L. Casterline
who would "gladly learn and gladly teach"
and taught me to do so as well

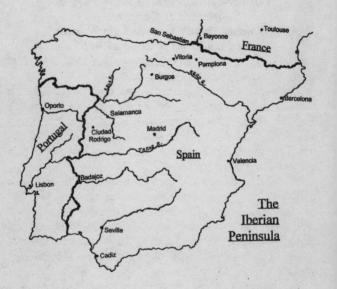

San Sebastian • Bayonne • Toulouse

France

• Vitoria • Pamplona

• Burgos

EBRO R.

• Barcelona

Oporto

Salamanca

Portugal

Ciudad Rodrigo

Madrid

TAGUS R.

Spain

Valencia

Lisbon

Badajoz

The Iberian Peninsula

Seville

• Cadiz

Prologue

Northern England, 1808

"Do you, Rachel Alison Cameron, take Edwin Michael Brady to be your lawful wedded husband . . . ?"

The minister intoned the rest of the words as Rachel stole a glance at the handsome, dark-haired man standing beside her. Mr. Brady—Edwin—had been so attentive, so charming. Still, a streak of panic coursed through her. Could this be right? Would she be blessed with a marriage as good as her parents' had been?

She glimpsed her uncle's pudgy profile on the other side of Edwin and felt her aunt's nearness at her own side. The Brocktons were the only family she had, and *they* wanted this. Had Aunt Jessie not been singing the praises of Mr. Brady—Sergeant Brady—for weeks now? He was so handsome, so charming, so kind. Rachel was such a lucky girl. And on and on.

Yes, he was certainly all of these things, but somehow she wished they had just had time to know each other more thoroughly. However, Edwin was moving on to a new posting, and her aunt urged that the marriage take place forthwith. Rachel knew very well her aunt and uncle would be glad to rid themselves of a burden they had never welcomed.

"Miss Cameron?" the minister prompted just as her aunt shoved a sharp elbow in her ribs.

Rachel jerked her attention back to the clergyman. "Oh. I . . . I . . . do."

There. She had done it. It *was* what she wanted, was it not?

Aunt Jessie had made all the arrangements for this wedding, urging that a special license be obtained so the marriage could take place in the inn rather than in church and without the three weeks' wait for reading the banns. Thus she and Edwin stood in the best parlor of The Black Swan to exchange their vows.

Like most young women, she had long dreamed of marrying and having a family—someday. The dream had always been vague—"when I grow up, I want to be . . ." And now, at seventeen, it seemed she *was* grown up. So why did she not *feel* any different? Why was she so wary of the future?

The minister droned through the last words, the ring was on her finger, and the proper papers were signed.

"Well!" Her uncle clapped Edwin on the shoulder. "Congratulations, my boy."

Aunt Jessie stooped to bestow a kiss on Rachel's cheek. "I hope you will be happy, child."

The gesture and words were the warmest the bride had ever had from her father's stepsister.

Rachel knew very well her happiness was not uppermost in her aunt's mind. Aunt Jessie had made no secret these last three years and more of the imposition she felt at being saddled with her stepbrother's orphaned daughter. After all, did she not have a daughter of her own nearly the same age?

"There ain't no way that great hulking Leah can shine next to Miss Rachel." Rachel was embarrassed when she overheard one of inn's grooms say this to a chambermaid.

"La! An' don't you be lettin' Miz Brockton hear you say such!" the maid had replied. "She fair dotes on her darlin'."

"Yeh. Well. The sooner she gets Miss Rachel outa here, the sooner any o' the gents is likely to look at 'her darlin'."

The maid had laughed, and the two drifted out of earshot. Rachel brushed a wisp of hair away from her cheek and looked at the middle-aged matron who came in once a week to help with the laundry. The two worked together on a near-freezing February morning.

"Joey's right, you know," Mrs. North said in a very matter-of-fact voice.

Rachel felt herself blushing. She held up hands raw from wringing sheets in cold water in the unheated laundry shed and indicated her faded and worn dress and scuffed shoes.

"Even if he were, I doubt I present a picture to attract a man worth having." Rachel truly believed what she was saying. "Leah is a larger person than I, but she has lovely clear skin and blond hair. She is quite handsome, I think."

Mrs. North sniffed. "And spoiled rotten by her mum. You wait. You'll do with your dark hair and big eyes."

Rachel never knew exactly why, but soon after this, her aunt decided to change her duties. Instead of laundry, kitchen, and housekeeping chores, Rachel was to wait on customers in the taproom. Moreover, she was to have a more attractive outfit to wear and tie her hair up with a pretty ribbon. She, her aunt, and Cousin Leah were in the room the two girls shared when the new clothing was presented.

"Is it not . . . uh . . . cut daringly low in front?" Rachel asked hesitantly, feeling very bold in questioning her aunt.

"Try not to be such a ninnyhammer," Aunt Jessie said, jerking the neckline on the bodice lower and tightening the midriff laces to push the girl's breasts higher. "Men like to see what they might be getting."

"But I do not—" Rachel began.

Aunt Jessie interrupted. "No argument from you now—you hear? How else do you think you'll find a husband? For all your airs, you are not some gentry lady with a dowry and all. And you cannot expect to be boarded and coddled here forever."

Rachel swallowed her anger. She knew very well that she earned her keep here. "Yes, ma'am."

Sitting on the edge of the bed the two girls shared, Leah folded her arms across her chest and pushed out her lower lip in a pout. "I don't see why you are so worried about finding her a husband. What about me? I'm your daughter. And you're doing this—giving her new clothes—just when those nice looking soldiers have come, too!"

Aunt Jessie turned immediately to soothing her daughter's ruffled feathers. She put her arm around Leah's shoulders. "There, there, pumpkin. Your day will come. And we'll find you some nice local *boy."*

"But, Mama! That Sergeant Brady looks so handsome in his regimentals," Leah wailed.

"Yes, he does." Aunt Jessie caressed Leah's cheek. "But he's not for you, sweeting. I'll not have my baby carried off to God knows where."

Rachel jerked herself back to the present, her wedding day, as Uncle Phillip poured wine and passed it around.

"A toast to my bride." Edwin Brady's blue eyes locked with her gaze. He slipped his arm around her waist, pulled her close, and gave her a quick kiss.

This erased—at least for the moment—some of her trepidation. She felt the familiar warmth of his embrace and knew everything would turn out fine. How could it not? Had Edwin not assured her repeatedly of his love, even before the subject of marriage had come up? And so what if the subject had, in fact, come up only after she adamantly refused to allow him liberties beyond a few chaste kisses?

Her uncle beamed expansively and her aunt smiled triumphantly as the party drank the toasts.

" 'Tis nearly noon, my love." Her new husband's open endearment brought a blush to Rachel's face. "If we are to reach our next posting by nightfall, we must be off."

He shook hands with her uncle and the minister and bowed graciously to her aunt and to Leah. She saw Leah blush as Edwin deliberately winked at her.

Now that the moment of parting had come, panic threatened to engulf Rachel. Here she was, going off with a stranger, leaving the comfort of the known for the doubt of the unknown. She remembered this feeling well, for it had been the same when, following her father's death, she had been sent here three years ago.

She gave herself a mental shake. There was no longer a place for her at The Black Swan. That had been clear for some time. Now she embarked on a new life with a man of easy laughter and engaging manners. They would face any obstacles together and their love would be both their strength and their reward.

Brady handed his new bride into the hired coach and climbed in himself to sit next to her. God! The chit was a beauty! Dark brown hair. Big hazel eyes. And she was all his. Could he even wait until they reached their destination to take her? But he had better force himself to do so. After all, the girl was a virgin—he was sure of that. Her kisses were not those of a woman of any experience.

He sighed at the thought of what it had taken to get her into his bed. Marriage. Then he smiled at the tacit conspiracy that had achieved this end. Her aunt and uncle had been so anxious to be rid of her that they had even parted with the blunt to pay for a special license.

He laughed inwardly as he recalled Mrs. Brockton's machinations in throwing Rachel in his path at every turn—like the time she had sent Rachel to the root cellar, knowing full well Brady would be waiting outside. That was the first time he had kissed her.

He remembered her trembling eagerness in his arms. Even now the thought of her latent passion was stirring his own physical reaction. He put his arm around her and pulled her close, using his other hand to lift her face to his. He saw a flash of apprehension in her eyes.

"Everything will be fine, my love. You'll see." He kissed her, allowing his lips to linger on hers. When he felt her response, he deepened the kiss, probing, exploring. Hesitant at first, she then acceded to his silent urgings.

Ah, yes, this would be a fine bedding indeed.

One

Spain, April 1812

Rachel awoke with a start. Uncertain what had jerked her out of a fitful slumber, she lay listening for a moment. Quiet. It was too quiet. Artillery that had boomed incessantly for hours now—and intermittently for a fortnight—had ceased its agonizing howls.

Was it over?

Had the allies succeeded in taking Badajoz?

She rose to her knees on her bed—a pallet she had laid atop a layer of straw on a dirt floor in an abandoned sheep-herder's hut. She drew back the fragment of canvas covering the single window.

Dawn.

Well, almost dawn anyway. The rosy fingers of dawn, as Homer had described it in an account of another war in another time and another place.

She shook her head as though to dismiss that fanciful thought and listened again for the sounds of war. With the big guns silent, only an occasional rifle shot announced that sporadic hostilities continued. There was a faint glow of fire in the direction of the city, but it did not appear to be a huge conflagration.

Fully awake now, she reached for her shoes, sturdy half boots that served her well. Following the drum with Lord Wellington's army was very hard on shoe leather. She stirred the fire in the stone fireplace, added a few pieces of precious fuel, and set the kettle to heat water for tea.

She heard a rustling in the loft above and a babe's whimpering. The Bradys shared these elegant quarters with another soldier and his wife and child, and considered themselves inordinately lucky not to be out in the elements, as were most others of ranks below officer status. It had been raining rather steadily ever since the siege had started on St. Patrick's Day.

"They ain't back yet?" Clara Paxton asked needlessly as she climbed down from the loft with her son astraddle one hip.

"No. I think it will be some time yet before we know anything."

"At least the cannon stopped. My Joe, he hates artillery—theirs, anyway." Clara sighed and added, "I don't suppose the supplies have come in, either. We're about outa food. How about you?" She set the toddler on his feet. He immediately plopped himself on his little bottom and began to yowl.

Rachel handed the fussy child a crust of stale, dry bread. "Not much left. A bit of cheese and some bread—and it has gone to mold. Maybe enough tea to color the water."

"At least it'll be hot." Clara offered her own remaining tea to add to the kettle.

The two couples had become acquainted when the Bradys, as part of replacement forces, had joined the 51st Foot some eight months earlier. They were of an age, and the women had gravitated toward each other. This was not the first time they had shared makeshift quarters and limited supplies.

"I'll see if I can find some vegetables or something when I go out," Rachel said. "No telling when the supplies will arrive."

"I heard they was havin' trouble with the bridge."

"I heard that, too. Storm damaged several boats. Too bad the French destroyed the old stone bridge." Rachel had watched some weeks ago as British engineers fashioned a pontoon bridge of planks laid across boats in the river. Ingenious—but not up to all that Mother Nature threw in the way. "Sometimes I truly believe the elements themselves favor the French," she muttered as she poured two steaming mugs of the brew.

They sat in companionable silence on stools at a rickety table that comprised the room's only furniture.

Clara gripped her mug in both hands to warm them. Her clear blue eyes took on a dreamy look. "Wouldn't a real English breakfast of bacon and eggs and porridge go wonderful 'bout now?"

"Don't torture yourself." Rachel finished her tea and stood.

"You going back to the hospital already? It was late when I heard you come in."

"I didn't mean to wake you."

"You didn't. I never sleep well when Joe's gone like this."

"Oh." Rachel swallowed the last of her tea. "Well, I am going now. Mac sent me home to get some sleep. He thinks we will be very busy today."

"I just hope you don't find my Joe—or Mr. Brady— among your patients," Clara worried aloud.

Rachel put her hand on her friend's shoulder. "I do, too."

She pulled her shawl over her head and stepped out into the still, damp air. She picked her way carefully to the hospital which, in this instance, was a convent outside the city walls. Because the convent had been raided repeatedly by the French and the Spanish who sided with Napoleon, there were but a few nuns in residence.

She was grateful that MacLachlan, the regiment's chief medical officer, had insisted she return to her own quarters for some much needed rest. This was sure to be a very long, very distressing day. With only the first of the wounded having arrived the evening before, it had already been apparent that allied casualties would be horrendous. She had heard two of the surgeons talking with a colonel whose broken arm they had set and bandaged. Quietly going about her business of tidying the dressing station, Rachel had listened unashamedly to their exchange.

"The order to storm the city came in something of a hurry, didn't it?" asked Lieutenant Ferguson. "I mean, after all, you've been digging trenches and putting armaments in place for two weeks. Suddenly, tonight . . ."

"Well, as I understand it, his lordship received word the French were sending reinforcements from Seville. It was vital that we take the fortress before they arrive."

"Frogs forced the Peer's hand, eh?" asked MacLachlan.

The colonel nodded. "A night attack—and in this miserable damned weather, too. Not to mention being short on supplies and decent equipment. None of these factors helped our cause. Still, our lads pushed on." The colonel ended on a note of pride.

"Our first casualties have been in rather bad straits," Ferguson said with what Rachel knew to be characteristic understatement.

The injured man ran a hand across his eyes as though to erase an unwelcome vision. "The forlorn hope," he said. "They were magnificent! The first waves were beaten back and the next ones had to trample over fallen comrades to press on."

Rachel drew in a silent, horrified breath. The *"forlorn hope"* were soldiers and officers who volunteered for such missions. Their hope of surviving was slim, but those who did were more or less guaranteed promotions.

". . . and all the while," the colonel was saying in a ragged voice, *"those infernal French were on the wall yelling obscenities and picking off our lads as though they were shooting targets at a fair."* He heaved a sigh. *"But we made it. And at least with this rain, we will not have the worry of a musket starting a fire in the field and roasting the wounded before we can get to them."*

Ferguson nodded. "If only the weather would also discourage the battlefield ghouls who manage to strip and rob the dead and wounded within minutes of their falling."

The colonel shrugged, then winced at the movement. "One of the hazards of war."

Rachel knew he spoke only the truth, but she still found her anger rising whenever she dealt with naked and near-naked wounded carried in from a battlefield. No, they were not all heroes, but everyone deserved to have basic human dignity respected.

Now, picking her way around mud puddles, she observed increased activity as she neared the convent. The wounded, some crying out in pain, were transported in squeaking peasant carts. Some staggered in under their own power, or supported by fellow soldiers, their way impeded by both other wounded and the soggy weather. Her feet kept sliding, and she dreaded having to deal with injuries encrusted with mud as well as blood. At least she would be able to do something besides sit and wait and worry about Edwin.

She recalled vividly MacLachlan's initial skepticism when she had offered her services soon after she and her husband joined the regiment. It was not unusual for women accompanying the army to perform nursing duties, but most who did so were older and hardier-looking than she was.

Captain MacLachlan, a large man with a smattering of gray in his red hair, had cast a doubting look at her rather petite frame. "What's a pretty little lass like you want with hospital work?" Despite his less than friendly demeanor, Rachel warmed to him, for there was something about him—besides his heavy Scottish accent and his being a doctor—that reminded her of her father.

The "hospital" in that case had once served as a shed for shearing sheep and storing bales of wool. There was still a faint odor of lanolin mixed with the mostly unpleasant odors associated with a military medical station on the campaign trail. Some attempt had been made to fortify the large, open barn against the elements. Still, sunlight and wind made their way through chinks in the walls. Rachel remembered MacLachlan sitting at a small table he used as a desk

*in one corner of the room. He laid his pen down and stood
to tower over her, his hands on his hips.*

*Aware of not only his doubting scrutiny, but also the lis-
tening ears of others, Rachel had taken a deep breath and
squared her shoulders before answering his question. "I
want to be of some use, sir."*

*"I'd have no trouble makin' use of that one!" a man in a
nearby bed quipped. There was some general laughter.*

*MacLachlan gave the fellow a quelling look. "In that
case, maybe you are well enough to rejoin your regiment,
O'Mara."*

O'Mara lowered his eyes and muttered incoherently.

*"That's what I thought," MacLachlan said. He turned
back to Rachel. "Now, what did you say your name is?"*

*"Mrs. Brady. Rachel Brady. My husband is Sergeant
Brady with the 51st."*

"I see . . ."

*One of the men tending the wounded hurried forward.
There was something vaguely familiar about him.*

"Mac. Could I have a word with you?" the man asked.

*MacLachlan looked surprised at the interruption, but he
excused himself to Rachel and stepped aside to confer with
him. They spoke in low tones and both men glanced at Rachel from time to time. She heard MacLachlan exclaim, "You
don't say!"*

*Finally, MacLachlan turned back to her. He gestured to
his fellow medical officer. "Mrs. Brady, this is Lieutenant
Ferguson. He's one of our best surgeons."*

*"How do you do, sir?" She dipped her knees in a polite
curtsy.*

*"You were at Portsmouth when we brought back so many
of those suffering the Walcheren fever," Ferguson said.*

*"Oh, yes. I thought you looked familiar." Rachel was
slightly embarrassed at not recognizing him immediately.*

*"Ferguson says you work well with wounded—and that
you aren't squeamish," MacLachlan said.*

"No, I am not." She hoped she sounded confident.

"He also tells me your father was Duncan Cameron. Is that true?"

Rachel glanced at Ferguson in surprise. "Why, yes, it is."

"Cameron and I studied medicine together in Edinburgh. He was a good man—and a very capable doctor." MacLachlan ran his fingers over his chin as though he were stroking a nonexistent beard. "So . . . patching up broken bodies runs in your blood, eh?"

Warmed by his comments about her beloved papa, Rachel gave him a tentative smile. "One might put it that way. I believe I may be of some help to you, at any rate."

Over the next several weeks, she had gained the respect of the entire medical staff. Even Wellington's new chief medical officer, Dr. James McGrigor, heard of the woman who could work wonders.

"Your methods are unorthodox, to say the least," McGrigor observed during a tour of regimental hospitals, "but if you were a man, you'd make a fine doctor, my girl."

Rachel gave him an arch look. "And what has one's gender to do with trying to heal a wound or an illness?"

She had just successfully treated a man who suffered a terrible burn from his shoulder to his wrist when he was caught between a horse and a hot artillery piece. The doctors and surgeons were all occupied with overwhelming numbers of far more seriously wounded at the time. She had spread a coating of honey on the burn and wrapped it tightly. A few days later, the burn was healing nicely and the man returned to his duties.

"Where'd you learn that trick?" MacLachlan asked later.

"From a woman," she replied, knowing she sounded a trifle smug. "Mrs. Addison. She lived in a cottage not far from my uncle's inn. She taught me much about herbal cures and the like."

"A midwife?"

"Among other things. Local folk came to her for all sorts of ailments. She would stitch them up, set broken bones, give them salves and potions. People and animals alike."

"That so?" He raised an eyebrow in mild interest.

"Addy had a fierce respect for life—any living thing."
Addy had been the only person who truly cared about a
scared young girl who had lost both parents and been
shipped off to indifferent and uncaring relatives. Lost for a
moment in warm memories of her friend and mentor, Rachel
chuckled softly.

Mac—he had been "Mac" since her second day—gave
her an inquiring look.

*"Once a man accused Addy of being a witch. Swore she
put a hex on his mule when it died."*

"And . . . ?" Mac prompted. *"I should think that a serious allegation in a country village."*

"The villagers ran him *out of the parish! Very possessive
of their Addy, they were."*

*"Understandable. Some of those country remedies are
quite effective—as you have just proved with young Hankins
and his burn."*

"Thank you, sir."

She had beamed at his praise, for she received precious
little praise or appreciation in other areas of her life. The
acceptance and esteem of these medical men, especially Ferguson and MacLachlan, filled a need she had scarcely recognized before.

The crack of a whip shattered her thoughts.

"Look out, lady!" shouted the driver of a mule-drawn
cart that seemed to be sliding erratically in a river of mud.

Rachel jumped out of the way and was relieved to see
the man regain control. She hurried on to the hospital.

The dining hall and chapel of the convent had been turned
into wards of the hospital. In the central courtyard separating
these and the nuns' dormitory, the surgical tent—actually, it
was merely a tarpaulin to fend off the rain—had been set
up along with makeshift operating tables—doors set upon

barrels. Rachel tried to avoid looking at the severed arms and legs flung haphazardly near those tables. The sight was not unfamiliar to her, but she still found it difficult to look upon with any degree of equanimity. However, she would no longer rush out to vomit repeatedly as she had the first time. Amputation was a drastic action, yet it was decidedly the most effective way of dealing with serious leg and arm wounds in a battlefield setting.

Musicians, customarily assigned to transport wounded men to the hospital during battles, now brought their precious human cargo to the courtyard, where the men's wounds were assessed as to urgency. Patients often had to wait, and they were generally in excruciating pain all the while. A gulp of brandy or whisky prior to surgery and a piece of wood to bite on were the only concessions to their agony.

Rachel was part of the team assessing wounded as they came in this morning. As was her wont in dealing with maimed and injured men, she also offered comfort where she could—wiping this one's brow, cleaning that one's wounds in preparation for the surgeon, and providing water to the desperately thirsty. She had learned to carry a canteen of water with her constantly. Soldiers used their teeth to tear open the packets of shot and powder for reloading their muskets and rifles. Thus the mouths of the wounded often resembled black holes and the gunpowder made them inordinately thirsty.

Distracted by a commotion at the entrance to the courtyard, she straightened from bending over yet another thirsty young man. Two men of an infantry regiment came in, carrying a third man in a blanket. Despite the urgency of their mission, it was apparent they were taking great care with their burden. She hurried over to them even as one of them began to call for help.

"Hey! Doc! Over here!" A note of panic laced the voice of a young corporal whose uniform proclaimed him one of the famous Connaught Rangers.

"The major's been hurt bad," explained the other—a sergeant in a like uniform—as they tenderly laid the wounded man on the cobbled pavement of the courtyard. Rachel knelt beside him and began to assess his injuries.

Ferguson finished with his current patient, directed the bandsmen to take the man to the operating tent, then turned his attention to the new arrivals.

"It . . . it looks bad," she said to Ferguson. "He has lost a great deal of blood."

"Damned French saber got him right in the head," the young corporal said. "Beggin' your pardon, ma'am."

A gash above the wounded man's left ear had bled profusely, but Rachel knew it was probably not the worst of his injuries. Nor was it.

"He took a bayonet in the chest." The sergeant was older and calmer. "And a musket ball in his upper leg there."

The injured man's breath came in ragged spurts. Ferguson knelt beside him, unbuttoned his torn tunic, and examined him briefly. Looking over Ferguson's shoulder, Rachel gasped as she perceived the extent of the man's wounds. Ferguson took one look at the torn flesh and seeping blood and shook his head in resignation. "Sorry, fellas. He won't make it through the day."

"He's still alive! You gotta do something!" The corporal's voice rose. "The major can't die."

Ferguson gazed at the younger man with infinite sadness, and his voice was gentle. "I'm sure he was a good man, Corporal. But we've lost hundreds of good men this day. This one hasn't a prayer of surviving—probably won't last the hour even—and we simply have to deal with those who will."

The younger man looked as though he would explode with anger. The other simply looked down at the injured man with a bleak, resigned expression.

Rachel was touched by the younger man's dedication and devotion to his commander. Only a few officers elicited such a degree of respect among the men they led into harm's way. She placed a hand on the young man's arm and said softly, "We shall do what we can, Corporal."

"Don't let 'im die, ma'am. Please don't let 'im die. Major

Forrester took that bayonet for me." The boy's voice ended on a sob, and he turned away in embarrassment.

The sergeant put his arm around the corporal's shoulder. "Come on, Pete. Let's go." He turned to Rachel and Ferguson. "We'll come back in a couple of hours."

Rachel looked down at the unconscious man. Beneath his pallor, his complexion was deeply tanned and sported a mass of freckles. His hair, matted with blood, was a chestnut color. He had a straight nose, a rather square jaw, and a solid, muscular build. She thought he was probably of medium height when he stood.

"Such a shame," she murmured, feeling tears in her eyes.

"They all are." Ferguson sounded grim.

Silently, Rachel agreed, but there was something about this Major Forrester. . . .

An hour later, when there was a lull in the traffic of incoming wounded, Rachel thought to check on the infantry major. To her surprise, he was still alive. He remained unconscious and his breathing was still raggedly uneven, but she thought his pulse seemed a bit stronger. She went immediately for Mr. Ferguson.

"The man's a fighter, I'll say that for him," Ferguson said. "We may as well stitch up the head wound to keep him from reopening it." He again examined the wound in the major's chest. "This one will without a doubt kill him, though it may take longer than I thought at first. The wound itself will do it—or infection in it or in the leg, which he'd probably lose anyway."

Rachel gently cleaned the ragged edges of the flesh around the gash in his head and assisted Ferguson as he stitched the wound closed. The major's hair was matted with blood and sweat, but she felt an inexplicable urge to touch it. Besides the metallic odor of blood and the smell of gunpowder in his clothing, she caught a whiff of sandalwood. His shaving soap, perhaps. The man groaned and tried to pull his head away, but he remained unconscious and Rachel, surprised at his innate strength, managed to hold his head firmly only with difficulty. Ferguson finished tying the last stitch, and she wrapped a bandage around the man's head. As she tied the ends, Ferguson looked down and shook his head.

"Have him moved to the dead room," he said with a sigh of resignation and turned away to other duties.

The dead room was a side chapel off the nave of the church attached to the convent. The hopeless cases were taken there to breathe out their last.

The corporal and sergeant, accompanied by a third man, returned just in time to hear this last comment.

"This here's Henry—he's the major's batman," the corporal explained, introducing a short, wiry fellow who appeared to be in his forties.

"We are *not* taking Major Forrester into any death chamber," Henry announced in what seemed a rather protective manner. He barely acknowledged her presence.

"Does he have adequate quarters, then?" Rachel asked, observing that here was another person in whom the major had inspired extraordinary loyalty.

Henry looked chagrined. "We . . . uh . . . have a bivouac of sorts. We arrived after the siege had begun and officers' quarters were already assigned." His voice trailed off.

"But you do have adequate protection from the elements, do you not?"

Most wounded officers, after initial treatment by a surgeon, were then released into the care of their own servants. A major, she knew, would be entitled to have as many as seven servants accompany him. The quartermaster also reserved the best quarters for officers. However, something in Henry's tone had given Rachel pause, and when he did not answer her question immediately, a shiver of apprehension assailed her. This patient would probably die in spite of any efforts to save him, but consigned to the general neglect of the so-called dead room, or forced to deal with inadequate shelter, he stood no chance at all of surviving.

Rachel was vaguely aware that they had attracted the attention of two bandsmen who often helped with wounded, a Welshman named David and an Irishman named Kelly.

She repeated her question to Henry. "Will he have adequate shelter?"

Henry ran a forefinger around his apparently too tight collar. "Uh . . . not really, ma'am. At least not until I can locate some—maybe in the city. The major's tent was lost along with one of the mules on a mountain trail." Henry looked utterly despairing, but his voice was firm and authoritative as he added, "However, I have no intention of seeing him carted into some dismal room to await an end that *might not* be inevitable."

"Hmm." Rachel looked thoughtfully at the wounded man. She had no idea why this one's plight affected her so, but it did. Perhaps it was young Pete's devotion. Perhaps it was the whiff of sandalwood—her father had always smelled of sandalwood as well as his pipe tobacco. "Do any of you have any special skill at caring for someone in his condition?" she asked.

Each admitted with some embarrassment that he did not.

She heaved a sigh of regret for the wounded major. And, then to her utter astonishment, she heard herself saying, "Well, there is nothing else for it. You must bring him to my billet. We can care for him there. At least he will keep dry that way."

It would be crowded with another pallet on the dirt floor of that one-room hut. She had no idea how Clara and her husband would react to this addition to their household, but she was quite sure Brady would object. He usually took sharp exception to anything that disturbed his own comfort. Still, she could not just let the man die without doing all in her power to prevent such a turn.

"You can set up your bivouacs near us and help tend him," she said. The presence of strangers nearby might at least defer Brady's more vocal complaints.

This suggestion seemed to give the sergeant and the corporal a measure of hope.

Henry, however, appeared to be having second thoughts. "But—but—doesn't he need a doctor's care?"

"I will care for him—with your help, of course," she replied.

"You?" Henry's disbelief was clear. "With all due respect, madam, the major requires professional care."

One of the bandsmen, Kelly, wore a wide grin. The other snorted and pressed a finger into Henry's chest. "Better take what you can get, mister. As it is, your man will be getting one of the best."

"But she's a *woman,*" Henry said in almost a wail.

David grinned, too. "An' a very handsome one at that. She also knows what she's doing. I've seen her work."

"Thank you, David." Rachel felt a rush of gratitude to the normally taciturn young Welshman.

He blushed. "Nothin' but the truth, ma'am." He looked belligerently at Henry. "Consider yourself—no, *him*—lucky." He pointed at the major. "Come on, Kelly, we got more work to do."

As the two left, the opposition seemed to fade in Henry's stance. "Very well, madam. It shall be as you say." But his tone was grudging.

Two

While the batman went off to retrieve necessary items from the major's gear, Rachel informed Ferguson of what she planned regarding the wounded man.

"You're wasting your time," Ferguson said as he bent over yet another patient.

"Perhaps. But I have to try."

He straightened and surveyed the activity around them. "We are not shorthanded at the moment, so go ahead and do what you must." He gestured to a stack of supplies. "Take what you need there."

"Thank you, Captain."

He touched her shoulder and held her gaze. "And don't take it too hard if—when—he doesn't make it."

She nodded, a lump in her throat. All this human devastation around him, yet Ferguson had taken notice of how she might react to the loss of one patient. Captain Ferguson had comforted her through that first devastating loss in the Peninsula. She had witnessed death in the past, but always before, it had come from old age, a debilitating disease, or an accident, never from the organized inhumanity of war. He had been so very young, her first soldier death in Spain. Delirious with pain, he called for his "mummy" repeatedly. Rachel sat quietly talking to him, letting him think *she* was his mother until death finally came for him. Since then she had comforted other dying men and grieved for the losses their wives and mothers would suffer. Somehow she sensed—and perhaps Ferguson did, too—that if she lost the battle for Major Forrester, it would be as devastating as that first loss had been.

She gathered what she thought she would need—what she thought could be spared. Then, with the sergeant and the corporal again carrying the major in a blanket, she led the way to the sheepherder's hut. Thank goodness the rain had stopped, at least temporarily. Their patient groaned a time or two, but he seemed to remain blessedly oblivious to what was happening to him. They arrived at the hut just as Henry arrived from another direction, leading a loaded mule.

"Is that a folding cot?" she asked of Henry, pointing to a contraption on the mule.

"Yes, ma'am, it is."

"Good. That will keep him off the damp earth."

Rachel pushed the door open and called, "Clara?"

There was no answer.

She quickly cleared space for the cot against the wall opposite the pallet she shared with Brady. She helped Henry set up the cot as the other two patiently waited, their arms obviously strained by the major's weight. Despite the gentleness with which they laid him on the cot, he moaned incoherently at this abuse of his person. Rachel pinned up the canvas over the window to let in more light and stirred the seemingly dead coals in the fire. She was pleased to see they were very much alive. Moreover, the kettle was full of water that was still warm.

"Remove his clothing," she said as she laid out supplies and instruments.

"All of it?" Pete asked in a shocked tone.

"Probably." She smiled at the boy's naive response. Did he think a married woman—not to mention one who tended wounded soldiers—had never seen a man unclothed? "I need access to each of his injuries."

She poured hot water into a basin and carried it over to the cot. Henry had produced a pillow and draped a blanket strategically across the major's torso. Three helpless looking men hovered over the prostrate form on the cot.

"I shall need only one of you to assist me," she said with a gesture toward the door.

Henry took charge. "Sergeant, perhaps you and the corporal would be so kind as to get the rest of the major's gear and bring it here, and let Thompkins know where we are. He can tether the horses among those cork trees," he said, waving his hand.

"We'll do that," the sergeant said, ushering his companion out with him.

Rachel knelt beside the cot and began to sponge away the blood and dirt around the wound in a firmly muscled chest sporting a mat of reddish brown hair. She ran her hand gently along his rib cage to determine if there were broken ribs as well as internal injuries. She was surprised at the degree of her own awareness of his masculinity. She dealt with dozens of patients far more impersonally than this!

"Ah, this explains his labored breathing," she said.

"What?" Henry stood anxiously at the major's head, observing her every movement.

"He has at least two broken ribs." She rinsed her cloth and cleaned around the torn laceration across his abdomen. "He must have turned or ducked at just the right moment— or the assailant was confused."

"Why do you say that?"

"Corporal Collins said Major Forrester took a blow intended for him, and it appears his ribs took the brunt of the thrust, though the blade also sliced across his abdomen."

"Is that good?" Henry sounded dubious.

"It could be," she said guardedly. "Mr. Ferguson thought vital organs had been hit, but if they were spared . . ."

"Then there *is* hope?"

"A thread, perhaps." She continued cleansing the tissue. Then she looked up at Henry with a smile. "I *think* this injury is not as serious as it first appeared. However, I shall need to close this laceration. Then we shall bind his ribs tightly."

Henry's Adam's apple bobbed up and down, but the man gamely assisted her. He held the ragged edges of the cut together as she stitched, then held the major's upper body free of the cot so she could slip a cloth beneath him to bind the rib cage. Again, the major groaned incoherently and feebly tried to push her hands away.

"There. There," she murmured softly. "Just be patient, sir. I promise you will feel better."

The gentleness of her tone seemed to soothe him. As she reached around him to drag the cloth into place, her face came very near his. She felt his breath on her cheek and smelled the familiar sandalwood. She was pleased to hear his breathing take on a healthier tone as soon as the ribs were bound, and she wondered fleetingly at the brief catch in her own breath. As she drew the blanket up to his chin, he seemed to relax a bit.

Emitting what sounded to Rachel like a sigh of relief, Henry wiped his master's brow as Rachel stood and wrung out the cloth she had used to cleanse the chest wound. She took the dirty water to the door and flung it to the side, then filled the basin with more hot water. "Now, the leg," she said, a determined note in her voice.

She glanced at the major's face to find a pair of gray-blue eyes riveted on her. When he moved his head, she saw pain flash across his eyes.

"Wha—" he started.

"Shh. You have been seriously injured, sir. Mr. Henry and I are endeavoring to put some of the pieces back together." She motioned for the batman to come within the major's line of vision.

"I . . . see," he said weakly, his breathing erratic. "Well . . . carry . . . on . . . then."

She raised the blanket enough to expose the wound above his knee, but still preserve Henry's sense of propriety. Forrester's legs were covered with soft hair slightly lighter in color than that on his chest. She had a fleeting thought that, with legs as well formed as these, the man must show to good advantage in tight pantaloons. She sponged the dried blood from around the wound, which was about the size of her palm. The ball had torn through a good deal of muscle tissue, but there was no exit wound.

"The ball is still in there," she said to Henry. "Come hold his leg while I probe for it." She touched the patient's shoulder and held his gaze. "This is going to hurt, Major Forrester, but that thing must come out."

He nodded.

"Shall I give you something to bite down on?"

"No. Just . . . do it," he croaked hoarsely as Henry moved around to do her bidding.

She poked her finger into the torn tissue and felt around for the foreign object. The major took in a deep whistling breath which she knew must be extremely painful in itself, given his broken ribs.

"I'm so sorry," she murmured. Then her finger touched the piece of metal. It was lodged against the bone. But the question was, was the bone broken? She expanded her probing and said again, "I'm so sorry."

This time her apology fell on deaf ears. Her patient had fainted.

"Good." She glanced briefly at Henry. There were beads of sweat on the batman's forehead and upper lip; his eyes were suspiciously bright, and he had a rather greenish tinge to his complexion. "Don't you dare faint on me," she said sternly.

He took a deep breath and shook his head, but said nothing.

With her invasion of the injured area, it had started to bleed again. She wiped at the blood and reached for the instrument with which to extract the misshapen metal ball. She had to make two stabs at grabbing the ball, but finally had a firm hold and extracted it quickly. She heaved a great sigh, unaware she had been holding her breath, and heard an answering sigh from Henry.

She took advantage of her patient's insensibility to probe for any additional debris, but found none. Again, she wiped the area free of new blood, spread basilicum salve on a clean cloth, and wrapped the whole in a thick bandage. She tied a clean cloth around his leg to hold it in place.

"Will he lose the leg?" Henry asked. "I heard the surgeon say he would."

"I hope not. We shall know in time—perhaps as soon as tomorrow. And I am still worried there may be internal bleeding from the other wound."

"I . . . I apologize for what I said earlier." Henry's tone was very stiff. "It is apparent even to me that you do know what you are doing."

"Thank you," she said, unable to keep her exhaustion from showing in her tone. "I knew what had to be done—I have seen it done dozens of times—but I must admit this is a first for me."

Henry's eyes widened in surprise at this admission.

There was a commotion at the door. Rachel opened it to find Clara struggling to carry both her son and a canvas bag.

"Oh! I'm glad you are back," Clara said. "I've news. Both our men are safe. I saw Mary Parsons. Her husband was wounded as they broke through, but he saw both Joe and Mr. Brady and—" Her voice trailed off as she observed the other two people in the room.

"This is Mr. Henry—and Major Forrester." Rachel gestured to each and quickly explained the situation to Clara. "I—I hope you don't mind. I just could not leave him to die without doing *something.*"

Clara set her son on the floor and her bag on the table, then gave Rachel a quick hug. "Of course I don't mind. Nor will Joe. However," the ever-practical Clara added with a glance at the bag she had brought in, "we've precious little food, you know. Mind you, *some* of the supplies have begun to catch up with us, but that's all I could get."

"The major's rations will, of course, be added to yours," Henry said. "As soon as the rest of his gear arrives, we shall sort it out. I know he would not want to burden you unnecessarily." Henry took a lingering look at the major and then left, promising to return soon.

"Well, that solves that problem." Clara pushed a lock of red hair off her forehead and began to sort out her treasures to make a nourishing soup. "Now—" she pointed at Rachel. *"You* get some rest. I can see you're exhausted. I shall keep an eye on your patient as I get us some food under way."

Grateful for Clara's quick understanding, Rachel settled herself on the pallet. "What did you learn of Edwin and Mr. Paxton?" she asked from her horizontal position.

"They were both fine when Private Parsons saw them last, and the worst of it was over by then. I expect they'll be back sometime tonight."

"We'll see . . ." Rachel remembered only too well the looting and wild revelry after the taking of Ciudad Rodrigo a few weeks before. She had been shocked to learn her own countrymen reacted so when a besieged town put up a prolonged fight. And Badajoz had fought very long and very hard.

It was dark when Rachel awoke. She had actually slept an hour or so. She checked on her patient, who seemed to be sleeping normally, then sat to share the soup and some bread with Clara.

Clara held her son on her lap and spooned mashed vegetables into his rosebud mouth. Rachel smiled as Clara coped with small flailing arms and the child's tendency to wear as much food as he actually swallowed. Benny had been a source of joy to Rachel as well as his parents, though Edwin merely tolerated the toddler. Once, Rachel had tried to apologize for her husband's indifference.

"Oh, never mind," Clara had said. "Lots of men are like that. Just wait'll you have your own. He'll come around."

Rachel was not sure of this at all, but she let the matter drop.

Between spoonfuls, Clara said, "Mr. Henry seems very devoted to his employer."

"Yes, he does. So do the men who brought the major to hospital."

"Could be he's one of those rare beings—an officer deserving of such regard." Clara shared the typical rank-and-file soldier's disdain for officers as a general class. "Nice looking fellow, he is," she added.

Rachel pretended shock. "Clara! For shame."

"I may be married, but I'm not blind."

"I suppose you are right." Rachel feigned casual interest in this line of discussion. She did not understand the depth of her concern for a man who had been totally insensible during most of her acquaintance with him and had scarcely spoken two words in her presence.

As Clara continued to feed Benny, Rachel rose and stood looking down at Major Forrester, thinking to find an explanation in his countenance. As she stood thus, Henry returned, accompanied by a younger man and a boy whose olive skin proclaimed him to be Portuguese or Spanish.

"How is he?" Henry asked.

"About the same," Rachel answered. "He has not stirred much."

Henry introduced his companions. "This is Thompkins and Juan. Thompkins is Lord Jacob's groom and Juan joined us about a year ago. He takes care of the goats."

"Goats?" Rachel said vacantly, trying to absorb the fact that the man in the cot was a lord of some sort.

"Sí," the boy said shyly, holding up a covered container. "Here is milk for your tea—or *para su hijito."*

"For your son," Henry translated, addressing Clara.

"Milk?" Clara said wonderingly. "How marvelous!"

The three looked at the sleeping figure on the cot. Each of them seemed to need to reassure himself of the major's continued well-being.

"We are setting up our camp about twelve yards that way." Henry pointed over the major's cot. "And here's some meat and vegetables that may prove useful to you—and his lordship." He handed Rachel two packets as he turned to usher the other two out ahead of him. "I shall return in an hour or so to sit with him."

"Very well." Rachel sensed a burning need in the man

to be able to do something, however little. Besides, the major would undoubtedly prefer that his long-time batman perform the more personal services required for a convalescent.

She tried with little success to rouse the patient to get some of the soup into him. She *did* manage to give him some water, but he was barely aware of swallowing and fell back immediately.

Clara took her son to bed in the loft and Henry returned to sit, quietly reading, at the head of the major's cot. A pole with a candle on it had been driven into the dirt floor nearby.

Rachel lay down again on her pallet, but sleep did not come immediately. She reviewed everything she had done for the major. Could she have done more? Probably not, she decided. *Should* she have done what she had? Her conscience shouted *yes!* but common sense and experience told her there would be a price to pay when her husband returned.

And where *was* Edwin? Was he hurt? Surely not, according to what Clara had heard. But what was he doing? No. She would not allow her mind to go down that route. She had learned not to ask questions to which the response was likely to be a lie—or a shock.

Finally, she fell asleep, only to be awakened by a flash of cold air as the door opened.

"What the—?" a male voice asked in astonishment.

"Oh! Mr. Paxton." Rachel sat up quickly and Henry stood.

A weary-looking Sergeant Joseph Paxton took in the entire scene, then shifted his gaze to Rachel. "For a moment, I thought I had stumbled into the wrong billet."

She laughed softly. "No. This is the right place."

"Joe?" Clara called as she scrambled down from the loft. She threw herself into her husband's arms so violently he nearly dropped his musket. "Oh, Joe, I was so worried."

"No need to be." His voice was gruff.

Rachel thought him embarrassed in front of strangers. Rachel introduced Henry and explained his and the major's presence, which Joe accepted with great equanimity.

"Are you hungry?" his wife asked.

"Famished," he replied. "And see what I have." He pulled a bottle of wine from his knapsack.

Clara dipped him a bowl of the soup that still sat in the edge of the fireplace and Rachel produced four cups. She poured a small measure of the wine into each, handing one to Henry.

"Did you see Edwin?" she asked.

"I saw him about noon, I think it was. He was . . . uh . . . in another part of the city from me." He looked away, apparently unable to meet her gaze.

"But he was well?" she persisted, uneasy at Joe's hesitation.

"Yes. He was fine. Lots of fellows still checking out buildings, you know." Again he refused to meet her gaze.

Her heart sinking, Rachel knew what Joseph Paxton was *not* saying. Her husband was caught up in the looting and general mayhem they had heard of earlier. This siege had gone on for so long and the British had suffered so in building their trenches and bulwarks that they now sought terrible retribution on the town that had abetted the enemy. She tried to close her mind to the rape and murder of innocents that must be occurring even now only a few hundred yards away. While she desperately tried to save one life, her husband was actively engaged in needlessly destroying others.

When the Paxtons had gone to bed, Rachel sent Henry to his own bed as she watched over their patient. Having learned to knit during the winter, she sat knitting a scarf in the uncertain light from a single candle and the meager light from the now subdued cooking fire.

Paxton's inadvertent revelations triggered thoughts she usually managed to avoid bringing to the surface. The early months of her marriage had been happy ones, she supposed. Now she sometimes wondered if her happiness then had not been a product of her own naivete. The first rust on her shining knight's armor appeared when she discovered the shady means by which recruiters often met their quotas. She and Edwin had just finished having supper in the public room of an inn when they were joined by three other men, one of them a newcomer to the recruiting team. All three were decked out in the smart looking uniforms of their infantry regiment.

Sergeant Johnson, a man about Edwin's age—late twenties—introduced the new man. "This here's Simon Cantwell. He's to join us."

"He's new at gettin' rubes to take the King's shilling." Teeter, Johnson's constant companion, grinned knowingly.

"Is that so?" Edwin seemed only mildly interested.

Cantwell nodded.

Johnson sat back and hooked his thumbs in the belts that crisscrossed his chest. "I told 'im the best way's simply to give 'em a few tankards of ale—an' drop the coin in one. When the poor jerk hits bottom and takes that coin in hand, the deed is done. He's yours."

"Gotta keep him drunk, though, 'til he signs in front of the magistrate," Teeter said, gesturing to a barmaid.

"It helps to have a friendly innkeeper on your side, too—eh, Brady?" Johnson gave Brady a knowing look and laughed. " 'Course, you *could* resort to kidnapping."

"Too risky," Edwin said. "Your average Johnny Raw can be had with stories of brave deeds and the glory of war as well as plenty of food and drink to be had in the army."

Johnson nodded. " 'Specially the young ones. The army likes 'em young. Apprentices tryin' to flee their masters are perfect candidates."

"Sounds easy enough," Cantwell said.

"It . . . it all seems rather dishonest," Rachel said to Edwin, who gave her a look that clearly said she had stepped out of line. This was man talk.

She had spoken softly, but Johnson heard and snorted. " 'Tain't as bad as the navy's press gangs, now, is it?"

After that, she never inquired too closely about Edwin's recruiting ventures, but she was glad when he was posted to another duty.

The major moaned from his cot, increasingly restless in

his sleep. She put aside her knitting and quickly moved to his side. His cheek felt feverish to her touch. She rinsed a cloth in cold water and placed it on his brow. Lifting his head to give him a drink of water, she murmured nonsense words to him softly so as not wake those above. He quieted somewhat, but was still fretful. She returned to her knitting, but with a watchful eye on him.

Sometime later, his thrashing about became stronger and he mumbled incoherently, obviously delirious. Then he paused and called out clearly.

"Celia? Oh, God, Celia. No-o-o. No. Celia. Please—no."

The tone was pure anguish and Rachel thought Celia had much to answer for. His wife, perhaps?

She knelt beside the cot and wiped his brow, speaking softly to him as one would to a sick child. She held on to his hand.

"Do you need help?" Clara asked in a low voice from the top of the ladder up to the loft.

"No. He seems quieter now. I'm sorry he woke you."

" 'Tis of no matter. Call if you do need help."

"Thank you."

She released his hand, but as soon as she did so, he became agitated again. She pulled the stool around to the side and took his hand in hers again. Or, rather, she placed her hand in his, for his was a large hand with strong fingers. A scar ran across the back of his hand, which she traced with her fingertips, wondering how he had come by it.

She also wondered at the surge of sadness and protectiveness she felt at his vulnerability. She was often moved by the plight of injured men, and she had never become accustomed to having death steal a patient from her. Yet somehow this man struck a deep chord she had not known was within her.

"Death, you will *not* have this one," she whispered fiercely and gave his hand a gentle squeeze.

She still sat in that same position when Henry returned to take over the watch.

"Has he regained consciousness at all?" the batman asked.

"No. He's been very restless and called for someone named Celia."

She saw Henry press his lips together tightly. Then he said, "That is ancient history, to be sure."

Painful ancient history, Rachel thought as she disengaged her hand from the major's, startled at her own sense of mild loss in breaking contact with him. Pleased that he remained calm, however, she removed her shoes and lay down on her own pallet. She slept fitfully.

She dreamed of Edwin Brady—he of the laughing charm that had been so attractive to a girl not quite seventeen. She felt his arms around her and his lips nibbling her neck just below her ear. Then the vision changed. It was not his wife he nuzzled, but another—a Spanish beauty—and Rachel stood off to the side witnessing this in tableau. The other woman looked at Rachel and laughed wickedly.

Rachel felt a hand on her shoulder and was instantly awake.

"I—I'm sorry, Mrs. Brady, but Lord Jacob seems much worse . . . and . . . and I don't know what to do," said a very worried Henry.

She sat up and wiped her hands over her face, trying to erase the dream and come to terms with reality. She glanced at the window to see faint light around the canvas there. Morning. At least Major Forrester had made it through the night.

Slipping her feet into her shoes, she went to the basin to wash her hands and face remembering her father's words. "Too many people dealing with the sick forget that cleanliness is next to godliness—and we need all the help from God we can get!"

She felt the major's brow.

"He's burning up with fever," she said, keeping her voice soft despite her alarm.

"I know." Henry was obviously frustrated at his own helplessness.

"Light that other candle and hold it so I can see better."

Henry did as she bade and held the candle close as she pulled back the blanket to examine the wound to the major's chest and abdomen. She placed her hand on the skin there. It felt warm, but not unduly so. She then examined the leg wound. The skin around the bandage was an angry red color and fiery to the touch.

"Oh, dear," she murmured.

"Bad?"

"It's infected." A rotten sweet smell of decay arose as she removed the bandage.

With warm water and a clean cloth she washed the wound as thoroughly as she could and rebandaged the leg.

"Now we hope—and pray," she said as she discarded the old bandage in the fire and threw out the dirty water.

Clara climbed down from the loft.

"Did we wake you?" Rachel asked, apologetic.

"Not really," Clara said. "I needed to . . . uh . . . go outside."

She disappeared for a few moments, then returned to begin bustling about to prepare breakfast. She put the kettle on for tea, then brought a packet to the table. As she unwrapped it, the smell of spoiled meat assailed their nostrils.

"Oh, not again!" Clara exclaimed in revulsion. "This meat is all maggoty! You'd think since the commissary people drive our beef on the hoof, it would at least be fresh when we get it!"

"Yes, one would think so," Rachel agreed, looking over Clara's shoulder. "Is it so bad that you cannot save any of it?"

"Oh, no. I'll just wash it good and use lots of pepper, the way the Spaniards do."

Rachel frowned, trying desperately to recall something from the depths of her memory.

"No, wait," she said, staying Clara's hand. "Cut off a small piece and leave the maggots to work in it, then do what you will with the rest."

"What do you want with meat that has maggots in it?"

Clara asked in amazed repugnance. "I swear, Rachel, you are the strangest woman I ever met. You wouldn't let me throw out that moldy bread and now you want to save meat with maggots in it?"

"Just for today. I may have need of it—them—later." Rachel took the bit Clara had cut off and rewrapped it loosely as Clara scraped and washed the rest thoroughly.

Henry had observed this exchange with some interest, but he did not say anything.

"Mr. Henry," Rachel said, "I hate to leave you to tend Major Forrester alone, but I really should report to the hospital this morning."

"Never mind," he said. "I shall be fine. " 'Tis but my duty, after all."

Clara looked up. "You need some sleep, too, I'm sure, Mr. Henry. I shall be glad to watch over your patient for a few hours. Lord knows I won't be going anywhere and Joe is reporting to his lieutenant."

Reluctantly agreeing to this plan, Henry returned to his own camp and Rachel—with instructions to Clara to try to get some more broth into their patient—made her way to the hospital.

The rain had stopped the previous afternoon and the ground was quickly drying out. There was a smell of spring in the air. Mother Nature had taken up her age-old practice of renewing life even as humanity seemed caught up in death and destruction.

Three

"Did your patient make it?" Ferguson asked as soon as Rachel arrived at the hospital.

"Yes, he did," she said proudly, then added with a note of caution, "but I think he is not out of danger yet." She described the major's condition in detail.

"That leg could still kill him," Ferguson warned, "but the cut in his belly must have been far less serious than it appeared when he came in."

"I think so. Perhaps the blade caught on part of his uniform. It was broken ribs that were causing the labored breathing."

"McGrigor was right—you'd have made a fine doctor." The admiration in Ferguson's voice warmed Rachel.

She spent the rest of the morning changing bandages and feeding patients too weak to perform that task themselves. There were still some wounded straggling in, but the hectic pace of yesterday was gone and the surgeons were less busy at their operating tables. New patients coming from the city frequently smelled of stale brandy and wine.

"Crazy fools don't even watch where they're shooting," Mac said in disgust. He pointed to a man whose foot had just been amputated. "That drunken jackanapes dropped his musket—loaded, mind you—and shot off his own foot!"

"Oh, how awful," Rachel said. *And unnecessarily stupid,* she thought.

"They're tearing the town apart." A young bandsman who had just brought in a cart with three wounded soldiers was clearly shocked. "I never seen anything like it. Two of our 'brave' fellows were making sport of shooting at a couple of little boys who were running away. And the women—even little girls—"

"That'll do, son," Mac admonished with a glance at Rachel.

She knew her own shock and horror must have shown in her face. And her husband was still out there. No. She could not allow herself to think about that. Surely Edwin would return soon. Why, he might already be in the sheepherder's hut.

She continued to perform various duties, but her mind kept drifting between imagined terrors in the town and concern for the patient she had left in the hut. Finally, early in the afternoon, she returned to her own billet—tired, hungry, and heartsick at the human devastation in the hospital and the wild tales she had heard of debauchery in the city.

She arrived back at the hut to find both Clara and Henry highly agitated.

"Thank goodness you're here." Relief was clear in Clara's voice.

"He's in a bad way," Henry said sadly. "Outa his mind, he is."

Hurriedly, Rachel removed her shawl and placed a packet of additional bandaging material on the table, then washed her hands, tossed out the water, and refilled the basin with hot water. Even before she touched his brow, she could feel heat radiating from Forrester's fever-ridden body. She pulled back the blanket and lifted the edge of the bandage on his chest and abdomen.

"No problem here," she said, "so it must be the leg again."

Removing the bandage not only revealed the infected area, it released the familiar odor of such.

"Ugh!" Clara said. "Poor man."

Red streaks shooting up the major's leg struck fear in Rachel's heart.

"Oh, God," Henry cried. "He *is* going to lose the leg—or worse."

She closed her eyes very briefly. *Please, God, no. Not him. Not now.*

She tried to sound calm. "He may well do so. But I want to try something. If this does not work, we shall bring the surgeon here to amputate."

"If *what* doesn't work?" Henry sounded suspicious.

"The maggots," she said bluntly.

Comprehension dawned on the other two.

"No!" Henry said. "I will not allow it."

Clara was disbelieving. "You cannot mean to do what I think you mean."

"Look." Rachel stood, put her hands on her hips, and glared at both of them. "This man is going to lose his leg—perhaps his very life. The infection is too deep to be removed by ordinary means."

Henry raised his voice in protest. "And you think introducing vermin will help? What an absurd idea."

"Is there no other way?" Clara grimaced, her repugnance clear.

"What about using more of the basilicum salve?" Henry suggested.

"That will not remove the infected tissue which is poisoning his whole system."

"I suppose it *is* worth a try," Clara conceded. "A big strapping man like that—and a lord yet—he wouldn't look kindly on losing his leg if there were any means of saving it . . ." Her voice trailed off.

Henry considered this, then shrugged in resignation. "Very well. I do not like it, but I . . . I assume nothing could make matters worse."

Nearly gagging herself, Rachel swallowed hard as she dumped the crawling mass onto the wound and quickly put a very loose covering over it to confine the "beasties."

"We should know in several days," she said.

"Several *days?*" Henry's voice rose in surprised impatience.

"I think so. Meanwhile, we must try to get some more broth and liquid into him. Also try to keep the fever down by sponging his body frequently. Willow bark tea is said to help with a fever. I have the willow bark, but I wish we had some laudanum for the pain."

"I shall look for some when I go for supplies," Henry said. "If there is any to be had, I promise I shall find it."

Clara and Henry looked on quietly as Rachel finished cleaning up. Their patient had been restless as she worked on him. Now he opened his eyes, but they were clearly unseeing.

"Robbie!" he called. "Do be careful. Watch it! That Devil's a wild one." He groaned in obvious pain, but Rachel could not tell if it was current or remembered pain.

"No, Robbie. Don't . . . tell . . . Papa. Must save . . . Devil."

Rachel looked at Henry for an explanation.

"Robbie was—is—his brother. Robert Forrester, Marquis of Lounsbury. When they were boys there was a horse named Devil."

"What happened?" Rachel asked, wondering why the Lounsbury title was faintly familiar to her.

"The two boys decided to ride it—Robert was about ten, I think, so Lord Jacob was perhaps six or seven. The horse *was* unmanageable—even the grooms feared it—but somehow those children got it into their heads that *they* would ride Devil."

"Children rarely foresee danger," Clara observed.

"Lord Jacob received a broken arm in the adventure, but they told their father it happened in a fall. Which was true enough, perhaps. When Robbie fell from the bucking horse, little Jacob stood over his brother and tried to grab the reins. The horse's hoof clipped the child's arm before a groom managed to subdue the animal."

"But the stable hands knew what had happened," Rachel interjected.

"They were sworn to secrecy."

"I don't understand why," Clara said.

"The children were afraid the marquis would destroy the animal. He would have, too."

Rachel recalled the corporal's saying Forrester had taken the bayonet for him. "So even then he was putting himself between danger and others."

"Yes. He's always been one to protect and save those in danger or need. His brother Robert is like that, too. Strange."

"Strange?" Rachel repeated.

"Their father never cared for anybody but himself." Henry seemed suddenly aware of having said too much and busied himself with smoothing out the major's bedclothes. He left soon afterward, saying he would bring the major's rations to them later.

"While he is gone," Rachel said, "I intend to have a bath."

"A bath?" Clara sounded scandalized. "With the major lying right there?"

"He will not even be aware of what is going on."

"Still—"

"Come. We shall string a rope from those pegs on the walls and hang a blanket between us and the major—and just in case your husband or mine—or Henry—returns unexpectedly. We shall keep watch for each other." Rachel held up the rope.

"I admit the prospect of being clean is very enticing . . ." Clara said, entering into the spirit of Rachel's plan. "I did wonder how we should manage, what with your patient and all."

"Of course, it will be only a washing up, not a real bath, but just being clean—and with clean clothes—will make us feel more the thing."

An hour later the two women sat enjoying their new cleanliness along with cups of weak tea as the babe played on the Bradys' pallet. Suddenly, Rachel became aware of the major on the cot. He was moaning softly and thrashing about, particularly with his injured leg.

"Is . . . is he coming to?" Clara asked. "Is he in pain? Are those . . . those *things* hurting him?"

"I *think* he remains unconscious. As to his pain, he surely has his share of that. A fierce headache and sore ribs at the very least. But I think what is most irritating is the itch."

"The itch?"

Rachel reached into one of her bags for a bottle of brandy. "Lieutenant Ferguson said he might need this for pain, but I think it might serve another purpose as well."

Curiosity shone in Clara's eyes, but she said nothing as Rachel soaked a cloth in the brandy and proceeded to wipe the reddened area outside the bandage on the major's leg wound.

"There," she murmured as to a child, "that feels a little better, doesn't it?" Then she added in a more cheerful note. "And since you are awake—well, after a fashion, at any rate—perhaps you are ready for something to eat."

Clara seemed to have read her mind, for she handed Rachel a spoon and held a cup of broth dipped from the soup kettle at the edge of the fireplace. Rachel propped up the patient's head and shoulders with one arm and spooned a bit of broth into his mouth. He swallowed convulsively several times, then heaved a long sigh and turned his head away.

"I know," she said. "Not exactly roast beef and Yorkshire pudding, is it?" She removed her arm, surprised at the sense of inner warmth she had felt at holding him so, and pleased to see his restless thrashing cease.

Clara had taken her son for a walk in the fresh air when, sometime later, Henry returned to check on his master. He handed Rachel a packet of food.

"Corporal Collins and Sergeant Humphrey are outside," he said. "They came to check on Lord Jacob."

"He is sleeping, as you can see," Rachel replied, "but they are welcome to see for themselves."

The two were invited in and stood looking down in concern at their commander.

"Is he gonna get well?" Fear and concern laced Collins's voice.

Rachel realized the corporal's emotions paralleled her own. "I cannot say for sure," she admitted, "but I sincerely hope so."

Suddenly, the door of the hut crashed open. Startled, Rachel looked over to see her husband standing framed in the doorway.

"What in bloody hell . . . ?" he growled, tossing his knapsack on the pallet he shared with his wife and leaning his musket in the corner behind the door.

"Oh, Edwin, you're back," Rachel said brightly.

"Oh, Edwin, you're back," he mimicked. Then his voice turned cold. "Yes. I'm back—and find my wife entertaining half a ranger company. Would you care to explain yourself, *Mrs.* Brady?"

"Uh, Collins and I were just leaving," Sergeant Humphrey said. "We'll check on the major tomorrow, Henry."

The two made a hasty retreat, leaving the batman and Rachel to face her husband. Rachel sighed inwardly at seeing Edwin was half drunk. He was never a happy drunk. All the abuses an unfeeling world had heaped upon him seemed especially haunting whenever he was in such a state. She tried to stay calm and matter-of-fact.

"This is Mr. Henry. He is the major's batman. We brought the major here simply because he would have died immediately in the hospital." She bit her lip.

"So you turned *my* billet into a private hospital for some confounded officer?" He slurred the last word.

"Well, what difference did it make?" she asked, unable to quell her umbrage—or her embarrassment. "You were not here. Clara and Joe don't mind—"

"Oh, they don't, eh?"

"No, they don't. And I've already explained that Major Forrester would have died—"

"Forrester? Did you say Forrester?" He looked intently at the prostrate form and what could be seen of a head swathed in a bandage.

"Major Lord Jacob Forrester," Henry announced as though he were introducing an arriving guest at a ball.

Brady went red, then white with rage. He grabbed Rachel's arm and shoved her out the door. "I would have a private word with you, dear wife."

He stomped beside her, never loosening his grip on her arm. Brady had always—at least since the honeymoon was over for him—been a man of volatile temper, but Rachel had never seen him in quite such a rage. There was something deeper, more visceral to his emotions at the moment than she had ever seen previously.

About thirty feet from the hut, on the opposite side from where Henry had set up the Forrester camp, was a stone fence. Brady marched her over to the fence, where he swung her about.

"Just what the hell were you doing bringing Forrester into my billet?"

"Trying to save a man's life—just as I would hope someone might do for *you,* if necessary," she said, edging away from him.

He reached out to grip her chin painfully. "Don't you be giving me any of your sass, woman."

"Edwin, please." She tried to reason with him. "You're hurting me."

He stood close enough that she could smell the stale liquor and his own musky sweat—as well as a mixture of . . . what? Spicy food and some exotic perfume.

A sick feeling invaded her stomach. She remembered vividly the snatches of stories in the hospital—stories of women with earrings torn from their bleeding ears and other jewelry snatched from their bodies, leaving scratches, cuts, and broken fingers. Women and young girls raped wherever they were found. British soldiers literally falling down drunk and firing at anything—and anyone—that moved. Why, even Lord Wellington had barely missed being killed by a bullet fired indiscriminately. And Edwin had been a part of all that—had he not?

Brady snarled an obscenity. "I'll hurt you a damned sight more if you don't get that bastard out of my quarters."

Edwin Brady under the influence of drink rarely responded to reason. But she simply did not understand the depth of his rage this time, so she chose to ignore his swearing. A truly sober Edwin was usually more careful of his language.

"Edwin, do you *know* the major? I do not recall your mentioning his name—ever."

"Oh, yes, I know him. The Marquis of Lounsbury is . . . is the biggest landowner near Brixton, where I grew up. I know I've told you that."

"In West Devon?" she asked. "But I thought Henry said the major was from Gloucestershire."

"He is. But the damned Forresters have holdings all over southern England. Arrogant, clutch-fisted popinjays—the whole lot of them."

"Judging by what his batman and the two men who brought him to hospital have said, Major Forrester does not strike me that way," she ventured.

His eyes narrowed. "Are you contradicting me?"

"No. I merely said that is not the impression I had from others."

"Your impression is irrelevant," he said with a sneer. "Now, you get rid of him. It's bad enough you spend so much time in that damned hospital shirking your duties to me, but I will not tolerate your bringing that smelly mess into my own quarters."

"Edwin, the man was dying! And he may not make it yet. He cannot be moved without endangering him further."

"Are you refusing to do as I tell you?" His voice was menacing, and she knew if she confronted him directly he would immediately unleash his fury on her—and lord knew what else he might take it in mind to do.

"No . . ." She groped for a response that would appeal to his self-interest. "I just think you might not want to deal with the consequences if he died because *we* moved him. MacLachlan told me Lord Wellington's aide had asked about Major Forrester. And I imagine his brother could wield some influence with the Horse Guards."

Her mention of army headquarters in London seemed to give him pause.

"Bloody damned hell!" He glared at her. "See what you've got me into! Trust a stupid, ignorant woman to really muddle things up."

"I do not see any reason to carry on so—"

"Oh, you don't?" His hand shot out and he slapped her across the face. "That'll teach you to go behind my back."

Deeply hurt, but not shocked—this was not the first time he had struck her—she put her hand to her stinging cheek and stepped away from him. "I did not go behind your back. Your back has not been present for three days!"

"And *that* is none of your business," he sneered, but he did not hit her again, probably because Clara and her son were approaching the hut. The last time Brady had struck his wife in their presence, the Paxtons had subtly let him know they thought such a man beneath contempt.

He grabbed her arm and pulled her to him in what—from several feet away—might appear to be an embrace. She pushed against him, but he held her and, jerking her face around toward him, kissed her, brutalizing her lips in his fury.

"You're in luck, dear wife. I've only come back for some supplies and clean clothes. Morton and I and three others are to accompany Lieutenant Hoskins on some sort of scouting mission. We leave at dawn."

"A scouting mission," she repeated dully, unable to think beyond her bruised lips.

"Old Nosey's way of breaking up the fun in the town." Using but one of the army's endearing terms for their commander-in-chief, he gestured toward the city with his head.

"H-how long will you be gone?"

"Who knows? Hoskins may know, but he didn't tell us. At least ten days, I'd say. And—get this, woman—when next we meet, you'd best not have Forrester hanging on your skirt. Is that clear?"

She merely looked at him.

"I said *is that clear?*" he ground out.

"Oh, it's clear, right enough," she said, not bothering to disguise her hurt and anger.

"I warned you about sassing me." His voice was harsh, but he also seemed mindful of the watching Clara. He lowered his voice to almost a whisper. "And don't be saddling me with the Paxtons again. I don't like sharing quarters with a coward."

"A coward?" Her tone was disbelieving.

"You heard me." But he did not explain. Nor did he seem to recall that the idea of sharing quarters with the Paxtons had originally been worked out—at Brady's suggestion—between the two *men*.

They reentered the hut just as Clara did so. Henry rose from his stool as they came in.

"Henry, you need not stay longer. I shall watch over our patient," Rachel said.

Henry gave her a curious look, and Rachel felt embarrassed at the possibility of Henry's observing the color in her still stinging cheek. "As you wish, madam. I shall return after midnight, then, so you may get some rest."

"Thank you, but that will not be necessary. Just come in the morning, if you please."

"Yes, madam."

Henry was barely out the door when Edwin growled, "At least you had sense enough to get rid of *him*."

Clara gave Brady a questioning look, but said nothing. Rachel did not respond to the comment. Holding a soup bowl in one hand, she dipped to the bottom of the pot to bring up a generous portion of meat and vegetables for him. A thick slice of bread and a hunk of cheese completed his meal—or almost. He poured from his canteen a brimming cup of what her nose informed her was brandy. She closed her eyes, hoping more drink would not merely make him meaner.

Clara set about feeding her son as Rachel sorted through the clothing she had washed some days before. Women who followed the drum learned early on to take advantage of opportunities to do laundry, no matter how inconvenient the timing might be. She laid out her husband's clothing. He would stuff things into his knapsack himself and strap on a rolled blanket later.

She also spooned a little more broth into her patient and was pleased when he took some water. She sensed Brady's silent glare as she tended the injured officer.

When Joe Paxton came in a few minutes later, Rachel silently breathed a sigh of relief. Edwin was unlikely to create a scene in front of a man who had already tacitly expressed his disapproval of Brady's approach to husbandly behavior. The two men chatted amiably enough. There seemed to be some restraint on Joe's part, but Edwin was exerting himself to be charming.

Rachel listened in vain for any indication of friction between them that would explain why Edwin wanted separate quarters from the other couple. Joe politely accepted Brady's offer of brandy, but took very little and then switched to tea as he played with his son while Brady cleaned his musket. The two women sat on the Bradys' pallet, talking quietly even as Rachel devoted an attentive eye and ear to the major.

His breathing sounded more shallow, and she wondered if he might be regaining consciousness. He began to moan softly and thrash about. She rose to tend him.

"I hope he's not going to do *that* all night," Brady growled. "I need to get some sleep. The last three days have been very wearing."

Rachel could not bring herself to look at her husband—or at the Paxtons, who she knew were well aware of Brady's participation in the rioting in the city. She laid a hand against the major's cheek. It felt warm, but not dangerously so. She wiped his face and neck with a cool cloth and gave him another dose of the willow bark tea.

"I think you'll be able to get your sleep, Edwin," she said dryly, knowing full well once he fell into an alcohol-induced state of insensibility, almost nothing could wake him.

Her tone, however, was not lost on him, for he gave her a hard glare.

When the Paxton family took themselves off to the loft,

Edwin, too, decided to retire. "And you're coming to bed with me," he ordered Rachel.

"Oh, but . . ." She gestured futilely to the figure in the cot.

"You'll hear him if anything goes wrong. Now, come on. A husband's got certain rights, you know." His voice was low, but insistent.

"I . . . I shall lie down with you," she whispered, "but I can't . . . we mustn't . . ."

"Why the hell not? Are you denying me my rights?" He dragged her down beside him and began to fumble with the front of her dress.

"No, of course not." She searched for something to put him off. She could not face the idea of making love with Major Forrester lying only a few feet away—unconscious or not. "I . . . I . . . my courses," she whispered, hoping a show of shyness would put him off.

His hand stilled on her breast. "Your sense of timing is truly wonderful." He gave her nipple a vicious little pinch and rolled away from her. Soon enough he was snoring.

Rachel lay beside him, feeling humiliated. True, it was unlikely the Paxtons had heard them and the major was clearly unaware of *anything,* but *she* knew—and despaired of the state of this marriage.

She remembered a time when she had thought Edwin Brady handsome and charming, a time when she had trembled at his kiss. Now she did not even want him to touch her. She had even lied to him just now about her monthly courses.

Well, *was* it such a lie? They were certainly due. She lay mentally calculating.

Good heavens! They were overdue. *Way* overdue.

Oh, God. Not now—in the middle of a war.

Brady was right. Her sense of timing was truly wonderful.

Four

Her mind in turmoil, Rachel rose to sit by the unconscious major. She undid her hair from its customary tight bun and combed it out. When the major began to stir, she bent over him to check his bandages. All was in order; the streaks on his leg had progressed no farther. She fed him some broth, gave him more water, and wiped his face with a cool, wet cloth.

"Tomorrow I shall get Mr. Henry to help me give *you* a bath," she said very softly.

He made a low noise, almost as though he were responding to her voice. So she began to talk to him, spilling out her life story in a burning need to unburden herself.

"I—my life was not always like this," she began as she braided her hair in a single nighttime plait. "As a child I was very happy. My mama and papa were wonderful. I remember our laughing *so* much! Even after Mama died when I had but eight years, Papa did not allow the laughter to die. He said she lived on in our laughter."

She told him of her gentle, gracious mother, who always seemed kinder, sweeter, more refined than the mothers of her friends. And more fragile. She had not survived her second pregnancy.

"So then there was just Papa and me. He said I must be his capable son as well as his beautiful daughter." She laughed self-consciously. "Papa always thought of me as beautiful."

She paused, thinking of the only man who had ever loved

her unconditionally. The major stirred, turning his head as though seeking the sound of her voice, yet he remained unconscious. She continued her narrative in a barely audible murmur.

"When Papa died—he caught a fever in the terrible influenza epidemic of '06—I went to live with Papa's stepsister's family. Then I met Edwin. I know you will find it hard to believe now—I do myself—but Edwin brought laughter back into my life. At least for a while."

Again, she sat in thoughtful silence. She glanced at her sleeping husband and tried to remember when the laughter had stopped. She wondered what else she might try to restore it. She knew the main fault must lie within her husband's character, but surely she could help him—if she could just find a way.

"Maybe a babe—" But no. They had been there before.

In the first year of the marriage, she had hoped desperately for a babe. Convinced a child would settle her husband down and they might become a stable family, she was wildly happy when she discovered herself with child. However, Edwin was far less than enthusiastic about his impending fatherhood.

"I don't need any more brats in my life."

"More brats?" she asked, mystified.

"You forget I was the eldest of eight children."

"But this won't be the same."

"Close enough, I'm sure." He gave her a hard look. "Can't you *do* something?

"Wh-what do you mean?"

"Don't you have a potion of some sort to take care of it?"

"You . . . do not want our child?"

"Ah, sweetheart . . ." He came to enclose her in his arms and nuzzle her neck, speaking softly. "I do—someday. But don't you see it's just not a good idea for us now?"

"Nevertheless," she said, her tone adamant as she twisted away from him, *"now* is when it is happening for us."

"Fine!"

He had stomped from their rented lodgings and returned

in the wee hours of the morning staggeringly drunk. She got him into bed even as he faded into oblivion. He was violently ill when he finally woke and she might have felt sorry for him had she not herself been in the throes of morning sickness.

Three weeks later she miscarried, though she had done nothing to effect that outcome. In fact, she had wanted the babe intensely and she mourned its loss profoundly. Edwin had been contrite and caring during her recovery, but he could not hide his relief. After that, there was an unbridgeable gulf between them, but she suspected he hardly recognized it existed. Now, she feared bringing a babe into this world to follow the military drum. Perhaps when they returned to England . . . but no. This new life was not going to wait until then.

Well, so be it. She would not be the first woman to give birth on the campaign trail. And Edwin would have several months to adjust to the idea. Still, she thought she might not tell him quite yet.

Major Forrester moaned softly, bringing her back to the sheepherder's hut.

"You want to hear more, then?" she asked indulgently. "Very well."

She launched into a monologue about her childhood as the daughter of a doctor in a mid-sized town in Scotland. She told him of attending Miss Ogilvie's Day School For Young Ladies and of accompanying her father on house calls, of music and dance lessons, and of sharing her father's passion for research, as well as his love of history and literature. When this topic ran out, she recited passages from Shakespeare, Milton, and that modern poet, Mr. Wordsworth. Finally, as slits of light began to appear around the canvas-covered window, her patient seemed to have fallen into a restful, healing sleep.

The pain enveloped him—like one of those dense fogs in London where one fought to discern vague shapes and identify muffled sounds. Jacob Forrester had never felt so out of touch with himself and his surroundings. Pain dominated his whole being. He tried to concentrate on something else.

He recalled the woman bending over him. Pretty. Brown hair. He could not remember the color of her eyes. All he could pull through the pain was the compassion he had seen in them just before that sharper, most excruciating pain had sent him over the brink.

Even this enveloping fog of pain was preferable to *that*. Escape. How to get away from it? Then he heard the soothing music.

A siren's song luring him to the peace of death?

No. Not music. A voice. A voice offering comfort. He allowed the soothing tones to wash over him and push the pain to a lower level. Then the voice stopped and the pain rushed forward again.

He struggled to reach for the hope, the comfort embodied in that disembodied voice. Was it the pretty lady with brown hair? He felt lost, deserted. He was a small boy again, banished to a dark cellar after being beaten. What for? Ah, yes. He and Robbie had gone exploring. Nurse had been distraught. Robbie tried to assume the blame. The beating. Father kept a strap for just such occasions. Then Robbie was sent to the room the boys shared; Jacob to the cellar. No Robbie for companionship. No toys, no books for diversion. Just fear. Fear then; pain now. Unendurable agony from which he struggled to escape.

Then the voice started again. He felt the pain receding into the background once more—still there, but no longer center stage.

Finally the pain and the voice faded into sleep—not Hamlet's sleep of death, but Don Quixote's satisfying, healing sleep.

To avoid any further confrontation with her husband, Rachel deliberately did not try to rouse him until the last possible moment. He hurriedly donned clean socks and his discarded outer clothing of the night before.

"Why didn't you wake me earlier?" he grumbled. "Hoskins will be at me for being late. Not to mention Morton's smirking."

Rachel had never quite understood the relationship between Edwin and his friend Morton. On the one hand, they spent a good deal of time together both on and off duty. Rachel knew—and worried—that Brady owed Morton a substantial sum in gambling debts from their ongoing card games. On the other hand, Edwin seemed to resent Morton, for the two constantly competed, each trying to be "one up" on the other, whether in military or leisure activities.

For her part, Rachel simply did not like Morton much. Not that he had ever done anything overtly to earn her dislike. However, the way he looked at her sometimes made her uncomfortable. There were rumors Sergeant Morton cheated at cards, but when Rachel mentioned this to her husband, Edwin had dismissed the idea contemptuously.

"Silly women's gossip. He's just had a streak of luck which is bound to turn—and in my favor. Believe me, the man sharp enough to cheat Edwin Brady hasn't been born yet!"

When Brady and Paxton had reported to their respective duties, Henry arrived to take over the major's care. He brought with him a container of still warm milk. Clara voiced her intention to do some laundry now that the weather had changed for the better. When Rachel mentioned to Henry that she had promised Major Forrester a bath, the batman was aghast.

"I shall take care of that particular duty, madam," he had said stiffly.

"Very well." She acceded to his male sense of propriety. She could not stifle a yawn. "Try to get some more broth into him—or perhaps some milk. He needs nourishment. And water."

"Yes, madam. If you will pardon my bluntness, Mrs.

Brady, may I suggest that the biblical injunction, 'physician, heal thyself,' might be most appropriate at the moment?"

"Hmm?"

"You've obviously had but little rest."

Touched by his concern for her, she said, "It was rather a long night. I shall just have a short nap." She removed her shoes, lay down on her own pallet, and was almost instantly asleep. She awoke in midafternoon with a small hand patting her cheek.

"Oh, Benny!" Clara admonished her son in a quiet tone. "I'm sorry, Rachel."

Rachel sat up and stretched, then hugged Benny briefly. "Never mind. 'Twas beyond time for me to be up. I must check in with Mac. But, first, how is our patient here doing?"

"Actually, quite well, I think. Mr. Henry said he was conscious earlier, but I was not here. Major Forrester even took some broth and tea with milk." Clara had continued to keep her voice soft.

"That is surely a good sign," Rachel responded, feeling hopeful about his possible recovery. "Where *is* Mr. Henry?"

"He went into the city to see if the looters left anything in the way of foodstuff."

Rachel put her shoes on, combed out her hair, and quickly twisted it into her customary, efficient bun. She looked at Major Forrester and was surprised to see he was clean-shaven. The planes of his face stood out rather starkly. Henry had been busy as she slept. As she bent over him, the welcome smell of sandalwood arrested her attention. It caught her off guard, sending a curious tingle of excitement through her.

She changed his bandages, but he did not waken. The head wound was healing very nicely, as was the slash across his abdomen. She held her breath against the odor as she removed the old bandage on his leg wound. Gazing at the repulsive, moving mass of ghastly white and grayish-yellow, she could hardly believe she had done that to another human being. However, it *seemed* to be working. The infection was apparently being contained. She quickly retied the covering cloth.

Later, when she checked in with MacLachlan and Ferguson, she discovered far fewer patients requiring their care.

"What happened?" she asked.

Ferguson answered. "We sent those who were permanently disabled—and could be moved—back to Lisbon to be shipped home. The rest will either be well enough shortly to rejoin their regiments, or they, too, will be shipped home—assuming they make it." He lowered his voice. "Some won't. Would not even have survived a journey to the port."

"But most will," she said confidently.

"I hope so. By the way, how is your private patient faring?"

"He's . . . uh . . . coming along nicely, I think." She hesitated to tell these men of science of the precise step she had taken to control the infection.

"No infection?" Ferguson seemed to have read her mind. "I thought sure he would lose that leg."

"Well . . ." Needing their validation, she took a deep breath and explained.

"You did *what?*" Ferguson's astonishment was clear. "Mac, did you hear that?"

"Hear what?" Mac had been momentarily distracted by a patient.

Feeling some trepidation, Rachel explained again about using the maggots to cleanse the wound.

"Good grief!" Mac said. Then he stroked his chin thoughtfully. "Hmm. I *have* heard of such. Is it working?"

"I . . . I think so. The infection does not appear to be spreading."

"If Forrester survives at all, he will owe you his life," Ferguson said.

"And his eternal gratitude if he does not lose the leg," Mac added. "Be certain you keep a close watch on that. Call us, if need be."

"I shall." She was grateful neither surgeon ridiculed her efforts despite their surprise.

"Unless you mean to stay behind with him, you've not a lot of time," Mac informed her. "Word is Wellington intends to pursue the French right on to Salamanca—maybe even to Madrid. We shall be moving on in a fortnight or so."

"By then he will surely be out of serious danger." Her voice held more confidence than she felt.

When she returned to the hut, she found both Mr. Henry and Sergeant Paxton had arrived before her. Clara was in a high state of excitement.

"Mr. Henry has wrought a miracle," Clara announced.

"You found some laudanum," Rachel guessed.

"Yes. I did that, too." He held up a small vial. "But Mrs. Paxton refers to new quarters."

"New quarters?"

"In the town." Clara's eyes shone as she hugged the child on her hip. "We'll be in a real house, won't we Benny?"

"We are moving up in the world," Joe said with a grin.

"How can this be?" Rachel was well aware that officers were not regularly assigned to share quarters with enlisted persons.

"I simply explained that you ladies have been extraordinarily helpful in tending the major," Henry said. "We shall effect the move tomorrow morning. Sergeant Humphrey and Corporal Collins have offered to help."

"I . . . I see." Overwhelmed by this news, Rachel had a fleeting thought of her husband's injunction about new quarters. But there was really no point in her staying in the hut by herself—and besides, who knew for sure when Brady would return? She removed her shawl and placed the back of her hand on the major's cheek to check his temperature.

His eyes opened immediately.

Was it touching him or that penetrating gaze that affected her so?

"Oh! You have come back to us," she said, too brightly.

"You were not . . . a fantasy," he murmured.

"No." She gave a nervous little laugh.

"I dreamt of snakes crawling . . . then there was an angel . . . and music . . ." His voice ended with a wince of pain.

"He has been conscious from time to time," Clara offered. "He did eat a bit, but has little appetite."

" 'Tis the pain," Henry said. "We . . . I waited for you to come back before giving him the laudanum."

Rachel gave the batman a grateful look, for this statement showed her, as nothing else could have, that Mr. Henry no longer harbored doubts about her nursing abilities.

She checked the wound on the major's midriff, then lifted the blanket from his leg. He made a noise of obvious protest at this action, apparently embarrassed.

Henry laid a hand on his master's shoulder. " 'Tis not unseemly, my lord. Mrs. Brady knows about such matters."

It crossed her mind to wonder what Henry meant by "such matters," but she quickly completed her examination. "No change," she said.

"Is that . . . good?" Major Forrester asked.

She nodded. "At the moment, it is."

He grimaced and sucked in his breath, in the grip of pain. She mixed a bit of the laudanum with milk and, as Henry held the patient's head and shoulders up, Rachel put the cup to his lips. It was some time before the painkiller took effect and he slept.

The next morning, the Paxton-Brady-Forrester enterprise moved within the city walls. Upon seeing their new lodgings, Rachel thought Mr. Henry's powers of persuasion must be quite remarkable indeed. Henry looked embarrassed when she complimented him on his achievement.

"While I should like to have you think so well of me, the credit really belongs to Lord Jacob."

"Oh?"

"Yes, madam. You see, Lord Jacob served in India with

Lord Wellington. His aides know the general likes to take care of men who have served him well."

"Well, whatever the reason for our being here, these are quite the fanciest quarters I have enjoyed since I became associated with His Majesty's Army."

The accommodations were actually in a modest house on a side street. Its location had allowed it to escape the worst of the ravages of the looting following the siege. Some "removables" had obviously been taken, for the rooms had been ransacked and furniture overturned. Rachel and Clara, along with help from Joe and Thompkins, managed to put the place to rights in short order.

A drawing room, library, dining room, and kitchen occupied the ground floor. The first and second floors boasted bedchambers and dressing rooms, with servants' quarters on the top floor. There was even a small, empty stable in the rear. Amazingly, the place seemed totally deserted.

Major Forrester was, of course, allotted the best bedchamber, with Rachel in one directly across the hall, and the Paxtons in another on the same floor. Sergeant Humphrey and Corporal Collins again transported the major with great care. Rachel had given him another dose of the laudanum to ease his journey.

Within an hour, they were all in place, with Thompkins and Juan in quarters above the stable, which now housed the major's cattle—three horses, two mules, and three goats. Clara immediately set about the task of preparing lunch, which they would all share in the large dining room. Thompkins and Juan were initially shy about joining the others, as was Henry, to some degree. However, Joe, Clara, and Rachel contrived to make them feel at ease, and soon it was a relaxed "family" group around the table.

Juan found the Paxton baby fascinating and happily babbled to the toddler in Spanish.

"Juan misses his family," Thompkins explained.

"He has a family? Why is he not with them, then?" Clara asked.

"They were killed—massacred by guerrillas siding with the French. The whole village was wiped out."

"The poor child," Rachel murmured.

"How did he escape?" Joe asked.

"He was out taking the goats to pasture. Lord Jacob found him trying to bury his family."

"Oh, my." Clara cast a lingering look of sympathy on the boy who could not be more than eight—nine at the most.

Juan seemed to sense he was suddenly the center of attention. He looked up to smile shyly, showing white teeth against his olive skin.

Clearly changing the subject, Clara said, "I wonder that this house was so deserted."

"Juan talked with a neighbor," Thompkins replied. "Seems 'tis owned by a widow who lived here with her two daughters and a young son. Before the siege was in place, she left to join her sister further south."

"But they must have had servants," Rachel observed.

"They did, but they ran off when our troops broke through and the looting started."

"Probably the least we can do is try to leave their home in good condition," Joe Paxton said.

Rachel was struck by his generosity of spirit, and again she wondered about Edwin's accusing the man of cowardice.

The next few days settled into a routine, with Joe going off daily to regimental duties. Wellington's threats to hang anyone further involved in looting and pillage had restored order, and the troops returned to regular drills as they awaited the order to pursue the enemy to the north and east. Clara managed most of the household duties, for Rachel still reported to the hospital every day, though she also shared with Henry the care of the major. Ferguson came at Rachel's request to check on Forrester's condition.

"It is too early to be absolutely sure," the surgeon said, "but I think you may have actually saved this leg! At the very least, the infection seems to have been arrested."

Major Forrester spent more and more of each day fully awake now. Although Rachel could tell he still experienced a great deal of pain, he refused to resort to the insensibility offered by large doses of laudanum.

"I will not rely on that seductively dangerous stuff," he said. "I have seen men—and women, too—destroyed by such."

Only occasionally would he resort to a small dose of the drug. Meanwhile, he was also eating better and was recovering enough to become impatient with his inactivity. At one point, Rachel arrived in the room just as he had pushed himself to a sitting position.

"What *are* you doing?" she demanded.

"I should think that to be quite apparent, madam. I intend to get out of this infernal bed. Now, if you would be so kind as to hand me that dressing gown and then leave the room . . ."

Having by now some familiarity with the man's sheer willpower, Rachel silently handed him the gown lying on a chair. Then she stood back, arms folded across her chest. He glared at her and slowly pushed his good leg from beneath the blanket. When his foot touched the floor, he positioned himself to swing the injured leg next to it.

Suddenly, he blanched, and beads of perspiration popped out on his forehead and upper lip. With a groan, he fell back against the pillows.

She gently helped him reposition both legs on the bed. "Just as I thought. Too much, too soon."

"Nobody likes to hear 'I told you so.' " He sounded testy, but there was a glint of humor in his blue eyes.

"Then behave yourself," she said as though speaking to a naughty child. "You will merely prolong your recovery, you know."

"Yes, ma'am," he said with exaggerated contrition. "I shall do as you say—*if* you will consent to read to me again."

She smiled, for reading from his much-used treasure of books had become one of the most enjoyable aspects of caring for him. "Very well. Perhaps from the Sermon on the Mount, since you seem in need of some humility?"

"I had in mind *The Iliad*—great warriors engaged in deeds of glory."

"Do you not mean grown men behaving as spoiled schoolboys and thus wreaking havoc on others?"

His laugh turned into a wince of pain and he put a hand to his still tightly bound chest. "You do have a point, but there is greatness as well as pettiness in Homer's characters. Do you not agree?"

"I would venture to say that describes much of humanity—greatness as well as pettiness," she said. She tapped the book. "However, the actions of these men are usually understandable, if not always laudable."

They continued in this vein for quite some time—until Henry brought up the major's supper tray. She would read a passage, which he often interrupted to offer a comment, which would in turn elicit her response.

At one point, he paused in midsentence and said, "I say— how do you come to know this work so well? 'Tis not usually part of a female's education."

"My father loved Homer's works. I do not ever remember *not* knowing of them."

"Interesting," he said, waving at her to continue.

Later, Rachel could not recall a more satisfying or enjoyable afternoon in her entire life.

Five

Major Lord Jacob Forrester lay in his bed, unable to sleep. Pain was a constant companion, but, despite the late hour, it was not pain that kept him awake. The house had long since quieted down. He himself was on the mend enough that he no longer needed round-the-clock care. He had long since sent Henry to his bed.

So here he was, alone with his thoughts, which seemed of their own volition to turn to Rachel Brady. *Mrs*. Brady, he reminded himself. Not since Celia had he been so drawn to a woman. And this one was just as unavailable as Celia. With this memory came another flash of pain. Not the immediate sensation of physical pain, but remembered pain of the heart, of the spirit.

Perhaps it was time—past time—to face that pain and try to put it behind him once and for all.

He supposed he had fallen in love with Celia the moment he had seen the squire's golden-haired daughter through what he then thought of as adult eyes. He had been eighteen that summer, home for the school holidays. She was a blue-eyed China-doll beauty of sixteen, not old enough to have a real come-out, but allowed to attend local assemblies and group outings under her mama's watchful eyes. Jake knew Celia's parents encouraged his attentions. After all, the son of a marquis—even a younger son—would be quite a catch for their daughter. So the youngsters had occasionally been accorded discreet moments alone.

He smiled at the memory of the sheer ecstasy of their

awkward first kiss. Fleeting as it was—a bare touching of primly closed lips—he had nevertheless felt himself to be a bold knight wooing his lady fair. Robert—he had not been "Robbie" for some years—had been gone that summer. He had been sent along as part of the entourage of the King's emissary to Russia and Turkey.

Jake remembered telling his father, "I would have liked to accompany my brother."

"There was no need for you to do so," the marquis responded. *"You* will not be the one in Parliament one day."

Jake puzzled over this briefly, for it was not unknown for lesser members of a lord's family to fill seats in the House of Commons, and he knew very well the marquis controlled three such seats. He was also hurt by the comment, which he had interpreted as yet another indication of his father's extreme preference for his heir over his other children—Jake and his sister.

He and Penelope had known since the cradle they were accounted lesser beings in their father's eyes. They were the children of his second marriage, a marriage contracted with a much younger woman of unimpressive background in large part because he wanted a mother for the heir. He had cared so little about his new family that he had overlooked the taint of Jewish blood in his wife's family and even allowed her to name his second son for her beloved father.

At the beginning of what he came to view as his summers with Celia, Jake had missed Robert's company. Four years separated the marquis's sons, but the two boys were close, and Robert had never seemed to mind having his younger brother trail after him. Jake's loneliness dissipated when he discovered the joys of idealistic knightly love. He missed Robert far less then. He returned to school in the fall full of dreams of winning great honors to lay at his lady's feet.

Robert had not been around the following summer, either. He had been on the town during the Season and then off to an extended hunting party in Scotland. Celia had returned home from her first year away at school with more polish and poise than she had shown previously. Now, nearly twelve years later, Jake knew she had been on the verge of womanhood and eager to try out her winsome ways on someone with whom she felt safe—Jake.

He danced with her at every social gathering that offered such entertainment, and he was frequently her partner for the suppers at these affairs. He knew the local gossips had begun to link their names, but Jake had no objection to the idea of being linked to Celia for life. His father was apparently indifferent to the idea.

"Just remember the gel is gentry," the marquis said. "Take care you are not caught in parson's mousetrap."

Jake had drawn up in fine adolescent umbrage. "Celia— Miss Dalrymple—is not like that."

"Maybe not. But her father is. He's a very ambitious man. All I am saying is be careful. You *are* my son."

With a great show of indifference of his own, Jake had replied, "You need have no worry. We are merely friends."

Jake had then all but dismissed his father's unwelcome warning. Despite that just friends comment, he spent more and more of his time with Celia. She seemed to bask in his attention. They went riding and driving, always properly accompanied by a maid or a groom. They spent hours strolling the gardens of her father's fine house. During inclement weather, they were together in the drawing room with her mother and two sisters.

Mrs. Dalrymple watched the relationship with an indulgent eye, but both she and her husband had subtly but definitely made it clear they considered their daughter and her would-be suitor far too young to be making any permanent plans.

Jake was not dismayed at being thus warned off—for now. He had yet to finish his education. After the university, he would proceed to the Inns of Court to study law. He and Celia would have time enough—a lifetime—to be together. Meanwhile, there were occasionally stolen kisses and whispered endearments.

Then that summer, too, was over and they returned to their respective institutions of learning. The Dalrymples had gone away that Christmas season and, while Jake was sorry to miss Celia's company, he welcomed the time with his own family, especially with Robert, who no longer merely tolerated him as the younger brother. The two young men enjoyed each other's company as that of sincere friends, not mere relations.

Penelope, however, teased Jake about Celia in the manner of bratty younger sisters. "Do you not pine away for your lady love, Jake?"

The question had come unexpectedly at breakfast one morning. The marquis had already left the table, and his wife always took her morning cocoa and toast in her chamber. So it was just the three younger Forresters at the table in the family dining room.

"I have no idea what you are talking about." Jake did not intend to discuss such personal business with either sibling—yet.

Penelope laughed. "Oh, the beauteous Celia Dalrymple, of course."

"The squire's daughter?" Robert asked.

"The squire's daughter," Penelope confirmed and laughed again. "I vow—you should have seen them this past summer, Robert."

Jake rolled his eyes. "As usual, Penelope's overactive imagination is allowing her to create a raging tempest from the softest of breezes."

"Are you saying there is nothing to this breeze?" Penelope's voice rose in disbelief.

"That is precisely what I am saying," he lied, and added in a more sanctimonious tone, "And you, missy, would do well to refrain from sullying another young woman's name with idle gossip."

"Hmmph!" Penelope rose disdainfully and flounced from the room.

Robert looked at him questioningly. "You sure?"

"Now don't you start, too."

Robert put up his hands in a defensive gesture. "Hey! I have not met the female in question. Well . . . not since she was—maybe—eight years old. Big teeth. Skinny arms and braids."

"Believe me, that description no longer fits," Jake said, then changed the subject.

Several months later, he remembered the conversation and wondered what might have happened if he had told Robert the truth. But by then it was too late.

At the end of the school term that spring, Jake had joined some friends on a sailing holiday. This was extended as the young men learned of first a racing meet that it would be criminal to miss, and then a pugilistic contest that was said to be an historic match. When Jake finally joined his family in London, the season was well under way.

"I have met your Miss Dalrymple," Robert announced as the two brothers shared cigars and brandy on the terrace after the rest of the family had retired.

"She is not *my* Miss Dalrymple," Jake said, still reluctant to discuss his feelings for Celia.

"Oh? Glad to hear it." Robert blew a puff of smoke and sipped at his glass.

Jake felt a sliver of warning prickle the hairs on the back of his neck. His mouth felt dry. "Why?"

"I find her to be a very attractive, accomplished young woman . . . and if you are not interested . . . ?" Robert's voice trailed off in a question.

"I did not say that . . ." Jake said slowly, trying to think.

"I thought you were merely friends—given your age and all. Father said as much as well."

Although Jake felt distinctly uncomfortable, his response was at least technically correct. "I suppose we are."

"There is no understanding between you?"

Honesty compelled his answer. "No."

"Good. I would not want to edge out my own brother."

Jake swallowed hard. "You . . . uh . . . you intend to offer for her?"

"Yes. Now that I know you have no special interest in that direction."

"And if I had?"

"Well—that would make for a very awkward situation, for I fear I am in love with her."

"In love? *You?*"

Robert laughed. "Surprised me, too. Especially as it happened so fast."

Jake was forced to listen for several minutes as Robert waxed on and on about the woman he loved—the very same woman Jake loved. Why had he not been more honest and forthcoming with his brother earlier? Why had he wasted all that time sailing with Bentley and the others?

Still, Robert had not yet offered. Nor had Celia accepted. Given the tentative promises she had made last summer, Jake knew poor Robert was in for deep disappointment and heartache. He loved Robert enough to want him spared that. But he loved Celia enough to be glad she would refuse Robert's offer.

However, she had not refused the offer. Or had not been allowed to refuse it. Ten years later, he still wondered about that.

Robert had wasted no time in approaching her father and then making his offer to Celia. He had returned to the Lounsbury town house positively euphoric.

"You are to wish me happy, brother."

Jake thought he might be ill. He swallowed past a lump in his throat. "She—Celia—accepted your suit?"

"That she did. The announcement will be made at her come-out ball, and we shall be married in the autumn."

"I . . . see. Well, congratulations, Robert. I hope you will be very happy." Part of him had been truly sincere in that hope, though the news had shattered his own hopes of happiness.

"Thank you. I am sure we will be. It is truly a love match, you know." Robert seemed both proud and embarrassed at this admission. "A love match is not exactly common in our circles."

"No, I don't suppose it is."

They had chatted amiably for a few more minutes before Jake was able to make his escape. Thank God Robert's own elation had blinded him to his brother's reaction to the news. Unable to face the idea of being thrown in company with the happy couple just yet, Jake announced the next morning that he was going to the country for a few days with some friends.

"You will return for the Dalrymple ball, will you not?" his mother asked. "I mean, it might appear odd if you were to miss it, what with the announcement and all."

Jake avoided meeting his mother's eyes. He knew she sensed his despair. She always seemed to know more than one might wish her to. "Yes, Mother. I shall return for the ball."

He had gone to the Lounsbury hunting lodge, taking with him the ever-faithful Bentley, friend of his school days and the only person in the world who knew the extent of Jake's devastation at his brother's happiness. Viscount Bentley, heir to an earldom, listened to his friend and offered words of solace for two days. Then he took a sterner approach.

" 'Tis time, lad, you pulled yourself together."

"I know." Jake heaved yet another long sigh. "But everything has gone topsy-turvy . . ."

"Yes. However, life *does* go on." Bentley waited, but Jake made no response. "So—what will you do? I seem to remember you planned to study law."

"I am just not sure what I want now."

"Well, you cannot spend your life at the bottom of a bottle." Bentley paused, seemingly in thought. "There's always the church for younger sons such as you."

This brought a faint smile to Jake's lips—the first in nearly three days. "You see *me* as a vicar of the church?"

"No, but you have to do something, don't you?"

"Not really. I have an inheritance from my maternal grandfather—I'm the only grandson, you see. There's a property in Wiltshire and some investments as well."

"Independently wealthy, are you?" Bentley teased.

"Enough. I could become one of Prinny's crew."

"Not your style, old man. I know you. You need some sense of purpose."

"There's always the army as a calling for us younger sons."

"Good God, man! Be serious."

"I am." Suddenly, Jake realized he *was* serious. He had always been intrigued by things military. He remembered as a child marching around with a stick for a musket. "I *am* serious," he repeated calmly.

"Well I'll be—you *are*."

Two days later, not giving himself time to change his mind and giving no one else an opportunity to change it for him, he purchased a commission as a lieutenant in the famous 88th Infantry, the Connaught Rangers. Asked why he had chosen infantry instead of the more glamorous cavalry, he shrugged.

"I am not even sure myself. Perhaps because wars are always won or lost by those poor devils pressing forward, one step at a time."

Before he could take up his post with the army, though, there was the Dalrymple ball to be endured—and what he knew would be a painful interview with Celia.

Because the Dalrymple town house was a very modest residence, the squire had rented the ballroom in one of the city's leading hotels for his eldest daughter's debut in society. The decorations were lavish and the catered supper sumptuous. Jake had steeled himself for this affair, but even two stiff brandies before his arrival had done little to ease his heartache. He was determined that no one—save possibly Bentley—would sense his despair.

He would even dance with his prospective sister-in-law—but only once, and it would be a lively country dance at that. Celia, however, had determined otherwise. She was surrounded by would-be partners when he approached.

"Here, Lord Jacob, I have saved *this* dance for you." She pointed with a long-nailed finger at the line he was to sign on her card.

It was one of those stately dances in which couples spent long pauses waiting their turns as others performed. He gave her a direct look and reluctantly signed. He made some small talk with one or two of the group and then drifted away—or managed to remove himself.

Determined to appear totally natural, he danced with other women, but scarcely noted who they were. When it came time for the dance with Celia, he tried to steel himself anew against the sweet anguish of being so close, of touching her. He said nothing as he partnered her through the opening steps.

During the first pause, her hand decorously on his arm, she tightened her hold ever so slightly. "I must speak with you, Jacob."

"I should have thought, in view of the announcement to come this evening, that everything to say between us had already been said." He gazed at her directly, hoping none of his own emotional turmoil showed in his eyes.

"Please. Do not make this harder for me."

The pleading note in her voice broke through his wall of reserve. "Very well. Say what you must."

"Not here! I am not engaged for the next dance. It will not look amiss if we seek some fresh air on the terrace."

Jake considered this. He would *not* be an instrument of pain to Robert. However, Celia was right. The terrace offered a semipublic environment where a number of couples were to be found at any time. He nodded his agreement.

He escorted her onto the terrace with only the barest of touches, but even that sent a shock through his body. They stood at the balustrade separating the terrace from a garden a few steps below. Neither said anything.

He cleared his throat. "You had something to say?"

"Yes." She reached a hand toward him. He stepped back to avoid the contact. "Oh, Jacob. I am so sorry. I never meant to hurt you."

"Did it not occur to you that *someone* was likely to be hurt when you switched your affections from one brother to another?" Then, unable to hide his cynicism, he added, "But you are doing quite well for yourself. You will be wearing the robes and jewels of a marchioness."

"Please, Jacob. You were never so cruel. I . . . I had no choice."

"No choice?"

"Once Robert spoke to my father, the decision was made. Papa insisted . . ."

"Since when has your overly indulgent father ever refused you anything?"

She did not meet his gaze. "I . . . Mama insisted as well. She thinks it a splendid match."

"And you do not?" he challenged in a disbelieving tone.

"I . . . did not say that."

"So what *are* you saying? That you are being forced to marry my brother, the future Marquis of Lounsbury? *He* thinks he has a love match!"

"Not forced, exactly. But this is clearly something I must do for my family. For my sisters, you see." Her voice took on a tragic note. "My feelings are not to be considered."

"Nor mine, apparently." His blunt tone became bitingly sarcastic. "You poor dear—sacrificed on the altar of family ambitions."

"Please, Jacob. Do not hate me. I love you."

"Do not—I pray you—ever say that again."

"But I do love you." Tears swimming in her eyes made then a dark silvery blue in the dim light. "Truly, I have no choice."

"That may be so—now. But you *did* have a choice before. And know this, Celia," he said fiercely and grabbed her arm in a harsh hold, "Robert is never to know any such thing. Never. Do you understand?"

Anger flashed in her eyes. She jerked away. "I shall handle Robert." She sounded decidedly smug—then petulant. "You seem far more concerned about his feelings than about mine."

"Perhaps I am." He was surprised at the truth of this statement, but did not bother to examine his reaction.

That was the last time he had spoken with her privately. By the time of the wedding, the second Forrester son was enroute to India, where he had eventually so distinguished himself as a promising officer that he caught the attention of a young lieutenant colonel named Arthur Wellesley, later to become Lord Wellington.

In the intervening years, Robert had kept up a steady correspondence with his younger brother. Much of his communication dealt with Jake's property and business affairs, which Robert oversaw. But always there was a good deal of personal information as well. Robert had written proudly of the births of his three children. Jake was, in fact, godfather to the heir who bore the name Nathaniel Jacob, though the godfather business had been handled by proxy.

Robert had also written of their father's death and consulted Jake about the dowager's wish to live on her own permanently in town. When Jake had been home on leave twice, it had been natural for him to stay with his mother and thus avoid spending any but minimal time in the company of his sister-in-law, with whom he was always carefully polite, if not truly cordial. He had noted with gladness that Robert seemed still to be besotted with his wife.

All in all, he surmised, things had not turned out too badly. He had learned to accept his losses and no longer dwelt on what might have been.

He shifted in the bed and winced as a very real physical pain shot through his leg.

Across the hall, Rachel, too, engaged that night in a good deal of introspection. Perhaps she should return to England for the birth of her child. But where would she go? She entertained no illusions about being welcomed by the Brocktons. Her only visit with them since her marriage had been extremely uncomfortable.

Aunt Jessie had been wholly preoccupied with Leah who was about to produce the Brocktons' first grandchild.

"I'm sorry, Rachel, but I must help Leah. I'm sure you understand," her aunt had said as she left Rachel on a daily basis to coddle her pregnant daughter. "While I am gone, would you mind terribly . . ." And always there was a list of chores for her guest to perform at the inn.

Rachel had been glad to leave.

Nor could she go to Brady's family. During their brief courtship, Brady had mentioned his family only in passing. Shortly after the marriage, Rachel had asked again about her in-laws. She had persuaded Edwin to take a rambling walk one balmy evening outside the village that was their temporary home.

"My mother died when I was but eighteen," he answered brusquely.

"But your father?"

"Dead to me." His tone was bitter.

"Oh." Rachel, who had been extraordinarily close to her own father, found this hard to understand. "But . . . but . . . you have brothers and sisters."

"There were seven after me."

"Seven brothers and sisters!" She clapped her hands in glee. "I do *so* look forward to meeting them."

"Well, don't look too hard," he said. "You are most unlikely to meet them at all."

"Why? They are my family, too, now."

"I . . . I . . . have nothing to do with them."

"You quarreled?"

"Uh . . . yes."

"How sad." Then she added in a brightly optimistic tone, "Perhaps I can help you mend the rift."

"No!" The word exploded from him. "Don't you understand? I do not *want* it mended."

"Surely you cannot mean that."

He stopped, grabbed her shoulders, and shook her roughly. He ground out each word fiercely. "I intend never to see them again. You are to put this idea wholly and completely out of your mind. Forever. Do . . . you . . . understand?"

"Yes, Edwin." But she did not understand—not really.

However, this had put an end to her silly dream of belonging to a real family when she married.

Now it seemed she and Edwin were to make their own family. There was a bittersweet quality to this thought, for she knew it was not likely to be the storybook family she had dreamed of having. Only recently Edwin had said how glad he was not to have a stone hanging around his neck such as the Paxtons had in their brat. Surely he would come around, though. Fathers always did, did they not?

And surely she could find some way to recapture the happiness they had shared in the beginning. Those early months had been full of laughter and ever-changing locations and new friends. Edwin had proudly shown her off, reveling in what he saw as the envy of other men. And she had reveled in such attention, for not since her father's death had anyone appreciated her for herself.

Except for Addy, of course—but that was different.

There had also, in those first weeks, been the wonder of the intimacies of the marriage bed. That first time had been a disaster—for her, if not for Edwin. He had been so eager and expressed such satisfaction she willingly overlooked the pain, glad just to see him so happy. Later, she had come to welcome their couplings, especially when Edwin would take the time to be sure her body was ready for his entrance.

As she considered it now, it had been a very long time since he had expended such effort. No wonder her eagerness had diminished.

It also occurred to her now that she felt truly close to Edwin only when they engaged in sex. Perhaps that was why she usually welcomed his overtures. She needed that sense of closeness, the feeling of easy acceptance of her person.

Suddenly, she knew exactly what had prompted her thinking along these lines. This afternoon, discussing the adventures of Achilles and Hector with Major Forrester, she had felt just such harmony of mind and spirit with another human being as she had dreamed of all her life.

She closed her eyes as though doing so would shut out that shocking revelation. A married woman had no business feeling this way about another man. She would have to ensure any future interaction with him was strictly impersonal.

Six

The next day Rachel spent the morning at the hospital. When she returned, she found Clara in the kitchen, cleaning up after the midday meal as Benny played at her feet. Rachel helped herself to leftovers of a rice dish and some fruit.

"You look a little tired," Clara said. "Are you not sleeping well?"

"N-not really. But I am fine. Perhaps I will have a little nap this afternoon. It is so nice to have these days when we are not trudging along next to a supply wagon."

" 'Tis that." Clara agreed, giving her friend a doubtful look.

"But first I have one more disagreeable task to perform."

"Is it something I can do for you?"

Rachel gave a rueful little laugh. "I think not. It is time to cleanse the wound in the major's leg."

Clara shuddered. "Take out those things, you mean?"

"Yes."

"Well, let me put Benny down for his nap, and I shall do whatever I can to assist you. Mr. Henry has gone for supplies. He should return soon, though."

"You go ahead with Benny and I will get started with the major."

Rachel went into the pantry, found what she wanted, and then filled a basin with hot water and carried it up the stairs to Major Forrester's room.

"Ah, Mrs. Brady." He eyed the basin in her hands. "Come to torture me some more, have you?"

"As a matter of fact, sir, you wrong me terribly. I hope to relieve you of some of the torture you endure so very uncomplainingly."

"If you mean to remove these infernal worms that are driving me mad, you are welcome indeed, madam."

Because of the warm weather, he was covered with only a thin sheet which did little to hide the vigorous, naked form beneath it. Rachel tried to ignore that observation as she lifted the sheet decorously to expose the wound above his left knee. She loosened the binding, then held her breath as she removed the bandage. A wave of nausea threatened her. She stood and turned away, swallowing hard.

"Is something wrong?" He sounded apprehensive.

"No." She took a deep breath. "No. I forgot to bring the instruments and clean bandages."

She went to the adjacent dressing room to retrieve these items. As she did so, she noted that Henry would make an excellent housekeeper, judging by the neat orderliness she found there. She took another deep breath and returned to the major's bedside.

She bent closer over the open wound. The smell of decay was not as pronounced as it had been during previous changes of bandage. Moreover, the tissue had taken on a healthy deep pink tinge.

"I am sorely afraid this is going to be painful, Major."

Jake tried not to notice the compassion in her oddly colored eyes—were they gray? or green? or brown? He also tried to ignore the gentleness of her touch on his upper thigh. Most of all, he tried unsuccessfully to tear his gaze away from the cleavage of her well-formed breasts as she bent over him.

Good God! Had the woman no idea what she was doing to him? Even before she had turned back that sheet, he had been aware of her closeness. There was the smell of sunshine and flowers about her. Then she bent close. He sucked in his breath and tried to think of something mundane to divert the reaction of his body. No good. He could feel himself hardening and knew damned well the thin sheet would not hide his erection.

He was profoundly embarrassed. "I—I do apologize, Mrs. Brady."

He was grateful when she did not express shock or pretend ignorance. She straightened and patted his arm.

"Never mind, Major. It is not an unknown occurrence in a hospital. Shall we get on with relieving you of your unwelcome guests?"

"Oh, yes, please, ma'am," he said, trying deliberately to sound like an agreeable schoolboy. He steeled himself against the pain about which she had warned him, but could not suppress a groan as she wiped something against the surface of the wound.

Rachel had used a damp cloth to wipe away most of the maggots. She tried to control her own nauseated aversion to the task while simultaneously being as gentle as possible in the procedure. Perspiration poured from his face, and his teeth were tightly clenched.

"Just a little more," she said, knowing full well the worst was yet to come.

Clara came in just then. "What may I do to help?"

"There is a basin and a pitcher of water in the dressing room," Rachel said. "If you were to wipe his face and neck with a damp cloth, I am sure the major would welcome such."

Clara quickly went about this task and Rachel began the business of probing for remaining creatures, fully aware that Major Forrester felt acutely every touch of the instrument she used. Finally she removed the last one.

"There. Done." She let out a deep breath, unaware until now she had been scarcely breathing.

"Thank God," the major said hoarsely.

"Do not be too thankful just yet," she warned.

Before he could react verbally, she poured brandy into the open sore.

"A-a-h!" he cried. "Are you trying to kill me, woman?"

"No. Merely disinfect the wound. It is over now. I shall put a poultice on it and we shall hope for the best."

Clara watched closely as Rachel prepared the poultice. "Ah. So *that* is why you saved that moldy bread."

"Yes. I have no idea why it works, but it seems to draw the poison out of a wound."

Clara looked doubtful. "Are you sure? It seems rather dirty to me."

"I'm sure. My father learned this technique from an old ship's surgeon. And I saw Addy use it as well." Rachel had told Clara of Mrs. Addison's kindness to a friendless young girl.

"Well . . . if you say so. . . ." Clara did not sound at all convinced.

Major Forrester also looked at her rather skeptically. His face was still ashen from the pain earlier. "Surely, having brought me to this point, you are not planning to poison me?"

She smiled, pleased that he was able to tease. "Not today, at least. Maybe later—when you get really cantankerous."

"I shall try to be on my best behavior, then."

She finished tying up the bandage and bent over to gather up the waste. She felt the blood drain from her head and nausea rise from her innards.

"I—I—excuse me," she said hurriedly, and fled from the room. She heard the major call, "Mrs. Brady, are you all right?"

"Rachel?" Clara queried.

She barely made it to her own room and the chamber pot. She was vaguely aware that Clara had followed her. Finally, she ceased wretching and sat back on her heels.

"Here." Clara handed her a glass of water.

"Thank you." Rachel rinsed her mouth, then took a deep swallow of the liquid.

"Now you just stay here and rest," Clara ordered. "I shall finish cleaning up in there."

"Tell him . . . tell him I'm sorry."

"He knows that," Clara said gently.

Rachel lay on the bed, momentarily spent. She could hear Clara going in and out of the major's room and the low murmur of their voices. Soon, she also heard Henry come up the stairs and his greeting of the other two. She had no thought of going to sleep, but she supposed she must have done so when Clara arrived some time later.

"I have brought you some tea and toast," she announced, setting a tray on the bedside table.

Rachel noticed there were two cups for the tea. She watched silently as Clara poured both cups and handed one to Rachel.

"Thank you. You are so good to me, Clara."

"You need to take better care of *yourself,*" Clara said brusquely. She pulled up a chair and gave Rachel a penetrating look. "Have you told Mr. Brady about the babe?"

Rachel felt her eyes widen in surprise. "How did you know? I only suspected myself a few days ago."

"Living as closely as we have been doing, there is not much that remains secret, you know. I've seen the signs that you probably were too busy to notice. Also, it's not been so very long ago that I went through it."

"I *should* have noticed, though." She told Clara of the earlier pregnancy and her miscarriage.

"Then it is doubly important that you take care of yourself," Clara insisted. *"Does* your husband know?"

"N-not yet. He . . . he will not like the idea."

"And he'll blame you," Clara said grimly.

Rachel was embarrassed at Clara's assessment of Edwin, but she could not deny the truth. "Probably. I just need to find the right time to tell him."

Clara patted her hand. "Best do it sooner than later, my dear."

"I know."

The two women sat in companionable silence for several minutes as Rachel nibbled at the toast and both drank their tea. Rachel was touched by Clara's concern. She had never had such a close female friend—such a close friend, period.

She was determined to treasure this relationship, no matter what Edwin Brady said.

"Is Mrs. Brady unwell?" Jake asked from his bed when Clara came in to finish cleaning up.

"Not exactly. Just tired out, I think. A woman in her condition's got no business spending all those long hours in that hospital."

"In her condition?" he repeated dumbly. Good God. He had been lusting after a woman who was not only married, but one with child!

Clara merely nodded and went about her business.

"When is her husband due to return?"

"Any day now. But she'll not get much support in that quarter." Clara suddenly seemed self-conscious about the conversation. "I'm sorry, Major Forrester. I shouldn't have said anything at all. Sometimes I just talk too much. Rachel wouldn't want—"

"I shall say nothing to upset her. I probably had no business asking," he replied.

"It's just that we are so used to talking over you and around you . . ."

He smiled. "Like a piece of furniture, am I?"

"Oh, no. That is not what I meant. I meant—well—more like one of *us.*" She colored up at this admission. "At home, Joe and me would never know a real lord, of course. But here—" She floundered in embarrassment.

"Out here such distinctions seem to mean much less, do they not?"

"I—I suppose so. But Joe and me—we would never presume, my lord—"

"I did not think you would. Now, Mrs. Paxton, since we are, in effect, all living here as some sort of patched-together family, suppose you call me Jake? Nobody in Spain goes around 'my lording' me—except Henry, of course. I cannot seem to break him of the habit."

"Oh, my lord—I'm just not sure that would be proper at all."

"I insist."

"Oh, but sir—"

"Mrs. Paxton! Are you going to refuse a simple request from a wounded man?"

"Very well. Jake it is. I'm Clara, and my husband is Joe." She paused and her eyes twinkled. "My pa used to say the nobs always get their own way."

He chuckled at this. "Be sure to tell Mrs. Brady of our new arrangement."

"Rachel. Her name's Rachel."

"Yes, I know. Henry told me. He also informed me of precisely the lengths she has gone to in saving my life and limb."

"Rachel is a very generous, giving person."

"I am aware of that, too. And I want her to know if she ever needs anything, she has but to ask me."

Clara gave him an understanding look. "That is very nice of you, but I doubt Rachel will feel you owe her anything. She is that used to doing for others."

"Still, my offer is always open."

"I'll tell her."

Jake shifted in the bed. "Henry also told me your husband is with Grant's 94th."

"That he is."

"If he's of a mind to do so, would you ask your Joe to spend some time with me after the evening meal? I need to get a military man's view of what is going on."

"Certainly. Joe will be glad to visit with you."

Jake could tell she was pleased to have her Joe distinguished so by a high-ranking officer. Actually, Sergeant Humphrey and Corporal Collins had informed him of matters with his own regiment, and he had no doubt his officer friends Hastings and Travers would call soon. Still, it would not hurt to get yet another perspective. A lowly Lieutenant Jacob Forrester had learned early on the value of listening to men of lower ranks.

* * *

Rachel looked in on her patient later in the evening, but true to her plan to put some distance between her and the major, she did not stay long. She found him chatting amiably with Joe Paxton. Joe had drawn up a chair near the bed and sat lounging back in his seat with one foot on his other knee. He started to rise as Rachel entered.

"No, no, Mr. Paxton. Keep your seat, please. I did not mean to interrupt."

"A pretty woman is always a welcome interruption." The major's eyes twinkled as he added, "That is, unless you come to inflict more torture upon me."

She pretended to take offense. "Major Forrester! You insist upon wronging me." She addressed Joe. "See what abuse I suffer—and all from having performed a mission of mercy."

"Ah! Mercy, was it?" Forrester quipped. "Well, I must say the quality of mercy in this instance was mightily strained."

She smiled. "Nor did it 'droppeth as the gentle rain from heaven,' my lord. Actually, I merely meant to check on your current degree of pain."

He turned serious. "Discomfort, but no real pain."

"Good. With Henry's help you may finally make it out of that bed tomorrow. Good night, my lord. Mr. Paxton."

"Did Clara not inform you that henceforth we shall use Christian names in our 'family'?" the major asked.

"Yes, sir, she did."

"I see. The notion is too democratic for your sensibilities, is it?"

"Not precisely. Here, it makes little difference, but outside these walls, well . . ."

"Outside these walls, our paths have not crossed in the past, so it can make little difference there, either."

"He's right, you know," Joe said.

"Very well, gentlemen." Her tone reflected her reluctance, but she emphasized their names with, "Good night, Jake. And Joe."

The major winked at Joe. "She's as much of a high stickler as Henry. Good night, Rachel."

Joe gave a sympathetic chuckle as Rachel left the room. She was not comfortable using the major's name. Nor was she comfortable with the little thrill she had felt at his use of hers. This business undermined her resolve to maintain distance between them.

The next day she again spent the morning in the hospital. Most of the patients there were, like the major, now on the mend. The critical cases had been removed to Lisbon for transport home or to a holding hospital farther behind the front lines of the campaign.

Back at the house, she joined the others for the midday meal. Henry was full of news of the major's having walked about his bedchamber for several minutes that morning.

"He is determined to rejoin the regiment as soon as possible," Henry reported.

"Tell him not to be in too great a hurry," Rachel cautioned.

"There doesn't seem to be any need for urgency," said Joe, who had popped home for this meal and the Spanish siesta time that followed it. "The general hasn't given the order to move out yet."

"Surely he will give us some warning. I will hate to leave this house." Clara's longing for a more settled life was evident.

"I know, my dear." Her husband clearly understood her feelings. "As soon as Boney's people are pushed back to Paris, we will be able to go home." He paused and gave her a speaking look. "Or you could take Benny and go home yourself now. Lord knows that would probably be best."

"We have been over this before, Joe. Benny and I are *not* leaving you here alone."

"I would not be alone, exactly. I heard today that our

forces are expected to be near thirty thousand in a matter of weeks."

"But still outnumbered by the French and *their* Spanish allies," Henry said.

Clara raised her chin. "Benny and I are staying here."

Her husband shrugged. "So be it."

Later, as she climbed the stairs, Rachel wondered at this exchange. She knew Clara's family would welcome her and her son. Clara's father was not a rich man, but he was a merchant of more than modest success. Her parents had disapproved of Clara's following the drum, but they had not cut communication with their daughter. In fact, they urged her to come home in every missive. To which Clara inevitably replied that, with Joe, she *was* home. Rachel thought Benny's arrival had complicated matters for the Paxtons, but they seemed to be managing well enough.

She paused before the major's door and took a deep breath. How was it that the mere prospect of seeing him heightened her senses? She knocked and entered at his bidding, leaving the door ajar.

"Good afternoon, Major," she said cheerily.

"Jake," he growled.

Henry peered around the dressing room door. "We may have overdone it this morning."

" 'We'?" Forrester growled again. "Do you have a mouse in your pocket, Henry?"

"I beg your pardon, my lord?"

"Oh, never mind." The major thumped his pillow into place and then winced from the exertion.

"Serves you right for being so cranky," Rachel said, carefully removing the pillow and fluffing it. "Now, raise your head." As she replaced the pillow, she noted his face was clean-shaven and not so gaunt looking as it had been.

"You'd be cranky, too, were you confined to a bed as I have been."

"Well, you are looking better, sir, and judging by your foul mood, you must be feeling much more your usual self."

He grinned sheepishly. "Saucy little thing, aren't you?"

"I came to change that bandage for you," she said, trying to bring the conversation to a more impersonal level.

He looked uncomfortable. "Do you not think Henry might take over that task now?"

"Perhaps. Just let me see how that poultice is working."

As Henry stood by with clean bandaging, she removed the old dressing and pronounced herself very pleased indeed with the results. She showed Henry precisely how to apply the poultice and hold it in place. It was agreed that Henry could perform this task on his own the next day.

"Though I think you might leave the poultice off then— just place a clean bandage on the wound."

"Yes, ma'am," Henry replied.

"And you, sir, may dispense with my services," Rachel said with more cheer than she felt as she rose from kneeling beside the bed.

"I must confess to very mixed feelings at that prospect," the major replied. "Henry is not nearly as pleasant to look upon as you are."

Henry, pretending to have hurt feelings, responded in an exaggerated accent. "Oi does me best, I does."

"And you do very well," Rachel assured him.

Major Forrester reached a hand toward her, which she grasped before even thinking. He held her gaze steadily. "Mrs. Brady—Rachel—I want you to know I am well aware of the extent to which I am in your debt."

"Oh, but—"

"No. Do not diminish and disparage. You probably saved my life—and you certainly saved my leg. I am most grateful for that."

"Certainly I *helped* to do so . . . but a good many others were involved, too."

"I know. But I also know where most of the credit belongs. If ever you need anything—"

She gave his hand a quick squeeze and released it. "I—I appreciate your feelings, Major. Jake," she said on seeing his frown. "And your offer." Then she added in a lighter tone, "Just see you take proper care of our repair work."

"Oh, I shall. Henry and I are going riding tomorrow." He laughed aloud at the startled looks they wore. "Well— maybe the day *after* tomorrow."

"You can at least sit out in the courtyard then. We are having fine weather now."

Just then they heard the great oaken door of the front entrance bang open and the muffled sound of boots on the stairs.

"Rachel!" called a voice she recognized immediately. "Where the hell is my wife? Rachel!"

"Excuse me." She hurried out to the hallway and pulled the major's door closed, hoping he and Henry would not hear the ensuing conversation, but knowing it was a vain hope.

"I'm right here, Edwin," she said calmly, standing at the top of the stairs as he ascended them.

"And just what do you think you are doing in this place? Did I or did I not give you specific instructions when I left?"

As he reached the top stair, she stepped back, for the smell of brandy was so strong it sent her stomach churning.

"Is that any way to greet your long-lost spouse?" He grabbed her and pulled her close. As his mouth descended toward hers, she fought rising nausea. She turned her head.

"Please, Edwin." She braced herself against his chest and took a deep breath. He released her.

"What the hell's wrong with you?" He made no attempt to keep his voice down. "And why have you seen fit to disobey me?"

"It—it was not practical to do as you wanted," she replied softly, knowing full well it was unlikely he would listen to reason.

" 'Not practical'?" he sneered. "Since when do *you* judge my orders as practical or not?"

Rachel was burning with embarrassment. "Edwin, please. Can we just go in our room to discuss this privately?"

"No, by God! We'll discuss it here and now. I want to

know why you are tucked away in this house with his high and mighty lordship and the holier-than-thou Paxtons when I strictly forbade it."

"Perhaps to sleep in a real bed and sit on something besides the dirt floor or a shepherd's stool?"

"What your husband provides isn't good enough for you—is that it?"

Rachel was losing patience with his ranting. "Oh, Edwin, or heaven's sake, be reasonable."

"I've *told* you about giving me your sass," he snarled and swung his arm to give her a backhanded slap.

The blow knocked her off balance and she grabbed futilely for the railing.

"Edwin! No-o-o," she screamed as she lost her footing and fell head over heels to the bottom of the stairs. She put her hand to her stomach in an instinctive gesture as darkness closed in.

Seven

"Henry! Quick! See what's going on," Jake ordered as he threw back his sheet and reached for the dressing gown lying at the foot of the bed.

Henry was obviously torn between obeying the order and helping his employer with the still difficult task of getting out of bed.

"Go!" Jake ordered again.

"Yes, sir."

Henry opened the door, then stepped out of the room. Behind him Jake managed to don the dressing gown and even to stand on his own, but he had to grab the bedpost when he tried to exert weight on his injured leg, which promptly gave way.

"Damn!" he muttered.

Henry returned. "Here, let me help you, my lord."

"What happened?" Jake asked, allowing Henry to take some of his weight.

"Mrs. Brady fell down the stairs."

"Is she injured?"

"I don't know, my lord. She was just lying there. Her husband was with her—and Mrs. Paxton."

"Help me to the door. I have to see." He could not have explained, even to himself, the depth of this *need* to see that Rachel was all right.

As he reached the opened door, he could hear the others coming up the stairs. Soon a dark-haired head appeared above the top step, then the man's body. In his arms lay Rachel's still figure.

Jake could not help glaring at the man.

"What are you starin' at?" Brady snarled. "This is none of your business."

Clara, right behind them, hurried forward to open Rachel's door. "In here."

"She's not . . ." Jake could not bring himself to finish the sentence.

"No," Clara said, apparently reading his mind. "She's just unconscious. I've sent Mr. Thompkins—Sam—for a doctor."

Jake now saw only Brady's back, but that brief glimpse of the other man's face was troublesome. Brady kicked the door of the other room closed. Jake turned reluctantly back to his own bed, cautioning himself to remember that the man was right—it really *was* none of his business. What happened within a marriage was of no concern to an outsider.

"Henry, find out what happened," Jake said. "And when the doctor arrives, ask him to have a look at my leg."

"Did you do something to it when you moved so abruptly?"

"I wrenched it pretty hard, but, in truth, 'tis but an excuse to ask him about Ra—Mrs. Brady." Somehow, it seemed safer to think of Rachel as "Mrs. Brady" now.

Henry had, at Jake's instruction, left the chamber door ajar so they would know when the doctor arrived. Jake lay staring at the underside of the canopy of his bed, scarcely aware of the throbbing in his leg. His mind seemed riveted on the image of Rachel's inert body as her husband carried her up the stairs and into the room across the hall. Then his mind's eye moved to the face of the man Brady. There was something about that face. . . .

"Henry, do you happen to know where Brady is from?"

Henry turned from the window that looked out on the courtyard. "The doctor is arriving now," he announced, then answered Jake's question. "I *believe* Mrs. Brady once mentioned Devon."

"Devon." Jake mulled this over for a few minutes and allowed himself to sort through his thoughts aloud. It was a habit of long standing. "A long distance from Scotland."

"Yes, sir. Mrs. Brady lived in the north of England when they met. He was a recruiter."

"Hmm." Jake's mind still dwelt on that face and Devon. "My father, as you know, had a property in Devon, but I do not recall anyone named Brady . . . of course, I visited that property only three or four times in my entire life."

"May I ask what is troubling you, sir?"

"I am not sure. I have a feeling I should know that face."

"Well, the man's been in the army several years. Perhaps you connected with him sometime in the past."

"Perhaps . . ."

They heard the arrival of the doctor across the hall, and then silence for a good while. Jake thought it seemed the whole house was holding its breath.

Edwin Brady watched in horror as his wife went tumbling down the stairs. It was almost as though it were happening in some slowed dream time. Then he jerked himself into action and raced down the stairs. He knelt beside her and cradled her inert body to his chest.

"Oh, God, Rachel. I'm sorry. I didn't mean—"

"What happened?" Clara asked in alarm as she came from the kitchen in the back of the house. "I heard a scream. Oh! Rachel!"

"She . . . she fell," Edwin explained lamely.

"Down the whole flight of stairs?"

"Yes. She's unconscious."

"I'll send for the doctor."

"Let's wait to see if that's necessary," Edwin said, but Clara had already gone. "Officious damned woman," he muttered.

As he maneuvered to gather Rachel into his arms, Clara returned.

"Let's get her to bed," she said.

"Just show me where."

He stood rather awkwardly, then carried Rachel to the room indicated, noting the opened door across the hall as he did so. Forrester. Just what he needed now.

He laid Rachel on the bed and knelt beside her. "You'll be all right, sweetheart, I promise," he said softly.

Clara rummaged through a dresser drawer and came back with a nightgown in her hand. "With her unconscious as she is, you'll have to help me get her out of those clothes and into this gown before the doctor arrives."

"Of course." He resented Clara's take-charge attitude, but this was obviously not the time to argue with her.

Together they removed Rachel's outer dress and Clara loosened her stays and removed her undergarments, then slipped the gown over her head and, with Brady's help, worked it down over her body.

"That's an ugly bruise on her face," Clara said, giving him a penetrating look. Her tone was challenging. "She get that in the fall?"

He shrugged. "Must have." By God! A man had no need to justify punishing his own wife to some near stranger!

As Clara reached for the cover to draw it over Rachel, the patient groaned and opened her eyes.

"Oh, Clara. Oh. I hurt so very, very much."

"Try to stay calm. I have sent for the doctor."

"Clara, I . . . I feel strange. Am I bleeding?"

"Bleeding?" Edwin asked brusquely. "Of course not. You just got the wind knocked out of you."

"Clara? Would you see . . . ?" Rachel asked.

Clara pulled back the blanket, lifted the gown. "Oh, dear. You're right. You *are* bleeding. Let me get a pad of some sort to put under you. But do lie very still, Rachel. We shall try to save your babe."

"Babe?" Edwin growled in astonishment. "Are you saying she's with child?"

"Please don't be angry, Edwin," Rachel pleaded. "I was going to tell you—when the time was right."

"There would be no 'right' time for such news. And you know it. What *were* you thinking?" His voice was cold, accusing.

Clara straightened from placing a folded sheet beneath Rachel's lower body. "You are not helping the present situation, Mr. Brady. Besides, it is rather common knowledge that no woman comes into this condition alone."

"I don't need—"

His retort was cut off by the arrival of Captain MacLachlan.

"Ah, Mrs. Brady. What have you got up to here?"

"I—I fell down the stairs," she said.

"And you should know she is with child," Clara informed him.

He raised his brows at this news. "How far?"

"Two—two and a half months," Rachel answered.

"Two and a half months?" Edwin repeated in a challenging tone.

"Sergeant, if you will just wait over there as I examine the patient?" The surgeon pointed to a chair off to the side, and his tone made it clear this was no mere suggestion.

With Clara standing watch over the procedure, MacLachlan made short work of his examination, checking first for broken bones. When he was finished, he drew up a chair and sat beside his patient. He took Rachel's hand in his great paw and gazed at her compassionately.

"I am very sorry, my dear. You are, in fact, losing this babe."

"No. Oh, no-o-o." Rachel's anguished wail filled the room. Tears flowed freely from the outer corners of her eyes onto the pillow as she twisted her head from side to side in her emotional pain.

Clara grasped her other hand. "Rachel, I'm so sorry."

"Are you sure, Mac?" Rachel asked, but she seemed to know the answer before the doctor responded.

He nodded, his expression solemn. "I know it is of little

consolation to you now, but you are young and healthy. There will be other babes for you."

Rachel merely turned her head away as though she were refusing to listen. The surgeon and Clara continued to offer words of comfort.

Brady sat mulling over the astonishing news of his wife's pregnancy. Two and half months? Why, that meant she had lied to him several days ago when she had refused his advances. Refuse her own husband, would she?

Finally, the surgeon stood and took his leave of Rachel.

"Sergeant Brady, may I have a word with you outside?" Again it was an order rather than a request.

Outside the room, the doctor took a belligerent stance in front of Brady. Edwin felt intimidated by the man—a huge fellow of perhaps six and a half feet with shoulders that could have supported an ox.

"Now, look here, Brady. That little woman did *not* get that bruise on her face from any tumble down the stairs— and we both know it. I'm inclined to think she had some help in that fall, too."

"I don't know what you're talking about."

"Don't try to gammon me. You know exactly what I'm saying." MacLachlan thumped him on the chest. "And know this, Brady—if it happens again, I will take a very personal interest in the matter."

"What happens between a man his wife is of no concern to you."

"I'm making it my concern in this instance." The surgeon gave him a hard stare, and Brady found himself unable to hold the other's gaze.

Seething with frustrated anger, Brady asked, "Are you finished having your say?"

"No. One other thing. She is a very sick woman now. She needs complete bed rest for at least a week. Mrs. Paxton has promised to care for her. And you are to leave her alone for at least a month. Do you get my meaning?"

"A month? A whole month?"

"A whole month." The doctor did not bother to hide his

disgust. "You could cause her further injury. And, I swear, if you do . . ." The threat was very clear.

Brady heaved an angry sigh. "So be it. A month."

They simply stared at each other for a moment. Then Forrester's batman came into the hall. Had he heard this conversation? Well, so what if he had? Forrester and his lot were nothing to Edwin Brady.

"Captain MacLachlan, while you are here, would you please have a look at his lordship's leg?"

"I'll be glad to." The surgeon also seemed glad to be shut of Edwin Brady.

"Will she recover properly?" Jake asked the question as Henry was closing the door behind the surgeon.

"Mrs. Brady, you mean? Yes, she will, though she has suffered a miscarriage. That's always hard on a woman."

"A sorry bit of bad luck, that," Jake said. He felt profoundly sorry for Rachel. His intuition told him she would mourn such a loss even as she would a living child.

"I think more than luck was involved." MacLachlan's voice was filled with disgust.

"Yes, we heard it," Jake admitted. "Unfortunately, it was over before I could fairly move."

"Not much you could do anyway, especially given your own physical condition at the moment. 'Tis not unusual—and certainly not illegal—for a man to treat his wife so."

"One wonders why a generous, giving woman would choose to align herself with such a brute," Henry observed.

MacLachlan stroked his chin. "Who knows? She must have been very young when they married. Perhaps circumstances forced her to such a choice. Women simply haven't the freedom of choosing that we men have."

"True," Jake said, thinking of Celia's argument and wondering if there might be a parallel there.

"Now, you wanted me to look at that leg wound?"

"While you are here."

MacLachlan removed the bandage and examined the injury. "You've reopened the wound, but the bleeding seems to have stopped. Mrs. Brady saved that leg for you, Major. I would have amputated immediately."

"I know. I am most grateful to her."

"Of course, your own fine constitution helped—along with a good deal of sheer will, I suspect." MacLachlan rose. "I'll be checking on her again in a day or so. I shall look in on you as well."

"Thank you, sir."

MacLachlan had left some laudanum for Rachel. Clara mixed a small dose with water and gave it to her.

"This will help you get some rest."

"Thank you." Rachel's voice was dull, lifeless even to her own ears.

With tears in her eyes, Clara put her hand on Rachel's. Her voice was infinitely gentle. "Try not to dwell on what might have been. It must have been God's will."

"I know, but it is just so hard to accept."

"Of course it is."

Brady returned to the room then.

"Mrs. Paxton, will you excuse us, please? I would like a word with my wife." His words were polite enough, but his manner bordered on rudeness.

"Why, surely," Clara said, casting a worried look at Rachel.

"Don't worry. I will be fine," Rachel assured her.

"Why should she worry?" Brady snapped.

"I'll bring your supper up later." Clara closed the door softly behind her.

Edwin took the seat Clara had vacated. He simply stared at Rachel a few minutes, but she was not sure he was actually seeing her.

"I didn't mean for this to happen," he finally said.

"I know."

"Why didn't you tell me about the babe?"

"I didn't know myself until just you before left."

"But you could have told me then," he insisted.

"I—I suppose I just did not want to deal with your anger," she said wearily. She could feel the laudanum beginning to take effect and wished he would postpone this confrontation.

"So is that why you lied to me?" His voice had turned hard.

"Lied to you?"

"When I tried to make love to you."

She could not meet his gaze. "Partly," she whispered.

"Rachel, I will not tolerate your lying to me."

Now she looked at him directly. "And I will no longer tolerate your striking me."

"Then don't provoke me," he said dismissively.

She raised herself on her elbows. "Provoke you? Edwin, when you've been drinking it takes almost nothing to set you off."

"That's not true, and you know it. I have never hit you without cause. Now I'm sorry you fell down the stairs, but you can hardly blame me that you lost your footing."

"Had you not hit me, I would not have lost my footing."

"This discussion is going nowhere, Rachel. Just see you never lie to me again—or I promise I will make you very sorry indeed."

Despite her exhaustion, her words were clipped, adamant. "Then know this, Edwin Brady—if you ever—ever again—raise a hand against me, *I* shall contrive to make you more than just sorry." She lay back, spent.

"And just what do you think you could possibly do?" His tone expressed disbelief and contempt.

"If nothing else, I *could* easily slit your throat when you are in one of your drunken stupors. But most likely I would feed you some potion that would, at the very least, make you extremely and painfully ill. You know I possess sufficient knowledge of herbs."

"You wouldn't have the nerve," he sneered, but she thought there was a trace of fearful doubt in his tone.

Her voice was calm, devoid of emotion, but firm. "Yes, Edwin, I would. I will not be hit again."

Something in her demeanor must have penetrated, for he gave her a look that was at first startled, then speculative.

"I—I don't have to put up with this nonsense," he blustered. "You are obviously not quite yourself. I'll go away now and let you rest. I shall see you in the morning."

He rose and left the room.

Rachel lay still, trying to make her mind go blank. She allowed the drug to sweep away all unpleasantness—at least for a while.

Sergeant Edwin Brady left the house feeling very put upon indeed. He was madder than hops at Rachel, but what could he do with her lying there? How would it make him look if he heaped abuse on the head of a woman who had just suffered a miscarriage? He had to get away. Not only was he wholly inadequate as a nursemaid, he also did not want to spend too much time in close proximity to Jacob Forrester.

He sought the company of his friend Morton, finding the man in a posada—a Spanish pension or inn where Morton and several others were billeted. The entire place of business had been appropriated by the British army and duly Anglicized by English soldiers. Ralph Morton was in the common room of the posada throwing darts with Privates Harvey Willis and Fred Potter.

"Ay, Brady," Morton greeted him. "Thought you went to find your wife."

"I found her," Brady said, disgruntled.

"And you're back with *us* already?" Morton's question was both leering and ridiculing. He grinned knowingly at Willis and Potter. "Our friend Brady seems to be having woman problems."

"And wouldn't you like to have problems with one as looked like that?" Willis retorted.

"I think I'd know how to keep her happy," Morton said.

"You just *think*," Brady responded, nettled. He stepped to the bar, ordered a drink, and carried it to an empty corner table.

Soon Morton finished the game and joined him. The two privates left the posada with joking comments about finding a willing woman. As Morton planted his muscular body in a chair across the table, Brady was struck anew by the incongruities of the man. Things just did not seem to fit with Morton. He was several years older than Brady and the two privates, yet sought to spend most of his free time with the younger men. He had a broad, flat face and a receding hairline. His nose was misshapen from having been broken one too many times. He looked like what he had been in civilian life, a street ruffian, yet he had smooth, long-fingered hands that looked almost feminine.

"Want to tell Uncle Ralphie your troubles?" Morton asked.

"Damn women who won't do what they're told," Brady grumbled. "I *told* her I wanted nothing to do with Forrester."

"Forrester. That major with the Rangers? *He's* the one she's taking care of?"

"The very one. The whole lot of them moved into the town together while we were gone. Forrester, the Paxtons, and my wife."

Morton raised an eyebrow. "Sounds cozy."

"Too cozy. And after I told her to get shut of that lot."

"Well, make her do it now. Women have to do what their husbands tell them to do."

"It's not that easy." Brady told him of Rachel's fall and miscarriage, carefully omitting his role in the accident.

"Sounds like a plushy billet to me—and the major must be footing the expense. What is your gripe about that?"

"I got no use for Forrester. And the Paxtons are not my sort at all."

"Thought goody-two-shoes Paxton was your bosom beau."

"We shared quarters—that was all."

"So what have you got against Forrester—other than his being a bloody officer?"

"I . . . uh . . . met him once, years ago." Brady was not about to share details of that particular event of his youth with the likes of Ralph Morton.

"Bested you in a fight, did he?"

"Not precisely."

"Does *he* remember *you?*"

"I don't think so—and I'd just as soon keep it that way."

"Best get your woman outa that house then."

"I know that," Brady said impatiently. "But I have to wait now until that meddling doctor says she's recovered enough to move."

"Sounds a right proper mess to me." There was little sign of sympathy in Morton's tone.

Brady signaled the harried bartender for more drinks. When they arrived, he took a deep swallow of his and said, "I am heartily sick her disapproving what I do—*and* disobeying my orders. You're damned lucky not to be saddled with a woman out here."

"If you're serious about that, it shouldn't be too hard to rid yourself of her."

"What are you saying?" Brady was genuinely shocked at what he thought Morton was suggesting. Soldiers killed, but cold-blooded murder was something else entirely. Although—had his wife not threatened him with such?

Morton gave him a look of exasperation. "Not what you are thinking."

"What then? I couldn't just desert an Englishwoman here on the Peninsula. I'm not looking to be court-martialed and flogged. Officers might turn a blind eye to a soldier abandoning a French, Spanish, or Portuguese woman—but an *Englishwoman?* I doubt that very much."

"True. But there is another way of dealing with a wife you no longer want."

Brady gave a derisive laugh. "Oh, sure. I could hie myself back to England and get Parliament to grant a bill of divorcement"—he snapped his fingers—"just like *that.* 'Well, you see, General, I need to shed this woman.' Can't you just see the Peer agreeing to my having leave for that? Not to mention the cost. Where do you think I'd get the hundreds—no, thousands—of pounds it would cost—on a *sergeant's* daily pay?"

"There's always the poor man's divorce . . ."

"You mean *sell* her? I've heard that's not exactly legal."

"Maybe not, but it's still done, and English authorities generally tolerate the practice."

"I'd have to think about that quite a lot."

"You do that," Morton said. "Look, if you need a place to sleep, you can roll up on the floor in our room."

"Thanks. I'll do that. You bunking with Willis and Potter, are you?"

"Yes."

Brady finished his drink and shook his head, trying to clear it of Morton's suggestion.

Sell his wife?

What a preposterous idea!

Eight

That conversation with Morton flitted in and out of Brady's mind over the next few days. However, he found himself curiously reluctant to examine the idea too closely. True, he often chafed at the responsibilities of seeing to the needs of a woman. Moreover, his resentment had grown in the last year or so. Equally true, he was extremely angry with Rachel for contriving to put him in Forrester's path. In all fairness, however, she had had no idea of his antipathy to the entire Forrester clan. Besides, she *was* an attractive woman—and she was *his*. Did he truly want to give her up? Things would be back to normal as soon as he could get her away from Forrester and the Paxtons.

Forrester.

Just what perverse fate had landed a Forrester—this Forrester—in the same corner of the world as one Edwin Brady?

He thought back to the events of his youth that made this current situation so very uncomfortable.

The first had occurred during his seventeenth summer—nearly twelve years ago in Devon. He and Victor Kenwick, the squire's son, had been home from school. It had not occurred to Edwin in those days to wonder why the Marquis of Lounsbury would trouble to send a tenant farmer's son away to be educated. True, it was not a first-rate education such as the marquis had accorded his own sons, but it was such as to allow a boy from a tenant farm to aspire to a better station in life—perhaps as a steward, even. Obviously, the marquis had observed that the boy Edwin was a cut above local farm yokels.

The summer before, Edwin had happily lost his virginity with one of the dairy maids on the home farm of Raleigh Manor, one of several Lounsbury holdings throughout England. Anna. He still recalled fondly her saucy, flirtatious manner and her smooth white flesh. A year later, he desperately hungered for another taste of what he had so enjoyed as a mere boy of sixteen. He and Kenwick had talked of little else but "finding a girl" for several days.

The two had been out fishing that day and were returning home through a corner of the Lounsbury woods, when there she was on the lane ahead of them. Anna. Anna, who had been oh-so-willing last year.

"Hey, there. Anna," Edwin called.

She turned. "Oh, Edwin. I heard you was back."

He hurried to catch up with her, and Kenwick was right beside him.

"That I am. And hungering mightily after what only you can give." Edwin gave her one of his practiced smiles that had been moderately successful on taproom maids in town.

She sidled away from him. "Well, as to that, I'm afraid you'll have to look elsewhere."

"Ah, now. You don't really mean that. We had such a good time last summer. And I was looking to having it again." He reached to caress her arm and she tried to move away from him. "Kenwick here would like a taste, too."

Kenwick had moved to block her flight. She suddenly appeared very apprehensive, but not yet truly frightened.

"I—I'm to be married," she announced, just as though that should mean something to Edwin. "Me and Jim Jenks are promised."

"Ah, that's nice," Edwin said smoothly as he slipped his arm around her shoulder and held her tightly. "But ol' Jim won't miss what he don't know about." He bent to kiss her, but she twisted her face away.

"Please. Let me go. I don't want—"

"You wanted it enough before. Victor and I promise you'll like it now, too—don't we, Kenwick?"

"We surely do!" Victor agreed eagerly.

"No!"

It was real fear in her voice now, and for some reason that gave Edwin a sense of power that heightened his desire. She pushed at him, but he held her arms.

"Now don't be fighting us, or we might have to hurt you."

"Over there—under that tree is a good spot." Victor pointed as he put an arm around her from the other side. The two males thus propelled her balking female form in that direction. "Quick. I can hardly wait," the squire's pudgy son urged.

Edwin grinned at the other's bulging crotch. "I see. Well, me first, my friend. Me first."

"No!" Anna screamed again. "No! No! Please. Don't do this. You're hurting me."

They threw her onto the ground. She struggled futilely to get away and screamed again.

"Hold her down for me," Edwin said, "and see if you can shut her up." He tossed up her skirts and attempted to wedge his knee between her legs, even as he fumbled with the flap on his breeches.

He suddenly became aware of the sound of a horse coming through the brush just an instant before he felt a stinging lash across his upper back.

"Let her go," a voice ordered.

Despite his shirt and jacket, the sting of that lash managed to take his attention from Anna's luscious body.

"I said *let her go*," the rider repeated and raised his riding crop again. "The girl quite obviously does not welcome your advances."

"She's just playing hard to get," Edwin said. "Besides, this is of no concern to you."

Victor had straightened and released Anna's shoulders. "Give it up, man. That's Forrester. The marquis's younger son."

As Edwin also loosed his hold on her, Anna struggled to her feet and straightened her clothes. Tears stained her cheeks, and Edwin now had the grace to feel somewhat ashamed of himself. "Ah, well, no harm done—eh, Anna?"

She glared at him, then addressed the young man on the horse. "Thank you, my lord."

He nodded. "You go along home now. I doubt these two will bother you any more."

She hastened to do his bidding, practically running in her effort to put distance between herself and her assailants. Forrester looked down at them with unconcealed contempt.

"There is little honor or manhood involved in forcing a female." He looked from Edwin to Victor. "What kind of scum would hold a woman down while another raped her?"

Edwin saw Victor's face turn beet red, but the squire's son merely looked at the ground and said nothing. Edwin shifted his gaze to the man on the horse.

"I repeat, it was none of your business. The girl was asking for it. I would have had her moaning in ecstasy in another few minutes."

Forrester nudged the horse forward, forcing Edwin to step back. He poked Edwin's chest with the riding crop.

"Her screams clearly suggested otherwise." Again he stared at each of them in turn. "If either of you two noble gentlemen *ever* so much as touches an unwilling woman in this parish again, I promise you will pay very dearly for your action. Now you get your worthless, cowardly hides out of my sight before I decide to horsewhip the both of you."

Edwin had seethed for days, dreaming of vengeance against his interfering lordship. In the end, his rage was fueled by an even more serious grievance against the Marquis of Lounsbury and his sons.

Six months later, he had been called home to the bedside of his extremely ill mother. He somehow knew as soon as he looked into her dark, sunken eyes that she was dying. Her husband, the farmer Mullens, told him she had the wasting sickness. She was surrounded by her family, which included Edwin's seven siblings, ranging in age from sixteen-year-old Mary to a toddler of almost two, baby Charlie.

"I . . . I need to speak with Edwin alone," his mother said with a pleading look at her husband.

"You sure about this, Bess?" the farmer asked.

"Yes, dear. It's time."

Her husband herded the others out, and Edwin was alone with his mother. He drew up a chair to sit close to her, hating the lump in his throat and the tears that threatened.

"What is it, Ma?"

She gazed at him, her eyes bright with tears of her own. "Edwin, I love you. I have always tried to do right by you."

"I know, Ma."

"I loved your father, too."

Something about this comment struck him as strange, but the woman was extremely ill. He patted her hand. "He knows, too, Ma."

She grasped his hand in a surprisingly tight grip. "No. You don't understand. Not Thaddeus Mullens. Your real father. Though I grew to love Mr. Mullens, too."

He was stunned. "My—my *real* father? Are you telling me—?"

"Mr. Mullens took me in and married me a few months before you were born. Lounsbury arranged it all."

Suddenly a number of incidents and casual comments of his youth made sense to him. He also understood now why he had always felt so much closer to his mother than to his father—that is, to Mullens. Nor was the bond with any of his three brothers and four sisters particularly strong.

"So who—"

"Lounsbury. The marquis is your father. I was one of the upstairs maids. He had just lost his wife, and he was so handsome. And charming. I was young and foolish. So very foolish . . ."

Edwin sat in stunned silence for several minutes, trying to absorb all this. Then he spoke slowly.

"That's why he sent me away to school."

"Yes. He said he would never acknowledge you, and he never has, but he did see that you—and I—had a decent home. He sent Thaddeus and me to this estate, and we've had a good life. He saw to it you had a proper education."

"Proper, but not the best—that was reserved for his *real* sons." *Just good enough for a bastard,* Edwin thought bitterly.

"I—I'm sorry," his mother whispered. "I thought you should know."

He relinquished her hand and sat back in his chair, his thoughts muddled—and bitter. He recalled the incident with Forrester and the girl this past summer. That arrogant son-of-a-bitch was his brother! And he—Edwin—had been merely following his inherited instincts—tumbling a Lounsbury servant.

"Edwin? Please . . . don't hate me, darling."

"I don't hate *you,* Ma. But Lounsbury has a lot to answer for."

"What he did is not unusual," she said. "And he did better by us than many a peer might have done."

"He could have married you—given me my proper name."

Even in her weakened state, her voice showed the strength of her shock. "Married *me?* A housemaid? Oh, no, dear. Not Lounsbury."

" 'Tis not wholly unknown," he argued.

"For him, it was. And truly, it would have been no life for me, either."

"Well, what about *me?* I'm his son. I have as much of his blood as those two popinjays who occasionally show themselves here!"

"But you are *my* son, too," she said gently. "And I have loved you dearly."

"And that is supposed to make up for the life that might have been mine? I'm sorry, Ma. Love is not enough."

Her tears flowed in earnest now.

Mullens came back into the room then. He stood looking helplessly from his wife to Edwin. He put a work-roughened hand on the young man's shoulder.

"I know that came as a shock, son—"

Edwin jerked away and stood so abruptly the chair toppled over. "I'm not your son. I never was." He ignored the pain in the other man's eyes.

"You were—you are—our firstborn son," Mullens insisted quietly.

Edwin was lost in helpless fury now. He was angry at a turn of fate that had *him* born on the wrong side of the blanket. And he was angry at these two for hiding the truth from him all these years.

He lashed out in a sneering tone. "I suppose this farm was your reward for taking in his noble lordship's whore and passing off his by-blow as your own?"

Mullens was a big man, and at not yet eighteen, Edwin had not reached his full growth. The farmer straightened now and slapped Edwin across the face.

"No!" His mother reached a supplicating hand toward the two men. "Please. Thaddeus—Edwin, don't—please."

"You will apologize to your mother this instant!" Mullens ordered.

Edwin knew he had gone too far. "I'm sorry, Ma. I didn't mean it."

"I know, dear." She sighed heavily and exchanged a meaningful look with her husband.

The next day, his mother died. Edwin stayed at the farm only long enough to see her properly buried.

He had always hated the farm. While this one provided the family a decent, if not lavish, existence, it required never-ending, back-breaking labor. Even as a small boy he had chafed at the thought of such a life for himself. And now to discover he should have been born to something infinitely better . . . !

So he had packed a bag with a few meager belongings

and the only presentable clothing he owned and simply left. He had never looked back.

He had departed the farm with no clear plan in mind. He knew only that he was *not* returning to school. He possessed something over three guineas. That would see him through for a time at least. He drifted for several days before he managed to work up enough courage to face the Marquis of Lounsbury.

He arrived at Lounsbury's principal seat in Gloucester-shire only to have a sour-faced butler tell him the marquis was not at home.

"When do you expect him to return?" Edwin asked with as much civility as he could muster.

"Not for a few weeks."

"Can you tell me where I might find his lordship? I—I have some rather urgent business with him."

"Parliament is in session. He has gone to London." The man shut door abruptly.

As he reversed his trip down the long, long driveway, Edwin looked back at the huge, luxurious edifice that was but one of several homes owned by the Marquis of Lounsbury. *I might have grown up* here, he thought.

In London, he found an equally sour-faced butler at the Lounsbury town house.

"Wait here. I will see if his lordship is receiving. You said the name is Mullens?" The butler's tone reminded Edwin that a proper gentleman—which he had a *right* to be— would have had a calling card to hand the servant.

Edwin fidgeted in the entranceway as the butler disappeared down a long hallway. The entrance was all white marble and highly polished mahogany. There were a number of paintings on the wall of a stairway rising to the floors above and several large, expensive-looking oriental urns within view. The place screamed quiet, confident wealth.

He heard a voice say, "Mullens?" There was a pause. "Well, show him in."

Edwin was shown into an elegant library he thought must surely contain as many volumes as his school library had boasted. The marquis sat behind a huge desk—mahogany, Edwin noted—but the man did not rise as his guest was shown in. Lounsbury appeared to be fairly tall. He had deep blue eyes beneath heavy black brows that contrasted sharply with the shock of white hair he sported. He raised one brow.

"Ah, I expected your father when Jeffers announced a Mr. Mullens. That will be all, Jeffers."

The door clicked shut on the departing butler.

"My *father?*" Edwin asked with what he thought to be sophisticated irony.

The marquis did not even blink. "I see she told you."

"Yes."

They studied each other silently for a moment. Edwin had not been invited to sit, and the longer he stood, the more nervous he became.

Finally, the marquis spoke. "You've grown. I last saw you about five or six years ago. Just before you went away to school. I must say, there is not much of a Forrester look about you, though you do have your mother's fine coloring. Pretty girl, she was. I was sorry to hear of her death."

"Perhaps the Forrester heritage runs more than skin deep, sir."

"Perhaps . . ." The older man picked up a paperweight and turned it over and over in his hands. "Well. Why are you here? What do you want?"

"Is it not enough to want to be known to one's father?"

"Your father is Thaddeus Mullens, as far as I am concerned. If you think to extort further consideration than I have heretofore provided, I would strongly advise you otherwise."

"Extortion is rather a dirty word, your lordship." Edwin could not help the tinge of irony to the title of address. "However, I believe I am entitled to have certain expectations of the man whose seed spawned me."

"You are a nervy bastard—I will say that for you—coming here like this." The marquis stood—he *was* a tall man—and, placing his palms flat on the desk, leaned toward the man in front of him. "But know, sirrah, I provided for your mother and I saw to your education. I rather think that is more than sufficient payment for an occasional bit of fun between the sheets."

"An occasional bit of—" Edwin felt the blood rushing to his face as his fury intensified. "Why, you—"

The marquis uttered a derisive, mirthless laugh. "Surely you did not fancy it was anything else? She was a maid, for God's sake."

As that ugly laugh ground its way into Edwin's very soul, he silently vowed that someday Lounsbury—a Forrester, at any rate—would pay dearly for this humiliation. Someday—if it took forever.

Not trusting himself to respond, he simply gave the man an ironic bow and turned toward the door.

"Here!" the marquis called.

When Edwin turned back, the older man had taken a bag of coins from a desk drawer. He tossed it toward Edwin, who instinctively caught it.

"Buy yourself some decent clothes, boy. Then report to Simpson, my steward on the estate in Yorkshire. He has been expecting you these two years or so. And do *not*—ever—accost me again. If you do, I shall have you arrested and transported."

With that, Edwin's humiliation was doubled—along with his desire for vengeance.

Edwin Brady Mullens had henceforth become merely Edwin Brady, Brady being his mother's maiden name. His pride forbade he follow the marquis's orders. He had drifted aimlessly for several months before finally drifting into taking the king's shilling with His Majesty's Army. His first posting had luckily been in a training facility near a village called Bothwick-on-the-Bay in East Anglia. When the captain in charge of the company to which he was assigned discovered Brady had rather a fine education, he arranged for the young man to be assigned to a clerical position.

During his two-year stay in Bothwick, Brady became acquainted—and generally well-liked—in the village. He found himself eagerly received by certain mamas and their enticing daughters. Nor was his ability to charm confined to females. He was also popular with other young men. Seeing his persuasive abilities at work, certain army officers saw him as a natural choice for a new recruiting team.

So he said his good-byes and for the next few years he went on the road as a recruiter. Bothwick, though, was home for him now, and he returned periodically with stories of an exciting life beyond the village and his own successes out there. As he progressed in rank, he regained some of his self-confidence and pride.

However, over a decade later, he had never forgotten that vow. The marquis was dead now, as was Thaddeus Mullens. But here was Jacob Forrester, unexpectedly close at hand. Surely he could make use of such an opportunity.

The question was—how?

Nine

Physically, Rachel recovered quite rapidly. She could not—*would* not—be confined to a bed for a whole week. On the third day, she arose and visited with Major Forrester briefly. She was pleased to see him up and seated on a chair, his injured leg propped on a stool.

"Mac told me you were doing well," she said, taking the chair he offered. She could hear Henry bustling in the dressing room.

"Dr.—Captain—MacLachlan, you mean? He told me the same of you. But . . . should you be out of bed already?" There was genuine concern in Forrester's gaze.

"I am fine. Truly. It seems neither of us is a very 'patient' patient." She managed a weak smile.

"I—I was sorry to hear of your loss," he said, somewhat awkwardly.

She felt his basic sincerity and could not help noting her own husband had offered no such words of comfort. Brady had returned the day after the accident, pretending that all was well. He had shared her big four-poster bed for two nights now, but scrupulously kept his distance. He left early in the morning and returned late at night. She thought she should probably care more than she did about his prolonged absences.

As a matter of fact, she found it difficult to care about much of anything now. When Clara came to her room babbling of matters dealing with the house and local neighborhood, Rachel forced herself to even monosyllabic responses.

She knew Clara was concerned about her. Clara was another who seemed more in tune with Rachel's feelings than was Edwin Brady.

She brought her mind back to formulating a response to Major Forrester. "Thank you, Major. I—I suppose it was meant to be . . ." She knew her voice sounded dull, but she had little inclination to alter it. He gave her a penetrating look.

"Henry!" Forrester called.

The batman hurried from the dressing room. "Yes, my lord?"

"Find me that copy of *Lyrical Ballads,* please."

Henry produced the book, and Forrester held it out to Rachel. "Here. I want you to have this. There are some fine works here."

"Oh, my lord—I could not possibly accept such a gift." Rachel knew how much he treasured the few books he had brought to the Peninsula.

"I insist." He thrust it toward her again. " 'Tis not an improper gift. You may find some comfort in the words of Mr. Wordsworth and Mr. Coleridge."

She held his gaze and knew she could not refuse his gesture. "I—very well. I shall treasure your kindness." As she took the slim volume, their hands touched, and she found the contact strangely comforting.

They talked of other matters for a while, then agreed that they would both venture into the courtyard on the morrow.

Jake watched sadly as Rachel left the room. That teasing sparkle was gone from her eyes, and the sense of energy in the way she walked and held her shoulders was no longer there. He wanted—oh, so badly—to see again the friend who sparred with him over the antics of ancient Greek warriors.

Henry had told him that, according to Mrs. Paxton, Rachel was taking the loss of the babe rather hard—just as Jake had supposed she would. However, he thought there might be even more cause for Rachel's distress. After all, he and Henry had heard much of that altercation before Rachel fell. He felt again that impotent anger at the man who seemed so blind to the treasure he possessed.

'Tis none of your concern, Forrester, he told himself. *Leave it. Just leave it.* But his mind kept drifting back to that haunted look in her eyes.

Lord! It would be a happy day when he rejoined his regiment. At least there he would deal with problems about which he could actually *do* something. Here, he not only was physically powerless to do much, but he had no moral right to interfere in the relationship between a wife and her husband. The fall had clearly been an accident—precipitated by Brady's temper—but still an accident.

As he lay in his bed brooding, he heard a commotion below. First a knocking on the outer door, then Clara's exclamation of "Oh, my goodness!"

This was followed by her calling "Mr. Henry! Can you help us?"

Henry had been belowstairs for a while. Jake listened intently from above.

"We need to get him to his room," Clara said.

Him? Who? Jake wondered. Then he heard Rachel's shocked voice.

"What—oh, Edwin! What on earth happened?"

A male voice Jake did not recognize responded. "Well *you* might ask. Couple of fellows worked him over good."

"If you can remove his outer clothing and put him to bed, I shall take over from there," Rachel said.

The sounds receded behind the closed doors of Jake's own room and the room across the hall. He waited impatiently for Henry's arrival.

"What happened?" he asked as Henry entered and closed the door.

"Bit of poetic justice, I'd say." Henry's voice held grim satisfaction.

"Explain."

"Well, sir, it appears Sergeant Brady met with an accident."

"An accident?"

"You could call it that. Seems two Rangers caught him in an alleyway and thrashed him rather thoroughly. You should see his face. Black eye, bruises, a torn lip. Probably took several blows to his midriff and ribs, too."

"Rangers?" Jake mused.

"Yes, sir."

"Humphrey and Collins, you think?"

Henry nodded. "That was my guess, too. They were that angry about hearing of Mrs. Brady's fall—especially after that earlier incident."

"What earlier incident?"

"Right after the siege. When Brady came to the hut—you were still unconscious. Mrs. Brady turned up with an ugly bruise on her face."

"My God! He beats her?"

"I am not sure to what extent, my lord. But on that occasion, at least, I'm fairly sure he slapped her. And of course, the other day . . ."

"Seems he was given his just deserts, then," Jake said.

"That was certainly my view, sir."

Clara had gone for warm water and Henry had retreated to the major's room, leaving Rachel alone with her husband and his rescuer.

"Sergeant Morton, please tell me what happened."

"I come upon it only at the very end. Two men. Rangers, I think. I figured you might know 'em."

"I?" she asked in wonder. "Why?"

"Well, that Forrester fellow is a Ranger, too."

"But Edwin has nothing to do with the major," Rachel said, totally mystified.

"Mebbe so . . ."

Clara returned then with a basin and clean towels. As the two women set about cleansing Brady's face, Morton excused himself and left. Rachel was glad her husband seemed only semiconscious during their ministrations. He groaned occasionally, but was otherwise quiet.

Late that afternoon when MacLachlan came to check on Rachel and the major, he examined Brady, too, while Rachel stood at the bedside.

"You've bruises, but nothing's broken—not even your nose. You'd be fit for duty right now if we'd a battle in the offing."

Edwin looked at though he would like to protest this judgment, but he said nothing to the surgeon.

MacLachlan stood and gave Rachel a stern look. "I thought I ordered bed rest for you."

"I did as you said for two whole days. I could not endure just lying there any longer."

"Well, mind you don't overdo it," Mac said, then muttered darkly, "Lord, deliver me from independent women!"

"Amen, doc," Brady said, but MacLachlan simply glared at him and gathered up his medicine bag.

At the door he put a hand on Rachel's shoulder. "Remember what I said. Do *not* be overextending yourself. You take care of *you,* too."

"I shall, Mac. Thank you."

Brady lay listening to this exchange. He ached all over. What did this damned butcher boy surgeon know of the matter anyway? Brady mentally replayed the incident and nursed the renewal of his anger.

He had recognized Forrester's toadies immediately, but he had been surprised at their attack—and its apparent cause. He recalled their taunts.

"Like to bat women around, do ye?" the older one had said, smashing his fist into Brady's face.

"How ya like being at the disadvantage?" the younger one had asked with a swing at the gut that doubled Brady over and elicited a loud grunt.

"Not your concern," he panted. "She's my woman." He

tried to get in a strike or two himself. However, with two of them working on him, he was rather ineffectual and was knocked to the ground.

"She's an angel of mercy," the bigger, older fellow said.

"An' if you hurt her again, we'll come after you again. May even finish you for sure." The younger man aimed a kick at Brady's stomach.

Even as he tried to protect himself from their repeated blows, he could not believe this was over *Rachel*. Now, several hours later, he was still puzzled. What the hell was going on with her and those damned Rangers anyway? Not that he suspected anything really out of order. Hell. It was apparent Forrester was too incapacitated to do anything, even if he were so inclined.

Besides, Brady knew Rachel well enough to know any sort of illicit affair with another man was out of the question. Had he not observed her repulsing even the slightest of advances in the past? No, that was not the issue. At least . . . it never had been before with her.

Had she somehow set those two on him, though? He recalled her earlier threat. Or maybe Forrester had done so. Hadn't Paxton said Rachel almost single-handedly saved Forrester's life? Pity, that . . . but would Forrester see this as a twisted means of repaying her?

That idea did not quite fit, though. He knew little enough of Forrester, but he had to admit the man would probably deal with an issue up front and in person, not send others to handle the unpleasantness.

Still, the fault for the pain he felt every time he moved could be laid directly in Rachel's lap. And by God! no woman was worth that sort of aggravation.

"Close that door and come over here," he ordered.

Her sigh as she did as he told her annoyed him even further.

"And don't be giving me the martyr act, either," he said.

"Edwin, I know you are uncomfortable and I am sorry for your pain, but—please—try not to be so cross."

"And well you *should* be sorry," he accused. "This is all your fault."

"My fault?"

"I *told* you to get away from Forrester. Now his noble lordship's flunkies have done this to me. Cowards. An' it took two of 'em."

"Edwin, are you sure?"

"I know what happened and I know what they said." However, he felt no need to explain any further to her about the humiliating beating he had received. "Now, you set about getting our things together. I'm finding us another billet as soon as I can move without hurting all over."

He did not tell her he had no desire to spend time around the major—that he feared Forrester might connect a boy named Mullens with a man named Brady. This simply was not something his loving wife needed to know.

Brady's determination to move them to different quarters distressed Rachel mightily. She simply did not understand what seemed wholly capricious behavior on his part. However, it was a wife's duty to do her husband's bidding. She had felt so at home in this house with what the major had called their patched-together family. She would miss them all terribly—Juan's touching smile, baby Benny's babbling. Thompkins, Henry, and Joe. But most especially would she miss Clara and the major. Their friendship had filled a void she had hardly been aware of before. It had been hard to tell Clara the news.

"You're leaving? *Why?"*

"Edwin insists we do so. He has found us another billet near some folks of his own regiment."

"But we are so comfortable here—and Lord knows it will last only until the army is on the move again," Clara said.

"I have presented that argument to him repeatedly, but he is adamant."

"What about *you?* You are not well—"

"I am fully recovered now—and regaining more strength every day," Rachel said. "You must not worry about me."

"Well, I certainly shall worry about you," Clara said indignantly, "and I shall make a point of checking up on you from time to time." Tears shimmered in Clara's eyes.

Rachel felt her own tears threaten. She knew that only a few days earlier this change in her life would have been incredibly wrenching. Now, she seemed somewhat numb. One more loss would not make much difference. Intellectually, she knew she should care greatly, but emotionally she seemed to view everything from a distance—or through a veil. She was simply unable to allow herself to care. Caring brought loss, which brought overwhelming pain. It was best to insulate oneself against loss to start with.

She waited until the last day to tell Major Forrester. As he had before the beating, Brady was gone from early morning until late evening. She knew military duties occupied only a portion of the time he was absent. She and Major Forrester sat together at a small table in the shade of a large tree in the courtyard. Henry had helped Forrester make his way laboriously down the stairs and out to the courtyard for two afternoons now.

"I shall be leaving in the morning," she announced abruptly.

"Yes, I know." His voice was quiet. "I wondered if you intended to tell me."

"I suppose Henry—or perhaps Clara—told you."

"Actually, both did. They—we—are concerned about you."

"I am fine," she said hastily. Well, it was true. She was fine physically, was she not?

"Remember my offer. Should you ever need anything—"

She could hardly bear the compassion she saw in his gaze. She had this terrible urge to throw herself in his arms and sob out her loneliness, her anger, her grief. She tore her eyes away from his.

"Thank you, Major. I doubt it will be necessary, but it is comforting to know help is available if one needs it." She deliberately used his rank and spoke in a distancing, formal tone.

He reached across the table and grasped her hand. "I mean it, Rachel," he said softly.

"I—I know." She disengaged her hand, equally aware of her reluctance to do so and of the impropriety of not doing so.

Clara's voice broke in. "May I interest you in some lemonade?" She bore a tray with a pitcher and glasses. "Where is Mr. Brady? I told him you were in the courtyard, Rachel."

"He has returned so early?" Rachel asked vacantly. "I had better see if he needs anything." She rose and hurried into the house.

Brady sprawled on a sofa in the drawing room and eyed his wife as Rachel came in.

"You are home early." She sounded nervous.

His tone was sarcastic. "None too soon, apparently. That was quite a little tête-à-tête you were having with the lord of the manor."

"We were just talking."

"I thought I told you to stay away from him."

"I was merely saying good-bye."

"That vow of obedience you took rests heavily on your shoulders, does it, dear wife?"

"Not necessarily. But it should not negate simple civility to others."

He started to admonish her for being too saucy, but in fact there was little spirit in her tone. He decided to let it pass. "Is our gear ready?" he asked.

"Most of it. There are a few items in the kitchen yet."

"I borrowed Morton's mule. I'll go and get it first thing in the morning. See you have everything ready when I get back."

"Yes, Edwin."

He looked at her to see if there was any sarcasm in her expression, but her gaze was as flat as her tone.

Later, he took the evening meal with the rest of the house-hold, having first ascertained that Forrester would have a tray in his room. Going up and down stairs more than once a day was apparently too much for him yet. Brady was aware that his presence at the table was somewhat stifling to the others, but he refused to let it bother him—and he refused to make any effort to put them at ease.

Thank God he'd be shut of this lot tomorrow.

The next morning Rachel waited in her room for Edwin to return with the mule to carry their gear to the new quar-ters. She had already said her good-byes—there was no point in prolonging the process.

Soon enough Edwin arrived and they began to carry things down to the animal tied in the front of the house. They were returning for the second load when Major For-rester's door opened and he and Henry emerged.

"Oh." Forrester started at seeing them. "I thought you had gone."

"Almost," Rachel said, feeling a lump of regret in her throat.

"Do you need some help? Henry will be glad to—"

"We'll manage," Edwin growled, propelling her into the room that had been theirs.

They waited while the major and his batman negotiated the stairs before carrying the last of their goods down. As they tied the final bundle on the waiting mule, Clara ap-peared at the door with Benny in his customary place on her hip.

"We couldn't let you go without a last good-bye." She leaned the toddler toward Rachel and said, "Kiss Auntie Rachel good-bye, Benny."

Benny planted a wet, slobbery, but ever-so-sweet kiss on Rachel's lips. Rachel hugged the mother and child, unable to trust her voice.

"Time to go," Edwin said abruptly.

She turned and followed as he led the mule down the

street. She looked back once and waved to Clara, still standing there clutching Benny.

Their new quarters were a small, cramped room on the third floor in the home of a middle-aged couple who ran a wine shop on the ground floor. Even on the third floor, the smell of stale wine permeated everything. Rachel was given restricted use of the kitchen, and the Bradys could take their meals at the kitchen table. She went about the task of trying to arrange their possessions in the room so they had at least a path to the bed.

"There is very little storage room here," she noted.

"What? Are you criticizing already?" Edwin asked, his tone harsh.

"I was not being critical. I simply observed—"

"You were complaining. It's hard to please, you are."

"Edwin, please—you are being unfair."

"So now I'm unfair, too. First I don't provide quarters elegant enough for you and then you find some other charge to level at my head!"

Taken aback by the vehemence of his tone, she looked at him in surprise. "Edwin, I do not understand—"

"No, you don't. And you don't even try to," he flung at her. He stuffed some gear into his knapsack and picked it up along with his musket. "I'm to report to Hoskins again. I'll be back later. And *you* stay put while I'm gone. I don't need you running all over the town."

Given his mood, she did not dare ask how much later. She wondered at the urgency of their making this move just now, but she hesitated to ask about *that,* too.

Despite the fact that it was still officially springtime, summer heat was upon them and it was swelteringly hot in the upper stories of the wine merchant's building. Having climbed the three flights of stairs twice in moving their possessions to the room, Rachel was exhausted. Still, it was too hot to stay in the room beneath the roof. She found her knitting and the book Major Forrester had given her. With these and her journal, she made her way back down the stairs. In a small garden, she sat on a shaded stone bench and read for a while, then tried to bring her journal up to date. She soon tired of that, though, because she found the events she recorded so disheartening.

After a sparse luncheon of bread and cheese, she returned to the garden, wondering why Edwin had not come back for the midday meal. When he finally did show himself, it was well after even the late-dining Spaniards had had their evening meal. Rachel had stretched out on their bed to wait for him. As usual, there was the smell of brandy about him.

Rising, she asked, "Would you like me to get you some food?"

"No. I ate with Morton. You could help me with these boots." He lifted a foot toward her.

She struggled to pull off first one boot, then the other. He lay back and closed his eyes.

"Have you any idea how long we will be here?" she asked.

"How should I know? I'm not privy to officers' talk."

"I—I just thought you might have heard—"

"Well, don't think. Now let me get some sleep."

This turned out to be the pattern of her days for the remaining weeks in Badajoz.

At one point, Rachel mentioned going back to her hospital work.

"No. Absolutely not," Edwin shouted. "I'll not have you cluttering up my quarters with your strays again. And what's more, you stay away from the Paxtons and Forrester."

"But—why?"

"Because I said so. That's why."

She found herself feeling more and more disconnected from the life going on around her. She felt empty and lethargic. She knew she was reacting to the loss of the babe, but it was more than giving up on her long-cherished dream of family and motherhood. She tried to talk with Edwin, to explain her need to return to the hospital work. He refused to discuss it with her. And somehow—at some point—she had lost not only the ability to communicate with her husband, but the desire to do so as well.

One day when she had gone to replenish their supplies from the commissary station, she encountered Clara, who was on the same mission.

"Good morning, Rachel," Clara said brightly.

"Good morning." Rachel tried to look and sound equally cheerful.

Clara gave her a penetrating look. "Are you well?"

"Very well, thank you."

"We miss you. The major grumbles at not having anyone to argue with."

Rachel felt a faint smile touch her lips at the memory. "How is he? Healing nicely, I assume."

"Yes. He walks on his own now—with a walking stick, mind you. He works very hard at getting back full use of his leg."

"I am glad to hear that." Rachel paused. "And the others?"

"Everyone is fine. Jake—the major—is teaching Juan to play checkers."

"How nice." Rachel listened as Clara chatted on. Benny was sporting a new tooth. Joe had presented his wife with a fine woolen shawl. Henry and Thompkins were engaged in a petty squabble over their respective duties to the major. Rachel tried not to be too interested. It was easier if one did not care too much about others.

She excused herself and hurried home, but as she parted from Clara, she saw Sergeant Morton watching her from across the street. That night, Edwin upbraided her about the incident.

He grabbed her elbow and swung her around to him. "I told you to stay away from the Paxtons."

"I merely spoke with Clara on the street. I would not be rude."

"You just remember to do as you're told."

She did not reply and he released her. With an occasional snide comment, Edwin let her know she was shirking her wifely duties, but he did not press the issue. When he pronounced himself mightily glad that his month of enforced celibacy was over, she could not even summon much reaction to what she knew in her heart to be a lie; she knew it was unlikely he had remained celibate at all.

Nor could she welcome his advances with any degree of enthusiasm. She returned his kisses mechanically, but felt nothing. When he placed his hand between her legs, she dutifully accepted his caresses and adjusted her body to allow his entrance. Finally, it was over and he rolled off her.

"What the hell's the matter with you?" he asked. "I might as well be making love to a stone fence."

"I'm sorry," she said, but she did not *feel* sorry. She did not *feel* much of anything.

Ten

By the end of June, Wellington had moved his forces out of Badajoz in the direction of Salamanca. Jake had resumed his duties with his regiment, though he still favored the injured leg when he walked. However, he spent much of his duty time in the saddle.

He had seen nothing of Rachel once she left the house they all shared. Now, on the trail again, he caught only an occasional glimpse of her, but fearing it would cause trouble for her, he did not single her out for attention. After all, she was another man's wife. An enlisted man's woman. One did not breach certain unwritten laws of military custom.

The battle of Salamanca in the third week of July was a hard-won victory for Britain and her allies. When it was over, Jake joined his friends Captain Hastings and Lieutenant Travers for dinner. Hastings and Forrester had been at Oxford together, albeit in separate colleges, and had become truly close friends only here in the Peninsula. Travers, some four years younger, had joined the 88th as a replacement after the battle of Busaco some two years earlier.

"Good God!" Hastings exclaimed. "If we have many more victories like these two, the French will surely hold the field!"

"The Peer himself said something very like," Travers agreed.

"Good job Boney keeps raiding his armies in Spain of seasoned veterans and sending raw recruits in their place," Jake said.

Hastings reached for the wine flagon to refill their glasses. "Even so, the French here are ably led—more's the pity."

"Not ably enough this day," Travers exulted. "Did you hear the figures?"

"We have nearly five thousand dead and wounded," Hastings responded in a glum tone.

Travers nodded. "Yes, but we crushed a force of forty thousand French soldiers in a matter of forty minutes!"

"That will look good in the dispatches anyway," Jake observed. "Perhaps Parliament will provide the wherewithal to push the Bonapartists back over the Pyrenees."

"That—and this march to Madrid." Hastings sat back in his chair and lit a cigarillo.

Travers sounded querulous. "Far be it from me to second-guess the Peer, but I simply do not see the point of this mad dash to Madrid, spreading ourselves out so."

Jake exchanged a knowing look with Hastings and answered, "Politics, my good man. Politics."

"Politics?"

"Think. Would you not give a pretty piece to see the look on Napoleon's face when he learns the British have taken over Madrid, the very capital of the land he gave to his brother Joseph?"

"Ah, I see the point now," Travers said.

"Still, in my never very humble opinion," Hastings offered, "we will not linger in Madrid, what with reinforcements for the Frenchies already on their way."

"You may be right," Jake said.

And so he was.

The British enjoyed a triumphant entry into the capital city. The populace welcomed them by hanging banners and tapestries from their windows. Riding tall in the saddle, Wellington was the target of girls eager to touch him or kiss him. Failing to kiss him, they kissed his horse instead. Jake noted with amusement that afterward the Peer traveled through town only in closed carriages. A grand ball brought out the city's notables in great finery and the Spanish showered Lord Wellington with honors as the ousted Joseph fled east toward Valencia.

For his part, Jake spent most of the time in Madrid wandering the streets of the city, admiring the magnificent houses, beautiful public plazas, and fountains. Once he encountered Hastings and Travers with a bevy of young ladies and was persuaded to join them. Later that night, as he drifted off to sleep, he saw himself wandering those streets with a dark-haired Englishwoman, one with dark eyes of an intriguing, undefinable color.

Rachel. Why was it she haunted his dreams so? Why did he have a feeling of something unfinished there? She was a married woman, and that was that. Why, he had not even seen her for some weeks now.

From the triumphs of the hard-won victory at Salamanca and the ecstatic welcome in Madrid, Lord Wellington turned his attention north to the fortified town of Burgos. Jake knew what the general had in mind. Capture of Burgos would be a major step in pushing the French beyond the mountain range that divided France from Spain.

Burgos proved to be a much harder nut to crack than Badajoz had been. Again, the weather allied itself with the enemy. Autumn arrived early and torrential rains flooded the trenches, rendering much of the siege machinery useless. Fevers and agues—as well as French bullets—attacked the men.

"Finally!" Captain Hastings announced in late October. "Four weeks later, he has at last called it off."

"What? Who?" Lieutenant Travers looked up from a letter he was writing at a small portable desk. The three were sharing a large tent. A smaller one had been assigned their servants.

"Wellington has called for a retreat from Burgos. We are cutting our losses and returning—temporarily, mind you—to Portugal."

" 'Tis unfortunate," Jake said, "that the campaign this year ends on such a note of failure. Overall, though, we have not done so badly."

"Forrester!" Hastings challenged. "We've lost two thousand men in the last four weeks! The French have lost three hundred."

"I know," Jake replied calmly. "And we lost upwards of five thousand each at Badajoz and Salamanca. But we still hold those positions, and French losses were even greater than ours there—*and* we have shipped nearly twenty thousand prisoners back to England."

Travers was clearly confused. "So are we winning or not?"

"Too early to tell, but it looks as though we have made some progress," Jake said cautiously.

"Still, no one likes the idea of retreat," Hastings grumbled.

Rachel passed through the summer and early autumn still feeling disconnected and isolated. Indeed, she *was* isolated. Denied her work with the wounded and forced to avoid her friends, she drifted from day to day. She no longer cared as much about her personal appearance as she had previously. If Edwin failed to show up for a meal, she sometimes simply forgot to eat. When the supplies failed to keep pace with Wellington's advances, Rachel felt the deprivation much less than her fellow travelers.

During the battle of Salamanca, she shook herself out of her malaise enough to report to MacLachlan and offer her services, despite her husband's objections.

"Please, Edwin. You must allow me to help. I do nothing but wait when you are gone. And I *can* be of use in the hospital."

"Oh, very well," he said finally. "Do as you please—so long as you are here when *I* need you."

MacLachlan had been far too busy to welcome her with open arms. He merely said, " 'Tis a blessing you've come, lass." He promptly assigned her to care for patients as they came from his makeshift surgery.

She quickly fit into the rhythm of the hospital work, reacting almost automatically in some instances. As she comforted the injured and dying, she began to lose some of the self-absorption that had engulfed her recently.

However, when she returned to her own quarters—a tent the Bradys shared with two other women and eight men—the sense of detachment reasserted itself. It was, after all, the means by which she coped. She knew the others saw her as aloof and haughty. But if she did not make them her friends, she would not suffer their loss, would she?

After Salamanca, the army moved erratically across much of western Spain, first east to Madrid, then north to Burgos, then west. If the regiment engaged in a skirmish, Rachel was occasionally needed to help with wounded. Otherwise, she was wholly occupied with the rigors of the trail and camp life at night. There was precious little opportunity for privacy, a fact Rachel welcomed and one to which Edwin seemed indifferent for the time being. Rachel—in her strangely detached way—suspected he found solace in the arms of a certain Spanish camp follower.

During the retreat from Burgos, Rachel spent a good deal of time thinking about—and trying *not* to think about—her marriage. She felt as though she and Edwin were in a state of limbo, each waiting for some cataclysmic event to set their future course. She embarked on a futile search for a solution to the breach between them. She must have done something to turn him against her—but what? Another question also haunted her. How could the gulf between them be bridged without Rachel's losing her very self in the process?

The retreat from Burgos involved great hardship for the whole of Lord Wellington's forces. Supplies had not arrived. Soldiers and their families were often hungry, reduced to eating acorns at one point. Guards had to be set on the oxen needed to pull the baggage and artillery carts to prevent the men from dining on the draft animals. However, the areas they passed through had enjoyed a good harvest of grapes that year. Hunger pangs became much less gnawing to those drunk on new wine. Officers found themselves fighting to keep their drunken regiments on the move.

Nor had the weather improved. The final days of October and early days of November threatened winter on a daily basis. Rain slowed progress as the routes became veritable rivers of mud. Often the men had to add their own muscle to that of bullocks pulling artillery and baggage carts to extricate them from the mud. For the women, every effort to keep clean was immediately frustrated. The nights were cold and all too often the bed clothing damp. It seemed to Rachel that *everyone* suffered from coughs, fevers, and sniffles.

Every day some woman said, "Oh, my, I'll be glad when we reach the winter quarters!" and a dozen others agreed with her.

In general, the regiments traveled separately from each other, taking turns at the advantageous lead. Only occasionally did Rachel see Clara and Benny with the supply wagons of Paxton's regiment.

One evening the two regiments chanced to be camped near each other. Clara, with Benny in her arms, braved Edwin's surliness to visit Rachel. For once it was not raining, so the two women sat on camp stools near the fire, but outside the ring of others gathered there.

"Are you well?" Clara asked in genuine concern.

"Aside from the same aches and sniffles we all have, yes. And you?"

"We are fine. So far Joe has come through every skirmish without a scratch. And Benny has not yet contracted any of those horrid childhood sicknesses. Touch wood." Clara put a finger to her forehead.

Rachel smiled, then held out her arms to Benny, who readily allowed her to hold him. "I'll bet you are a handful on this trail," she said over the child's head.

"That he is!" Clara said. "He wants 'down' all the time—and in this mud!"

"Dow-w-n," Benny said.

"That's his new word," his mother explained. "That and 'horsey'—for which I have Major Forrester to thank!"

"Major Forrester?"

"Yes. He came by one afternoon when Benny was being rather fractious and took him up before him on his horse. Now Benny thinks every horse offers a potential ride."

"I see." Rachel paused. "The major is well?"

"Yes. He asked about you."

"How nice," Rachel said politely, then changed the subject.

The two women chatted amiably for a few more minutes. Then Clara departed to put her son down for the night.

"What'd *she* want?" Edwin growled, coming over to Rachel as soon as her guest left.

"Nothing—just to visit," Rachel replied.

"Just nosing around, you mean." When Rachel did not respond to this mean-spirited comment, he went on, "Don't you be encouraging her now, you hear?"

"Yes, Edwin. But I do wish you could explain why you have taken the Paxtons in such dislike."

"I don't need to explain anything," he said.

And that effectively ended the discussion.

Brady was annoyed that Rachel had apparently not shunned the Paxtons as he wished her to. He was also annoyed by her request for an explanation of his antipathy toward the other couple. How could he explain—without putting himself in the wrong—that Paxton had seen him, along with Morton and two others, assaulting a woman and her adolescent daughter in Badajoz? Paxton had been alone, and with four armed men in Brady's group, there was little Joe Paxton could do about the situation at the time. Brady had seen the disgust in Paxton's eyes, though, and he saw it again every time he encountered the other man.

Besides that incident, there had been the earlier silent disapproval of both Paxtons when Brady had disciplined his own wife. Edwin Brady did not need some sanctimonious male-milliner passing judgment on *him*. Or have the man's nosy wife do so, either.

Still annoyed the day after Clara's visit, Brady was lost

in thought, marching along with his company, when he became aware that Morton had come up beside him.

"Saw the Paxton woman in your camp last night," Morton said. "You gettin' chummy with them again?"

"No. And what's it to you if I was?"

Morton stepped slightly away and gave him a look of mock innocence. "Hey. Nothin' to me. Nothin' at all. I just thought you were rid of that lot."

"Well, I thought so, too."

"Didn't you tell your wife?"

"Yes, I told her." Brady did not attempt to curb his testy tone.

"Ah, well—some women are harder to control than others, I suppose." There was a false note to Morton's sympathetic words.

"You got that right."

"Well, whenever you get tired of tryin' with yours, you let me know—won't you?"

Brady gave him a blank stare and Morton moved off after a while.

The truth was, after four years, Edwin Brady *was* rather tired of trying to deal with Rachel. She was never openly hostile toward him, but she obviously no longer saw him as her knight in shining armor. Hell. She didn't even respect him half the time! It was damned hard to live with a woman's silent but continual disapproval.

And he dared not beat her into submission. Her own threat had hit home. He was not at all sure she really *would* harm him as he slept or feed him a potion, but that was just it—he was *not sure*. And then there were those damned Rangers—Forrester's toadies. He had seen them a time or two since Badajoz. No one had said anything, but their threat to finish the job of that beating hung heavy in the air.

He hated feeling so curbed by others. And now here was Morton with his sly innuendoes about handling women! As though *he* knew anything . . .

* * *

Wellington's army spent the winter in several villages along the frontier dividing Spain and Portugal. Problems with distribution of supplies having been resolved, the troops lived in relative ease. Soldiers drilled and practiced maneuvers during the day, but their evenings were usually free. Scouting teams were sent out on a regular basis to keep tabs on enemy positions, but neither army was inclined to wage war against the elements as well as their opposing military faction.

The Bradys were quartered in a small inn that boasted only six guest chambers, but the couple had one of these to themselves. The hospital personnel set up in another village entirely, so Rachel was not involved in that work during these months. After they were settled in, she learned the Paxtons were in a village some ten miles from where the Bradys were billeted.

During the late summer and autumn, she had begun to regain her inner strength. She was determined now to make an effort to put her marriage back together. However, each time she tried to reach across the chasm between them, Edwin rebuffed her. He refused to discuss any of the issues that troubled her—or to explain his own attitudes and feelings.

"What is there to discuss?" he asked. "You know what I want—not that it seems to matter a whole lot to you."

"Of course it matters—" she started to defend.

"Do we have to discuss this now? I was about to join some fellows over at the Montenegro." He named the inn at which she knew Morton was staying.

"W-will you be playing cards again?" she asked hesitantly.

"Probably. Why?" His tone was belligerent.

"I—it's just that we have not much money left . . ." Her voice trailed off.

"You let *me* worry about such matters," he ordered.

"Do be careful, though, won't you?"

"I *said* I will handle it," he snapped.

She also tried to increase their level of physical intimacy, but to her surprise, had little success there either. She refused to beg him to make love to her, but she was puzzled by his general indifference to her physically. She could only conclude that his needs were being satisfied elsewhere for the most part. She was just as puzzled by her own reaction, which bordered on *relief.*

Not that he ignored her entirely. But when he did approach her, it was not truly making love. It was just to satisfy a momentary urge—and it was all about *his* satisfaction. She tried to bear the situation patiently, but could not help feeling deeply hurt. Under the circumstances, she was wary of becoming pregnant again, and she took steps to avoid such an event. Certain herbs were effective, and she made sure she had a plentiful supply of them.

Still, she saw their lack of intimacy as a problem. He did not.

"I don't see what you're complaining about," he said. "Don't you think I can tell when you're faking it?"

"Edwin!" She felt herself flushing with embarrassment. It had been hard enough to bring this matter up with him. And now to have him speak so bluntly . . .

"Well, don't you?"

"I—I don't—"

"Don't lie. Of course you do. Most of time you can hardly bear to have me touch you."

"Edwin, that's not true—"

"Of course it is. Not that it matters much any more."

"Not that it—? Oh, Edwin. What has happened to us?"

"You tell *me,*" he challenged. "But do it some other time, eh? I need to get some sleep now."

These exchanges, along with the dullness of her days, served to undermine any gains she had made in self-esteem.

There was also the matter of money. It seemed no matter how frugal she was, there was never enough. Whenever she questioned Edwin about their finances, he became irritable and accused her of hounding him with constant complaints.

More and more, he left her alone. During the day, of

course, he was occupied with military duties. He spent most evenings with his men friends—or so he said.

Yet he became angry when she began to form a friendship with one of the other women quartered at their inn. Nellie Bingham was the middle-aged wife of another sergeant in the 51st.

"They're not our kind of people," Edwin said.

"That sounds rather arrogant," Rachel replied.

"Are you calling me arrogant?" Surprise and outrage warred in his tone. He raised his hand to strike her, then slowly lowered it.

"Not *you*—but that comment."

"I'm sick of your criticizing me." He grabbed his coat and left. He did not return until dawn.

Baffled by his behavior, she resolved to keep trying to placate him. Then one day she realized abruptly how truly isolated she had become—and lonely. Even when he was in the same room with her—indeed, in the same bed—they were not together. She concluded that, if this was to be her life with Edwin, she would have to make another life for herself outside the one she shared with him.

She began by inviting Nellie to have tea with her. She felt inordinately liberated in doing so. What was more, she thoroughly enjoyed the other woman's company.

"Ah, my dear, I've been an army wife these thirty years and more," Nellie told her. "My John and I served in the colonies, then India, now here. 'Course, John was in a few other places, too, where he couldn't take me."

"India? Lord Wellington was there, too."

"That he was. He wasn't Wellington then. Just plain Colonel Wellesley—though his brother was a lord, you know. My John served with the Peer there. Not many of 'em here can say that."

"I believe Major Forrester served there as well," Rachel said.

"You're right! He did. Fine man, Forrester. Came out there a green lieutenant, but learned real quick-like. Got along right well with the natives."

Rachel could not have explained precisely why, but Nellie's confirming her own opinion of Forrester as a fine man pleased her.

The next day, she encountered the major himself for the first time in weeks.

Rachel wrapped herself tightly in a woolen shawl to ward off the January cold and set out on a vigorous walk. Edwin was off on some sort of training mission, so she had the entire day to herself, and this walk was first on her agenda. Having no errand or goal in mind, she felt wickedly self-indulgent. She had walked for perhaps a quarter of an hour when she heard a horse behind her and voice call her name.

"Rachel? Mrs. Brady? Is that you?"

She turned. "Major Forrester. Good morning, sir."

"This is a pleasant surprise," he said. He dismounted to walk beside her, and she noted he scarcely favored the once-injured leg at all.

"No trouble with that wound now, I see," she observed. Flashing across her mind came an unbidden thought—she had not remembered how handsome he was. No, *handsome* was the wrong word. Attractive, maybe. Friendly. Comfortable.

"None at all," he answered. "Thanks to you."

"Oh, well . . ." She waved her hand in a dismissive gesture.

"I should have known you would refuse any credit." He was silent for a moment, then asked, "And you? Are you well?"

"Oh, very well." She made her voice sound light and cheerful. "Lazier than sin with so little to do, but otherwise all goes well."

"That is army life all right," he said. "Long periods of routine boredom and short spurts of intense activity."

She looked up at him to find his gaze rather intent on her. She glanced away. "Perhaps that describes most lives, sir. I daresay most of us devote the major portion of our days to relatively meaningless details—things that must be done repeatedly."

"Probably," he agreed.

"May I ask what brings you to this particular village? I was told the 88th was closer to headquarters."

"So we are—which makes us convenient errand boys for the Peer. I'm delivering a message to Colonel Markwell."

"You'll find him that way." She pointed off to the left. "The third house on the right. It has green shutters."

"Thank you." He started to remount, then checked himself. He dug into a bag behind his saddle. "Here." He handed her two large oranges. "Lord Wellington and several others just returned from the south. They brought these back with them."

"Why, thank you. Thank you very much. Fresh fruit is such a treat at this time of the year."

"You're welcome." He held her gaze for a moment and seemed on the verge of saying something else, but then swung into the saddle again and took up his reins. "It was nice to see you again, madam."

"Yes. Good-bye, Major. And thank you again."

He waved and proceeded in the direction she had pointed.

Jake rode off reluctantly—but it would not do to take up too much of her time. There *were* other people out and about. They would have seen her talking with a strange man—and an officer at that.

Seeing her had been a shock. His heart ached at observing how thin she was. And while the brisk January air had set roses in her cheeks, there were dark circles under her eyes. Despite her protestations to the contrary, all was *not* well with Rachel Brady.

With a vague whisper of fear, he wondered if she might be seriously ill. He would make it a point to check on her from time to time. He could do that much.

Why? he asked himself. He was not checking on other women following the drum here in the Peninsula.

Other women have not saved my life, he answered himself impatiently.

Ah, and that is all it is, is it?

He refused to consider this impertinent question.

Eleven

Time weighed heavily on the often idle hands of soldiers in the allied armies. During daylight hours, the officers managed to keep their men occupied with drills and training. Evenings, however, were another matter. Members of the British, Portuguese, and Spanish forces, as well as the King's German Legion, tended to gather in their own inns and wine bodegas. However, occasionally they invaded each others' territory and fights would often spill out into the streets.

Such bursts of energy were offset by activities of a spectator nature. Boxing matches, pitting favorite pugilists of different regiments against each other, drew large audiences. Horse racing, when weather permitted, was a great pastime among the officers. The men of their commands enthusiastically followed the races, with a great deal of money changing hands afterward. Nor were horses and boxers the only things that twitted the British love of gambling. The outcome of any event, any game, might offer an occasion for laying a bet, whether it was darts, checkers, or cards—or even which of two cockroaches would arrive first at a certain crack in the floor.

Rachel knew Edwin was not immune to this spirit of gaming. In fact, he was so woefully addicted that they were often short on money for food, let alone clothing and shoes. She practiced every measure of economizing that she knew. They ate plain meals. She patched and mended until she was patching patches and mending mends.

It had not always been so bad. In their earlier years, he

had played cards for recreation, but gradually he was seduced by the element of chance. When he won, he was ecstatic and cheerful. When he lost, he became morose and surly—and preoccupied by anticipation of the win next time.

When he was paid, he usually gave her a certain amount for the household expenses. Often as not, he would be demanding some of it back within only a few days. She began to discover certain of their possessions missing—an ornate snuff box of his, a fine ivory fan of hers.

"Where is that gold locket you used to wear?" he asked one day in late March. They were alone in the breakfast room of the inn, the other residents having finished preparing, consuming, and cleaning up the remains of their own meals.

"W-why do you ask?" She had taken to carrying it in a pocket hidden in the inside of her dress.

"Well, we are short of money again, and I thought to sell it. It ought to be worth a few shillings—or Spanish dollars."

"No!" she cried. "That locket came from my mother! It was my father's wedding gift to her. It is all I have of them. You cannot mean to sell it. Please, Edwin, no. I beg you." She drew in her breath on a long, shuddering sob.

"Oh, for God's sake, stop your blubbering! You can keep the damned thing." He took a deep swallow of his breakfast ale and muttered, "Maybe I should just sell *you*. You might be worth almost as much as the locket anyway."

"Edwin! Don't even talk like that!" Sure he was not serious, she was nevertheless shocked he would even voice such an idea aloud. However, she knew it was not entirely unknown for a husband to sell his wife.

"Now you're even telling me how to talk?" He slammed his mug on the table and rose. "I'll be back tonight."

But he did not return that night, or the next.

She worried about his absence. It was not the first time he had stayed out all night, but this was his longest unexplained absence since they had left England. When he did return, it was late in the afternoon of the third day. He was cheerful and apologetic and he carried a bottle of wine,

which he insisted they would share to show there were no
hard feelings between them now.

Rachel did not really want the wine, but she was willing
to smooth over the situation if he wished. Maybe this would
set them on the road to true reconciliation. Hope springs
eternal, she thought. Unused to drinking alcoholic bever-
ages, she thought this particular red wine was not only quite
strong, but it tasted rather strange, yet Edwin seemed to
relish it. She would not allow her lack of experience to ruin
her husband's peace offering.

"Come on," Edwin said when the bottle was empty.
"We're going to the Montenegro. There's a party over there."
He pulled her upright.

"Oh, Edwin, I'm not sure I can." She felt dizzy and un-
steady on her feet.

"Sure you can, sweetheart." He put his arm around her
waist. "The fresh air will bring you around."

"Very well. If you shay so." Edwin was being so sweet,
and he held her close all the way to the Montenegro.

It was going exactly as he had planned, Brady exulted to
himself. He thought once she might have seen him lacing
her glass with the drug, but apparently she had not. He had
had some reservations about this scheme, of course, but now
it seemed the perfect solution. He would not be the first
man to escape from an impossible situation in this manner.
And, after all, it was probably better than simply deserting
her here in a foreign country. It was one thing to desert a
woman in England, where she would have the support of
family and parish. It was quite another to just leave her in
the midst of a campaign a continent away.

So he had eventually acquiesced to—even welcomed—
Ralph Morton's suggestion two nights ago. They had been
drinking and playing cards, with Brady occasionally offering
disparaging comments on the character of complaining
women.

"Maybe you just don't know how to handle yours." Morton winked broadly at Harvey Willis and Fred Potter, his usual companions. The two chuckled appreciatively.

"Think you could do better, do you?" Brady asked belligerently.

"Probably," Morton said calmly. "But come. We're here to play cards, ain't we?"

Brady sulked silently, but he called for more drink and agreed to continue playing. Three hours and several drinks later, Morton laid down yet another winning hand.

"I don't know how you keep doing that," Brady said with an edge to his voice.

"Luck, my lad. Just plain luck." Morton's tone was jovial, but also condescending.

"I wonder . . ." Brady muttered, but he motioned for Willis to shuffle the cards again.

Morton stayed Willis's hand.

"You're gonna give me a chance to retrieve my losses, aren't you?" Brady asked, barely aware that he seemed to be whining.

"You're into me for quite a sum already," Morton said. "Six guineas and more."

"Six guineas is a lot of blunt on a sergeant's take of a shilling six per day," Willis said.

Potter whistled. "Two months pay—not even figuring the expenses they take away from us!"

Brady glumly considered this, but he wanted another drink—and he wanted to continue the play. "Look. You know I'm good for it."

"Not the way your luck's been runnin'." Morton peered at him from beneath brows that were incongruously bushy, given the man's thinning hair.

Brady stared back at him, holding the other's gaze as Morton idly played with the coins stacked in front of him. Brady hated Morton's smirking almost as much as he hated Rachel's jawing at him.

"Tell you what I'll do," Morton said. "You're always complaining about that wife of yours. I'll buy her from you for what you owe me."

Brady saw Willis and Potter drop their jaws at this suggestion now that it seemed serious. Always before, such an idea had been posed as a *joke,* for God's sake.

"Wha-at? I can't—you don't mean—"

"Of course you can," Morton said smoothly.

"You want me to sell you my woman for six guineas?" Brady raised his voice in surprised outrage. He was vaguely aware they had caught the interest of others in the room.

"Very well. I'll make it ten."

"Jiminy!" the youthful Potter exclaimed. "That's more'n three months' pay!"

"Hmm." The idea was preposterous, but Brady found himself considering it. Hadn't he idly threatened Rachel with such two days ago? It would be nice to be free of always dealing with the millstone of a woman about one's neck. "I just don't know . . ."

"Well, you think on it. Ten guineas." Morton flipped a coin at Potter. "Fred, get us another drink, will ye?"

"Sure thing."

Brady sat silently until Potter returned with the drinks. Then he said, "I couldn't just sell her to you outright."

"Don't see why not," Morton said. "You hear of men selling their wives all the time. English papers are full of such stories."

"It is not such a common occurrence at all," Brady insisted. "I've personally only known of one such incident— and it occurred over twenty years ago."

"Still, it's done. And I'm offering you ten guineas."

Brady looked away from the man's penetrating stare. He took another long swallow of his drink.

"It'd have to be done in a proper manner," he said slowly.

"What d'ye mean—proper?" Morton asked.

"Well, at home these things are done like cattle auctions—at the market fairs, you know?"

"You want to hold an *auction?*" Morton challenged.

"Well, I just think it should *look* like a proper auction," Brady argued. "Wouldn't be anyone else that 'ud have ten guineas to spend on a woman. In England selling a wife is legal only if the sale is public. I know that much."

"Uh . . . I don't think they're really *legal* even then," Willis put in.

"You stay outa this," Morton growled, and Willis shrank back into himself. "They may *not* be legal in the strictest terms," Morton added persuasively, "but everyone recognizes the results—including the courts."

They all sat in silence for a few minutes.

"Well, Brady?" Morton prompted.

"I don't know . . ."

"Don't be tryin' to hit me up for more blunt. Ten guineas—and that's it."

" 'Tain't that. I just don't know how I'm gonna get Rachel to go along with the idea."

Morton laughed. "Oh, you'll think of something."

And so he had.

Major Lord Jacob Forrester straightened the coat of his dress uniform and turned toward Hastings and Travers.

"I am ready." He picked up his saber and attached it properly to his belt.

"Don't we three look fine as five pence?" Travers asked. "Ladies, be on guard this night!"

The three of them once again shared quarters, this time rooms in the house of a blacksmith and his wife. They were preparing to go to a ball given by Colonel Ashworth of the Second Division. There had been several balls in the last months to relieve the tedium of winter. This would be one of the most elegant.

"I think Colonel Clark's pretty red-haired daughter has her eye on me," Hastings said jokingly, "so don't either of you be trying your luck there."

Travers snorted scornfully. "Don't you just *wish* it were so?"

They heard a loud knocking at the door downstairs, then

Señora Ramirez called up in Spanish, "Major Forrester, you have a visitor."

Jake descended the stairs with Hastings and Travers behind him to find a very agitated Corporal Collins awaiting him.

"What is it, Collins?" Jake asked.

"C-could I have a private word with you, sir?"

Jake motioned Collins out the door and followed. When he had closed the door, he asked again, "What is it? We were just on our way out."

"He's gonna *sell* her, sir!" The young man was obviously highly agitated.

"Hold on. Who is selling whom?"

Collins took a deep breath. "That Brady fellow. He's selling his wife to another man in his regiment."

"He what—? Ridiculous. Men do not go around selling their wives in this day and age," Jake said, trying to comprehend the absurdity of such an idea.

"I'm telling you, sir, he's doing it. Tonight. At an inn called the Montenegro."

"How did you come by this information? Perhaps it is just a rumor."

"No, sir, it ain't. These two fellows—Potter and Willis—they told me so themselves, and they're mates of the man what wants to buy her. Only Brady, see, he says it has to be a proper auction and they're doin' it tonight. Word has got around—lots of fellows plan to be there."

Jake felt his gut tighten. Good God. That Rachel—sweet, kind, proud, spirited Rachel—should be subjected to such humiliation.

"She don't deserve that, sir." Collins voiced Jake's thoughts precisely.

"I'll take care of it," Jake said, vowing silently to kidnap her from beneath the buyer's nose if necessary.

"If you don't mind, sir, could me an' Humphrey come with ye?"

"Find yourselves some mounts. No. Never mind. You and Sergeant Humphrey may use my extra horses."

"Thank 'e, sir."

Jake went back into the house, where Hastings and Travers regarded him questioningly.

"I need all the money you have to spare," Jake said without preamble as he led the way back upstairs. Neither of them questioned this unusual request.

As he dug around in his gear to find his own money pouch, his friends went to their rooms to do the same. Soon they met again at the bottom of the stairs.

"Here." Hastings handed him a small bag of coins. "I think it's about twenty guineas."

"I've only ten, but you are welcome to it." Travers handed over his hoard.

"Thanks," Jake said. "And I have nearly thirty. Let us hope that is enough."

"For what?" Hastings and Travers asked in unison.

"To buy a woman."

"Buy a woman?" Hastings gave him an inquiring look. "Since when does one Jacob Forrester need to *buy* a woman? And at such an outlandish price?"

Jake quickly explained. His friends were aghast. Both had met Rachel only briefly, and they were well aware their friend owed his life to her. Still, they seemed to have reservations about the intended rescue.

Doubt brought a frown to Hastings' brow. "You sure you want to do this, Forrester?"

"Yes, I'm sure. Why would I not be?"

"Well . . . 'tis just so unusual. I mean, involving yourself in the off-duty life of enlisted."

"The generals won't like it," Travers added.

Jake paused briefly. They were right. There was that necessary gulf between officer ranks and enlisted. It existed to maintain the discipline vital to a smooth fighting machine. Then his mind returned to Rachel, her gentleness, her quick smile, her empathy for another human being in pain.

"That is a risk I shall have to take," he said. "God knows

it will not be the first time some commander has been un-happy with me."

"Ever the rebel, eh, my friend?" Hastings clapped him on the shoulder. "Or is it Sir Galahad? I seem to remember your rescuing some poor soul at university when others were picking on him."

"Helman, you mean?"

"The very one."

"He did not deserve the treatment he was getting." Jake said defensively. "And neither does Rachel—Mrs. Brady." He saw Hastings and Travers exchange a look at his use of her given name. "No, it's not what you are thinking, either."

"As you say," Hastings said. "So—you are determined to fly to her aid?"

"Yes."

Travers exchanged another look with Hastings, then said, "We're coming with you. There might be trouble."

Thus, with Collins and Humphrey on Jake's extra mounts, five riders dashed toward the Montenegro some twelve miles away.

Jake could hardly tear his mind from what Rachel might be suffering. Collins had described Morton as something of a brute—a man of questionable ethics and one most other men tried to avoid crossing. That Brady should even think of turning a woman like Rachel over to such a one!

Oh, God, he prayed silently, *please let me stop it. Please let me be there in time.*

Rachel accompanied her husband to the Montenegro in something of a daze. She wanted to sleep, yet she seemed to see the two of them approaching the inn as though she watched strangers from a great distance. She stumbled twice, but Edwin's arm about her waist supported her.

The taproom of the inn was extremely crowded. The pa-trons were mostly men, but there was a scattering of women. Rachel blinked several times, knowing she should recognize these people—some of them, at least—but the faces all blurred before her eyes. She could not understand why her brain was taking so long to register details of the scene. The voices seemed blurred, too, with several people talking at once. She felt she was in a dream-like scene—but there was a sense of apprehension, too, that was more like a nightmare. If only she could just curl up and sleep.

"Here she is!"

"Prime bit of goods, that is."

"Hey! You need a rope." A cackle of female laughter punctuated this comment.

"Here. Use this." There was a sound of ripping cloth. Rachel was vaguely aware of someone tying strips of cloth together. Then a loose loop was lowered over her head. A hoot of laughter accompanied this action. She looked around vacantly, but could not register the faces. Yes. There was one she knew. Edwin's friend Morton. She did not like the look of raw hunger and triumph she saw there. She leaned closer to Edwin.

"It—it's so warm in here," she said, thinking she was speaking softly to him alone.

"Likely to get real hot for you before the night's over." There was that female cackle again.

Rachel heard herself emit a giggle, but she had no idea what was so funny. She shook her head, trying to clear it. Somehow she needed to understand what was happening— but it was such a blur of sounds, colors, and motions. Was she going to be sick? Was it that possibility that caused this faint feeling of panic and fear?

"Come on. Get on with it!" That was Morton's voice, sounding authoritative and annoyed.

Get on with what? she wondered indifferently.

"Stand 'er on the table so's we can see," a disembodied voice called out.

Rachel felt herself lifted onto a table that was not quite steady. She looked down vacantly on a sea of upturned faces that were indistinguishable to her. She concentrated on keeping her balance. *Must not fall. Must not fall.* She tried to find Edwin's face among the blur. Then she heard what sounded like his voice, but it came from a great distance, almost like an echo.

"Start the bidding."

"I got seven shillings," said a drunken voice.

"Two pounds," said another.

"Five guineas," called out yet another.

Rachel looked around, but she could not see what on earth it was they were bidding on. She tried to find Edwin again. She must tell him she really had to go home now.

She felt a draft of cool air as the door of the inn opened. Ah, that felt good. She tried to look around to see who had come in, but her head just did not work very well.

"Ten guineas!" The voice was loud, decisive. Morton. What would Ralph Morton think worth giving up *ten* guineas for?

The crowd was suddenly very quiet. All eyes seemed turned toward the door, but Rachel just could not make any part of her body function to see what or who commanded their attention. Also, she felt very wobbly up there on the table.

"Guess she's mine for ten guineas." It was Morton's voice again, sounding self-satisfied this time.

"Fifty," called a voice near the door.

A ripple went through the patrons of the inn.

"What'd he say?"

"Fifty. My bid is fifty guineas," the voice said.

Did she recognize that voice? Major Forrester's? No, it could not be his. Not in the Montenegro. Then whose?

"Now see here!" Morton again. He sounded blustery. "Brady, are you tryin' to cheat me?"

Why would Edwin cheat his friend? Besides, had she not heard it was *Morton* who was given to cheating?

"Take the fifty," someone shouted.

She did not follow what happened next. Suddenly, strong hands were around her waist, swinging her from the table. The noose was lifted from her neck and she was picked up bodily. She smelled sandalwood.

"Here, Travers. Pay the bastard."

It *was* the major's voice, but it sounded as though it came from under water. Suddenly everything just faded away, but, inexplicably, she felt safe—wherever she was.

Twelve

Jake knew the instant he saw her that Rachel had been drugged. She seemed to be in a daze, staring vacantly around her. When he got closer, he saw the pupils of her eyes were reduced to little pinpoints even in the dimly lit room.

"Here! He can't come in here and queer our business this way." The man named Morton was obviously out of his mind with fury—why else would he presume to talk so in the presence of an officer?

"I believe I just did," Jake said. "And unless you wish to see yourself court-martialed for insubordination, you will say no more."

"Give it up, Morton," someone said. "That's Forrester—ol' Nosey's fair-haired boy."

The one called Morton glared at the three men in fancy dress uniform and the enlisted man who accompanied them in more nondescript attire. Something in their stance must have dissuaded him, for he turned away with a curse about "bloody damned officers who think they own the world."

That phrasing—"Give it up, Morton. That's Forrester"—triggered something in Jake's memory, but he stored it away. He would think about it later. Right now he had to get Rachel away from here. Away from the crowd who had been like a pack of hyenas waiting for their turn at a kill. Away from lascivious eyes measuring, weighing her.

As he turned to carry her toward the door, he caught sight of Edwin Brady. Jake wanted to plant his fist in the man's handsome, weak face. He saw Travers give Rachel's husband the money. Brady was counting it even as Jake exited the inn with his burden. Travers and Hastings followed.

"What now?" Hastings asked.

Jake thought fast. What now? He had not planned beyond simply rescuing her. "You two go on to Ashworth's ball. You will be late, but I doubt you will be refused admission."

Laughter lay under Hastings' tone. "No. Not likely. A military ball here in Spain or Portugal is not exactly like attending an assembly at Almack's in London."

"Here, Hastings." Jake handed over the limp body of Rachel and then mounted his horse behind the saddle. "Hand her up to me now."

Hastings did so, and Jake settled her on the saddle in front of him. He reached his feet awkwardly for the stirrups.

"Is Mrs. Brady hurt, Major?" asked Collins, who had been left outside to hold their horses.

"I think not." At least not physically, he thought. How on earth would a woman like Rachel react when she regained full consciousness?

Trying to balance Rachel's limp form and guide his horse properly made the return ride far longer for Jake than the dash to the Montenegro. Hastings and Travers, at Jake's urging, went on to the ball. Jake knew he could trust their discretion, as well as that of Collins and Humphrey. But there was that whole room full of leering faces they had left behind. This incident would spread like wildfire through the entire Army of the Peninsula. Poor Rachel.

He rode with one hand on the reins and the other holding her securely. She remained unconscious, her head resting against his chest. Occasionally he felt a wisp of her hair brush his chin and caught an herbal scent that must have been from whatever she used to wash her hair. He could not define his jumbled emotions. There was, of course, intense, unwavering anger directed at the men who would do this to Rachel. He tried to tell himself it was the same reaction he would have had against those who abused any innocent person. To a certain extent, it was. However, he knew very well that with no other such victim would he have felt this fierce sense of protectiveness, this intense gratitude that she was safe. He hugged her closer.

It occurred to him he had never consciously touched her before, beyond clasping her hand once or twice. So why did having her here in his arms feel so familiar—so absolutely right?

Whoa, Forrester. She is still a married woman. She belongs to another.

No. She belongs to me now. He sold her. I bought her.

Then it hit him.

He *had* bought her. What the hell was Jake Forrester—officer in His Majesty's Army—going to do with a woman on the campaign trail?

What was he going to do with her tomorrow? Tonight?

"Collins. Humphrey." He called to his only companions now that the others had ridden off at his own bidding.

"Yes, sir?" both answered.

"Do either of you know where Sergeant Paxton is billeted? He is with Grant's 94th."

"I do, sir." Humphrey named the village accommodating most of Paxton's regiment.

"I want you two to ride over there and ask Mrs. Paxton to come back with you to my quarters."

"Tonight, sir?" Collins asked.

"What about her boy—and her husband?" Humphrey added.

"You're right," Jake replied, aware he had not thought beyond the fact Rachel would need her friend when she awoke.

"Tell them—discreetly, mind you—what happened and ask them to come in the morning. I will send some sort of conveyance for them. I think Mrs. Brady will probably sleep now for a long time."

They parted at a fork in the road and Jake went on alone with Rachel for the last two miles. Arriving at his own billet, he was glad to see the adult members of the Ramirez family had not yet retired. Señora Ramirez frowned and shook her head when Jake appeared at the door with Rachel in his arms. The señora waved her finger in a negative gesture and spoke in rapid Spanish.

"No. No. No. No women, Major. I told you. My children—"

"You do not understand," he said in his almost fluent use of her own tongue. He explained to her that Rachel had been mistreated and she needed help. He even told the señora of Rachel's saving his own life and his obligation to help her.

He watched as the woman's expression softened at hearing Rachel's story.

"But I have no room for the lady," Señora Ramirez protested.

"She may have my room this night," Jake replied. "I will sleep on a cot in the other room—or on a chair. I do not think she should be left alone. I will make other arrangements for her tomorrow. Henry and I will see to her now."

He could tell Señora Ramirez still had misgivings, but she shrugged her shoulders and gave in to his plan when her husband assured her it was all right to do so. She muttered something that sounded to Jake like, "Oh, these English. What next?"

Jake carried Rachel up to his own room, where he found Henry dozing by the fire.

"Wha—" Henry roused himself. "Mrs. Brady?" he asked in surprise.

Jake explained what happened.

"I knew that Brady fellow was a bad piece of news. That devil's by-blow should be horsewhipped," Henry said vehemently.

"That he should." Jake put Rachel down on the bed and removed her shoes. He noticed her cotton stockings had been much mended. He lifted her as Henry drew back the covers and the two of them tucked her into bed, having removed only her shoes and shawl.

"You say she was drugged, my lord?

"I believe so. Probably a heavy dose of laudanum."

"That means she will sleep a good long while."

"That is what I thought, too," Jake agreed, "but I do not

want her to be alone when she awakens. I have sent for Mrs. Paxton."

For the rest of the night, Jake and Henry took turns sitting with the sleeping Rachel. It was well after midnight when Hastings and Travers returned. They looked in on Jake and expressed no surprise at finding Rachel there. They spoke softly.

"The story is already out," Hastings said.

"Damn!" Jake muttered. "How?"

"Who knows? Someone in that inn just could not wait to be the bearer of such a tale."

"We did what we could to put the best face on it," Travers said.

"Thanks. I appreciate that, but I doubt it has a positive face."

Travers nodded and his tone was sad. "What a thing for a good woman to have to live with."

"Right," Hastings said. "Luckily, however, she seems to have no connections with the *ton,* so she will be relatively safe from clacking tongues when she returns to England."

The other two went on to the room they shared down the hall. Jake sat mulling over the entire incident. He heard again that voice. "Give it up, Morton. That's Forrester. . . ." The words floated like a wisp of fog in the shadows of memory. "Give it up, Morton . . ." No. There was something wrong about the picture. "Give it up . . ." He closed his eyes and leaned his head against the back of the chair. "Give it up . . . man!" That was it!

Then it came to him. The forest. A young woman and a man—a boy really, scarcely older than himself at the time. Jake had been—what?—sixteen? He remembered vividly the faces of the other two young men, one embarrassed and chagrined, the other enraged. And now he also recalled that enraged countenance all grown up—Brady!

The name *Brady* did not sound right to him, but for the life of him, he could not recall a name that *would* sound right. Maybe it would come to him later. However, he had no doubt Rachel's husband had been the would-be rapist on that long ago afternoon in Devon. Once again, he wondered how a woman like Rachel had come to be tied to such a man.

Early the next morning, Sergeant Humphrey brought Mrs. Paxton—alone—to the house where Forrester was billeted.

"I came as soon as I could," Clara said.

Jake rose from the chair at Rachel's bedside. "Thank you for doing so. I am sorry to take you from your family."

"Well, Joe has his duties, you know, and Mrs. Stevens offered to watch Benny for me. I will stay as long as Rachel needs me."

"She has not awakened yet," Jake said, "though she has seemed more restless in the last hour or so. I assume Humphrey told you what happened?"

"Yes, he did. I would dearly love to wring that Edwin Brady's neck," she said grimly.

"I fear you would have to stand in rather a long line for that privilege."

Just then Henry came in. He welcomed Mrs. Paxton and then asked, "Has Mrs. Brady regained consciousness?"

"No." Jake looked from one to the other of them. "I do so reluctantly, but I must leave you two to this duty, as I have a staff meeting this morning and Lord knows what *it* will lead to."

"We can handle things here, my lord," Henry said, "especially now that Mrs. Paxton is here."

Jake and Henry gathered up clothing and items for Jake's toilet and left Clara alone with Rachel. Jake cast a compassionate look at the figure in his bed. He hated leaving Rachel, but he knew she would probably welcome Clara's presence more than his own under the circumstances.

It was rather late in the morning when Rachel finally awakened. She opened her eyes slowly; the lids felt heavy and rather scratchy. She quickly closed them again. The sun was far too bright—and the window was in the wrong place! Pain pounded in her head. She could not suppress a groan.

"Oh. Are you awake then?" a female voice asked.

Her eyes flashed open. "Clara? What are you doing here?" She glanced around in surprise. "Wha—what am *I* doing here? And—and—*where* am I?"

"You are in Major Forrester's room."

"Major Forrester's—" She tried to absorb this news. "Good heavens! How did I get here?"

Moving her chair closer to the bed, Clara took Rachel's hand in her hers. "How much do you remember of last night?"

"Well . . . I do remember Edwin came home with a bottle of wine. He—he had not come home the night before, you see." She felt a little sheepish and disloyal in admitting this even to Clara. "It—the wine—was in the nature of a peace offering, I think." Rachel wondered about Clara's expression, which reflected both fury and skepticism. "I did not want it—not really—but he was so sweet about it . . ."

"That blackguard!" Clara muttered. "Did the wine taste strange to you?"

"Well, yes, it did. But as you know, I am not accustomed to drinking wine, and Edwin said it was fine." Rachel felt an inkling of apprehension slither through her.

"What else do you remember?"

"We went to the Montenegro—I think that is where Edwin's friend stays. I *think* I saw him—the friend—there. But . . . but I do not remember anything else."

"You do not remember the sale?"

"Sale?" Apprehension was there in full force now. She struggled to recall anything after their entering the taproom of the Montenegro. "I remember only a great number of people all talking at once and very loudly. I—I seemed to be looking *down* on them."

"You were. Oh, my dear, dear friend."

The gentleness and anguish in Clara's tone and her tightened grip alarmed Rachel. "What is it? Has Edwin been hurt?"

"If only it was so simple." Clara proceeded to tell—in what Rachel later thought of as the gentlest possible terms—of the events of the previous evening.

When Clara had finished, Rachel looked at her in disbelieving horror. She spoke in a near whisper. "He *sold* me? He really *sold* me? And—and I—I just *allowed* it?"

Clara gripped her hand even harder and gave it a small shake. "No. You did not *allow* it. You were drugged. Laudanum, probably—in the wine."

Rachel rose to a sitting position. "Oh, my God! Please. This cannot be true." She pressed her hands to her eyes to shut out the vision. Somehow, even as she denied and rejected what she heard, she knew it *was* true. Edwin, her own husband, who had once sworn to love and cherish her, had, in fact, treated her like a piece of disposable property.

Tears shimmering in her eyes, Clara slid from the chair to the edge of the bed. She gathered Rachel into her arms and held her as the shocking message sank in. Rachel could not withhold her sobs. The two of them rocked back and forth—one in stunned, disbelieving grief, the other in impotent fury.

Finally, Rachel pushed away. "I feel so very sick," she said in a voice devoid of emotion. "I am not sure which ails me most—my body or my soul."

"*Your* soul has no reason to suffer," Clara said fiercely. Then she added in her familiar practical way, "But we can deal with your physical sickness. I shall get you some tea and toast. There is a chamber pot in the dressing room there, as well as a wash basin and some water." She pointed to an adjacent room and left.

Rachel sat for some minutes on the side of the bed. Her head hurt horribly and she felt dizzy—so dizzy—and queasy. Finally, she stood and slowly made her way to the small dressing room, where she was promptly and violently ill. Strangely enough, she began to feel better almost immediately. The queasiness was gone, though her head still ached miserably. She rinsed her mouth and washed her face. The cool water felt refreshing. On her return to the bedroom, she found Clara waiting for her with the tea and toast.

"I brought you a poached egg as well." Clara had set the tray on a small table near the bed.

"Thank you." Sitting on the edge of the bed, Rachel drank some of the tea and nibbled at the food. Then she sank back into the pillow.

"You'll feel more the thing after a while," Clara assured her. "This is merely the effects of overindulging—even if the overindulgence *wasn't* your doing!"

Rachel smiled weakly at her friend's attempt at levity. How was it she had been so very lucky in choosing her friends and so very unlucky in choosing a husband? She closed her eyes, more from need to guard against the bright sunlight than from any sense of sleepiness. She needed to think, but she doubted she could develop an effective plan so long as she felt so very, very miserable.

Major Forrester sat through the staff meeting only half listening to the colonel and general, who were repeating their presentation of the week before. Clearly, Wellington intended to take the offensive this spring and summer. In view of the fiasco at Burgos last autumn, they would bypass that fortified city by swinging to the north and continuing toward the Pyrenees.

"The logical place for a major encounter this side of the mountains," Colonel Kingsley was saying, "is probably near Vitoria."

"Have we any reliable maps yet?" asked Major Tucker, one of the Third Division's regimental commanders.

"Unfortunately, no. Horse Guards has been woefully negligent in that regard. We must rely upon those our correspondents produce and those we have captured from the enemy."

Jake felt a great deal of empathy for the correspondents— men who regularly went out on scouting missions to track the enemy's movements and gather information on the strength, supplies, and equipment that might be brought against their own side. It was a dangerous mission, for the correspondents were in effect spying on the enemy. That they had to do so in their uniforms made the job even more difficult, but to be caught by the enemy and not in uniform meant being summarily executed. The uniform at least gave a man a chance of staying alive.

"One would suppose the Spanish would at least have adequate maps of their own country," groused another major seated at the table.

"Yes, one would." General Powers, sitting at the head of the table, responded to this perennial complaint. "But they are no better prepared than we are. I suppose they never thought of war coming to their own territory."

"So," Major Tucker said in a rather assertive tone, given that he was addressing a general, "we are to march into that mountain range with nary a clue as to how to get across?"

Powers was an imposing figure who carried himself with great dignity. "That is correct, soldier. What is more to the point, we will follow orders unquestioningly."

"Yes, sir."

Colonel Kingsley attempted to smooth this over by saying, "Our correspondents are in the mountains now making maps—*and* making friends. The local people up there are usually more inclined to favor us than the French. They are not happy about having a Frenchman on their Spanish throne. They know the mountains, and they will gladly show us through them."

Jake shifted in his chair, bored. So far there had been little in the way of new information. His mind reverted to the issue that occupied him for the last—what?—fifteen hours or so: what to do about Rachel.

His own expertise in legal matters was lacking in the extreme, but even he knew the legality of last night's transaction was questionable at best. The legal bonds of matrimony were not so easily broken. Still, though rare, wife sales did occur. Moreover, the courts had been known to recognize the results in some instances, despite the railing of newspaper editors and an occasional Member of Parliament against the practice.

The fact was, the sale *had* been made—and it had transpired in the presence of dozens of witnesses. Like it or not, Jake Forrester had bought himself a woman—and, short of reversing the sale, he must live with the results. Reversing the sale was not an option. Brady was unlikely to agree to part with the fortune that had fallen into his lap. Even if he would do so, what would prevent him from performing the same nefarious deed another time, with who knew what result for Rachel?

The meeting was breaking up. Major Tucker clapped Jake on the shoulder and nearly leered as he said in a too loud voice, "Ah, Forrester. I hear you went to an auction and bought yourself a pretty piece of goods."

Tucker's laugh struck Jake as obscene. Jake had never liked this man, who seemed to think the only way to elevate himself was to put others down.

"I beg your pardon," Jake said coldly, and pointedly removed the man's hand from his shoulder. "A decent woman was sorely wronged and the rest of us would do well to remember that." He looked Tucker in the eye, hoping his glare would warn the other off this topic.

"Sorry," Tucker said with an exaggerated show of innocence. "I had no idea it was such a sensitive subject for you." He walked away chuckling, and Jake wished he had struck that smirk right off Tucker's face.

Not here, Forrester. Not here, he told himself. It occurred to him that twice in fewer than twenty-four hours he had wanted to plant a facer on someone's countenance over Rachel Brady. Good grief. Perhaps those practice sessions in Gentleman Jackson's Boxing Saloon during his last leave would come in handy after all. He shook his head ruefully.

Word apparently got around that Major Forrester was a might touchy about that auction business, for no one else mentioned it to Jake for the rest of the day. In fact, they studiously avoided the topic.

However, he did not. Rachel dominated his thoughts throughout the day. What *was* he to do with her?

It was not unusual for men and officers to be traveling with women to whom they were not married. Women of this sort in the Peninsula, however, were usually Spanish or Portuguese nationals, though some were widows of fallen soldiers. They were not proper English women married to other living soldiers! Such women were tolerated, but rarely respected. They shared a man's bed, but rarely shared his life in any significant way. Jake found the very idea of having Rachel reduced to such a state wholly repugnant.

When he returned to his billet in the late afternoon, he was no nearer a solution to his dilemma than he had been that morning. He found Rachel in his room sitting in a chair, staring vacantly out the window.

"Good afternoon," he said, announcing his presence.

She returned his greeting and gazed at him briefly, then glanced away, apparently unable or unwilling to hold his gaze. "I—I want to thank you for what you did." Her voice was soft, and he thought she might be fighting to ward off tears.

"That is not necessary," he replied. "Against what you did for me nearly a year ago, this was a minor matter indeed." He stood in front of her, then half sat on the window sill, bracing his hands on either side of him to keep from snatching her into his arms, where she had felt so right the night before.

"No. It was not a minor matter, as I think you well know." She lifted her eyes to give him a challenging look. "It . . . it puts both you and me in a very awkward position."

He held her gaze and nodded. "You are, of course, right. But I honestly could do nothing else—and I would do it again in an instant."

"For which I do most sincerely thank you, Major."

She seemed withdrawn, yet tense. He wondered how she felt, what she thought about the events of the last evening. He sensed now was not a good time to press her on that issue, though, especially in view of the fact he had yet to sort out his *own* thoughts and feelings.

He deliberately tried to make his voice sound light-hearted. "Consider it a down payment on a debt of long standing."

"If there were a debt—and I challenge that view—your action alone has rendered it paid in full." She glanced away and spoke in a dull voice. "However, I should like you to know that if it takes me a lifetime, I will see you have your money back."

He moved from the window sill to squat in front of her. He took her hand, small, soft, and cold, in his own. "Rachel, look at me!" When she at last brought her gaze to his, he continued, "The money is irrelevant. I have plenty of money in England, though I admit to borrowing from Hastings and Travers last night."

"You—you did?" she asked dumbly.

"Yes. And they were eager to help in this emergency."

She was quiet for a moment, absorbing this thought. "I think we are both blessed in our friends." She gently disengaged her hand from his.

Pleased at the thought she might be including *him* among her own blessings, he stood and asked casually, "Speaking of which, where is Mrs. Paxton?"

"I sent her back to her family. I can get on myself now—though I am grateful to her for being here." She held his gaze again. "And to you for arranging that."

"Yes. Well. It seemed the right thing to do." He paused. "The question is, what is the right thing to do now?"

Thirteen

Rachel had spent the entire day in Jake's room, sleeping off and on, talking with Clara when she was awake. Twice Henry had looked in on them, once to bring the midday meal on a tray. Clara kept up the gossipy patter of the routine events of an army ensconced in winter quarters. Rachel only half listened. Her mind refused to let go of Edwin's betrayal and her need to make some sort of plan for the future.

After a while, she asked Clara to reiterate the details of the evening before. Clara willingly did so, apparently understanding another woman's need to comprehend every nuance of the incident. Rachel felt better physically in the afternoon; she was no longer queasy and the headache had lessened remarkably. Now she was merely tired. Needing time alone to think, she sent Clara back to her Joe and little Benny.

"You're sure you don't want me to stay?" Clara asked.

"No. No. You go on. I shall be fine now." Rachel hugged Clara tightly and said, "I do thank you for being here. I am glad *you* were the one to tell me such news."

She spent what was left of the afternoon deep in thought, beset by two sets of questions above all others. The first was *why? Why* had Edwin done such a despicable thing? How had she been so wrong about the handsome, amiable fellow the Brocktons had encouraged her to marry? What had she done to turn him against her? After all, they had been in love in the beginning—or had they? She was not even sure what love was at this point. Had Edwin ever loved her? Had she really *loved* him? Or was it a young girl's infatuation gone terribly awry? Could she have behaved any differently?

The second set of questions was *what now?* What did that sale mean? Was she no longer married, then? Foolish question. Only the Church or Parliament could dissolve a marriage—and neither institution did so for any but the wealthiest and most powerful. That being the case, would she have to go back with Edwin—assuming he would have her?

Welcome the advances, the exploring hands of a man who had sold her as he might a cow he no longer wanted? She shuddered at the very idea. What if he tried to sell her again? There might be no Major Forrester around to rescue her another time. The image of her would-be buyer, Morton, sprang before her, and she shuddered anew.

In truth, she was frightened. Nor was it only fear of returning to Edwin nor his giving her over to Morton that sent a chill through her. She was alone in a foreign land, where the language itself was a great mystery. She had no money, no means of support, no way of returning to her homeland on her own—and no home to which she could return if she got there!

There were, of course, many women in the very long "tail" of the British army. A number of these were wives as Clara was—as Rachel had been. Most, however, were camp followers—women who had taken up with soldiers in casual affairs and thus attached themselves to the army's baggage train. The majority were Portuguese and Spanish, though there were French women here and there who had been abandoned by their protectors in the wake of British victories. Most traded the favor of their bodies for a modicum of care and protection.

In other words, Rachel thought, they were whores. And that was precisely her status. Her husband had made a whore of her! She buried her face in her hands and wept yet again. Finally, she wiped her eyes and blew her nose. She sat staring blankly out the window until she was distracted by Major Forrester's greeting.

Now, he was asking about the right thing to do.

"I think there is nothing 'right' about this sordid business at all," she said in despair.

"I quite agree with you there." He sounded rueful. "However, we are faced with the consequences of actions beyond our control."

A knock on the door brought Forrester's, "Come." Henry entered, bearing a large tray. The major cleared the small bedside table and moved it near Rachel.

"I'll bring tea up later, my lord." Henry set the tray down and left.

"I arranged for us to have our supper here tonight," the major said, drawing up another chair.

"I—I am not very hungry," she said. Was he protecting her, or the rest of the household with this private dining arrangement?

"Still, you must eat something. Perhaps you would like a glass of wine?" He poured a glass of red wine from a small pitcher and held it out to her.

"No!" she said sharply. At his surprised look, she added, "I'm sorry. It was red wine . . . yesterday . . ."

"The drug was in red wine?"

"Yes."

"Shall I have Henry bring some fruit juice?"

"No. Water will be fine—and the tea later."

It was a simple meal of a thick rabbit stew and bread. Rachel picked nervously at her food, wondering if his lordship would expect her to share his bed later. She noticed with some resentment that he had a hearty appetite.

He made polite conversation throughout the meal, informing her that the army would probably be moving out within the week. She responded in kind with comments about the weather and mild winters in Spain.

Henry came to get the tray and returned with a tray of tea, apples, and cheese.

"Captain Hastings said he would speak with you in a few minutes, my lord," Henry said.

"That will be fine," the major answered. He settled back in his chair and crossed his legs, seemingly relaxed as Rachel filled their cups and handed him one. The aroma of tea enveloped them in a cloud of domesticity at variance with her turbulent emotions.

Rachel could stand the uncertainty no longer. "Wha—what is to happen to me?" She tried to make her voice sound conversational, but she knew the tension showed.

"I confess to some confusion on that point myself," he replied, giving her a direct look. "Much depends upon what you yourself want."

"What *I* want?" she asked bitterly. "Surely you know women have few choices in life, even in enlightened modern England. And here . . ." Her voice trailed off in light of the obvious.

"I will see you have *some* choice, at least."

She held herself silent, waiting for him to go on.

"For instance, it may be possible to force your husband to accept his responsibilities toward you—if you wish." Major Forrester let this idea hang between them, but gave no indication of trying to influence her response.

"I *have* thought of that," she admitted in a resigned tone, "but, in truth, I think it might make matters worse—and Edwin would likely find some way of doing this again." She closed her eyes briefly, trying to shut herself away from the shame and humiliation. Opening her eyes again, she saw only understanding sympathy in his.

"In time, I can arrange to send you back to your family in England," he offered.

"I—I have no family in England."

"Surely there is *someone*?"

"No, there is not. I have only an aunt—my father's stepsister—and she would not welcome me."

"Hmm. That complicates things."

"Really, my lord, you must not refine upon my problems.

You have done enough as it is. Perhaps Mac—Dr. MacLachlan—will be able to help me."

"Are you rejecting my help?" he asked in a lighter tone.

"No, of course not. It is just that—"

"Then say no more."

A knock heralded the entrance of the tall, lanky Captain Hastings, carrying a canvas bag. The captain bore a shock of blond hair, but his brows and mustache were incongruously dark. His brown eyes shone with friendly compassion as they settled on Rachel before he turned his attention to Major Forrester. The captain set the canvas bag on the bed along with himself, since the only two chairs in the room were occupied.

"It took some doing, but I've talked the señora into allowing Mrs. Brady to stay here."

Major Forrester grinned. "I never doubted the power of that Hastings charm."

"Yes. Well. It helped that the army will be moving out shortly and this is her last chance at seeing any of the ready for a while."

"What's in the bag?" Major Forrester gestured toward that object.

"Mrs. Brady's things. I went to Brady's billet as you suggested, but he had cleared out. Left his wife's clothes, but the landlady said he took everything else."

"Everything?" Rachel rose in some agitation to open the bag. She pawed through it, then breathed a sigh of relief as she brought forth her journal and the book Major Forrester had given her. She exchanged a look of understanding with him.

Forrester turned to Captain Hastings. "He left? Did he find new billeting then?"

Hastings shrugged. "I don't think so. I asked around. No one has seen him since last night. Hoskins—his lieutenant—is mad as hops."

"Desertion?" Major Forrester asked.

"I'd surmise that," Hastings said. "All that money, you

Take A Trip Into A Timeless World of Passion and Adventure with Kensington Choice Historical Romances!
—Absolutely FREE!

Let your spirits fly away and enjoy the passion and adventure of another time. Kensington Choice Historical Romances are the finest novels of their kind, written by today's best selling romance authors. Each Kensington Choice Historical Romance transports you to distant lands in a bygone age. Experience the adventure and share the delight as proud men and spirited women discover the wonder and passion of true love.

4 BOOKS WORTH UP TO $23.96— Absolutely FREE!

Take **4 FREE** Books!

We created our convenient Home Subscription Service so you'll be sure to have the hottest new romances delivered each month right to your doorstep — usually before they are available in book stores. Just to show you how convenient Zebra Home Subscription Service is, we would like to send you 4 Kensington Choice Historical Romance as a FREE gift. You receive a gift worth up to $23.96 — absolutely FREE. There's no extra charge for shipping and handling. There's no obligation to buy anything - ever!

Save Up To 30% On Home Delivery!

Accept your FREE gift and each month we'll deliver 4 bran new titles as soon as they are published. They'll be yours to examine FREE for 10 days. Then if you decide to keep the books, you'll pay the preferred subscriber's price. That all 4 books for a savings of up to 30% off the cover price! Just add the cost of shipping and handling. Remember, yo are under no obligation to buy any of these books at any time! If you are not delighted with them, simply return the and owe nothing. But if you enjoy Kensington Choice Historical Romances as much as we think you will, pay th special preferred subscriber rate and save over $7.00 off t bookstore price!

We have 4 FREE BOOKS for you as your introduction to
KENSINGTON CHOICE!

**To get your FREE BOOKS,
worth up to $23.96, mail the card below
or call TOLL-FREE 1-800-770-1963
Visit our website at www.kensingtonbooks.com.**

Take 4 Kensington Choice Historical Romances FREE!

YES! Please send me my 4 FREE KENSINGTON CHOICE HISTORICAL ROMANCES (without obligation to purchase other books). Unless you hear from me after I receive my 4 FREE BOOKS, you may send me 4 new novels - as soon as they are published - to preview each month FREE for 10 days. If I am not satisfied, I may return them and owe nothing. Otherwise, I will pay the money-saving preferred subscriber's price plus shipping and handling. That's a savings of over $7.00 each month. I may return any shipment within 10 days and owe nothing, and I may cancel any time I wish. In any case the 4 FREE books will be mine to keep.

Name _____

Address _____ Apt No _____

City _____ State _____ Zip _____

Telephone ( ) _____

Signature _____

(If under 18, parent or guardian must sign)

KN052A

Terms, offer, and prices subject to change. Orders subject to acceptance by Kensington Choice Book Club. Offer valid in the U.S. only.

4 FREE
Kensington
Choice
Historical
Romances
are waiting
for you to
claim them!

*(worth up
to $23.96)*

*See details
inside....*

PLACE
STAMP
HERE

KENSINGTON CHOICE
Zebra Home Subscription Service, Inc.
P.O. Box 5214
Clifton NJ 07015-5214

know. More than a year's pay for a sergeant. What do you think, Mrs. Brady?"

Rachel, surprised that he asked her opinion, answered slowly. "I—I am not sure. I suppose it is possible. Anything is possible. I clearly did not know him as well as I had imagined."

Hastings seemed discomfited at having embarrassed her. "I'm sorry, ma'am. No reason you *should* know."

"That other fellow—Morton?" Forrester asked.

"He's still around. Grousing about being cheated. But a witness saw Brady pay him what was apparently a long-standing debt." Hastings stood. "And that, my friends, is as much as I know. I bid you good night."

Rachel looked up at him and gave him a tentative smile. "Thank you, Captain, for bringing my things."

"My pleasure, ma'am." He bowed slightly and was gone.

Major Forrester, too, rose and went to the door, where he called for his batman. When that worthy arrived, the major told him, "Clear my things out of here, Henry. I shall share with Hastings and Travers for the time being."

"Yes, my lord."

Henry went about the task quietly and efficiently, darting only an occasional glance of curiosity at Rachel.

"Major Forrester," she said. "I must protest. I cannot force you out of your own room. Last night was one thing, but this is quite another."

"You are not forcing me," he replied. "This is the most sensible thing to do right now. We shall see what develops later."

With that, he, too, took his leave, and Rachel was left to wonder what that enigmatic comment might mean.

The next day, unsure of her status and embarrassed at the señora's possible reaction to her presence, Rachel was reluctant to leave the room. Answering a knock at the door, she found Henry bearing a tray with tea and bread and jam.

"Breakfast, madam," he said grandly. "Lord Jacob said I was to see to it for you."

"Why, thank you. How kind of both of you. But, please, Mr. Henry, do not think you must add *me* to your duties. If you will just show me around, I can do very well for myself."

"Yes, madam. You have your breakfast then, and I'll come back and show you the ropes, so to speak."

Henry did just that a short while later. Rachel thought they were both slightly embarrassed and unsure around each other. Acutely aware of being neither fish nor flesh in the major's movable establishment, she deliberately sought to reassure Henry she had no wish to usurp *his* position with the major.

The midday meal was an informal affair in the Ramirez kitchen. Rachel offered to help prepare the later meal and was politely refused. She returned to her own room and amused herself with her knitting and the book of poetry the major had given her. In the evening, she ate supper with all three officers, and they invited her to become a fourth for a card game.

The next few days followed this routine, with the only variation being an occasional walk in the afternoon by herself or in the evening with Major Forrester. She began to look forward to this special time with him.

One day Clara came to came to visit, pulling a laughing Benny in a small farm cart.

Rachel met them on the pathway and lifted the child high above her head. She twirled him about, and he screamed with delight. "Oh, Benny! How you've grown!"

She set the giggling child down, but he lifted his arms and said, "Up! Up!"

Clara laughed. "Now you have done it, Rachel! He will not leave you alone."

Rachel lifted and swung him again, then happily returned him to his mother who, with a stern "no," put him back in the cart and handed him one of the toys there to distract him. The two women ambled along aimlessly, Clara pulling the cart behind her.

"I had to come to see how you are doing," Clara said.

"I am dying of boredom with nothing to do."

"Enjoy it while you can. I hear we are moving out in a few days."

"I shall almost welcome the rigors of the trail," Rachel said.

"Unfortunately, I think you will face more than the usual hardships." Clara's voice carried a warning note that was not lost on Rachel.

"The talk is that bad, I gather?"

"It's a pretty unusual situation—a man selling his wife."

"Tell me the rest," Rachel demanded.

Clara seemed uncomfortable, but determined. "Well, there are those who think you've not done too badly in coming under the protection of the major."

"And by 'protection' they mean—?"

"Just what you'd think they'd mean," Clara said.

Rachel sighed. "I expected as much. But it is not true."

"It isn't?" Clara seemed only mildly curious. "Well, that'll probably change."

"Clara!"

"I'm sorry. I meant no offense. It's just that you are two very nice people and you have been friendly and . . ." Clara's voice trailed off into embarrassed silence.

Rachel patted her arm. "Never mind. I take no offense." But Major Forrester's, "We shall see what develops later" popped into her mind, and she felt herself blushing.

Clara looked at the sky and said, " 'Tis getting late. I must get our rations and take Benny home for his nap."

"It was nice to see you," Rachel said, genuinely glad of Clara's continued trust and friendship.

When Lord Wellington finally gave the order for the army to begin moving north, Jake was no closer to a solution to the dilemma of Rachel than he had been on the night of the sale. In fact, the situation grew increasingly complicated as he spent more and more time with her.

In their long walks, he asked about her family, and she told him of her childhood and youth. Some of this sounded vaguely familiar to him.

"Have you told me this before? I cannot believe I would have forgotten *all* of it."

She blushed prettily. "Well, yes. As a matter of fact, I *did* tell you something of myself once."

"You did?"

"You were in no condition to respond, but you seemed quieter if someone talked to you. At Badajoz, immediately after you were wounded."

"And you were the someone."

"I conjectured it was merely a female voice to which you responded." Her eyes twinkled mischievously as she looked up at him, and he wanted to kiss her right there in the middle of the village. "Many wounded soldiers cry out for their mothers or sweethearts, you know."

"Oh?" He pretended hauteur. "And you thought I was like all the rest?"

He was pleased when she picked up on the game and pretended to smooth his offended sensibilities. "Oh, no. Never." She paused. "I *knew* you were."

"Hmmph."

Her little giggle at this bit of foolishness told him, as nothing else had, that the resilient Rachel was on her way to recovery.

"So? Go on. Tell me more about your Addy," he urged.

As her story unfolded, he became aware it was true. She had no one to whom she could return in England. Not that he had doubted her before, but now he saw the situation in clearer terms. She expressed gratitude toward her aunt and uncle, but they sounded coldly indifferent to his ears.

"What of your mother's family?" he asked.

"I know nothing of them," she said sadly. "Papa rarely spoke of them. He said it broke Mama's heart when *her* papa disowned her."

"Do you know her maiden name?"

"Hendon."

"Hmm. It means naught to me, but my brother may know of it."

Her eyes twinkled again. "I thank you for the implied compliment, but I doubt anyone connected to a country doctor in Scotland would belong in such a rarefied atmosphere as a marquis occupies."

"Now don't you go all haughty on *me,* my dear," he admonished jokingly. "You have told me she taught you pretty English manners, and that she was different from the mothers of your friends."

"True, but—"

"And did you not say it was *she* who insisted on her deathbed that her daughter go to a proper school?"

"Yes, but Papa would have done that in any case."

They walked in silence for a while. Then he said, "There is a touch of Romeo and Juliet in the story of your parents."

"Yes. 'Tis wonderfully romantic—if somewhat mysterious now."

From that they went on to talk of Shakespeare, for Jake had lent her his copy of the bard's works and he knew she had been devouring the plays when he was away during the day.

Enjoyable as these sojourns were, their discussions brought him no resolution to the basic problem. He told himself yet again that Major Lord Jacob Forrester would have no use for a woman on the campaign trail. However, he resisted every suggestion that might remove her from his protection.

No, she should not join the Paxtons—nor her new friends the Binghams, either. There would be no provision for rations for her now that she had no husband in the picture. Jake, on the other hand, had never possessed the full contingency of servants to which he was entitled as a major. He had objected to taking on Juan, but there had been no choice in the matter of that small child. Nor did he see any in this matter of Rachel.

She had, of course, mentioned Mac, the doctor. But in Jake's view, the medical man offered nothing better for her than Jake himself could. He studiously ignored the twinge of jealousy he felt at the idea of her going over to the doctor.

When the call came to move out, Rachel's pitiful bag of possessions was added to his own pack animal.

For Rachel, the last days in winter quarters had become a time of healing—some, at least. She had not come to terms with the *why* of Edwin's betrayal, but she had begun to accept the consequences of it. She knew in time she would be able to move on. What other choice had she? For now, she would simply accept whatever else life threw in her path.

She desperately wanted to earn her own way. She was acutely conscious of owing a great—unpayable—debt to Major Forrester. So long as she was attached to his entourage, she would do what little she could to help—and what little Henry allowed her to do! Jake—or rather, the major—had been incredibly kind to her, especially in view of what people were saying.

Once the campaign was under way again, she would also continue her work with the hospital whenever possible. Only then would she be able to hold her head up. She knew the gossip and she had seen the stares—some curious, some slyly knowing—as she and the major walked of an evening.

One evening as they returned from a walk, it was later than usual. When they reached the door of her room, she turned to him with a sense of determination.

"Please come in for a moment," she said.

He gave her an inquiring look, but did as she asked. She closed the door and stood very near him.

"What is it?" he asked.

"I—uh—would you like to move back into your own room?" she asked in a rush.

"You mean—?"

"I know that cot cannot be comfortable for a big man

like you. Nor can sharing that crowded little room with your friends."

"But there is no other room in this house."

"I—I know."

"Rachel?" He put a finger under her chin to force her to meet his gaze. She noted his rare use of her name. "What are you doing?" he asked softly.

She swallowed, but refused to allow herself to look away. "I—I am offering to share your bed."

"Why?"

"It is what everyone thinks anyway. And . . . and 'tis but goods you bought and paid for." This came out more bitterly than she intended.

He simply stared at her for a moment, his eyes searching hers. Then he enfolded her in his arms, holding her close and laying his head against her own. "Oh, my dear girl. There is nothing—nothing!—I would like more."

Her head against his chest, she smelled the familiar sandalwood along with a faint odor of tobacco, the wool of his uniform tunic, and the not unpleasant smell of him alone. As they stood in total silence, she slipped her arms around his waist.

"I—I have nothing else to offer you." Her voice was muffled against his chest.

"You needn't offer me anything. Certainly not this—like this—like a—a—"

"A whore," she said flatly. "My husband made a whore of me."

"No! He did not!" The major's voice was harsh and he pulled away enough to look into her eyes again. "Do not—ever!—use that word in reference to yourself."

"But—"

"No." He put a finger against her lips. "Only one person could reduce you to such a level. You. And I cannot allow you to do that."

"I—I understand," she said dully and tried to move away, but he still held her firmly.

"No, I don't think you do. Rachel, listen to me. You are a

warm, giving person—and certainly one of the loveliest women of my acquaintance. But I will not have you this way."

"You don't want me?" She had humiliated herself only to have him reject her? How mortifying!

He gave her shoulders a gentle shake. "Of *course* I want you! Any man in his right mind would want you."

"My husband didn't."

"As I said . . ."

She smiled weakly and reached her head upward to kiss him on the cheek. "You are a fine man, Major Forrester."

"Perhaps. Perhaps not." He still held her close. "I want you to know this, though. When we make love, I want it to be because you are as wild for it to happen as I am. It will be entirely mutual and equal. And there will be no question of either of us 'owing' the other anything but supreme pleasure."

"When? Not if?"

"When," he said firmly.

And with that he kissed her properly—and very thoroughly. His lips were gentle at first, exploring, searching, but they quickly became firm, urging the response she readily gave. He pulled away—reluctantly, she thought.

He put her from him and stepped toward the door. "I must say good night before I lose my resolve."

"Good night, Major."

He turned back. "Under the circumstances, can you not bring yourself to call me by my name? 'Tis Jake, you know."

"Yes, I do know."

"If you continue to address me so formally, I shall feel compelled always to call you 'Mrs. Brady'—and, frankly, I do dislike referring to you by that blackguard's name."

"Very well, Major." She gave him a teasing smile. " 'Jake' it is. However, I think in company we should abide by the formalities. Do you not agree?"

"You drive a hard bargain, madam."

He kissed her quickly and was gone.

Fourteen

In the days that followed, Rachel tried to put the best face on the situation. Jake made no attempt to kiss her again, and she could not get beyond the obvious conclusion that he had been kind in his rejection, but it had been a rejection all the same.

While it had been a blow to her self-esteem, she admitted to ambivalent feelings about that scene. On the one hand, she had wanted him to want her, for she could not ignore her own heightened senses whenever he was near. On the other hand, danger loomed in taking the relationship beyond the friendship they already shared. She was not at all sure she could withhold her deeper self from this man—and it was imperative that she do so. She had made the offer thinking she could engage in a purely physical arrangement, preserving her inmost self in any such encounters.

Edwin had been able to inflict so much pain because she had given too much of herself. In the interest of self-preservation, she was determined she would never again be so vulnerable. Thus, a part of her was glad she had not been put to the ultimate test. Her own reaction to Jake's kiss told her clearly it had been a narrow escape. She now welcomed his cool pretension that nothing was changed between them, though occasionally she caught a puzzling look from him. When they chanced to touch hands or brush against each other, she thought he was just as aware as she of the resulting jolt.

Late April and early May gave forth several days of good

weather, which would produce adequate feed for the animals so necessary to transporting and feeding Wellington's army. The order came down for the troops to move out.

"Perhaps I should join the medical team now before we start on the trail," Rachel said as she and Jake walked out one evening.

"Why? Are you unhappy with us then? I hope neither Travers nor Hastings has said anything to discomfort you."

"Oh, no. No, they have not."

"Well, then—?" Jake left the question hanging.

"It is just that . . . well . . . maybe it would look better . . ."

"It would look better for you to travel with MacLachlan and Ferguson than with me? I fail to see any logic in that."

Put that way, Rachel saw little logic in it either. "Still, I should like to resume my work with the wounded."

"That should pose little problem," he said. Then he added, "I could hire one of the women to travel with us as your maid to preserve the proprieties."

"I doubt that would dampen the gossip. It would be merely an added expense—one that would put me even more in your debt. And I *am* quite used to doing for myself."

"As you wish," he said.

And they left it at that.

There were some minor skirmishes along the trail as the army, like some gigantic, many-legged insect, made its way north, veering to the east. Rachel knew these sporadic confrontations were far from "minor" to the men who lost limbs or friends in them—nor to women who lost husbands or lovers. For the most part, however, these days were filled with routine hardships of the trail. *Routine hardships,* she thought, was as contradictory a phrase as *minor skirmishes.*

Occasional thunderstorms provided a notable contrast to the more usual days of burning heat in terrain that offered little relief from the relentless sun. Rachel could often feel the perspiration between her shoulders, in the small of her back, and between her breasts. She kept her water canteen handy for not only herself, but the wounded on the wagons as well. Where land formations in the flatlands permitted, the men spread out in a great horizontal line across the countryside, with commanders holding their companies together in more or less orderly ranks. Each group was accompanied by its own set of camp followers and baggage wagons.

The quartermasters rode ahead each day to scout out quarters for the night. Sometimes these were in villages and the quartermasters would mark certain buildings with chalk for specific companies and would be on hand to direct traffic. Often, however, the army was required to camp in the open. Rachel actually preferred camping in the open rather than intruding into the lives and homes of local people. British soldiers paid their way and used their own supplies, unlike their French adversaries, who were forced to live off the land. Rachel knew the British practice of paying their way accounted for the welcome the allies, especially the British, received in the villages. Still, such an influx of people to be accommodated *had* to be disruptive, and she felt uncomfortable about it. Also, there was something clean and fresh about being outdoors.

"At least the men have tents now," Henry said as he and Thompkins were setting up camp during one of the early days.

"You did not always have them?" Rachel asked in some surprise.

"Officers had them because they supplied their own, but the men did not. 'Tis said the Peer argued long and hard for them. Parliament finally gave in."

Rachel paused in the process of unpacking cooking utensils. "Good heavens. Surely the government recognizes it is more expedient to preserve lives here than ship out new people all the time!"

"I'm told that was the argument that finally persuaded them," Henry said. "Some of the men grumbled about tents being more time and trouble than they were worth. But most are proud of them."

Attached to Forrester's group as she was, Rachel was determined that if she were to be considered a real member of it, she would have to make a place for herself. At first this had been difficult. Henry, perhaps taking his cue from his master, insisted on treating her as an honored guest. In fact, she thought Henry resented the intrusion of a female into what had been a strictly masculine household.

Henry was invariably polite to her, though, and he was mindful of her help to Major Forrester earlier. Rachel had twice heard him recounting to others her extraordinary medical skills. However, she was aware of being an extra to this small domestic group. She was given the tent that had heretofore been shared by Henry, Thompkins, and Juan. Initially, Henry had, at the major's direction, moved his bedroll into Jake's tent and the others slept in the open in good weather. When it rained, Thompkins, too, laid his bedroll in the major's tent, and Juan was glad enough to share hers.

During the first skirmish, a certain Captain Kenmore of the 28th Foot had been killed and, as was customary, his military equipment was auctioned off, the proceeds to be sent along with his personal effects back to his family in England. Thus did Jake acquire another tent for the male members of his entourage. He also bought another mule, explaining it would be needed later on.

Intensely grateful to Jake and his servants, Rachel wanted to make a genuine contribution of her own to their living situation. She did what she could in leading one of the three mules as Sam Thompkins handled the major's two extra mounts, Henry handled the other mules, and Juan was responsible for the goats. There was also a small dog named Poco, which trotted along at Juan's heels and slept in the little boy's bed. Rachel made a point of doing the washing up after a meal, but Henry refused her help on doing the laundry beyond taking care of her own things.

Gradually, though, she was able to take over some of the preparation of the evening meals, and it soon became apparent she was a much better cook than Henry.

"I don't know what it is," Henry acknowledged in a grudging but friendly manner, "but your beef stew is much tastier than mine."

"A bit of seasoning. Some herbs. That's all. I should be glad to explain."

Henry threw up his hands in protest. "No, no. That will not be necessary." He lowered his voice to a stage whisper. "I must confess I really hate to cook. The less I know, the less I am obligated to do."

"Well, then. You must simply allow me to help more—at least prepare the evening meals. I have always enjoyed cooking."

"Done!" Henry said.

Hastings and Travers often contrived invitations to supper, offering some treat of fruit or vegetables to add to the menu. By tacit agreement, they became regulars at Forrester's fireside for evening meals. With their servants— each had but one—there were nine people to feed. The servants always ate quickly and then returned to their duties, which now included the washing up. Rachel welcomed the chance to be useful, but she was glad the other meals were handled more casually.

Occasionally the regiment in which Sergeant Paxton served marched or camped close enough to Forrester's outfit that Clara and Rachel could visit. When this happened, Rachel was glad for Clara's company. She also enjoyed seeing Nellie Bingham from time to time.

Rachel was aware she was not universally liked by members of her own sex. There was a kind of hierarchy among the women following the drum. One's place was determined by the rank of the man to whom she was attached, for no woman could travel with the army without some firm connection to a specific soldier—though those connections in some instances were very fluid, to say the least. At the top of this social scale were wives and daughters of generals and colonels. If the husband or father also had a title in the peerage, his women folk were likely to assume these distinctions for themselves as well. Women married to men of lesser ranks were accorded a measure of respect. At the bottom were the women known to be legally unattached "camp followers." This was the group to which Rachel now found herself relegated. Overnight, she had gone from being a respectable—and respected—married woman to a person whose questionable morals might contaminate more upright members of the army community.

Everyone knew of the sale. Some men now viewed her as available, and if they chanced to catch her alone—that is, separated from others so voices would not carry—she was subjected to lewd suggestions. The second time this happened, Henry had observed the encounter from some distance. He worked his way through the stragglers following the marching columns.

"Do you know that fellow?" He gestured at the man who had just accosted her.

"Only by name. He is Dinkins. He was in my husband's regiment."

"Was he bothering you?"

"Well, yes, he *was* being rather uncouth in his suggestions."

Henry's lips tightened. "I shall inform Lord Jacob. He will put a stop to that."

"Oh, please do not do that," she replied. "Major Forrester has enough to do without dealing with someone like Dinkins. Dinkins has a foul mouth, but he is something of a coward. I doubt he will bother me again." Especially, she thought, in view of the fear she had seen in his eyes when she herself threatened to tell Forrester of his behavior. She had no intention of burdening Jake with such problems, but bird-witted fellows like Dinkins did not know that.

"As you wish, madam," Henry said. "However, I think his lordship would want to know . . ."

The women were harder to deal with because they were more subtle, more indirect with their disapproval. Some women had simply stopped speaking with her and looked right through her at chance meetings. Among these, a certain Mrs. Hardwent made no secret of her disdain for the disgraced Rachel.

Mrs. Hardwent was the wife of Colonel Lord Richard Hardwent, a baron with a very minor holding in East Anglia.

Colonel Lord Hardwent had come into his title only very recently, and his wife wore her new mantel of importance like a queen's robe, insisting that her servants—she and her husband traveled with eight of them—address her as "my lady" at every opportunity. She dressed fashionably—or at least in what had been fashionable in London the year before. She always wore a straw bonnet decorated with garishly colored artificial flowers, and she carried a lacy parasol that looked decidedly out of place in the midst of a military campaign.

On the trail, she insisted on riding her mule with the lead troops, regardless of which regiment led on a given day, because she had "a delicate aversion to dust." One of the colonel's men servants was required to walk at her side and sometimes carry the small lap dog she was never without. She was a plump little woman Rachel thought might have reminded one of an amiable pigeon, had there been an ounce of amiability in her.

Colonel Hardwent was attached to the 51st, Edwin Brady's regiment. As a sergeant's wife, Rachel had had very limited contact with her, but Mrs. Hardwent made it her business to single Rachel out a few weeks after the Bradys' assignment to the 51st. She sent a note to the hospital announcing she would receive the sergeant's wife at her quarters at a given hour in the afternoon. It was not a summons an enlisted man's wife could ignore.

Mrs. Hardwent—her ladyship—lost no time in preambles. "It has come to my attention you are spending a good deal of time in the hospital," she said, after inviting Rachel to sit and ordering a maid to bring them lemonade.

"Yes, ma'am, I am." Rachel's reply was brief, for she had no idea where the conversation was going.

"Well, my dear, I can certainly appreciate the generosity of your motives. I have myself long supported charity work in my parish at home. But you must know this is simply not something one thinks a woman of any refinement should be doing."

"I . . . beg your pardon?" Rachel was genuinely puzzled,

but she was also stalling for time to think. She was glad the maid brought the lemonade and the colonel's wife busied herself with the tray.

At last her hostess replied. "Surely you know it is not very ladylike for a young woman—married or no—to be in constant association with such vulgar persons as most lower-ranking soldiers are."

Rachel answered rather stiffly. "I happen to be married to one of those vulgar sorts, my lady."

"Oh, my dear, I meant no offense, of course. I am informed your husband is a man of some education—above the ordinary, so to speak." Mrs. Hardwent's words carried more apology than her tone.

"Yes, he is." Rachel saw no need to tell this woman the truth about Brady.

"You must see it will not be helpful to his military career to have his wife engaged in such demeaning activity."

Swallowing her anger at the woman's pretentious meddling, Rachel took a sip of the lemonade and put her glass down. "I am not sure I understand. Are you suggesting helping others is somehow demeaning?"

"Oh, no, of course not. But one need not subject oneself to the baser elements to be helpful. There are other things one may do . . ." Rachel noted the woman's failure to specify what those "other things" might be.

"I think," Rachel said slowly, feeling her way, "that we all make our contributions in life as we can."

"Oh, most assuredly. But our 'contributions,' as you put it, need not force a gentle female into dealing with such thoroughly distasteful matters." Mrs. Hardwent's attitude was at once firm and condescending. She rose and said, "I hope you will give proper consideration to all I have said."

"Oh, yes, ma'am. I shall certainly give it proper consideration."

Later, Rachel had shared an account of the interview with Dr. MacLachlan, but not with her own husband. MacLachlan had patted her on the shoulder and said, "Never mind.

Mrs. Hardwent is a bit of a busybody, but I think her husband rarely listens to her pronouncements."

Now, Mrs. Hardwent was one of those who went out of their way to let the disgraced Rachel know just how low she had fallen in the female pecking order. The behavior of Mrs. Hardwent and her ilk, however, simply made Rachel appreciate all the more the loyalty and good will shown by Clara and Nellie.

One day the commanders had called an early halt to the rigorous marching, giving the troops a chance to rest for a bit in an area with adequate forage for the animals. The women, along with a good many soldiers and servants, seized the opportunity to do their laundry and bathe in a nearby stream.

Rachel and Clara had found a spot along the bank where a number of the women pounded wet clothing against the river rocks to remove trail dust and sweat. It was hard, tedious work, relieved by gossipy conversation. Suddenly everyone's attention was arrested by an imperious voice calling out louder than the others.

"Some of us have done right well for ourselves," the voice said, "jumping from a sergeant's bed to a major's, that is."

Rachel had no doubt to whom the woman referred. Nor did anyone else, for all eyes had turned at once to see Rachel's reaction.

"That's Madge Selkins," Clara said softly and needlessly. "Pay her no mind."

Rachel knew the woman to be one of those negative sorts who thrived on creating controversy. Madge loved nothing better than stirring up fights among the men. Now she apparently was bored enough to want to do the same with the women. Rachel glanced up and pushed a loose strand of hair behind her ear. She gave the Selkins woman a questioning look. Madge's eyes glittered with something like triumph. Rachel went back to her scrubbing. "It is hard to ignore such a blatant attack," she muttered.

"I know," Clara sympathized. "But that sort *will* have their say—no matter how wrong or hurtful it is."

"Hey, Madge," chimed in another voice also obviously meant for other ears as well, "you think she'll manage to keep a major in her bed any better'n she did a sergeant?"

Nellie Bingham slapped a piece of clothing viciously against a rock and called out, "I don't suppose it occurred to you two know-alls that he might *not* be sharing her bed?"

Madge gave a derisive laugh. "No. An' it never occurred to us that pigs could fly, neither!"

Madge's friend, a woman named Florrie, added her false laughter. "It'd take a heap of humping to earn out fifty guineas, don't ye think?"

"You should know, Florrie," Nellie said. "But maybe you shouldn't always judge others by yourself."

"Listen, old woman—"

Florrie's response was interrupted by a blood-curdling scream from the bank where Clara had left her son under Juan's brotherly care.

"Escorpión!" Juan yelled. "Benny! *Escorpión!*"

"Oh, my God! No!" Clara ran to her son and scooped the screaming child into her arms.

Rachel followed her, pausing only long enough to grab a fistful of river mud. "Where is the bite?"

"Aquí." Juan pointed to a red welt on the smaller child's chubby thigh.

Rachel pressed the mud to the welt. "Bring him down to the water, where we can replace this with some that is cooler."

Clara did so, murmuring nonsense words of comfort to her crying son.

"The mud will help draw out the poison, I think," Rachel said.

"He won't—? He won't—?"

Rachel could tell Clara simply could not use the necessary words to express her worst fear.

"Surely not." Rachel was firmly reassuring. "I doubt the scorpions in this area are so very poisonous. It might make such a small body quite sick, though."

As Clara held the crying child, Rachel splashed cool

water on the injury to wash off the now warm mud. Then she applied a new pack of thick, cool clay. After a while, the child's sobs subsided to whimpering breaths. Rachel sent Juan back to the camp for a container in which to carry more of the mud for later use.

Other women had gathered around. Some watched silently and others murmured words of sympathy.

"Poor little thing."

"Tsk. Tsk."

A woman Rachel hardly knew patted her on the shoulder. "Good job you were here, Mrs. Brady."

Others voiced soft agreement with this sentiment. Rachel marveled inwardly at the abrupt swing in mood from their earlier acquiescence to Madge's taunts. She returned to her more immediate concern.

"He may have a fever," she told Clara. "Some weak willow bark tea should help if he does."

"Thank you, Rachel. I just don't know what I'd have done if you weren't here."

"Probably the same thing I did."

Rachel set about gathering up their things as Juan, having returned, helped her. He kept stopping to pat Benny occasionally and offer comforting soft phrases from his own musical language.

The next day there was still a red welt on Benny's leg, but he was himself again, cheerfully prattling and playing.

Fifteen

By mid June, the British-led allies had marched over four hundred miles in forty days. The march was long, hard, and fraught with danger. Although they were clearly in retreat, the French were not going willingly. They subjected the British and their allies to frequent skirmishes. For the journey, Wellington broke his army of eighty thousand into two groups to confuse the enemy as to which would be the main fighting force. He further attempted to confuse them by himself traveling with the smaller contingent and sending the larger group on a very difficult northerly route. Traveling in the larger group, Jake and his lot found they often had to forge their way through difficult terrain. They certainly were not traveling the so-called Royal Road!

Bypassing Burgos—site of defeat amidst last year's victories—Jake had mixed feelings about ignoring this town, and he thought the Peer must be experiencing the same emotions. Jake surmised that, even now, the general would love to take Burgos, but a long siege of the still well-fortified site would take far too much time. Moreover, it would detract from the commander's main objective by spreading his troops too thin. Wellington, Jake knew, was determined to push the French north of the Pyrenees, back into France. And the French, he had learned from a captured French officer, were now under the command of King Joseph, who had sent Marshal Soult back to Paris. Joseph was anxious to prove himself as a military leader by keeping the British forces south of the river Ebro. There had already been fierce, bloody fighting in several skirmishes.

Nor were French attacks the only danger. Mother Nature added her obstacles to their path. Melting snows in the mountains swelled streams to raging torrents. The river Esla posed the most difficult river crossing. Ten men—and a wagon load of equipment—were swept away in the first attempt. Many of those who made it across did so by hanging on to the stirrups and tails of horses ridden by officers and cavalry. Finally, with a contingent of the force on each side, the engineers were able to set up a pontoon bridge, allowing the rest of the army to cross in relative ease. On they marched, through forbidding terrain, on roads which were often little better than goat trails and were devastating to footgear—and feet.

They were just north of Burgos when they heard a tremendous explosion. It clearly came from Burgos, but it was some hours before Jake knew what had happened.

"Did you hear?" Travers asked excitedly when a rest had been ordered for the midday meal.

"We *all* heard that explosion," Jake said.

"No. I mean what caused it."

"So what was it?"

"One of our scouts said the French blew up the town and left! They prepared for a siege and then we just went on by. I'm thinking they couldn't take all their powder and shot with them—and they most assuredly did not want us to have it—so they just blew it up!"

Jake nodded. "I'm thinking you are quite right. With our troops already beyond them, the town was no longer of any strategic value to them. It is unfortunate, though. It might have been a nice town."

"Hah! I can't be sorry," Travers said. "We lost good men there last autumn."

"We lose good men in *every* engagement."

"I know, but—"

The call for officers to mount up and move their troops out again distracted Travers from his tale.

That evening, Jake was glad to see the supply train had finally caught up with the main force of the army. The replenishment of supplies was often erratic, though it had improved since the port of entry was now Santander on the Bay of Biscay. Previously, supplies had come from England to Lisbon or Oporto on the Atlantic coast of Portugal. At the ports they were loaded on mules and ox-drawn wagons to make their way to the folks who needed them—in this instance, desperately needed them, for the men had marched on empty stomachs this day.

"One must give Bonaparte his due," Jake observed. "An army really *does* move on its stomach. Or at least at the direction of that organ." He, Travers, and Hastings sat around their campfire reading and sharing news of home, for the supply train had also brought mail. The arrival of mail in an army camp always produced a festive atmosphere.

Jake had received a packet containing letters from his mother and his brother, as well as several newspapers and a book that the scholarly Robert thought would appeal to his soldier brother.

Hastings picked up the book and examined it. *"Pride and Prejudice?* By 'a lady'? I say, Forrester, your brother has a rather peculiar view of you, does he not?"

"Perhaps," Jake said absently, still absorbed in Robert's letter. He looked up. "But he usually does know what will appeal. This must be a rather extraordinary work."

"I think it is," Travers said. "I mean—my *mother* said it was. Even the Prince Regent liked it."

"Hmm." Hastings handed the book back to Jake. "Perhaps I'll have to read it when you finish."

"Because you value Prinny's judgment so?" Jake asked with a chuckle.

"No," Hastings answered shortly. "But I value *yours,* and if you think it worthwhile . . ."

"I shall let you know."

The letter from Robert was of particular interest because it was a response to one Jake had written in which he recounted the incident of the sale and his belated recognition of Brady. Having discussed in some detail affairs dealing with Jake's properties, Robert went on to describe the general euphoria over the victory at Salamanca and the triumphant entry into Madrid. "These successes have been well received," Robert wrote in characteristic understatement, "but we are still awaiting a truly decisive victory." He then went on to say,

> I have searched our own records here at Lounsbury and find no one named Edwin Brady who was ever attached to us. There was a maid named Elizabeth Brady, but she must have left our employ about the time Father remarried. I have no memory of her, and the ledgers do not mention her beyond 1781. I shall continue the search, however, and let you know if anything turns up.
>
> Hendon, by the way, is Aylesworth's family name.

"Good God!" Jake gave a start and reread the last line twice over.

"Bad news?" Travers asked.

"Uh . . . no. Just startling. My scholarly brother has quite a head for business. You will be happy to know he has passed along sufficient funds to allow me to repay you—with interest!"

"Now you *know* we ain't cent-percenter moneylenders." Travers sounded slightly offended.

Hastings grinned. "Now that idea has possibilities. We might go for Shylock's pound of flesh."

"I'll settle for another bit of that apple dumpling Rachel made," Travers said.

Lost in thought, Jake paid little attention to their banter. He had hedged on sharing Robert's observations with his friends, just as he had never told them of having encountered Brady in his youth. It had to do with protecting Rachel. He knew that much, though he was not sure how withholding information from Travers and Hastings had anything to do with protecting her. They were, after all, eminently trustworthy.

Aylesworth! Aylesworth was a duke! Was it possible Rachel had some connection to that family—one of the oldest in England? The idea seemed decidedly far-fetched. Still . . .

He waited until Travers and Hastings sought their own tents before broaching the topic to her. She had sat on the other side of the fire during most of the evening quietly knitting, though she had occasionally offered a comment. He moved his camp stool over to sit closer to her.

"Rachel, does the name Aylesworth mean anything to you?"

"Aylesworth. Aylesworth." She turned the syllables over carefully. "No. I don't think so. Should it?"

"How about the *Duke* of Aylesworth?"

"A duke?" She laughed. "Now why on earth should *I* be familiar with a duke?"

"That is his title. His family name is Hendon."

She looked startled. Then she laughed even more heartily. "Well, if there is any connection with my mother, I am sure it is *very* remote! Hendon is a common enough name."

"Perhaps . . ."

"Oh, Jake." Her eyes twinkled merrily. "You really must not try to make a silk purse from a sow's ear."

He pretended to take umbrage. "I am, madam, merely trying to solve the mystery of a woman named Rachel."

"Well, I should think you might have more success if you sought answers in the yeomanry rather than among the *ton!*"

"Perhaps . . ." he said again.

"Why is it so important?" Her tone was serious now.

"It might not be. I just thought . . . well . . . this war is not going to last forever. Word is Napoleon suffered a terrible defeat in Russia."

"The Russians defeated Europe's great conqueror?" One of the things he liked about her was that she would think to ask a question like this.

"Not so much the Russians themselves as their fierce winter."

"Winter?" she asked blankly.

"The Russian army, too, of course. The French were retreating with the Russians on their heels. But it was apparently the cold weather that did in Boney and his lot," Jake explained. "Tens of thousands of them simply froze to death."

"Tens of thousands?"

"That's what the dispatches say. The great conqueror went to Russia with an army of nearly six hundred thousand. He is returning to France with less than ten percent of them."

"How appalling," she said. "All those lives lost. All those grieving women . . ."

"It *is* appalling," he agreed. "A terrifying monument to one man's ego. But the point is, it may be a portent of the end. As I said, this cannot go on forever. Perhaps if we can find family connections for you . . ." He wondered if he really *wanted* to find such connections for her. Then he mentally chastised himself. Of *course* he did. What were her options, after all?

"Yes. I see your point." Her eyes held an unreadable expression. "However, I do not wish you to be unduly responsible. Something will turn up to provide direction for me."

Jake suspected this little speech held more bravado than confidence, but he offered no argument. For the time being, he would let Robert handle things. However, he, Jake, *did* feel responsible, and if Rachel thought he would abrogate that duty, she could damned well think again.

She bade him good night, and he remained by the fire for some time staring into the dying coals. He wondered idly if he would feel so strongly about another woman in the same situation. In a sense, his rescue of Rachel was a repeat of his rescue of Juan, was it not? And not unlike his rescue of that pretty milkmaid a decade earlier.

Yet he had been happy to see the milkmaid hurry home, and, while he felt some sort of brotherly affection—or was

it fatherly?—for Juan, he certainly did *not* find his senses
uncommonly stirred whenever the boy was near!

Very well. He admitted it. He lusted after Rachel. Perhaps
he had been a fool to turn down her sweet offer to share his
bed.

He immediately dismissed this idea.

No. Accepting her offer might have been infinitely satisfying for him, but he knew it would have destroyed her.

Her offer had been born of despair, not desire—despite
the warmth of her response to his kiss.

That response played over and over in his mind, telling
him that there was, indeed, unfinished personal business between them.

His mind drifted back to Robert's letter. His brother had
signed off, then added, "P. S. Celia sends her love."

Jake had been surprised to find he read that line with
absolutely no twinges of nostalgia for what might have been.
At last, he thought, he might be able to face his old love,
now his sister-in-law, with some degree of equanimity. It
was true, then—time did heal all wounds.

The addition of Rachel to Jake's entourage had not only
swelled the group in his camp of an evening, it had also
changed the tenor of the gatherings. There was less boister-
ous horseplay now, and the men made a more concerted
effort to display proper decorum. Jake noted to himself that
his quarters had always been the focal point of an eclectic
lot in the evenings. Officers of all ranks tended to drop
by—in part for the conviviality they found there, and in part
because they had discovered they could put their fingers on
the army's pulse here in an informal setting.

For it was not only officers who felt at ease in Major
Forrester's camp. Sergeant Humphrey, who had served with
Jake in India, was a frequent visitor, and the sergeant was
usually accompanied by the cheerful, likable Corporal Col-
lins and one or two others. Humphrey had apparently taken
Collins under his wing to teach him the special survival

skills needed in army life, just as he had done with a young lieutenant in India nearly ten years ago.

Jake remembered well preferring the company of Humphrey and other enlisted men in India. Men of his own rank too often held themselves aloof from lower ranks in their own army—and from the native people as well. He had once been called on the carpet for his unorthodox behavior.

Colonel Moulsson had been in India for over forty years and held rigidly to the old school of thought. One evening, the colonel had singled out the lieutenant during an informal gathering prior to a formal dinner that all officers were required to attend.

"Fraternization, my boy, destroys discipline. You must not fly in the face of centuries of practice."

"Have I done something wrong, sir?" the young Lieutenant Forrester had asked.

"Wrong? Well, not precisely. So far as I know, you have violated no regulations, but it has come to my attention that you spend an inordinate amount of time with a sergeant in your command, and—what's worse—with the natives."

"With all due respect, sir, I have learned more in six weeks with Sergeant Humphrey than I had in the entire year before. I am learning their languages and culture from the Indians. Fascinating it is, too."

Moulsson waved his hand in a dismissive gesture. "That is not necessary. Natives have to conform to our rule. Enough of them speak our language—there's no point wasting your time that way."

Jake knew he should just keep his mouth shut, but since when had that ever stopped him? "But I find it all very interesting, Colonel. I had no idea before coming here of the tremendous complexity of this country—their religions, the castes, their whole way of life."

"Most of it is a lot of tomfoolery. You'd do well not to clutter your mind with such stuff. Take my word for it, boy. Need to keep your distance. Keep that barrier between us and them."

"Us and them?"

"Officers and enlisted. Natives and their conquerors. Familiarity breeds contempt. Contempt leads to revolution. Just look what's happened in France. Keep the discipline, boy."

"Yes, sir."

Jake knew full well it would do no good to argue with this obtuse old man. Moulsson undoubtedly would not even recognize a parallel between the way the British in India treated the natives and the way the French aristocracy had treated the common people of France.

However, the colonel had not given him a direct order, now had he? So the independent young lieutenant had gone on doing exactly as he pleased. Of course, *Major* Forrester now mused, that young lieutenant had not advanced as rapidly in rank as he might otherwise have done.

Juan had become a favorite with the men who gathered in Jake's camp of an evening, a pet to be coddled. The boy usually sat quietly, hugging his dog, his bright eyes—so brown they appeared black—alert and interested. Rachel had cut down a Ranger tunic for the child, which Juan wore with great pride. Jake welcomed the men's attention to Juan. Having lost his entire family so brutally, the child was adopting a new family among these rough and tumble soldiers. Nor was it only on the boy's account that Jake approved the developing relationship.

One of the difficulties of the campaign trail was keeping up the men's enthusiasm. Army life was often boring, tiring, and dull. Commanders seized every opportunity to improve upon the *esprit de corps*. Marching chants and songs helped. Contests between companies and regiments diverted attention from sore feet, aching backs, and sometimes empty bellies. If the men wanted to make a pet of Juan, why let them!

One evening Corporal Collins sought out Juan who, as usual, sat on the ground next to his hero, Jake. His knees were drawn up with his arms around them, and the faithful Poco was stretched out nearby.

"Hey, Juan," Collins said. "I wonder if I could borrow your pup tomorrow?"

"B-bor—?" Juan looked in consternation at Jake.

"He wants to borrow your dog," Jake explained in Spanish.

"Poco?"

Poco was clearly a mongrel with some sort of terrier in his ancestry. Small and mostly brown and white, he had a large black spot over one ear and eye. Some of the men teased Juan by referring to his canine friend as a pirate. Hearing his name, the dog leaped up and licked at Juan's face. The boy giggled and clasped the dog to him.

"Yeah. Poco. I promise not to hurt him." Collins seemed to understand precisely what Juan's first concern would be. Jake's translation was unnecessary this time.

"No . . . hurt?" Juan said slowly.

"No hurt," Collins repeated.

The boy gazed at the young corporal solemnly. Then he nodded.

"Good boy!" Collins ruffled the little boy's hair and patted his dog. "I'll come get him tomorrow morning. You'll have him back in about an hour."

Juan looked to Jake to translate this, then grinned and nodded again.

"¡Gracias!" Collins said and quickly took his leave.

Jake suspected Collins did not want to entertain any embarrassing questions about why he wanted Juan's dog. Jake trusted Collins, though, and he doubted the young man would allow any harm to come to Juan or Poco. Jake shrugged and sent Juan off to bed. With Poco.

Jake did not think again of Collins's unusual request until late the following morning. Major Forrester's regiment was bringing up the rear of the column this day. He knew the lead column, whoever they happened to be, would be accompanied by the imperious Mrs. Hardwent with her frivolous hat and frilly parasol.

The woman was a source of annoyance to the men, who often had to break the rhythm of their pace to accommodate her. She also made frequent demands of them, which few felt they could ignore, coming as they did from a colonel's wife. Had she shown the least bit of appreciation for their kindnesses, they might have accepted her with greater tolerance. However, the woman made little secret of her view that most of the rank and file members of His Majesty's Army were not half so worthy of regard as the little fluffy white dog with which she traveled.

The day before had been a tough one, what with the hot sun and a rough road—and the supply wagons were late again. A disgruntled mood swept from one man to another, one company to another. Sporadic attempts at chants or songs died quickly. There was little sound but that of plodding feet and an occasional curse. Dust was a constant source of irritation.

Suddenly, Jake heard a ripple of laughter start at the head of the column. Then loud guffaws swept back among the marching men. Finally, he perceived the cause of this merriment. Trotting along from the front of the column to the rear came Juan's Poco in search of his master. The little dog had been outfitted with a makeshift straw bonnet on its head, complete with a huge orange flower. Attached to a strap around his belly was a stick to which a circle of pink lace had been attached to resemble a frilly parasol.

Jake, too, burst into laughter.

Soon enough, Poco found his little master, who also laughed and picked up his masquerading friend.

Spirits—and the pace—picked up for the rest of the day. Late in the afternoon, the heretofore separated elements of Wellington's great army were joined. Spirits rose even higher with the festive atmosphere of friends meeting after an absence, sharing recent weeks' events, and anticipating the coming battle.

The next morning, word passed down the column that Vitoria, sparkling jewel of northern Spain, lay only hours ahead. Most were keenly aware that the retreating Joseph— Napoleon's brother, the puppet to whom the French emperor had given the Spanish throne—would make a stand here. Known as the "Intrusive King" by Spanish subjects who objected to a foreigner as their leader, Joseph in retreat had stripped Spain of as many treasures as could be easily moved. Gold, silver, art treasures—and women—were crammed into his baggage train as he fled.

Late in the afternoon, Jake happened to be near the British baggage wagons along which Rachel walked, leading a mule and chatting with one of the less seriously wounded on a wagon. Henry was not far away. Jake had noticed that, lately, Henry usually marched near Rachel, just as though he, too, felt some need to protect her. Jake dismounted and walked beside her.

"It comes tomorrow, then?" she asked.

"It seems so," he replied.

"There has been a sense of anticipation among the men ever since the others joined us yesterday. One could even say eagerness."

"There always is before a battle," he said.

Rachel looked at him questioningly. "I do not understand that. Tomorrow, many will die—or be wounded. And yet there is almost a degree of merriment here."

"No soldier ever thinks *he* will be among the wounded or dying. We are near a goal here. This is what we have been marching toward—and we are almost there."

"Men! I suppose I will never understand what makes the males of our species behave as they do."

He laughed and gave her a teasing sideways look. "Perhaps you should concentrate on only one, then, to understand the whole."

She gave him an answering grin. "Perhaps I should. Have you anyone in mind?"

He gave a hoot of laughter at this. "Hoist by my own petard," he said, but he did not trust himself to answer her question.

After a pause, she asked, her tone serious, "What are our chances tomorrow?"

"Fifty-fifty, I'd say. We have more men under our command, but they have a far greater number of heavy guns. Like most battles, it will probably be reduced to two factors—luck and leadership."

"I have heard King Joseph seems very confident of both," she said. "Is it true he has built reviewing stands near the city so women and townspeople may witness his victory?"

He nodded. "That's what our spies tell us."

"Such self-assurance!"

"Such arrogance, you mean, do you not?" he asked.

"Sometimes there is a very fine distinction between confidence and arrogance," she said. "King Joseph brings to mind that ancient king who consulted the oracle at Delphi. He was told if he crossed a certain river, he would destroy a mighty empire."

Jake picked up the story. "Croesus. He crossed the river and his own empire was destroyed. He had neglected to ask which empire."

"Perhaps this Frenchman will have forgotten some important detail, too," Rachel said.

"We can only hope so."

Just then they topped a hill to find a lovely valley lying at their feet. It was green and lush, for the river Zadorra wound its way through it—and it looked deceptively peaceful, with grazing sheep dotting the countryside.

"Oh, how beautiful," Rachel said in an awed voice.

"It is that," Jake agreed. He pointed off in the distance. "That is Vitoria." He put his arm around her shoulder to direct her gaze. "Not that small village in the foreground—the town beyond."

Between the arriving allied army and Vitoria, the river made its sinuous way through the valley with four great bends, the sharpest of which wound around a hill that rose like an island in the valley. Another hill, larger and higher, with a small village at its base, jutted up between the river and the city. In addition, another stream flowed into the Zadorra at an angle. Jake's practiced eye took in all those obstacles—which were only those of Mother Nature. In the distance, he and Rachel could also see the camps of the French soldiers spread out between their own side of the great river and the city of Vitoria.

"It will not be easy. There are several bridges, but they

are likely to be heavily manned." The soldier in him was thinking aloud now, rather than conversing with her.

But she seemed to understand his need to do so. And he was struck by that fact—she always seemed to *understand*. He did not have time to consider *that* thought fully right now, though.

"Come," he said. "We must get down this hill and set up our own tent city before darkness overtakes us."

Sixteen

For Rachel, the morning of the Battle of Vitoria started early. After a fitful night, she woke to a cold, drizzling mist. As she stirred the nearly dead coals of the fire to life and set the kettle to heat water for tea, Jake joined her.

"You're up early this morning," she said.

"I could not sleep. Too many small matters demanding attention."

"This rain will put a damper on things, will it not?" she asked.

"It *could,* but I rather think our troops will view it as a good omen—a sign from God."

"A sign from God?" She did not bother to hide the skepticism in her tone.

"Yes, ma'am!" he said emphatically. "Our greatest victories in this campaign have been accompanied by rainstorms. Badajoz. Salamanca. Now this. Vitoria."

"This is not a victory yet."

"Yet." He grinned at her.

Rachel slid her gaze away from his and busied herself with the tea caddie. Apprehensive, even fearful, she did not want him to see the worry in her eyes. He would need a strong, positive outlook this day. She must not do anything to diminish it.

Soon the others joined them for what was a *very* sparse meal, the supplies not having caught up for two days now. Rachel knew many a soldier would go into this battle with hunger gnawing at his innards.

She reported to MacLachlan at the large hospital tent which had been set up to accommodate those wounded in skirmishes en route. These men would return to normal duties shortly. Others, more seriously wounded, had already been sent to holding hospitals nearer the ports. She found Mac at a table under an awning in front of the hospital. He was poring over a crude map, with Ferguson looking over his shoulder.

"That river poses a problem," Mac said. "We need to set up the hospital on the other side of it, but we cannot do that until our people are *on* the other side."

"By which time," Ferguson added, "we will already have need of its services."

"Luckily, it takes little time to set up the portable hospital." Rachel was trying to be encouraging.

Mac nodded. "Yes. At least the Peer agreed to that innovation when McGrigor proposed it."

"I still don't see why Lord Wellington turned down McGrigor's plan to use *ambulances* to transport wounded to us." Ferguson's tone was querulous.

"I don't know, either," Mac replied. "They have served the French well, while our poor fellows are still brought to us on a catch-as-catch-can basis."

"One would hate to think ol' Nosey rejected the idea solely because Napoleon adopted it first," Ferguson said with broad irony.

"Yes. One *would* hate to think that." Mac's tone was equally bland.

Rachel continued checking their supplies, ensuring that all the instruments the surgeons used would be clean—at least when they started.

They heard the first boom of artillery fire shortly after eight, but they received no new wounded until nearly an hour later. However, it was only a few, for Mac had been right in supposing that the river Zadorra would be a problem. Then someone arrived with the news, "We're across!" and the medical team packed up again and crossed one of the several bridges. At least the rain had stopped, Rachel noted.

They hurriedly set up their portable hospital in the courtyard of a convent which had once been a self-sustaining religious community outside the secular village of Arinez. The convent, Rachel learned to her horror, had been sacked some weeks earlier by the French, who suspected the abbess of providing information to the enemy.

"The poor woman was brutally tortured," Ferguson told her. "And several other nuns were abused in the most heinous ways."

"Good heavens!" Rachel said. "Why? The French are mostly Catholics, too."

Ferguson shrugged. "Apparently they see a huge difference between *French* Catholics and *Spanish* Catholics."

Rachel shook her head in disbelief. "So the nuns are all gone?"

"No. There are a few still here. Most fled, though. Of those that remain, some offered to help when they realized we were turning their facility into a hospital."

"How generous of them."

"Downright Christian, I'd say," Ferguson said.

The fighting went on all day, but those working with the wounded had no clear picture of how the battle progressed. Wounded soldiers were brought into the courtyard, where their injuries were quickly assessed. The lucky ones with flesh wounds were stitched back together and bandaged. Others had to wait until the beleaguered surgeons could get to them.

There were moans of pain now and then, but overall, the hospital was amazingly quiet. Rachel recalled how this had surprised her when she first came into a battlefield hospital. Stoicism in the face of pain was the normal circumstance, not the exception. She had witnessed more than once a man lying in apparent calm—with little or nothing to assuage the pain—as a surgeon removed his arm or leg.

She remembered one man in particular, a captain who was older than most men of equal rank. The captain had lain on the operating table totally alert as his arm, shattered at the elbow, was separated from the rest of him. He emitted a sharp intake of breath as the surgeon sawed trough the bone, but that was all. When it was over and the stump bandaged, he stood abruptly, but his loss of blood had made him faint. He leaned on a companion, but kept himself erect as he started to leave. Then he turned back.

"Oops! I almost forgot. Would you be so kind, Doc, as to remove my ring from that thing?" He pointed at the pile of severed limbs beside the table. "My wife would be most distraught if I lost that piece of jewelry. 'Twas her wedding present to me."

Today's wounded showed the same sort of endurance. Rachel wondered how the battle was really going. Isolated as they were in their own little pocket of frenzy, the surgeons and their helpers caught only snatches of information. Excited, often garbled comments from the wounded and their bearers allowed the medical team to catch glimpses of what was happening throughout the day.

"I never seen Frenchies turn tail and run like they was doin'."

"We jus' walked right acrost that bridge. Nary a shot."

"Them heavy guns on the hill got us hard."

"The bridges were intact and weakly defended. Such luck."

"Such stupidity on Joseph's part. Believe me, if Soult had been in charge, there would have been a different tale to tell!"

"Why was Soult not here?"

"I heard he was called—or sent—back to Paris."

"That was a piece of luck for us—having the able Soult replaced by the incompetent Joseph. Wonder why Napoleon allowed it?"

"Cannon fire is noisy and frightening, but rifle fire is far more deadly."

"At least we ain't gonna be hungry this day, what with all them dead sheep."

"Is it true? Did they get the colonel?"

Hurrying from patient to patient, Rachel heard this anxious question coming from one wounded Highlander to another as the newcomer was laid on the next pallet.

"Yes. He was a Highlander to the very end. Made us carry him up on a hill so's he could watch the regiment's action. His last words were 'I trust to God that this will be a glorious day for England.' "

Rachel was touched by this account of a brave man's death, but Lord! there were so many brave men maimed and dying this day!

In midafternoon, Ferguson took her by the shoulders and steered her into the cloistered garden attached to the chapel of the convent.

"You have been at this steadily for over five hours," he told her as he gently pushed her to sit on a stone bench. "You need a rest. Here." He handed her a piece of bread and some cheese.

She protested. "So have you, Mac, and the others, been here all day."

"Men are tougher," he said, sitting beside her.

"What a bouncer that is!" However, she gratefully accepted the food and a chance to sit, if even for a moment. "How is it going?" she asked.

"Still uncertain, I think, but it does seem Lord Wellington's attacking from four or five different directions has unnerved the French, despite their tactical advantage and greater weaponry."

She felt her brow wrinkling in confusion, but before she could formulate her question, Ferguson answered it.

"Apparently the French expected a single large frontal attack. By the time they realized their error, it was too late to change their own positions."

The center of the battle—site of the fiercest, most desperate fighting—was the hill above the village of Arinez. Rachel knew that in the center of this fighting were the Connaught Rangers—Jake's regiment. She had tried to keep herself so busy all day that she would be unable to dwell on this fact. Now, with a moment of rest, her worry flooded back to the forefront of her thoughts.

Ferguson rose. "I must go, but *you stay here* for at least another ten minutes."

She did stay for another five minutes and finished her snack. Then she, too, rejoined the battle being waged in the hospital to save lives and limbs. It occurred to her that their job was a bit like cleaning up a mess after a destructive child. The actions of this child called war were deliberate and deadly—but just as likely to be mindlessly repeated.

These generalized thoughts were abruptly terminated with the arrival of a particular patient. Corporal Collins was brought in with a musket ball still lodged in his chest.

"Damn! It hurts!" he said as the bearers set him down. Then he caught sight of Rachel standing nearby. "S-sorry . . . Mrs. Brady." His breathing was labored.

One of the bandsmen who had brought him in stood to face Rachel, his back to Collins. He gave his head a slight shake as though saying, "It's no use."

Rachel knelt beside the young man and opened his blood-soaked tunic to examine the wound. The bandsman was right. She schooled her expression before allowing her gaze to meet that of Corporal Collins.

"I ain't . . . goin' to make it . . . am I?" he asked in some surprise.

"Nonsense. Of course you will," she lied. "We merely have to do some patching here."

"P-patching?" He coughed and red bubbles appeared on his lips. She wiped them away with the edge of her apron and called for an orderly to bring a basin with water and a cloth.

"Thirsty," Collins whispered.

Rachel unscrewed the cap to the canteen of water she always carried on a shoulder strap when she worked with battlefield wounded. She held his head as he drank thirstily.

"W-will you . . . write to m-my . . . mother?" he asked. Rachel took his hand in one of hers as she wiped the black residue of gunpowder and sweat from his face. "Of course I will."

"Humphrey . . . has 'er direction." He coughed again. "Tell 'er . . . tell her . . . I won't be able to . . . pick the . . . apples. . . . She should get . . . Ned to—" He coughed again.

Rachel squeezed his hand and wiped his face again. She said softly, "Never mind, Pete. She knows."

He turned his head toward her voice, but his eyes were already clouding over. "Mama? Is . . . that you? It hurts . . . Mama."

"I know, darling." Rachel could hardly contain her tears. She leaned down and kissed him on the forehead.

He gripped her hand tighter. "Mama?" The word ended on a long, shuddering breath, and his hold on Rachel's hand relaxed. He was gone.

"Good-bye, Pete," she whispered, sliding her free hand across his eyes to close them. Now she allowed the tears as she continued to sit for a few minutes holding the limp hand of the boy who had been so full of laughing merriment just the day before. Finally, hearing someone call her name, she forced herself to rise and go about the grim business of fighting death on other fronts.

A very exhausted Major Forrester sought his own camp that evening. It was nearly nine when he did so, and he was struck by the relative quiet around him. The entire camp, not just his section of it, seemed somewhat deserted. Hastings, his arm in a sling, was there along with Travers. Fatigue showed in the faces of both the captain and the lieutenant. They were eating a meal put together by Henry and themselves.

Jake looked around, then asked, "Where is Ra—Mrs. Brady?"

"At the hospital," Travers answered.

"Still?"

"Still."

"If she is not back soon, Henry, you go and get her."

"Yes, my lord."

Jake went into his own tent and eyed his cot with longing. *Not yet, old man,* he told himself. *Have to see she's all right first.* He splashed cold water on his face, wiped away a good deal of the grime, and rejoined his comrades.

He accepted the filled plate Henry offered him. "I take it supplies finally caught up with us."

Hastings responded. "No. But it didn't matter. There are so many dead sheep around, there is plenty of meat available. Your enterprising Henry managed to get some vegetables from some farmer, too."

"What happened to you?" Jake pointed his fork at Hastings' arm.

"Nothing serious. Ball just grazed me, really. Tore a hole in my tunic, though," he said in disgust.

The three warriors then discussed the day's events, each attempting thereby to have a clearer view of the overall picture. By midafternoon, the British allies had broken through the center of the French defense. Two hours later came the news that King Joseph had ordered a retreat of all his forces. This brought on a general panic among the townspeople and the French army's followers. Both the retreating French soldiers and the pursuing allies were hampered by multitudes of civilians clogging the route—and then by their abandoned vehicles.

"I never saw anything like it!" Hastings noted. "There were hundreds of vehicles—peasant carts and fancy coaches and wagons and—you name it!"

"And all abandoned in short order," Travers added. "With local Spanish and our own forces crawling through all that loot like bees on fallen fruit!"

"I hear the Peer is mad as hops," Hastings said.

"He is." Jake set aside his plate. "It appears Joseph did, indeed, get away—and with the greater part of his army intact, though they abandoned most of their heavy weapons. Wellington wanted to pursue them immediately. We *might* have captured their whole army."

"Same old problem." Hastings offered the now fed Jake a glass of brandy. "Once the British soldier smells the possibility of plunder and loot, all order is gone!"

"And such loot it is this time!" Travers said. "Joseph and his lot had stolen most of the treasures of Spain. Gold and silver—from churches as well as homes. And paintings! Cut them right out of their frames and rolled them up for easy transport."

"Not to mention chests and boxes of jewelry and money," Hastings added, "as well as expensive clothing." He chuckled. "I saw one of our women disrobing right there on the road to put on a fancy ball gown! Right down to her very skimpy underthings, mind you! Don't know how she'll manage the long train on that gown when we resume the march later."

"Oh, she'll manage." Jake sat silently for a few moments, sipping at the brandy and letting his exhaustion mellow. Then a small motion outside the range of their light caught his attention. Rachel came into view, accompanied by a bandsman. Ah, Jake felt, rather than consciously thought, he could relax now.

"Captain MacLachlan said I was to see Mrs. Brady back to her quarters," announced the bandsman, who could not have been a day over fourteen. "The cap'n said to take 'er whether she wanted to go or not. So here she is." The boy ended on a note of triumph.

"Thank you, son," Jake said, setting down his glass and rising. He was alarmed by the degree of exhaustion in Rachel's movements and the stricken look in her eyes.

"Oh, Jake!" She stumbled and he caught her in his arms. She clung to him as though seeking oneness with another human being and totally oblivious to their audience. "Oh, Jake." Her voice caught. "He's dead. I couldn't save him."

"Who? Who is dead, Rachel?" He tried to keep his voice calm and reassuring, despite his alarm at her breaking down like this.

"Pete. Corporal Collins."

"Ah, God. No." Jake felt a familiar wave of regret and

anger at the loss of yet another good man. He held her even more tightly, sharing her grief. Finally, and reluctantly, he released her and guided her to the stool on which he had been sitting. He put the brandy glass in her hand. "Here. Drink this."

She dutifully drank, then coughed. "It feels warm all the way down."

"Yes. It's supposed to." He squatted in front of her and gestured for Henry to get her some food. When the plate was in her lap, she would have protested, but Jake ordered sternly, "Eat it." Only when she had tentatively, then hungrily, devoured most of it, did he say, "Now, tell us about Collins."

Her account of the young man's death saddened them all. They shared an anecdote or two in the quiet way of the living in the face of death. Then they sat silently, each absorbed in particular memories.

"Henry," Jake ordered at last. "Please go and find Humphrey and relay this news to him."

Half an hour later Henry returned to say simply, "He took it real hard."

"I thought he might," Jake said.

By then Travers and Hastings had sought their beds and Jake had insisted that Rachel retire as well. He thought fleetingly of "sleep that knits up the ravaged sleeve of care" and then worried idly that he had not gotten that quotation quite right.

Rachel awoke the next morning feeling much as she had the night before—tired, sad, and despairing. She shut her eyes against the daylight and snuggled back into the covers, but it was no use. She was awake. Might as well face the day after all. At least it was not raining this morning. She emerged from her tent to find Henry packing things in order to move later on. She greeted him and helped herself to a breakfast of leftover stew and tea.

"The major has gone already?" she asked.

"Yes, madam. Seems Lord Wellington is still of a mind to pursue the French immediately."

"Really?" She was somewhat surprised at this, given the general revelry and debauchery—the strange aftermath of battle—she had observed last night as she returned to camp.

"Lord Jacob said even if we don't get the call to move out, we shall probably move into the city."

"I see. I will be sure to leave my things in order when I go to the hospital."

"Right. Thompkins and I will see to the move—with Juan's help, of course." Henry smiled at Juan, who had just come in from tending his goats. "One of us will come and escort you to our new quarters."

On arriving at the hospital later, she found MacLachlan in a towering rage. She could hear his muffled shouts as soon as she came into the courtyard. Several other people stood in the courtyard, seemingly petrified as they listened.

"You stupid—blithering—incompetent—God-*damned*—idiot!" Mac was yelling. The language and tone were totally out of character for the big, gentle bear of a man. Mac was addressing someone inside the chapel, where quite a number of wounded lay on straw pallets.

"*What* on earth . . . ?" Rachel questioned Lieutenant Ferguson.

"Brewster," Ferguson said.

"The assistant surgeon?"

Ferguson nodded.

Mac's voice came through again. "You get your gear and get your miserable person out of this hospital right now. If I ever catch you even near a wounded man again, I'll see you flogged within an inch of your miserable, useless life."

There was a muffled reply, unintelligible to those in the courtyard, to which Mac responded, "Well, we can damned well do without the likes of *you.*"

The chapel door banged open and Mac came storming out. His eyes ran quickly over those assembled before him. His gaze rested on Rachel, and he looked a bit chagrined.

"I am sorry you heard that, Mrs. Brady."

She merely nodded and he went on.

"Brewster! No wonder the men call him 'Butcher Brewster'! He killed a perfectly good man this morning. Just killed him. Right there on the operating table. No reason for him to die. Hell! Bloody hell! He might not even have had to lose that leg—but Brewster just loves chopping off limbs. Thinks he's a damned woodcutter or something." He paused. "Sorry, my language . . ."

"Never mind. I'm sure you have cause to be upset." She knew Mac had probably not had more than two hours sleep the night before.

"Any first-year student could have performed that surgery without cutting into a major artery—and then he just allowed the man to bleed to death."

"Good heavens!" she murmured.

Mac seemed incapable of cutting short his rant. "They require tailors, shoemakers, and carpenters to serve a proper apprenticeship in England, but anyone—anyone!—can hire on with the army as an assistant surgeon! I tell you, it's downright criminal. Murder, it is."

"It does not seem a very rational approach," she agreed.

He was quiet for a moment. Then he gave her a grin that was at once rueful and grim. "He's not the first incompetent surgeon to join our ranks. But Lord! I hate losing men needlessly."

With that his tirade was over. Brewster made his retreat, and everyone else set about the business at hand. There were still wounded coming in from the battlefield, many of whom had been forgotten by their comrades in the frenzy of looting the riches in the French baggage train. Also, the hospital, too, would be moved into the city some four or five miles away.

The new hospital was set up in the city's largest cathedral. Rachel wondered what it was about religious facilities that always seemed to provide space for medical work. She knew that that was it—they provided ready *space*. However, it probably did not hurt to have God's immediate attention in what they were trying to achieve.

The tempo of their work tapered off in the late afternoon. Rachel was more than ready when Juan came with two of the mules to take her to their new quarters. The ride was not unpleasant. The temperature had cooled, and she chatted with Juan in a combination of broken English and broken Spanish. Poco trotted along beside Juan's mule.

Vitoria was a walled city with narrow, winding, cobble-stoned streets. Even in such a short time, Juan seemed to have learned his way. With many twists and turns, he brought them at last to a large stable and explained that it served their house and two others. Juan dismounted, opened the stable doors, and led both mules into the cool, dark interior.

"I . . . help señora down?" he asked her.

Rachel's eyes had not yet adjusted to the change from the light outside to the dim interior of the stable. She sensed more than saw the shape that materialized nearby.

"That won't be necessary," a voice growled, A hand shoved Juan aside.

Startled, Rachel twisted around. "You!" She was looking into the none-too-clean face of a slightly drunk Ralph Morton.

He grinned, his teeth showing lighter against the darkness of his face with a stubble of beard on it. "Yeah. Me, sweet thing. You were supposed to be mine—'n' now you will be." He reached for her, dragging her roughly from the mule.

"No!" Rachel screamed. She stumbled and would have fallen flat but for his hold on her. She felt her ankle turn in an excruciating twist.

"No!" Juan yelled and struck at the man, who merely swatted the child away as he would a fly, without loosing his grip on Rachel's arm. At this, Poco let out a growl and sank his teeth into Morton's leg. Morton swung his leg and aimed a vicious kick at the dog. "No!" Juan yelled again. He picked up his pet and ran for the door.

"Good riddance," Morton said. "Don't need no brat around for our business, now, do we?" He tightened his hold on her and pushed her toward an empty stall.

He pulled her tight against him and she could smell his long unwashed body, his foul breath, and the stale odors of tobacco and brandy. He bent to kiss her, but she jerked her head away.

"Let me go," she said, trying to hide the terror she felt.

"Not bloody likely, my pretty. I've waited far too long for this." He grabbed her hair, yanking it to hold her head as his lips settled on hers, bruising her mouth against her teeth, and muffling her scream.

He pushed her down into a pile of straw and covered her body with his. "You may as well lay back and enjoy this, for I aim to have what was *mine* to start with!"

"I was never—"

Her protest was cut off by his bruising mouth again. His rough beard scratched and burned her face. He fumbled with her skirt, but without much success as she twisted and turned beneath him and kept pounding her fists against whatever portion of his anatomy she could reach.

He paused and grabbed her chin to force her to face him. "If'n you keep fightin' me, woman, I'll hafta to hit you—an' I won't be gentle about it, neither."

She lay still for a moment, thinking she might catch him off guard if she relaxed.

"Ah, that's better." He tried to open the flap on his trousers even as he shoved one of his knees between her legs. "Jus' let me get little Ralphie out here to do his business," he grunted.

"No. Don't do this. Please," she begged.

"Can't stop now, pretty one." He pushed at her skirt again, trying to position himself against her as she began to fight him even more desperately now.

"I warned you." He drew back his fist to strike her.

The blow never fell.

Instead, a powerful fist slammed into his own head, knocking him against the side of the stall. As he lay there stunned, Rachel scrambled to her feet.

"Jake!" she screamed in relief.

"Wait out there," Jake ordered her. Stumbling again, she

did as he said, though she was still stunned by the attack. The pressure on her ankle sent pain jolting through her. She was frightened and horrified by what had almost happened, but she also felt shamed and a bit embarrassed.

Dimly she witnessed what happened next as though it were happening in a dream. Jake jerked Morton to his feet, and before the inebriated Morton could fairly position himself, Jake threw all his own weight behind a blow to the other man's face. She heard a horrible crunching sound. Morton uttered a low animal-like howl and tried to grab Jake in what would have been a bone-crushing bear hug. Jake sidestepped him and shoved Morton's head into the side of the stall.

Morton quickly brought himself upright to aim a kick at Jake's groin. It missed its target, but caught Jake's leg, knocking him to the floor. Morton sprang for Jake's neck, obviously intending to squeeze the life out of him. Bringing his knee up just as Morton lunged, Jake landed an unplanned blow at Morton's genitals. Morton rolled over, his body curved into a fetal position, whimpering breaths coming from his bloody mouth.

Jake squatted down and jerked the big sergeant's head around. Each word came out at a distinct clip. "If you ever so much as look at her again, I'll kill you. Do you understand me?"

Morton just stared.

"Do you understand me?" Jake ground out again.

Morton nodded. Like most bullies, he was a coward in defeat.

Jake rose, jerked the other man to his feet, and shoved him out the stable door. Morton stumbled, and Rachel saw him bent over in pain and fumbling to fasten his trousers even as he staggered away.

Jake, still breathing hard, turned to enfold her in his arms.

Seventeen

Jake hugged her trembling body close to his own. In the aftermath of what must have been helpless terror, she put her arms around his waist, buried her face against his chest, and sobbed wildly.

"Ssh. It's over, Rachel. You are safe now." He rocked her back and forth in his arms. "I will not allow you to be hurt. Please stop crying, love."

He was scarcely aware of using the endearment. Now that the crisis was over, he, too, was shaking with the aftermath of his own emotions—his fear for her and the blinding fury he had felt toward the beast who dared touch her, let alone hurt her. Her sobs subsided, and he rested his head on hers, taking comfort even as he gave it. He had no idea how long they stood there clinging to each other. Finally, she moved slightly and he lifted his head. He put a finger under her chin to look at her face. There was a bruise on her cheek and a small cut on her lower lip.

"Oh, Rachel." He could not suppress the anguish he felt as he brushed his lips tenderly against the bruise. "I'm so sorry this happened to you."

"Thank God you came when you did!" She shuddered. "Jake?" Her gaze held his for a long moment, then she moved her arms up to pull his head down to her own and kissed him, tentatively at first, then fiercely.

He was caught off guard only for an instant. Then he answered her need with his own, though mindful of her cut lip. Her mouth opened to allow him entrance. He drew in

a sharp breath and eagerly took what she offered. He withdrew only to feather light kisses over her eyes, her cheeks,
her nose. Then he sought her mouth again. And again she
responded with staggering intensity. He felt his whole body
bracing itself at the wonder of this moment—and in anticipation of more.

"Rachel," he murmured, "we . . . uh . . . we should . . .
perhaps . . ."

She pulled back and looked away, shy now. "I . . . I didn't
mean to—"

He put a quieting finger on her lips. "Please. *Don't* be
sorry."

She brought her direct gaze back to his and held it. "Oh,
I am not sorry. I . . . well . . . it seemed *right* somehow."

He hugged her closer. "For me, too." He touched his lips
to her forehead, then released her. "We must go in. Thompkins will be out soon to feed the animals."

"Yes," she said absently. She stepped back and, as she
did so, she uttered a sharp cry of pain.

"What is it?" he asked, alarmed.

"My ankle. I twisted it when he . . . he pulled me from
the mule. If you will just lend me your arm . . . ?"

Instead of doing so, however, he picked her up, one arm
around her shoulders, the other under her knees, to carry
her to the house some twenty or thirty yards away. She put
her arms loosely around his neck. He could smell that clean
woodsy odor of whatever it was she used to wash her hair.
Standing right outside the stable door were Juan and his
dog.

"Did that man hurt the señora?" Juan asked in his own
language, which he invariably used with Jake, though the
child's English was steadily improving.

"No," Jake said. "At least not badly—thanks to you. You
did well, Juan. That was quick thinking."

The boy blushed with pleasure at this praise, then murmured something about taking care of the goats. Jake carried
Rachel into the house and up the stairs to a bedroom on the

first floor. He called out to Henry, who came from the kitchen on the ground level.

"Get the medical kit, Henry. Unless I'm mistaken, we shall need to bind this ankle."

"Yes, my lord."

There were two bedrooms and a sitting room on this floor. Jake carried Rachel into the one he and Henry had decided earlier would be hers. Henry and the other two were lodging in the servants' quarters above. Jake knew he was extremely lucky to have such privacy, and he said a mental thank you to some follower of King Joseph who had hastily abandoned this house, however temporarily. He sat her down on a small sofa which, along with two upholstered chairs, a small table, and a huge bed, comprised the room's furniture. He knelt in front of her as Henry arrived with such medical supplies as they possessed.

"Now, about this ankle." Jake took her foot in his hand and began to remove the sturdy half-boot she wore.

"No. Really. This is unnecessary. I can take care of it." She was obviously embarrassed by such intimacy.

"Do not, I pray you, turn all missish on us, madam," he said in teasing sternness. " 'Tis your turn to be a properly behaved patient."

"Yes, sir," she replied with an excessive show of meekness.

He raised one expressive brow, but did not respond otherwise. He carefully removed the boot. He heard Henry's low whistle of dismay.

" 'Tis already swollen, my lord."

"Yes." Jake took her stockinged foot in his hand and felt along the ankle itself. He manipulated the foot, trying to be as gentle as possible. He heard her gasp, but she did not cry out. "I think there are no broken bones," he said.

"No, I do not think it is broken," she agreed. "It wants ice, but since that is unavailable, it should be wrapped tightly."

Henry coughed significantly.

"Can you remove the stocking?" Jake asked her, just as though he had read Henry's mind.

She blushed. "Yes. Don't look."

Jake was amused at this. Was this the woman who had kissed him so soundly only minutes earlier? He and Henry dutifully turned their backs and Jake heard the soft rustle of her clothing and a small grunt of pain.

"All right," she said.

The swelling was, of course, even more apparent without the stocking. Jake took a strip of bandaging material and wrapped it tightly around the ankle, tying it firmly. He was intensely conscious of the intimate nature of this act, for merely touching her bare flesh had heightened his senses.

"That should do. It feels better already," she said brightly. A shade too brightly, Jake thought. Had she felt it, too, then?

"I shall bring your supper, madam," Henry said as he replaced the rest of the bandaging material.

"Bring mine as well, Henry," Jake instructed, then addressed Rachel. "That is, if I may join you?"

"I should be delighted." She sounded polite but shy.

"Good. I will just remove some of this grime and return shortly."

When he returned, wearing only his shirt and trousers and a pair of comfortable slippers, he noted Rachel had washed her face, combed her hair, and removed the other boot. He also found Henry had not only delivered their food, but had pushed the table in front of the sofa and placed one of the upholstered chairs across from her.

"I see Henry is his usual efficient self," Jake said.

"He is more than efficient. He is a miracle worker. He even found me a walking stick!" She held up this item for Jake's inspection.

"Good for him. But don't praise him too highly, or I shall be forced to raise his wages."

"Not that you would not do so anyway."

Now she sounded nervous. Was this tête-à-tête a mistake then?

It was a simple meal of roasted lamb, boiled carrots, and

bread. Jake was surprised to see slices of fruit cake for dessert.

"Henry said he found it in the pantry," she told him.

They chatted amiably of mundane matters. Yes, the number of wounded brought to hospital had diminished. No, Lord Wellington could not yet issue an order to move out, as his troops were in no condition to follow such an order. There was to be an auction of looted goods later. They even discussed the weather—anything, apparently, to avoid talking about what had happened between them in the stable.

When Henry came to take away the tray, he brought another with the tea paraphernalia, as well as a bottle of brandy and two glasses.

"Will that be all, my lord?"

"Yes, Henry. Thank you—and good night."

When Henry had closed the door behind him, Jake left his chair to sit beside Rachel on the sofa. He put an arm around her shoulder, pulling her closer. "Now—where were we?"

"H-having tea?" she asked inanely and tried to reach for the teapot.

His hand stayed hers. "It will keep."

He kissed her slowly, deliberately, and was gratified by her response. There was no sign of the earlier nervousness, nor any reluctance in the eager way her lips sought his. He trailed kisses across her face and on the column of her neck. Her hands in his hair held him to her. Her breathing had accelerated, as had his own.

He caressed her breast, feeling the rigid nipple through the thin stuff of her dress and her undergarment. He was pleased that, like most of the younger women on the campaign trail, she was not wearing stays. She drew in a sharp breath as his thumb gently worked her nipple, but instead of withdrawing, she leaned in to him to encourage his touch.

He reached for the hem of her dress and ran his hand up her good leg, which still had a stocking fastened above the knee. He stroked the smooth, warm flesh above the stocking and felt his own body responding vehemently. He moved his hand higher to explore the moist depths there. He felt her tremble, but also noticeably relax to welcome his probing.

"Rachel?" he whispered. "Are you sure? There will be no going back if we continue this."

She took his face in her hands and held his gaze. "I know. And, yes, I am sure. I want you, Jake. I want this. With you."

He stood, gathered her to him, and carried her to the bed.

Sitting on the edge of the bed, Rachel pulled at the ribbons fastening her dress. Disrobing was a simple matter. Since leaving her father's house, she had never had a maid to see to her needs, so truly fashionable dress was simply out of the question.

"Allow me." Jake made short work of removing her dress and tossing it on a chair. "The shift, too," he said, removing the last barrier.

Rachel had never been aware of her body as a thing of beauty. Now, feeling Jake's eyes on her and hearing his appreciative intake of breath, she was both pleased and disconcerted. After all, he was not only a very attractive man, he was a lord, one of England's chosen. He had probably always had his pick of women.

"Beautiful," he murmured.

She pulled back the blanket and settled into the bed, watching as he removed the last of his own clothing and turned the lamp down, but not out. Shy about staring at him, she sneaked fleeting looks at him.

He chuckled. "It's all right, Rachel. I have no objections to your looking."

Her eyes drank in the sight of him. She was reminded of a drawing she had once seen of Michelangelo's David. The sculptor had depicted the hard, muscular body of a man—a warrior, not that of a young boy. Jake might have been the model for that magnificent work of art. She noted the scars on his body as he faced her, old ones she had seen before as his nurse, and the new ones on his midriff and thigh. As he stood by the bed, she reached to touch the scar on his leg.

"It healed nicely," she said, partly to prolong this moment, partly because she was nervous about what would come.

"Yes. I had excellent medical care." His matter-of-fact tone matched her own.

He lay down beside her, and she reveled in the simple miracle of bare skin against bare skin. He slipped an arm beneath her head and pulled her closer.

"You're sure?" he asked her again. "You can still change your mind. I will understand."

"Do *you* want to change your mind?"

"Good Lord, no! Do I *look* like I want to change my mind? Does it *feel* like I do?"

He punctuated his questions with a marvelous kiss. His hand stroked her body, bringing her to a fever pitch of desire. She was reminded of the poetic line "with my body I thee love," but she did not say it aloud. He touched, stroked, and probed, gently exploring, bestowing pleasure with every caress. Then his mouth followed the trail of his hands, kissing, licking, suckling, until she was fairly writhing in the pleasure-pain of anticipation.

"Jake . . . please . . ."

"Not yet, sweetheart."

She lay still for a moment. "Well, then—" Her tone was a teasing threat. She began to explore his body with her hands, curling her fingers in the soft, downy hair of his chest, running her hands over the hard muscles of his arms, chest, and belly, caressing the warrior's scars he wore so nonchalantly. She smiled at his hard intake of breath when her fingers floated in fleeting whispers of touch over his erection.

"Rachel!" he gasped.

"Ye-s-s?" she responded innocently. She increased the intensity of her stroking.

"Oh, yes!"

He positioned himself above her and made his entrance, his gaze holding hers all the while, except for an occasional searing kiss. Even through the sheer madness of her own passion, she was aware Jake was holding back, waiting for her. As ecstasy tore its way through her body, she murmured his name over and over. "Jake, Jake. Oh, Jake."

Reaching his own peak with a cry of pleasure, he collapsed against her. She lay savoring his weight, relishing the wonder of their oneness.

Then he roused himself. "Oh, God, I'm sorry, Rachel."

"Sorry?" She could not hide her hurt. "I thought that was truly remarkable, truly beautiful—and you are *sorry?*"

"It was remarkable—and beautiful. Oh, believe me, it was!" He rolled over beside her and held her close. "It is just that I didn't mean to . . . I meant to . . . to pull out at the last moment. And I didn't."

"Oh. You are worried we might make a babe?"

"Yes. I want no child of mine born on the wrong side of the blanket."

"I do not *think* that will happen." She explained about the special concoction she had continued to take, mostly out of habit, even after Brady was gone as an immediate presence in her life.

"Are you sure it works?" he asked skeptically.

"Well, I was not with child again after the accident at Badajoz . . ."

"Nevertheless, next time I promise to exercise more control."

He kissed her again as she savored the idea of a "next time."

And it came even that very night—twice.

The next morning, Jake rose early and kissed the still sleeping Rachel on the cheek. She murmured sleepily, but did not awaken. He stood at the side of the bed gazing down at her for a moment. She had never been so beautiful to him as she was in the sleepy afterglow of their lovemaking. He knew this night's pleasure would have consequences—consequences he had simply put out of his mind in the fever of anticipation and the euphoria of fulfillment.

Still, he would not have missed a moment—not even a second—of it, and already he looked forward eagerly to the next time. His body tightened at the mere thought. Jacob Forrester had certainly had his fair share of women in the past. He could not remember, though, ever losing himself in one. He had always managed a certain detachment. Last night there had been a sense of oneness, completion, and union that was totally new to him.

The fact remained—that sale business notwithstanding— she was legally married to another. One who had abused and abandoned her! Jake Forrester would no sooner give her up to her husband than he would let that animal Morton have his way with her. So where did that leave her? In what sort of limbo would she be required to live out her life?

He ran his hand through his already sleep-mussed hair, picked up his discarded clothing, and went to his own room. Henry had already brought up hot water for his shaving ritual. Jake sat patiently as Henry scraped twenty-four hours' growth from his face. Usually, Henry was full of chitchat in the morning, sharing news and views on anything from the Prince Regent's problems with his wife to the locals' stories of Lord Wellington or some extraordinarily clever achievement of Juan's. Today, Henry glanced once or twice at Jake's undisturbed bed, but did not open his tightly closed lips for anything beyond a "Good morning, my lord."

So, Jake thought, *the consequences begin already.*

That was the trouble with having servants who had been with one from childhood on. They knew everything and, if they were honorable and caring people—as Henry surely was—their opinions and regard became important to one.

Jake sighed. "All right, Henry. Out with it. I know you are just dying to ring a peal over my head."

Henry said tersely, " 'Tis not my place to do so, my lord."

Henry was suddenly the ever-so-proper servant? "When has that ever stopped you before?"

Henry sniffed. "I just hope you know what you are about, my lord. Mrs. Brady is not your usual run-of-the-mill lightskirt."

"*My* 'run-of-the-mill lightskirt'?" Jake challenged.

"I meant it in a general sense, my lord. She is a good woman."

"Yes, Henry, she is. And I promise you, I mean to see no harm comes to her—from me or anyone else."

"Very good, my lord."

"Now—if your tender sensibilities have been satisfied—send Thompkins over to that infernal hospital to explain that Mrs. Brady will not be there today. I doubt she will be able to stand on that ankle for any considerable length of time."

"I shall see it done, sir."

Jake could tell Henry was not completely mollified, but his batman would just have to accept the situation. After all, Jake and Rachel were the principal players in this scene, and had they not agreed there would be no turning back?

Given Henry's reaction, though, he wondered how Travers and Hastings would view this matter—or Humphrey. These were all men Jake liked and respected. On the other hand, their good regard was not important enough for him even to consider giving up what might develop between him and Rachel. Whatever that might be.

When Rachel woke, her first thought was to question where she was. Then the events of the previous afternoon and evening came flooding back to her. Her mouth was sore from Morton's treatment. There were ugly bruises on her wrist and arm. And her ankle would at first take none of her weight without sending a message of excruciating pain. She recalled with a shudder the terror she had felt as Morton tried to force himself on her.

However, all this faded to nothingness in the remembered wonder of Jake's lovemaking. She had not been unmoved by sex with her husband, especially in the early days, but she had had no true understanding of the heights to which she could be brought. Brady had made love *to* her; Jake shared the magic of it *with* her. If he never approached her again, she would still be grateful for this discovery of her own capacity for passion.

As she made her way laboriously down the stairs, the walking stick thumping out each step, she was nervous about seeing Henry and Thompkins. They must know Jake had spent the night in her bed. She had not considered that, had she, when she was so frantic to have Jake there.

Henry, Thompkins, and Juan were all in the kitchen when she came in. She was grateful neither of the adults treated her any differently than they had previously. By neither look nor nuance of tone did either man suggest any condemnation of her behavior. Of course, Juan was unaware of the initial moment of awkwardness she felt.

"Lord Jacob has already sent word of your accident to Captain MacLachlan," Henry informed her. "Thompkins here took the message."

"Thank you, Sam."

"I just told 'im you'd had an accident and twisted your foot. I figured you could tell 'im as much or as little as you please."

She felt rather humbled by this consideration of her reputation. And what had she herself done in that regard? Why, practically seduced Major Forrester into sharing her bed! However, she could not bring herself to entertain even a moment of regret for what had happened between her and Jake. What did it matter what others thought? In truth, most people assumed they had long since gone down the road they had traveled last night.

She felt happier this morning than she had for months—nay, years. She would clutch this happiness day by day, for who knew what the future would bring?

Eighteen

Wellington finally managed to get his army on the move again, but only after he threatened to hang anyone who continued the rape and pillaging that had gone on nonstop for nearly three days.

"He means it, too," Travers told Jake on the third day as the two of them returned to quarters in town. They had spent the day in the field, trying to get their own troops in order. "He's set up a scaffold in the main square."

"I have a candidate in mind to be his first lesson."

Travers gave Jake a sympathetic look. "I heard about that near thing with Mrs. Brady."

There was a uncomfortable silence as Jake wondered if the lieutenant had also heard about Jake's sharing Rachel's bed. Well, if he hadn't, he would find out soon enough when they took to the trail again.

"In any event," Travers was saying, "it looks as though we shall be on the move again soon."

"What a shame it couldn't have happened earlier. Who knows how many lives we might have saved?"

"You're right, of course," Travers agreed. "But I doubt any of our fine fellows will connect their greed here with a French bullet in those mountains."

"Those mountains themselves are going to be a hazard if we don't make our way through them before the snow starts."

"Hard to think of snow when it is so infernally hot here now."

Several days later, it was not snow but the mountains themselves that set great obstacles in their path. Because the French controlled the main passes, the allies were forced to seek other routes through treacherous terrain. Officers complained of inadequate or nonexistent maps and had to rely on local villagers to guide the troops through the mountains.

"Luckily," Jake told Rachel, "the Basque people are mostly sympathetic to us. Living as they have for centuries with abuse from the French north of the mountains and the Spanish to the south, they haven't much love for either of their neighbors."

"I think it helps that Lord Wellington insists that we pay for services and food we obtain from them," she said.

"The looting after battles notwithstanding." Jake's tone was ironic.

He had taken to sharing more and more of such views with Rachel. He also now shared his tent with her. Henry, Thompkins, and Juan were regularly in one nearby. Jake had been surprised at the alacrity with which not only his servants—from whom he expected nothing less—but also his friends had accepted this change in accommodations for Rachel. No one brought up the topic and all seemed to take it as a given fact of life.

As for himself, Jake reveled in the relationship. Beyond the intimacies of the bed, he found himself increasingly turning to her for simple friendship. She listened to concerns he could not share with Hastings and Travers—and kept his confidences. She offered sound advice when he presented a problem to her. She laughed at his witticisms, but, more importantly, she made him laugh. They argued over what they read. Jake thought Othello to be the consummate soldier; Rachel said he was the stupidest of men. They threw lines from the poems of Wordsworth and Coleridge back and forth at each other. The only other persons with whom Jake had felt so completely in tune were his brother and his mother.

Even as he took greater enjoyment in her company, his

concern for her grew. Life on the trail was grueling. The "roads" were often steep, rocky paths carved out of the precipitous inclines by the cloven hooves of goats and sheep. The mountains rose to dizzying heights on one side and the canyons sank to dizzying depths on the other. One wrong step and it was all over. Troops often had to traverse these ribbon-like thoroughfares in single file. Horses and mules were led, not ridden.

Exhaustion reigned at the end of the day.

Still, Jake thought, one could not but be impressed with the beauty and rugged grandeur of the scenery. The harsh terrain and the scarcity of fodder for the animals forced Lord Wellington to divide his troops into small groups, thus leaving them vulnerable to attack in frequent skirmishes. Nevertheless, the French were being steadily, inexorably pushed toward their homeland.

All wounded were carried forward with them now, and Rachel was often to be found near the wagons that transported injured soldiers. She chatted with them, even sang to them or with them, and Jake had held her as she grieved when death claimed one of "her" men.

When camp was set up at night, she was the one to prepare their meal, though likely as not Henry helped her. Afterward, as others did the washing up, Rachel would be off to write letters for the wounded, or to the families of the dead.

"You're doing too much, driving yourself too hard," Jake protested when she finally came to bed late one night.

"I know. But I could not let Ensign Cathcart's mother just read of his death in the casualty lists. The poor woman deserves more than that."

"So you made up a pretty story for her." He scooted over to allow her room in the bed, a pallet laid on straw.

"Hmm. I love it when you warm up the bed for me."

"Do *not* be changing the subject," he said, drawing her close.

"Well, I *may* have embellished the truth a *little*," she admitted.

"I'm sorry we lost him, but really, Rachel, Cathcart was both lazy and stupid."

"Perhaps he was. But his mother will feel better if she hears that he was brave and thinking of her at the end."

"Even if he was no such thing?"

"Even so," she said and yawned.

"You are a marvel." He kissed her. "Now do get some rest. The trail gets worse tomorrow."

"Hmm. Not possible . . ." Her voice faded into the deep breathing of sleep.

Jake lay awake a few minutes longer, treasuring her closeness. Then he, too, slept.

Despite the hardships of the trail and the sometimes painful losses in working with the wounded, Rachel was supremely happy these days. The medical work gave her a sense of achievement, and her nights with Jake were a wonderful time of discovery and fulfillment. For the first time in her adult life, she felt truly valued for herself.

In a small mountain valley that provided extraordinarily good feed for animals, a halt had been called early one day. Clara sought Rachel's company, and the two sat on the rocky ground, simply relaxing as Juan played with Benny nearby.

"You have the look of a well-loved woman these days." Clara grinned at Rachel's blush.

"As to that," Rachel said, "I am not sure *love* has much to do with it, but I am more . . . more *contented* now."

"I think it is love," Clara said firmly.

"I don't know. In truth, I hope it is not that."

Clara gave her a startled look. "You hope it is not love? For heaven's sake, *why?"*

"I have not been as lucky with love as you have. I used to envy you." Rachel looked off into the distance, but she did not see the play of sun and shadows on the hill across the way. What she saw were ugly scenes of her life with Brady.

"Envied *me?"* Clara asked.

"Yes. Joe not only cares for you, he genuinely *likes* you as a person."

"Yes, I think he does." There was no trace of arrogant pride in Clara's statement.

"And you have Benny, too." They were both silent for a moment. Then Rachel went on. She needed to sort this out for herself, and Clara was a good sounding board. Perhaps—someday—she could share this part of herself with Jake. But not yet. "When Edwin and I married," she began softly, "I thought I loved him. I truly *did* love him."

"Of *course* you did."

"And I was sure he loved me, too. Oh, it was going to be *so* wonderful." She paused. "Then—I honestly do not know what happened or when it changed. But it did. There . . . there were other women."

"I know. Joe told me."

"I mean even before we came out here. He would go off for days at a time, leaving me behind. One time it was for two whole weeks. He still . . . uh . . . came to me, you know, but he did not *like* me. Do you understand what I am saying?"

Clara put her arm around Rachel's shoulder. "Yes. I think I understand better than you do."

Rachel gave her a questioning look.

"Rachel, has it never occurred to you Edwin Brady married above himself when he got you?"

"Above himself? An innkeeper's poor relation? You must be joking!"

"Don't belittle yourself so," Clara said sharply. "You are smarter than he is. You have a better education—or you put yours to better use. That was probably hard for a man like Brady to live with."

"Well, I don't—"

Clara gave Rachel's shoulder a shake. "No. Hear me out."

"Yes, teacher," Rachel teased to lift the mood slightly.

"I think that, as a young man, Brady went through life on his charm—that pretty smile and handsome face. He has that kind of swaggering bravado that appeals to some men, too."

Rachel nodded.

"But it's all show," Clara went on, squinting against the setting sun. "There's no depth. And there is nothing shallow about you. You're beautiful. You're intelligent. You *care* about others. And people are drawn to the depths they find in you. Brady could not handle a wife who outshone him."

"You are suggesting he was simply jealous? Of his own wife?"

Clara released her hold on Rachel and looked around for her son. She caught sight of him and relaxed. Hugging her knees close to her chest, she continued. "No. I think there is nothing *simple* about it. Joe says a lot of men are like that—deliberately seeking women inferior to themselves."

"And a lot of women are smart enough to let them think they have found what they sought," Rachel said bitterly. "I just was not smart enough to do so."

"There you go again. My father used to say it was her Calvinist upbringing that made my mother assume guilt when it didn't exist. She was Scottish, too, like you."

Rachel laughed. " 'Tis hard to grow up in Scotland without its wearing off on one." She thought for a moment. "But that Calvinism lends toughness and resilience, too."

"Well, it certainly did so in you, my friend." Clara gave her a teasing smile. "I still say you are looking well loved."

Rachel waved her hand dismissively. "Perhaps some day. But not now. Perhaps never."

"Trust your heart, Rachel."

"I did that once—and look what it brought me."

"But your heart is all grown up now." Calling to her son, Clara stood and brushed dirt and pebbles from her skirt. "I have to go now. The men will be coming in soon."

As she returned to camp, Rachel only half listened to Juan who, with the ever present Poco, skipped along beside her, chatting of his day's adventures. She mulled over what Clara had said. Clara had some good points, but the fact remained that the best way to deal with pain was to insulate oneself against it in the first place. Friendship, not love. That was the answer. And friendship with good sex? She smiled to herself. That was icing on the cake.

Rachel was as much aware of the gossip now as she had been before Vitoria. Then, she had acted discreetly and tried to present a picture of proper decorum. To no avail. Gossips like Madge Selkins had had their say anyway. Now she did not flaunt her behavior to others, but neither did she take excessive measures to conceal it. What would be the use of doing so? After all, members of an army community lived in each other's pockets.

She adopted a "live and let live" policy. However, she did not want her actions to reflect on others.

"Might I have a private word with you, Mac?" she asked one morning soon after they left Vitoria.

"Of course." He steered her outside the tent he was using as a combination surgery, examination room, and ward. "What is it?"

"I . . . uh . . . suppose you've heard the gossip about me?"

"About you and Major Forrester, you mean?"

Rachel nodded, glad Mac was not dodging around the issue.

"What about it?" he asked.

"It—the gossip is not particularly nice . . ."

"Gossip never is, my girl. What *is* your point?"

"There are those who say you have no . . . no right to defile brave soldiers by having the likes of me tend them."

"Oh, for the love of—!" Mac said in impatient disgust. "Surely you are not crediting such drivel?"

"Well, the gossip is true—now." She felt herself blushing. "And I thought you might not want . . . well, you'd feel better if . . ." Her voice trailed off in embarrassment.

"My dear girl!" He gestured toward the tent. "These are the people Wellington himself called 'the scum of the earth'! They consider themselves lucky to be cared for. None of *them* has said anything untoward to you—*have* they?" His tone left it clear that if they had, they would hear from Captain MacLachlan.

"No. Oh, no," she assured him.

"Nor would any of those tattlemongers with overactive tongues be willing to do the work you are doing."

"No, I don't suppose they would."

"Well, then, let us stop wasting our time with this discussion." He clasped her shoulders to force her to look at him directly. "You are a valuable member of my staff. What you and the major do with your private lives is your own business."

"Thank you, Mac."

He released his hold. "However, if he harms you in any way . . ." The implied threat was only half joking.

She patted his arm and smiled. "He won't."

Sharing Jake's tent and his bed—he had happily given up the cot—meant sharing his dreams. She had been surprised to find the man she viewed as the consummate soldier was actually looking forward to life as a civilian.

"Will you not miss the military life?"

"Certain aspects of it, yes. But overall, I think not." He lay in bed watching as she brushed out her hair and began to work it into the single braid she customarily wore to bed. "Leave it loose tonight, won't you?"

She gave him an arch look, but quietly did as he asked. She lay down next to him and said, "Why?"

"Because I like the feel of it against my skin."

"No, I mean why will you be so glad to leave the army?"

He put his arm around her, hauling her closer, resting his head next to hers. In the interest of privacy and courtesy, they spoke softly, for voices carried from tent to tent in the still mountain air.

"Well," he said slowly, "like most men, I came into the army a green youngster wanting to get away from home and seek adventure. I suppose now I am just tired of fighting—though, in truth, it is a fact of army life that one spends very little time actually fighting."

"But a great deal of time *preparing* to do so," she observed.

"Yes. Someone once described it—accurately, I would say—as 'long periods of great boredom punctuated by moments of great fear.' Not a bad summation, eh?"

"For those who wait as well as those who fight." She kissed him. "But what sort of civilian life do you envision for yourself?"

Rachel was not sure why she asked this question. She usually refused to let herself think of the future, for she knew Lord Jacob Forrester's future could have no place in it for Rachel Brady, abandoned wife of a sometime sergeant.

"My mother's father had no sons. He left a rather large holding to her and stipulated that it would eventually go to *her* son and not be swallowed up in Lounsbury lands. He knew there was little likelihood his grandchild would ever have the Lounsbury title."

"So you will become a gentleman farmer?" she prodded.

"Something like that. I have a good steward, and Robert looks after things for me now. He also controls three or four seats in Commons. I may very well seek one of those."

"You want to join Parliament?" She was mildly surprised at this.

"Well—yes. I think so. If this prolonged war with the French republic has taught us nothing else, it has shown the need for reforms. I should like to be a part of that."

"And your mother?" she asked to shift the subject.

"She mostly lives in town since Robert's marriage."

"She dislikes country living?"

"She likes it well enough," he said. "I think she wanted the new marchioness to feel she could run the household her own way."

"A most unusual mother-in-law."

"What about you?" he asked. "Would you like country living?"

She knew the question was far more significant than his casual tone suggested. She answered carefully. "Yes. I believe I would. I liked the village people when I lived with my aunt and uncle. But I shall probably have to make my way in a city."

"You never know," he said lightly. He then turned his attentions—and his caressing hands—to satisfying his curiosity on a more immediate level.

Jake had little time in the next few weeks to dwell on this conversation, for the future was swallowed up by the frenzy of the present. Wellington had decided to launch his army at not one, but two important targets. The well-fortified town of Pamplona sat on an important crossroads to the Pyrenees. He dared not leave it in the hands of the French as he pushed into the mountains, for this would leave too large a force at British backs.

On the seacoast, San Sebastian was also well fortified and controlled the harbor of Passages, through which the Peer wanted his supplies to come as he pushed into France. These two sites were located only about fifty miles apart, but they were separated by impassable mountains—and the ubiquitous French troops. Both sites required long, bitter sieges. Nor were these the only places where hard-fought battles occurred. Jake knew names like Sorauren, Elizondro, Irurzun, and, most of all, Maya Pass, would be forever seared into his memory.

Wellington established his headquarters in a village called Lesaca, between Pamplona and San Sebastian, and it was here the main hospital was located. Jake was glad to know Rachel was there in relative safety, though he was sure she was still working too hard. Once again—at Jake's insistence—she shared quarters and rations with Clara Paxton. Nellie Bingham was billeted near them, and Jake had left Juan in Rachel's care.

The battles for the Pyrenees were turning out to be some of the toughest of Jake's career—and of Lord Wellington's. They began in mid-July and lasted until the end of October. Forrester, Travers, and Hastings spent much of their time in rather primitive bivouacs, though they occasionally made it

back to headquarters between battles. There, they would be
temporarily free of the booming guns, arduous marches, and
bloody fighting. There, too, they could pick up news from
home, for the mail managed to come on a fairly regular
basis to wherever Wellington was.

By mid-August, they were finally receiving in the Peninsula news of England's reactions to June's Battle of Vitoria.

"Listen to this." Jake addressed the rather large, festive
group gathered around his table in Lesaca. It included the
Paxtons, the Binghams, and Humphrey, as well as Hastings,
Travers, and, of course, Rachel, who sat close enough to
touch him from time to time. He waved the letter he was
reading. " 'Tis from my mother . . . oh, here it is."

> *The newspapers are full of the victory at Vitoria.*
> *The Prince cannot seem to contain himself in praising*
> *Wellington. I suppose you know he has named Wel-*
> *lington a Field Marshal now in addition to all the*
> *other titles the man now holds! (Sounds rather French*
> *to me, but I admit to a great deal of ignorance about*
> *military matters.)*
>   *The papers are calling this the decisive victory of*
> *the war in the Peninsula. I just hope they are right*
> *and that you will all be home safe and sound—soon.*
>   *Parliament has voted another great monetary*
> *award to your leader, too. I suppose they have already*
> *given him the highest* title *they can assign him. I*
> *mean, they* will *give pause at naming him a prince,*
> *will they not? Just think how out of joint Prinney's*
> *nose would be!*

"My father writes much the same thing," Hastings said,
"though less entertainingly than Lady Lounsbury does."

Rachel kept more or less abreast of the battles in the
Pyrenees through the wounded brought to hospital.

"I swear ol' Nosey must wear out more horses than all the cavalry put together. You never know when he's goin' ta show up."

"An' the troops always cheer like crazy when he does."

"I hear that really threw the Frenchies in a tizzy a time or two—wonderin' what in thunder we was cheerin' for."

"Once they thought we got reinforcements an' they turned tail and ran. Had us outnumbered, they did, too!"

"Seeing his lordship on a field of battle is as good as having a whole regiment with you."

"He sure ain't too happy with officers who don't follow orders."

"Fighting was so fierce at San Sebastian that when we finally broke through, most all the officers was killed."

Hearing this, Rachel said a silent prayer of thanks that Jake was then at Maya Pass. Then she heard another snatch of rumor.

"I hear we lost a whole regiment at that Maya Pass."

Please, God, no, she silently prayed and took some solace in this being but hearsay.

"I was two days gettin' here to hospital. Some poor fellas—they jus' bled out where they was."

"Villagers and wounded clogged the route. We could not relieve the 92nd as planned."

"We retreated so fast, we had to leave wounded behind. Put notes in their hands asking the French to take care of them as they would their own."

"They will," was the positive response to this cry of despair. "We do it for them." Rachel knew this to be true. She had tended many French prisoners herself.

"Looting at San Sebastian was worse than at Badajoz or Vitoria."

"Not enough officers left alive to control it."

"Some Spanish think it was deliberate. They are saying we destroyed the city purposely to weaken their trade when the war is over."

"Well, you must admit Spain and England have always been great rivals for control of the seas."

Finally, on the last day of October, came word of the breakthrough.

"Pamplona has fallen."

"Starved out, they were."

"Getting through these mountains would have been much easier if Boney hadn't sent Soult back against us."

"The Peer will handle Soult. You'll see."

"He's already pushed into France. He's there now."

"Plans to winter at Bayonne."

"That'll put a burr under Bonaparte's saddle. I'm told he's especially fond of Bayonne."

One last bit of welcome news MacLachlan shared when he learned it from a captured, wounded French officer. The allies had defeated Napoleon himself at a place called Leipzig.

"This may truly be the beginning of the end," Mac said. "The little corporal is returning to Paris."

In the first week of November, troops returned only long enough to gather themselves together to move out again. Once again Rachel was on the road—or what passed for a road—headed for Bayonne and winter quarters. But Jake was with her, so all was well.

Nineteen

Winter now became the enemy as the British and their allies forged their way through the last of the mountains and then fought their way across the river Bidassoa and then the river Nive. The French viewed both rivers as major barriers that must be defended at all costs, now that the British army was firmly established on the French side of the border. Marshal Soult—called back from his exile to Paris—seemed to think he had reached the deciding issue of his career. He should not only hold the line against the invading allies, but send them back to Spain.

For Rachel, the hardships of a winter march were profound, but she knew she suffered far less than many others. Men who had not been issued new uniforms in literally years were in rags. Once smart red tunics had faded to pale pink in the Spanish sun. The riflemen's green and artillerymen's blue uniforms were now nearly unidentifiable shades of gray.

A multitude of patches further obscured the means of recognizing who was wearing which uniform. Although tunics were the more distinguishable elements of the uniforms, trousers wore out more quickly and replacements had to be obtained wherever they might be found. Often, that was on the bodies of the dead—friend or enemy, it did not matter.

The marchers also desperately needed footgear. For many their boots had long since worn beyond use. The cobblers could not keep up with demand, even when they had sufficient materials. Many a soldier resorted to wrapping his feet in skins from newly butchered animals. The feet of men and women alike had repeatedly been cut, bruised, and blistered. For those in the rear of a column plowing through snow, they had but to follow the bloody footprints to find their way.

Despite the well-known efforts of Wellington to keep his troops well fed, they were too frequently hungry. Sometimes their bellies drove them to fraternization with the enemy.

"Though as to that, 'tis most often boredom that leads to excessive contact between our men and theirs," Hastings grumbled one evening.

"Boredom is a great motivation," Rachel agreed.

"Sentries on our side of a bridge start out making catcalls to those on their side and soon they are meeting in the middle, trading for liquor and tobacco!"

"Brothers under the skin," she commented. "Makes all the killing doubly senseless."

"Probably."

Rachel had learned of one such instance that underscored the truth of this. A group of French soldiers had lost a bullock, which was to provide their rations. The animal ended up in British hands. When the French approached under a flag of truce to claim their property, they explained that their rations had been short for some time. The British, suffering the same privation, agreed to return *half* the butchered animal—and then they sent along several loaves of bread as compensation.

"If only that kind of cooperation could find its way to the top," Rachel noted to Jake when she told him the story.

"If only," he agreed.

Finally, like a great animal going into hibernation, the army established winter quarters in villages near the city of Bayonne, but that town itself remained firmly in French hands. For the most part, the two armies left each other alone in the dead of winter, so Rachel's hospital work was considerably diminished.

Major Forrester had been assigned quarters in an inn, along with Hastings and Travers. Juan's herd of goats had been reduced from three to two in the course of the journey. Jake and the others assured him a wolf had got his pet, but Rachel knew they suspected the hungry wolf had had but two feet. Juan was now even more fiercely protective in caring for the remaining two. Rachel thought that, for Juan, the goats somehow represented a link with his dead family, and her heart went out to him. Of course, truth be told, this child had long since stolen a place in her heart.

Like Henry, Juan had appointed himself Rachel's guardian when Jake was not around. She knew the boy needed a mother—though, typical of little boys everywhere, he made a show of rejecting females. Once she had idly laid aside the bar of soap with which she had just washed her hands. When she turned around, Juan had picked it up and was smelling it in deep intakes of breath. Catching her looking at him, he shyly laid it aside.

Later, Rachel persuaded Henry and Thompkins to see that Juan had a proper bath. She surmised it was the first he had ever had, but he seemed quite proud of his newfound cleanliness.

With Napoleon's defeat at Leipzig and the British now firmly established on French soil, a sense of fatalism pervaded the remainder of the Peninsula campaign. Some of the fight had gone out of the French, despite Soult's determination to the contrary. Occasionally, new wounded offered proof that Soult was at least partially successful. Still, everyone seemed to have an eye to the end—and going home.

"What will happen to all these people with us when we leave?" she asked Jake one evening. She had been sitting on a settee by the fire, doing some mending.

He looked up from a month-old newspaper he had received only this day. "Which people?"

"You know. The Spanish and Portuguese women—and people like Juan."

"I hadn't really thought about it," he answered.

"Well, now that you *are* doing so, what do you think?"

"Hmm. I seriously doubt they will be loaded onto transport ships—unless they can prove a valid marriage."

Rachel was appalled. "But some of them have children of British fathers! Are you telling me they will simply be left at the docks? With their children?"

"Probably," he said. "So far as I know, native women who become camp followers have no claim on His Majesty's Army."

"What about British women who become camp followers?" she asked in a tight little voice.

Jake put down his paper and rose from his chair. Moving her sewing basket to the floor so he could sit close to her, he put an arm around her shoulder. She did not melt into his embrace as she usually did.

"Rachel, you must not worry about such a matter. I promise I will take care of you. You will *not* be abandoned."

This little speech having dissolved her resistance, she accepted the kiss he offered. "But it's so unfair," she said. "I'm sure many of these men and women mean as much to each other as—as—"

"As we do," he finished for her. "I'm sure you are right, but I haven't the means of chartering a ship for them—even in the extreme unlikelihood of the government's welcoming them to England."

"And Juan?" she asked, holding her breath in apprehension.

He showed no shred of hesitation. "He will come home to England with me, too."

"Oh, Jake, I'm so glad!"

"What? You thought I would just leave him—a child with fewer than ten years—alone?"

"I didn't know—I'm sorry." She could tell he was hurt by her doubt. She kissed him on the cheek and he enfolded her more tightly in his arms.

"I need to keep Juan around to feed my feelings of self-importance," he said jokingly.

"He does think of you as Roland, El Cid, and Sir Lancelot all rolled into one."

"Only because you keep feeding him those heroic tales of derring-do," he said.

"All little boys need a hero," she said. "I am glad he has you."

He nibbled at the sensitive area just below her ear. "And do you also know about the needs of big boys, oh wisest of women?" he murmured.

"Hmm. I shall try to work on that problem."

Rachel had touched on an issue that had occupied Jake's thoughts for some weeks now. There had never been any question about her returning to England with him—nor about Juan's doing so. And certainly it would be easy enough to provide for the boy. A bright lad, he would respond well to a proper education once he gained mastery of the language.

The big question for Jake was what to do about Rachel once they reached English shores. With every day he had her near, it was harder to think of the possibility of *not* having her near.

Jake had recently had a conversation with Humphrey, part of which had been most disturbing. The grizzled sergeant, baked by the sun on two continents, had asked to speak privately with Major Forrester one evening. The two walked out toward the stable, ostensibly to check on an ailing horse. They paused under a window that threw light onto Humphrey's leathery face. Incongruously, the man seemed shy—or embarrassed.

"What's on your mind, Sergeant?"

"Well, sir, I wouldn't want you to be thinkin' I'm takin' advantage or anything, but I've actually got a couple o' things in mind."

"Very well."

"You know that nun, Sister Luisa? She joined us after Vitoria?"

"Yes." Jake remembered several of the sisters of that destroyed convent joining the British—along with a number of Spanish and French women who had been abandoned in the French retreat. The British soldiers had been inordinately solicitous of the nuns' welfare. Luisa was a woman of late thirties or early forties. Jake recalled friendly brown eyes and rosy cheeks, but a nun's habit had precluded much further impression.

Humphrey looked at the ground and pulled at his collar. "Well, you see, sir, me an' Luisa—we want to marry."

"Wha-at?"

"We want to marry," Humphrey repeated much more firmly. "She never did want to be no nun. 'Twas her dad what made 'er. Seems Spanish men often do that to women in their families—jus' turn 'em over to the church—'specially if the woman ain't inclined to marry the man the family wants her to." This was rather a long speech for the usually laconic Humphrey.

"And she speaks English?" Jake asked, curious, but also in a bid for time to consider Humphrey's surprising announcement.

"Yes, sir. Quite well, too. They had an Irish priest at that convent."

"I see."

"Anyways, we know she can't come to England with us less'n we be married. An' there's some as disapproves of soldiers marrying local women."

"And for good reason," Jake said. He put a hand briefly on Humphrey's shoulder. "However, that rule was made to protect green boys from making mistakes that could ruin their whole lives. Not for the likes of you."

"Then you'll help us, sir?"

"I shall be honored to do so." Jake held out his hand. "Congratulations, Sergeant."

"Thank you, sir."

"You said there was something else, too?"

"Yes, sir. Touches on you more'n me."

"Is that so?"

Humphrey seemed hesitant. "This might be just rumor, Major, but I thought I should pass it on."

"And . . . ?"

"You know some of our fellows work rather close with locals."

"We get some valuable information from those sources," Jake said.

"That's why I thought there might be some truth to this—'specially as it comes from Ed Nelson. He's a good man. Seems they's a band of renegades in this area."

"English deserters, you mean?"

"This partic'lar lot has English, French, 'n' even some Spanish. They steal from local folk—treat 'em real bad—and also from both armies when they can."

"I knew that much," Jake said.

"Ed says he saw that fellow Brady with 'em."

Jake gave a start. "Is that so? Recently?"

"Yes, sir. An' Brady was makin' threats against the English in general, but you in partic'lar. 'Course, Ed said he was drunk at the time."

"Hmm. Thank you for telling me," Jake said.

"There's more, sir."

"More?"

Humphrey drew a circle in the dirt with the toe of his boot. "Seems Brady said as how he was gonna grab his wife back. Said that'd teach you—or something like that."

"Good God!"

Humphrey continued, "I haven't actually seen it—and I can't prove it—but I hear Morton has had some contact with them renegades."

"I'm not surprised," Jake muttered.

"I'd watch my back—an' keep any eye on Mrs. Brady—if'n I was you, sir."

"I will, Sergeant. I certainly will. And I do thank you."

"No, sir. If'n you can help me an' Luisa, it's me that'll do the thankin'."

"I'll do my best, Sergeant."

Jake had not told Rachel of this turn of events. He did not doubt the story for a moment, but he did not want her to worry. He remembered too well that haunted look about her after the sale. She had at long last begun to lose that look, and he certainly did not want to see it return. However, he did inform Hastings and Travers, as well as Henry and Thompkins.

Hastings, a little the worse for drink one night in the common room of the inn, said privately to Jake, "Too bad you can't marry her, isn't it? But I s'pose it wouldn't do. Forresters prob'ly *marry* only their own kind."

"Never mind the fact that Rachel is already married," Jake said sarcastically.

"But he 'bandoned her," the captain muttered through a case of hiccoughs.

"True. However, that does not negate the legality of her marriage." Jake used the tone of infinite patience the sober often use with the inebriated.

"Still. Too damned bad. You're obviously in love with 'er."

"And you, my friend, are obviously drunk. Come, I'll help you to your bed."

Later, Jake strolled alone in the crisp cold air of a mid-December night, sorting through this conversation. Hastings was right. He *was* in love with her. Truth to tell, he had been in love with Rachel ever since she took him to task about Achilles and Homer's other heroes. But Jake had been right this night, too. She was still legally bound to another.

But, he asked himself, would he marry her if he could? He had been reared as a Forrester to believe he would eventually marry someone of his own class—someone like Celia. Now, having known the depths of passion and affection and friendship that Rachel offered, he could not believe he had cared so profoundly for the superficial Celia. But he had. And society would have applauded such a match. Mismatch, that is. He would have come—eventually—to hate it, he told himself. He was surprised at this thought, but even more surprised it had not come to him years earlier.

The answer to that basic question, then, was *yes*. Society and family tradition be damned. Yes. He *would* marry her—if she were free. And—if she would have him.

He hurried back to the inn to find Rachel already in her

nightclothes, writing in her journal. She laid down the quill as he closed the door.

"Rachel, come sit with me here by the fire. I must talk with you."

"What is it? Has something happened? You are not being called out at this hour!"

"No. Nothing like that." He took the wing chair next to the fireplace and pulled her onto his lap.

"You're in a strange mood," she observed.

"Rachel, if you were free, would you marry me?"

"Jake! Whatever brought this on?"

"Would you?" he insisted in an urgent tone.

"I—I don't know—I—you have taken me by surprise. You've not been drinking, have you?"

He laughed. "Not enough to enter into it." He gave her a brief, tight hug. "Now tell me—would you marry me if you could?"

She was silent for such a long while that apprehension began to slither through him.

"Rachel? I cannot believe you do not care for me."

She put her arms around his neck and kissed him hard. She tasted of the mint tea she liked of an evening. "Oh, Jake. Yes. I do care for you very much. Very much. But—"

"But you wouldn't marry me if you could?"

"I—I just do not know. At least not now. We come from such different worlds. And . . . and I am *not* free. We both know that."

This bleak statement of fact hung like a dark cloud between them, and each was silent for a moment. Then Jake gave her a little shake.

"Rachel, listen to me. This war is going to be over in a matter of weeks—a few months at most. Less if Napoleon has the sense God gave a goose."

She gave him another quick kiss. "I know. Then we shall return to England and go our separate ways." She said it a shade too brightly, he thought.

"But I want you with *me*," he said. "I love you."

"Oh, Jake it would not work. Truly, it would not."

"Why?" he demanded roughly.

"The only way I could be in your life in England would be as your mistress—as I am here."

"My lover," he corrected.

"That, too. But I could not be a part of your family, now, could I? Men do not inflict their mistresses on their kinswomen."

What she said was true. Moreover, Rachel was not the sort of woman who should live the half-life of a mistress, available to a man when he could spare time from his "real" life.

She continued in a tone that was infinitely sad. "One day you will marry and have children. I could not bear to watch that happen. Nor could I be party to inflicting the pain of a husband's infidelity on another. What's more, I doubt you could do that, either."

Suddenly Jake realized the depth of just such pain as Rachel had once suffered—and that she was not yet over it. And she was right about him, too. He could not see himself as party to hurting an innocent person. He felt despair wash over him.

"I have no intention of marrying some flibbertigibbet of the *ton*," he declared. Then he added in a more subdued tone, "And you and I *could* have children . . ."

"Born on the wrong side of the blanket? Neither of us would want that."

"Then we will not have children. But I will *not* let you go. Besides, to what—or to whom—would I let you go? Certainly not to that blackguard Brady. Unless you can honestly say you simply do not want me, I am yours, my girl. And I intend to love you and take care of you."

"Oh, Jake. You sweet, wonderful, silly man. How could I not consider such an offer?"

But, he noted, even as her lips met his, she had not said she would accept it.

Rachel's emotions were in turmoil. She was supremely happy at Jake's declaration of love for her. At the same time, she wondered if she would be supremely selfish to agree to continue as his mistress. *Lover,* she reminded herself and smiled.

Really, though, what choice did she have?

Mac welcomed her as a volunteer member of his staff here in the Peninsula, but it was not as though she were considered a true professional. And in England, there would be no paid hospital work for a woman. Her needlework was not so refined as to allow her to work as a seamstress. She *might* have been accepted, as a single woman, in the position of governess in some low-ranking gentry home. However, for an abandoned wife and another man's mistress, that notion was out of the question. She knew very well it would be impossible to hide such information forever. Someone was sure to find out sometime.

No. She really had no choice but to do exactly as every fiber of her being wanted—to stay with Jake.

And if he one day wished to marry another and have a family? Have a wife who could act as his hostess to entertain members of Parliament?

The very idea of Jake in the arms of another sent a shock of pain through her. It was a bridge that might one day have to be crossed, but not now.

What disturbed her most was that fact of having no choice, of being at the mercy of another's whim—even another whom she trusted as she trusted Jacob Forrester. She had trusted Edwin, though, too, had she not? And her aunt and uncle? Would this happiness also turn to ashes and dust? She was back to the original point—as a woman, a woman without means, she simply had no choice but to go along with whatever life chose to toss at her.

Right now, what it was tossing was very acceptable indeed. Better half a loaf than none. . . .

Christmas came and went, with the British making valiant efforts to preserve their traditions and the gaiety of the season. New uniforms had finally arrived, and for many this added to their celebrations. There was a Yule log in the inn's common room, mulled wine, and carols. Rachel surprised her "family" and friends with a Christmas feast, including a roast goose and plum pudding. The French innkeeper and his wife had happily allowed her take over the kitchen and they, too, joined in the festivities, supplying the wine themselves.

The innkeeper's wife had confided to Rachel their preference for British guests. "French soldiers just take— steal—they no pay. Same with filthy Spanish. Spanish *real* bad to us French."

"I had heard that," Rachel said sympathetically. The two women communicated in a patched-together language of French, English, and Spanish. Over the few weeks the Forrester group had already been there, Rachel and Madame Aubert had come to understand each other quite well. "I am told Lord Wellington sent one company of Spanish troops back to Spain because he could not control their looting and mistreatment of local people," Rachel said.

"Tres bien!" Madame Aubert said vehemently.

Two tables were set up in the common room, and the guests included the Paxtons and Binghams as well as Sergeant Humphrey and his Luisa. Among the officers present were—besides Jake—Hastings, Travers, MacLachlan, and Ferguson. Everyone had insisted on bringing something to add to their feast. Rachel was determined that Henry, Thompkins, and Juan join them, too, along with the two men who served Hastings and Travers.

"That is very kind of you, Mrs. Brady," Henry had said when Rachel informed him of her plan, "but, truly, 'twould be most unseemly for servants to join the gentry, as it were."

"Nonsense," she replied. " 'Tis Christmas, and I insist. Besides, your presence will make the Paxtons and Binghams feel more comfortable."

"Well . . . put that way . . ."

Later, when she and Jake finally retired to their room that night, he embraced her and said, "You truly are a marvel, my love. That was a wonderful party."

"It was, wasn't it? But why do you think it such a marvel?"

"I know of no other woman who could have pulled such a disparate group of people into the congenial company we were," he said.

"They are all such nice people, though."

"That they are," he agreed. He was preoccupied with removing his boots for a moment, then asked, "What do you think of Humphrey's Luisa?"

"I think she is very sweet. She was one of those who offered to help with wounded at Vitoria." Rachel and smiled and shook her head. "The poor woman walked around with tears in her eyes all the time over the plight of injured men. It was nice to see her laughing now."

"We are encountering some difficulty in arranging for Humphrey to marry her."

"Nothing you cannot resolve, I hope."

"I hope so, too."

He gathered her into his arms again and lowered his mouth to hers. Any thought of the other couple's problems vanished in her response to his kiss.

A few days later, Rachel and Jake walked through the village, as was their wont of an afternoon, before darkness claimed their world. Often as not they were accompanied by Hastings or Travers. Sometimes Juan skipped along beside them with Poco. But this day, it was just the two of them, though Hastings had promised he would "be along in a few minutes." Rachel had her hand firmly tucked into Jake's elbow, and the two of them chatted of mundane matters.

Ahead of them Rachel saw a familiar and despicable figure—Morton. She had seen him from time to time since the incident in the stable in Vitoria, but had carefully avoided him. Now he disappeared from view between some buildings, one of which Rachel knew was rumored to be a brothel—though she also knew she was not supposed to know of its existence.

"Robert writes that Vauxhall Gardens is planning a grand pageant of the Battle of Vitoria as one of its attractions," Jake was saying. "Can you imagine how distorted *that* is likely to be?"

Rachel saw the gun first—a deadly pistol. Then Morton stepped from between the buildings and pointed the weapon at point-blank range at Jake's heart.

"No-o!" she screamed and shoved at Jake, throwing him slightly off balance and causing him to stumble.

She felt a piercing, fiery pain in her shoulder and Jake's arms around her to break her fall. She heard another loud report and had a fleeting thought of *He's killed Jake!* Then she heard and felt nothing.

"Rachel! Oh, my God! Rachel!"

Terrified at the blood spreading over her breast, Jake knelt with his body hovering over hers. He heard rapid footsteps pass him. He had heard the second gunshot, but in his initial shock had not determined where it came from.

"Damn!" he muttered, drawing his own pistol. Since Humphrey's warning, none of them walked out with Rachel without loaded weapons.

Hastings materialized from the direction of the first shot. "He's dead."

"Brady?"

"No. Morton. Is she . . . ?"

"She's alive," Jake said, standing to lift her. "Get Mac-Lachlan, will you?"

"Right away."

Jake carried her back to the inn, murmuring in several languages every prayer he had ever heard.

Twenty

"Thank God, it's not too serious," MacLachlan said. "The ball may have nicked her collar bone, though, and she will definitely not be able to use that arm much for a while."

The bullet had gone into the fleshy part of her shoulder, and MacLachlan had extracted it rather easily. Jake had had to steel himself to endure the sight of the surgeon's probing around in the wound, though he had witnessed dozens of such procedures in the past.

At last MacLachlan stood and washed his hands in a basin. Drying them, he said, "When she is ready to sit or stand, she will need a sling to keep pressure off the wound."

"I will see to it," Jake assured him.

"You might also see to getting a woman to help care for her."

"*I* can take care of her," Jake said defensively.

"I've no doubt you *can,* Major, but I think she will be more comfortable to have another woman for some matters."

Jake recognized the truth of this, but he could not tear Clara away from her child, and Nellie Bingham was ill with the grippe. He supposed he *could* ask Madame Aubert to help Rachel. Then his thoughts lit on Luisa, and he immediately sent word to her.

Actually, Jake thought, Luisa's nursing Rachel might be the solution to more than one problem.

Luisa was pleased to offer her services. She and Jake shared the "watch" in the sickroom until Rachel regained consciousness. Mac had been right. Rachel *did* appreciate the presence of a woman—especially in those hours when Jake could not be there. He knew she endured a great deal of pain and trying to perform ordinary tasks with only one hand was often frustrating.

"I have certainly gained a new appreciation for those men who have lost a limb," she told him.

Despite her obvious battle with pain, she refused after the second day to take any more laudanum. "I want to be alert," she declared. She directed both Jake and Luisa in very specific terms regarding poultices and other aspects of her care. MacLachlan pronounced himself quite satisfied with her progress.

Soon, she regained enough strength not only to leave her bed, but also to sit in the common room and receive a steady stream of visitors. Among the first of these were Clara and Joe, along with Sergeant Bingham.

"Nellie wanted to come, too," Bingham said, "but she's afraid she might still spread that fever she had."

"Do tell her I miss her smiling face," Rachel replied.

Hastings inquired after her on a regular basis. On the day she had first presented herself in company, he was there to see for himself that she was recovering nicely. Jake and Luisa hovered nearby to see that she did not overtax herself. Jake had come in from the field to find her downstairs receiving visitors. He cast an inquiring glance at Luisa.

"I could not keep her in bed," the Spanish woman said.

"Don't be angry with Luisa," Rachel told him. "This was my idea. And you mustn't be such a mother hen." She smiled to soften the rebuke.

"He just wants to keep you to himself," Hastings teased. "He always was a selfish brute."

"Jake tells me it was you who came to our rescue," she said in thanking him.

"I should have caught up with you sooner," he replied apologetically. "It might not have happened if I had."

"Possibly," she agreed. "But we cannot know that for

sure. I think . . . I think Sergeant Morton must have been rather twisted in his thinking."

Hastings snorted. "Out of his blooming mind, I'd say."

"In any event, I am sorry to have been the cause of his death, however indirectly."

Hastings exchanged a look with Jake before saying, "You were in no manner to blame for what happened, dear lady. His target appeared to be your companion."

"I think you may be right," she said.

Hastings gave her a cheeky grin. "I do hope you have learned that a pretty woman's frail body is a most inadequate shield against a bullet."

"Hospital work tends to underscore the idea *no* body is an effective shield," she replied.

He nodded. "Just so."

She chatted cheerfully with others as well as Hastings until Jake perceived that she was tiring. When he simply scooped her into his arms to carry her back upstairs, she protested. "Do put me down! I came downstairs under my own power."

"And you are going back under mine," he said.

Their small audience laughed.

" 'Tis my *arm* that functions improperly, not my legs!"

He leaned his head closer to hers and whispered for her alone, "I know. But I like the feel of you where you are."

She blushed furiously and subsided, her good arm around his neck.

A short while later, Henry brought up a tray with supper for Rachel and Jake.

"Rachel, we need to talk," Jake said when they had made a substantial dent in the food.

"I truly *am* getting better." She sounded defensive.

"Yes, you are," he agreed. He hesitated, then continued, "In a week or so you should be able to travel."

"Travel? Do not say the army is moving out already. It's still winter!"

"Not the army. You."

"I don't understand." There was something like fear in her tone.

He grasped her good hand and brought it to his lips. "I did not want to alarm you, my love." He proceeded to share with her the information Humphrey had brought him earlier.

"You . . . you think Sergeant Morton was working with Edwin when he tried to shoot you?"

"I just don't know. But he hit *you*—and I cannot risk that happening again."

She absorbed this, then said, "So you intend to send me away? Alone? Without you?"

"Without me—but only for a while. And not alone. With Luisa." Still holding her hand, Jake absently stroked her fingers with his thumb.

"I think you had better begin at the beginning," she said, sounding like a schoolmarm.

"Very well. I've written my brother. He will meet you—"

"You're sending me to *England*? Without you?" The trace of fear in her voice had turned to panic.

"Hear me out, Rachel. Please. If you stay here, you may be in constant danger. I have worried about you these last weeks—ever since Humphrey told me. So far we have been able to protect you."

"Captain Hastings was not there by chance, was he?"

"No, my dear, he wasn't."

"You should have told me," she said stubbornly.

"Perhaps I should have." But he did not really believe this. "However, that is beside the point."

"The point being—?"

"The point being that with us in the field, you will be vulnerable, especially as you will not be able to have the cover of working with MacLachlan."

"Henry—" She was grasping at straws.

"Is a fine man and a faithful servant. But he knows precious little of the use of weapons. And Thompkins has enough to do."

"I see." Her shoulders slumped in defeat and she winced at the pain that movement brought.

"Robert will meet you and find you a place to stay and I shall join you just as soon as I may."

"You have it all arranged? For how long have you been plotting behind my back, Major Forrester?" She was on the verge of anger now.

He clasped her hand tighter when she would have pulled away. "Planned, not 'plotted.' I have written Robert, but he's not had time to respond. However, he will not fail me. He never has."

She was quiet for a moment. "You . . . you said I was not to go alone."

"You will not go alone. Luisa will accompany you—as your maid."

"Luisa? As a *maid?*"

"Yes. Humphrey agrees it is a good idea, and she is willing to go with you. You see, we have not been able to arrange their marriage."

"If he were an officer, those generals would agree, I should think." She was temporarily diverted from her own problem.

"Right." In that one word, Jake displayed his own exasperation with the autocratic bureaucracy that was part of any military organization. "The army makes no allowance for a man's age and maturity—just his rank."

"That is so unfair."

"Yes, it is. But if Luisa is in England when Humphrey returns home—well, he may marry whenever and whomever he pleases on English soil."

"And she goes there as my *maid?*"

He could tell she was being won over. "Maid. Companion. Nurse. She will accompany an injured British citizen, and she will have proper documentation—Robert will see to that, too."

Rachel turned her hand so as to give his a gentle squeeze. "Your Robert sounds a marvelous fellow."

"He is. But it helps that he is a marquis, too." He rose and nudged her to her feet. He gently put his arms around her to hold her as close as her injury would allow. "You will go then?"

"Do I have a choice?"

He pulled back and put a finger under her chin to hold her gaze. "Yes, Rachel. You have a choice. With me, you shall always have a choice. I want you to do this, but if you refuse, I will do what I can to see that no harm comes to you."

"You drive a hard bargain, my lord." They both recognized this as an echo of something he had once said to her. They smiled at each other and kissed. It was a sweet-sad kiss, a foreboding of the parting to come.

"Will you do it? he asked.

"Yes."

Near the end of January, Rachel found herself on board a three-masted ship bound for England. She and Luisa, tears in their eyes, stood on the deck of the ship despite the cold, looking toward the dock where they had said good-bye to Jake and Humphrey. Both of them simply stood there until the dock was but a pinprick on the horizon. The *HMS Mary Eliza* had brought supplies and replacements to Lord Wellington's forces and was returning to Portsmouth with a cargo of English wounded and French prisoners, some of whom were also wounded.

Jake had arranged with the captain of the ship for the transportation of Mrs. Brady and her nurse-companion Miss Luisa Lopez. The captain was most accommodating in satisfying the request of the brother of the Marquis of Lounsbury. Captain Taylor had, in fact, turned over his own cabin to his two female guests. They dined with the ship's officers. The ship's surgeon, it turned out, had known MacLachlan in school and had visited his old classmate while the *Mary Eliza* was in port.

"Mac spoke very highly of you, Mrs. Brady," Mr. Johnson said at dinner the first evening.

"Did he indeed? How very nice of him."

"He told me of some rather unorthodox procedures you have used. At your convenience, madam, I should like to discuss those with you, if you would be so accommodating."

"Certainly, sir. I should be glad to talk with you."

Thus, when weather permitted, Rachel spent much of her time on deck talking medicine with the ship's doctor.

"Were your arm not in that sling, madam, I could use your expertise below deck."

Having experienced life in the lower decks during her journey to Portugal—what?—over two years before, Rachel could not but be glad for an excuse not to go there. Neither Rachel nor Luisa were very good sailors, though their bouts with mal de mer had been blessedly few.

Then, suddenly, it seemed, they and their luggage were being lowered to boats in Portsmouth, and in no time at all they were on solid English soil. The port authorities merely waved them on through. Jake's agreement with the captain had included seeing them to an inn for the night and arranging for a post chaise to convey them to London. Two and a half weeks after having said good-bye to Jake and Humphrey, the two women were deposited at the front desk of Grillon's hotel.

"Brady? Yes, ma'am. We have been expecting you." The clerk's deferential tone was explained by his next comment. "Your accommodation was arranged through the auspices of the Marquis of Lounsbury. He asked that we notify him immediately of your arrival." The clerk snapped his fingers at two uniformed young men and handed one of them a key.

Rachel and Luisa were shown into a suite of rooms, the most elegant Rachel had ever seen—and she was to stay here! The servant handed over the key and told them light refreshments would be served to them immediately and supper would be available later in the hotel dining room. He named the hour and left.

"I cannot believe this!" Rachel said. "That I should be housed in such luxury!"

"But of course," Luisa said in her prettily accented English. "My Will, he say—said—Major Forrester has very important family."

"I know, but—" Rachel made a sweeping gesture with her good arm.

" 'Tis quite nice," Luisa agreed calmly. Then Rachel remembered that Luisa had herself come from an important family in Spain. Perhaps she was used to such elegance.

When they went down to supper later, Rachel was very conscious of the dowdiness of the attire she and Luisa wore. Jake had tried to ensure that they had suitable clothing, but it was obviously hopelessly out of date. As they ate their meal in the secluded corner to which they had been shown, a waiter delivered a note to Rachel, presenting it on a silver salver.

Robert Forrester, The Most Honorable Marquis of Lounsbury, will call upon Mrs. Brady at eleven in the morning on the tenth of February, 1814.

"How very formal," Rachel said, sharing the note with Luisa.

"*Sí.* Yes. Such a one would not entertain a mere sergeant as our major has done."

Rachel recalled Jake's establishing a "patched-together family" in Badajoz and his insisting they use his Christian name. Oh, how she missed him! And she was very apprehensive about meeting his brother.

She had not wanted to come to England without Jake. However, she would have been a liability to him on the continent. He needed to be free of worry about her, and his solution to Humphrey's problem required her cooperation. Indeed, as she had come to know Luisa better, she was glad to help the older couple—and glad to have Luisa's company.

Luisa was barely of the age group into which Rachel's mother would have fit. She presented a rather plain countenance at first, but when she smiled, she was lovely. Warm brown eyes and shy dimples set her entire personality before one. Luisa's helpfulness to Rachel seemed to stem from genuine concern, not merely from her obligation to Sergeant Humphrey's benefactor. The two women had become fast friends on the voyage. Now, after a long coach ride and an eventful day in which new scenes and experiences demanded the energy of their attention, both women were exhausted and they retired early.

Promptly at eleven the next morning a knock heralded the arrival of their guest.

"Mrs. Brady? I am Lounsbury."

"How do you do, my lord? May I present my companion, Miss Luisa Lopez?"

Rachel and Robert said all that was polite, but she could tell he was sizing her up, just as she was taking his measure. He was not as tall as Jake, nor, in her opinion, as attractive. However, it was apparent the two men were brothers. Half-brothers, she reminded herself. They possessed the same shock of reddish brown hair and deep blue eyes. Jake had a darker complexion and more freckles—all that sun, she noted—but then Jake had described his brother Robert as a scholar. The marquis was dressed in what Rachel surmised must be the first stare of male fashion. He had apparently deposited an outer coat and his hat before coming upstairs.

She invited him to a seat in the sitting room. Refusing her offer of refreshments, he sat in a comfortable upholstered chair and crossed his elegantly clad legs. Rachel sat across from him, and Luisa took a chair unobtrusively at a table where she had been writing a letter earlier.

"As you undoubtedly know, Mrs. Brady, my brother has charged me with the not unpleasant task of seeing to your welfare until he returns to England."

"So he informed me."

"I have arranged for you to remove to furnished rooms in a respectable house as per his instructions. You are to receive a monthly allowance that will, I hope, maintain you and Miss Lopez adequately. I have the first month's allowance here." He reached into an inside pocket of his coat and withdrew a small packet, which he laid on the table at his elbow. "Subsequent payments will be delivered to you on the first of each month until such time as Jacob returns."

Rachel was embarrassed. She had not before felt herself a kept woman, but this talk of money brought home that fact of her life now.

"Thank you, my lord," she said quietly.

"My brother also instructed that the two of you should be dressed in more fashionable clothing than he knew to be available to you in recent months."

"He did?" Rachel was truly surprised at Jake's having thought of this matter.

Robert's smile was apparently in reaction to her surprise. It was almost Jake's smile and did much to soften his formal demeanor. "I have made arrangements with a certain Madame Celeste. I am told she has the dressing of several very elegant ladies. She has her instructions and will, of course, present her bills to me. This is her direction." He placed a card on top of the packet.

"Also," Lounsbury continued as though he were ticking items off a list, "I have engaged a couple, Mr. and Mrs. Ellison, to serve you. There are quarters in your building for them and they are already in residence. I believe they will be able to answer many of your questions about the accommodations and so on."

Rachel was overwhelmed. "I . . . you—and Major Forrester—seem to have thought of everything. I hardly know how to thank you."

"I am merely satisfying my brother's requests, madam. There is little enough I have been able to do for him over the years."

"I appreciate being the beneficiary of your sense of duty, then. I shall write Ja—Major Forrester—immediately and tell him of your courtesy."

"I shall call upon you from time to time to see how you are getting on," the marquis said.

She smiled, "Was that, too, part of his instructions?"

"But of course," he said in stiff surprise. Then he smiled that Jake-like smile again, his eyes twinkling. "However, I should have done so in any case." He rose to take his leave. "If you require anything, just send me word. My direction is on a card there." He pointed at the packet on the table.

She stood, too. "Thank you, my lord."

He took a step toward the door, then hesitated. "Uh . . . I assume you know you should not go about London unescorted? The two of you *may* go out together during the day." His glance included Luisa. "However, there are some sections of this fair city that are simply not so fair—and you'd not be safe even during the day. The Ellisons will be able to advise you—and accompany you as necessary.

"Again you seem to have thought of everything, my lord."

"I have tried to do so. Good day, ladies." He bowed to each of them and was gone.

"Good heavens!" Rachel said. "Jake told me his brother was a marvel of efficiency—but this is beyond belief."

"He performs the task of the . . . the fairy godmother," Luisa said.

"Well! Luisa, what shall we do first? Inspect our new home—or visit the mantua maker? Oh, there are *so* many things to do and see in this city!" She whirled around like a young girl in her enthusiasm.

Luisa smiled. "Our new home and the Ellisons first, then clothing, then sight-seeing."

"Yes, of course. Whatever would I do without you and Jake to organize my life?"

Twenty-one

Robert Forrester, Marquis of Lounsbury, left Grillon's hotel a very perplexed man.

"That will teach you to leap to conclusions," he muttered to himself.

The woman was not at all what he had expected—though, to tell the truth, he had little idea of what he *had* expected. For weeks—ever since Jake had written of his plan—Robert had wracked his brain for some way to discourage this affair between Jake and a married woman, for a way to protect his beloved younger brother from the clutches of some scheming female. Now, he was inclined to do all he could to help her—for Jake's sake, if not for hers.

Mrs. Brady was soft-spoken and, he was sure, a person of some culture and education. She seemed aware of her situation and uncomfortable with it. The light in her eyes when she spoke of Jake, though, was enough to make Robert envy his brother for a moment or two.

He wondered how long it would last. Jake's other relationships with women had been short-lived affairs, so far as Robert knew. This one seemed so hopeless. Well, it was none of his business.

His second mission this day—also at his brother's behest—was to obtain a report from the Bow Street Runners he had engaged to track down someone named Edwin Brady. The "Runners" worked out of a rather messy office, but they usually produced results.

Mr. Darby, the investigator with whom Robert had been

working, showed the marquis into a back room. It was bare, with only a table and three or four straight-backed chairs. Robert surmised its more customary use was to interrogate miscreants.

"I'm that sorry, my lord, but I've only a little of any substance to report to you," Darby informed him.

"Well, give me what you have," Robert said in a resigned voice.

Darby consulted a notebook. "I am conjecturing here, but it would appear that your man's name isn't Brady, but Mullens."

"Mullens?" Startled, Robert repeated the name to himself. "Mullens. Mullens. I *know* I should know that name."

"Right you should, my lord. 'Tis the name of a farmer on your Devon property—right where your brother remembered having met this Brady."

"What is the connection with the farmer?"

"Church records show a child baptized as Edwin Michael Brady Mullens in 1782. This must surely be the Edwin Brady your brother met in the Peninsula."

"So when did Edwin Mullens become Edwin Brady? And why?" Robert mused.

"This is purely a guess, sir—but I've learned to rely on hunches in this business—I'd say *Brady* might've been his mother's maiden name."

Robert slapped the heal of his hand against his forehead. "Of course. That's it!"

"What? You have something?" the Runner asked eagerly.

"We had a maid at Lounsbury named Elizabeth Brady. She left the year before that child was christened. It must be the same woman. She left to be married."

Darby flipped back a page or two in his notebook. "Yep. Mother's name was Elizabeth B. Mullens; father, Thaddeus Mullens."

"So Mullens became Brady," Robert said in an abstract voice. "I wonder if he married under a false name—or did he and his wife change their name later?"

"That we still have to find out," Darby said. "I'm hoping

military records will shed some light on it for us. Should. The military *loves* keeping records."

Robert stood. "Well, keep at it, Mr. Darby. And send me word as soon as you have anything."

"Yes, my lord. Uh . . . sir? There *is* one other interesting development."

"What?"

"Seems to be another party also looking into this Brady fellow," Darby said.

"Really? Have you any idea who? Or why?"

"The vicar who showed me the church record just said as how he'd had someone else asking about a month earlier."

"Interesting, indeed," Robert said.

Rachel and Luisa found their new living quarters to be all the marquis had suggested—and more. Their rooms were large and furnished in slightly faded, slightly outdated elegance. The Ellisons were an amiable pair who were eager to be helpful. The allowance had proved to be so very generous that Rachel promptly hired a maid to take over some of the housecleaning chores, since Mrs. Ellison also doubled as the cook. This step converted the Ellisons into her devoted slaves.

The trip to the mantua maker had offered up another instance of Forrester—or was it Lounsbury?—generosity. Rachel put her foot down and refused all but the essentials she and Luisa needed, much to Madam Celeste's disappointment.

"But the marquis, he say—"

"The marquis has no notion of our needs," Rachel said. "We shall have the day dresses and cloaks—and one gown of more elegance for each of us, but it must be of a practical design and color so as to be useful on many occasions."

"Yes, madam." Rachel overheard her say something to an assistant that sounded like, "I might as well have the dressing of a . . . a governess!"

Rachel merely smiled and reaffirmed her order. Later,

when the gowns were delivered, they were accompanied by a note from the marquis.

I have taken the liberty of following Madame Celeste's advice regarding your wardrobes. I feel certain you will find her taste for style and eye for color satisfactory and this will ensure your being adequately prepared for any eventuality.

Lounsbury

The package contained several garments besides those Rachel had ordered.

"Why, that arrogant, high-handed—" Rachel fairly sputtered. "And that . . . that woman! The very idea! Going behind my back like that!"

"You must admit, my dear, that the gowns *are* lovely," Luisa said.

"Yes, they are," Rachel agreed grudgingly. "And we are certainly prepared for any eventuality—though Lord knows what those might be! We are not likely to be presented at Court!"

"Oh, I don't think a court dress was included." Luisa was obviously trying to ease Rachel's displeasure.

Rachel laughed. "Oh, dear. I am an ungrateful wretch, am I not? Most women would be thrilled with so many new costumes."

She had to admit it felt much better to be able to go about without having people cast pitying glances at her dress. And she and Luisa *did* go about. They visited the city's landmarks—Westminster Abbey, St. Paul's, The Tower, Piccadilly. They even persuaded the Ellisons to accompany them to Vauxhall Gardens one evening. Rachel and Luisa were highly critical of the pageant depicting the Battle of Vitoria, but they all enjoyed the acrobats and animal acts.

Although the Vauxhall pageant was a gross distortion of actual events, it served to remind Rachel of precisely where Jake was and the dangers—very real dangers—he faced every day. One glance at Luisa told her that Luisa's thoughts, too, were in southern France.

The two women began every day by poring over newspaper accounts of Wellington's campaign. Each feared seeing a particular name on the casualties list, and each heaved a sigh of relief when she did *not* find what she was looking for. They learned that Wellington had bypassed Bayonne, leaving only a small force to lay siege there. A major encounter in late February at Orthez accounted for a terrifying list of casualties.

"Our fearless leader came very close to being captured," Jake wrote in a letter received in mid March. "His luck holds, however, just as it has on previous occasions, and his presence on a field *is* most encouraging to our men."

He went on to give her news of their friends. Juan asked about Rachel often and Henry grumbled about having to take over the cooking again. Clara and Nellie had most particularly asked him to send their regards. "So you see, my love, we *all* miss you dreadfully—but none as much as I do!"

Rachel had tears in her eyes as she finished.

"Will writes that they push on," Luisa said. "The French are being steadily forced back in the direction of Paris."

"I believe the *Times* reported that Soult had taken refuge in Toulouse," Rachel replied. "The article said it is a well-fortified city in the south of France, but rumored to have strong royalist sympathies."

"That cannot be good news for Bonaparte's republican forces," Luisa noted.

Rachel loved the fact that she could actually discuss these matters with Luisa—just as she had been wont to discuss them with Jake. Twenty years in a convent had certainly not meant twenty years of isolation for the former nun. Gradually, Luisa's story had unfolded. Banished to the convent by her angry—and adamant—father, young Luisa had cheerfully made the best of a bad situation.

"A nun's cell is no bad thing when the alternative is the bed of a man one finds repulsive," Luisa declared.

She had also told Rachel of the courage of the abbess who, along with their Irish priest, had actively aided the anti-French partisans. "Very brave—and very loyal, she was," Luisa said sadly. Luisa herself had carried messages on several occasions.

"I should say you were rather brave also," Rachel said.

"Oh, no. The nun's habit was like armor—no one suspects a—how you say?—meek—sister of such activity."

Rachel smiled and patted her hand. "I still say you were very brave."

Time weighed heavily on Rachel's hands. She tried to keep busy, but the sight-seeing excursions began to pall after a while. Having discovered Hatchard's book shop on one of their outings, she read several books. She took up embroidery, but found it rather pointless. She urged long walks on Luisa until that agreeable soul protested. She lived for the post, which was erratic and interminably slow from France.

Robert had visited, as he had promised. Apparently recognizing their isolation and loneliness, he suggested the two women might like to go to the theater one evening. Rachel was delighted with this idea. She had enjoyed the performances of the few traveling theater groups she had seen in those early years with Brady.

The marquis sent his carriage for them and arranged for them to be escorted by a certain Mr. and Mrs. Larson, a middle-aged couple who turned out to be amiable companions. Learning that Mr. Larson was the marquis's solicitor, Rachel conjectured to herself that the excursion was in the nature of an employee's duty for the lawyer, but it was a welcome outing for the wife, who was thrilled with their special treatment.

"How very kind of Lord Lounsbury to lend us his box," Mrs. Larson said as they took their seats in the magnificent Drury Lane theater.

"Yes, it is, indeed," Rachel agreed politely. She was overawed by the grandeur of the auditorium and by the elegant dress of many of the patrons. She did not want to appear too much the country bumpkin, but she could not resist trying to drink in every detail of her surroundings.

The play itself was a delightful bit of forgettable froth, a comedy of manners set in the last century. However, Rachel—and Luisa, too—was most appreciative of the diversion. They talked of their enjoyment on the way home and for much of the next day.

And then the loneliness and boredom set in again. One morning, a small item in the paper triggered an idea.

"Listen to this, Luisa. According to this article, there is a hospital for soldiers and veterans right here in the city."

"Is that so?" her companion asked absently.

"Would you be interested in volunteering to help there?"

"Oh, my dear. I am not at all sure that is something most women do in this city."

"We are not 'most women,' " Rachel replied.

"No, we are not, are we? Well, I have done it before—in Vitoria. I should not mind doing so again," the always cooperative Luisa said.

The two presented themselves to the hospital's chief administrator, a tall, thin, harried-looking man named Jonathan Fitzsimon.

Looking up from his messy desk as an orderly showed the two women in, Fitzsimon shoved a lock of bushy white hair off his forehead. "Yes? What is it?"

"Sir, this is Mrs. Brady and Miss Lopez. They would like to speak with you." The orderly left immediately.

Fitzsimon stood, but did not come from behind his desk. "Can I do something for you ladies?"

"Actually," Rachel said, "we thought we might do something for you, sir."

Fitzsimon looked them over keenly. He seemed to take in their fashionable dress and then sounded doubtful as he said, "And what might that be?"

Rachel explained that she had just come from the Peninsula, where her husband had been with the British forces, and that Miss Lopez had accompanied her back to England.

"We both have had some experience in working with wounded," she finished.

He heard her out in silence and then rubbed his hand across his chin in a gesture that reminded Rachel of Mac. "Hmm. I don't know. We've very few women in this facility. The patients can be a rough lot, as you might expect."

"We have no illusions about ordinary British soldiers, sir—nor any prejudices, either," Rachel said.

"Well, you might be of some help with the officers and thus relieve my people for other duties. You know, read to them, write letters, maybe."

Rachel carefully masked her annoyance at his condescension. "Yes, we could certainly do that, *too,* but I think you will find us quite capable of other duties as well."

He looked at her, his skepticism plain. "We shall see. You may come in two afternoons a week if you wish. Now, if you will excuse me . . ."

Rachel and Luisa hastily took their leave, congratulating themselves that at least he had not flatly refused their offer. They did begin working in the officers' wards, but soon they were lending their services with others as well.

Rachel was surprised and pleased to find several patients who remembered her from Ciudad Rodrigo, Badajoz, and other encounters. In a matter of days, word apparently filtered out to the doctors and Fitzsimon that Mrs. Brady was a force to be reckoned with.

One afternoon at the end of March, Rachel and Luisa were sitting in their drawing room when Ellison announced a visitor.

"A Mr. Carstairs, madam," he said, presenting her the man's calling card, which proclaimed him to be a solicitor.

"Show him in, please," she said, puzzled.

Carstairs was a rather portly gentleman of some years. He was dressed in conservative dark clothing and carried a portfolio. He looked from Rachel to Luisa, then back to Rachel. "Mrs. Brady?"

Rachel stood, extended her hand, and invited him to sit in a round chair near her own.

"Mrs. Brady, I represent the Duke of Aylesworth."

"Aylesworth?" she asked in surprise, then smiled as she recalled a ridiculous conversation with Jake in which that name had come up.

"Yes, madam." He glanced at Luisa. "Perhaps you would prefer to hear what I have to say in private."

Luisa took this none-too-subtle hint and gathered up her embroidery. "I shall just be in the next room." She closed the door softly behind her.

Rachel gave her visitor an inquiring look. Carstairs opened his portfolio and shuffled through some papers.

"I have encountered some difficulty in finding you, madam. Ah. Here it is." He read from a paper he held in his hand. "You are Rachel Alison Cameron Brady?"

"Yes . . ."

"Your father was Duncan Alexander Cameron?"

"Yes." Her curiosity was growing by leaps and bounds.

"Your mother was Margaret Mary Alicia Hendon?"

"Yes. Sir, I must ask you—what is this all about?"

The lawyer gave her a shrewd look. "Are you unaware that Margaret Hendon was the daughter of the late Duke of Aylesworth?"

"Wha-at?" She felt herself staring in utter surprise. "No. There must be some mistake."

Carstairs consulted his sheaf of papers again. "Margaret Hendon married Duncan Cameron in Edinburgh in 1787. She bore a son in 1788 who was christened James Alexander Cameron, but who unfortunately died that same year. In 1791 she bore a daughter christened Rachel Alison Cameron." He glanced up from his reading. "You, I believe." He went on. "In 1798, Margaret Hendon Cameron died in childbirth. The child also expired. In 1804, Duncan Cameron was carried off in an influenza epidemic and his daughter sent to live with his stepsister, a Mrs. Brockton. In 1808, that daughter contracted a marriage with one calling himself Edwin Michael Brady." He paused and looked up again. "This *is* correct, is it not?"

Rachel was in shock. The lawyer's dry litany of the facts of her life startled her. But, of course, the most amazing fact was her mother's identity. Her mother the daughter of a peer? Impossible! But there it was. And all the rest of the man's information was correct.

"Yes," she said, her voice sounding rather hollow. "It is correct, but—"

The lawyer smiled a mirthless, professional smile. "I think there has been no mistake, then, madam."

"I . . . this comes as such a surprise to me," she said, unable to organize her thoughts. "W-why have you—I do not understand—"

Carstairs returned his sheaf of papers to the portfolio. "My job was to find you, madam. I have successfully performed that task. The Duke of Aylesworth—your uncle—will undoubtedly wish to call upon you soon." He rose. "Good day, madam."

Still reeling from this information, Rachel could barely rouse herself to show him out politely.

"Luisa!" Rachel squeaked when she was sure the door had closed firmly on Mr. Carstairs.

Luisa hurried in from the adjoining room. "What is it? Did that man have bad news?"

"No. Oh, no." Rachel gave an almost hysterical laugh. "You will not believe this. Lord, I hardly believe it myself!" She proceeded to relate the information to Luisa.

Luisa clasped her hands. "That is good news—no?"

Rachel thought for a moment. "I hope so." She was more sobered now. She really had no idea *what* this news could mean to her. She spent the rest of the day and evening wondering about it, but finally resigned herself to a wait-and-see attitude.

The next day, just as Carstairs had promised, the Duke of Aylesworth called. He was accompanied by his wife. Ellison admitted the couple immediately, as Rachel had instructed, and Luisa again politely excused herself.

Rachel was nervous about entertaining such exalted company. The Duke and Duchess of Aylesworth were a handsome couple in their midthirties. Of medium height, he had a rather stocky but athletic build. His wife was probably as tall as her husband, but, because she was very slender, she appeared taller than her spouse. Both had brown hair, though his was darker than hers.

After initial greetings, the duchess gave Rachel an appraising look and said, "My goodness, Charles, she looks exactly like your mother! She might have posed for that portrait in the east drawing room."

"Quite right, m'dear," he said as all three seated themselves. There was a small, uncomfortable silence. Then the duke cleared his throat and opened the topic uppermost in all their minds. "Well, now, we seem to find ourselves in a most unusual situation."

"Indeed, your grace," Rachel murmured.

"I suppose we should begin by exchanging histories, so to speak. To that end, let me first say that the duchess and I are delighted to have found you."

Rachel was warmed by this opening, but she wondered just how delighted he might be when he had a full accounting of her history.

"I must admit, your grace, that Mr. Carstairs dealt me a prodigious surprise yesterday when he informed me of my mother's lineage."

"So," the duchess offered, "we have the advantage of you, dear, for we've known of you for nearly a year now—and we are *so very* glad to make your acquaintance at last."

Her husband took up the tale. "Your mother was some ten or eleven years older than I. In the way of siblings who have such a span of years between them, we were not very close. I was away at school when she and Cameron eloped. When I finally came home on holiday, my father was still furious. He had, of course, disowned her and forbade any mention of her in his presence ever again."

"Oh, my—" Rachel murmured.

"Yes. He could be a very hard man when he was crossed," the duchess said. "And I gather Lady Margaret crossed him severely when she refused *his* choice of husband and ran away with her own."

At least she spared herself being sent off to a convent, Rachel mused, for her mother's story had put her in mind of Luisa's.

The duke continued. "Some years later—I'm not even sure how—I learned of Margaret's death, but I did not know until my father lay dying that she had had a child."

"It was one of those deathbed confessions," his wife said. "In the end, he wanted absolution for his sin against his daughter, but as any restitution to her was impossible, it must be made to her daughter."

Rachel looked from one to the other of her guests. "Sin? Restitution? I am afraid you have me thoroughly confused, your grace."

"My father's last cognitive act," the duke said, "was to tell me of Margaret's child—and of the inheritance my sister should have had."

"How did he know of . . . of my existence?" Rachel asked.

The duchess answered. "Your father wrote him. Apparently, Lady Margaret had a touch of her father's stubborn willfulness. She refused to write him, but Dr. Cameron wrote a very short, very formal note at the time of your birth." She smiled. "Did you know your name—Rachel— came from your maternal grandmother?"

"No. Did it?"

"Oh! We shall such fun teaching you about your family!" the duchess declared.

Her husband gave a refined snort. "She may want nothing to do with us when she hears the whole of it."

"On the contrary, your grace. I have always longed for family." She could not hide the depth of feeling that showed itself with this statement. She saw the duke exchange an understanding look with his wife.

"Well, my dear," the duchess said, "you may find you should take care what you wish for before you are through. Our children alone—we have four of them—are quite daunting. And there are cousins in abundance. You are likely to be overwhelmed by family!"

The duke cleared his throat again. "You are getting ahead of things, love."

"Yes, dear," his duchess said in a parody of wifely duty, and Rachel immediately felt herself relax in their company.

"There is a legacy that is yours," the duke said bluntly to Rachel.

She responded dumbly. "A legacy?"

"It was part of the settlement when my mother and father married, and on her death in '94 it should have gone to Margaret and then to Margaret's daughter. My father prevented that turn of events."

"Did I not say he was a hard man?" the duchess put in.

Rachel was trying to absorb all this information when Ellison entered with a tray bearing refreshments. Lord! How different her life might have been! She noted absently that Mrs. Ellison had outdone herself and she must remember to thank her. She busied herself with the tray as the conversation came to a temporary halt.

When they each had sat back with their plates and cups, the duke continued. "When he was dying, Father insisted I find you and restore what was rightfully your mother's to start with."

"Charles would have done that anyway," the duchess interjected with a note of pride.

"We shall sort out the legalities later," the duke went on. "Right now, we want to welcome you to our—your—family, but in order to do that, there is a very important matter we must discuss. It touches on your marriage."

His voice had taken on a very grave note and Rachel felt fear clutch at her. So close. She had come so close to having a family to cling to.

"You . . . you know about the sale," she said dully.

"Sale?" He was clearly mystified, but he was not to be

deterred from his line of thought. "No, I know nothing of any sale. But I may know more of your marriage than even you do."

Rachel silently looked at the duchess, who gave her a look of profound sympathy.

"In trying to find you, we of course started with your father's medical practice, which led us to the Brocktons, and then to Brady—unsavory folk, all of them."

Rachel smiled weakly at this pronouncement. It was, after all, an accurate assessment.

The duke held her gaze steadily. "I am assuming that when you married Brady, you had no idea he was already married."

Twenty-two

Rachel felt her body go cold. She knew the color must have drained from her face, and she gulped for breath.

The duchess rose from her chair to sit beside the younger woman on the settee and put her arm around Rachel's shoulder. "Oh, Charles! You might have been more diplomatic in dropping that bit on her." She took the rattling teacup and saucer from Rachel's hand. "There, there, dear. Put your head down and breathe deeply. That's it. Really, Charles!"

"My apologies to both of you," the duke said, "but I had to know if Margaret's daughter had, indeed, been a party to such a heinous deed."

His wife sounded indignant. "Well, now you know."

"He . . . he . . . was already . . . already married?" Rachel gasped out the words.

"Yes, my dear." The duke's tone was much kinder now. "He had married a woman in East Anglia."

"Then *my* marriage was . . . was—"

"Not valid. He had married Anna Dempsey some years before. They have two children, as well."

"Children? He has children, too?"

"Yes. I believe the report said there is one of eight years and another of four, perhaps five years."

"Four or five? Oh, my heavens!" A quick mental calculation told her the ugly truth—that child had been conceived and born after her own supposed marriage.

"I am sorry, Rachel. We *may* call you Rachel, may we

not?" the duke asked as his wife hugged his niece even tighter.

Rachel nodded mutely, and he went on. "This information came to us, as I said, in tracing you through the various postings Brady has had."

"A wife. He had a wife. And . . . children. And he never said—oh, Edwin! How could you? Even you—?" Rachel ended on a wail.

"Charles, get her a drink of water—or brandy," his wife ordered the duke.

"In . . . in the sideboard," Rachel said, pointing.

Soon the duke put a glass in her hand and she dutifully sipped at the brandy.

Finally she said through her anguish, "I just find this all so very, very hard to understand. I had come to realize that Edwin was a weak man, but this—this borders on . . . on *evil.*" She stifled a sob, then added bitterly, "Why, I was not even his to sell!"

"Sell?" The duchess sounded puzzled.

"You mentioned a sale earlier," the duke prompted.

Rachel took another small sip of the brandy and set the glass aside. She had to tell them, though it would surely mean they would reject her. Slowly, hesitantly, she laid the whole sordid tale of her marriage before them.

As she related the details of the sale, she saw growing horror in the duchess's expression and growing anger in the duke's.

"Why, that . . . that is simply barbaric!" the duchess exclaimed.

"Forrester?" the duke asked. "So that is how you came to the attention of Lounsbury. I must admit that connection has puzzled us."

"Yes. Ja—Major Forrester asked his brother to see to our care."

"Our care?" the duchess prompted.

"Mine and Luisa's." She told them briefly of Luisa and Sergeant Humphrey.

"Well," the duke said, his tone decisive, "they need

trouble themselves no longer. Your *family* will see to your welfare—and that of your companion."

Rachel was embarrassed, but felt they simply had to understand the whole of it before making such a commitment. "I think you should know that Major Forrester and I . . . that is, we . . ." She could not say it.

The duchess finished for her. "Major Forrester took advantage of your plight?" she asked in a shocked tone.

Rachel felt her face growing very warm indeed. "No. No, he did not. That is . . ."

"Hmm. I . . . uh . . . see."

There was an embarrassed silence for several moments.

"So, you see, your grace, the situation is rather complicated. Many in the Peninsula know of our . . . uh . . . circumstances—and of that infamous sale. I think there is not much talk about it now, but should my name become linked with yours—well, it could become quite an *on dit*."

The duke smiled indulgently at Rachel and exchanged an amused glance with his wife. "I fear you underestimate the power of a duke, my dear. And perhaps you are unaware that the Duchess of Aylesworth is one of the *ton's* leading hostesses. I daresay anyone she favors will be acceptable to the other social lionesses."

"If they wish to remain on my guest list," the duchess added.

"There. You see?" he said.

"You are both most generous to me, your grace, but really, I—"

He held up a hand to stop her. "No. I spoke too hastily before. There is no need for the family to support you financially. You have the wherewithal to support yourself. The Patterson legacy was quite generous to start with, and it has grown through some prudent investments. You are a woman of independent means."

"However," his wife said, "the family will certainly support you socially. We came here today with the express purpose of offering you our hospitality for as long as you would care to avail yourself of it. You and your companion."

"This is all quite overwhelming to me," Rachel said. "I simply need some time to think it through."

"Of course, dear. Take all the time you need." The duchess patted Rachel's hand and suggested to her husband that their mission this day had been accomplished.

The duke rose. "I shall call for you tomorrow, Rachel—if that will be convenient for you? We shall sort out things with the solicitor to give you control of your affairs, and I shall introduce you to your banker."

"Th-thank you."

They set the time, and then the duke and his wife were gone.

Rachel sat benumbed. The good fortune of her inheritance was offset by the knowledge of her husband's perfidy. No. Not her *husband.* Never her husband. She felt dirty, soiled. Had the Brocktons known? Probably not, but she wondered how much difference it would have made to her aunt if she *had* known.

She recalled acutely the pain and sense of loss at her two miscarriages. No wonder Edwin had been indifferent to her pregnancies. *He* had children already. She had grieved mightily over those losses! But now at least there were no children of hers to bear the stain of bastardy.

"I heard the carriage drive away," Luisa said, poking her head around the door. "Oh, my dear, are you quite all right?"

"Yes. No. No, I am not." She dissolved into tears.

Luisa sat beside her and held her as she sobbed out her grief and rage. Finally, she fished around for her handkerchief, dried her eyes, and wiped her nose.

"They did not reject you, did they?" Luisa seemed prepared to be indignant on Rachel's behalf.

"No. Nothing like that. In fact, they are most gracious and most generous." She proceeded to tell Luisa the whole story. Luisa murmured an occasional exclamation in Spanish, but otherwise listened without interruption.

Simply talking about it helped Rachel grasp what had happened, and she began to see some of her options. The fact was she *had* options now. Just knowing *she* would be in control of her own life gave her a heady feeling.

The next day she found her options were impressive, to say the least. Aylesworth had described the legacy as a modest amount, but to Rachel it was a stupendous fortune.

"I think you would be wise, my dear, to leave your affairs largely in the hands of the men who have done so well for you up to now," the duke suggested.

"Yes, I agree," she said. "At least until I have a better understanding of such matters myself."

As he handed her from the carriage back at her own door, he said, "I nearly forgot. The duchess would have my hide." He handed her a note and then followed her in to wait for her reply.

The duchess was inviting her and Luisa to a small dinner party the next evening. There would be about thirty people present. Rachel was grateful the duchess had included Luisa for this, Rachel's first sortie into society. At least she would have an ally.

Rachel quickly penned her acceptance and handed it to the duke. "I see your wife wastes little time when she sets her mind to something, your grace."

He smiled. "She *can* be excessively determined."

And, indeed, this proved to be the case. Only later did Rachel realize with what care the Duchess of Aylesworth must have chosen her guest list to launch her husband's niece into society. Several factions were represented among both the women and the men. Among the latter were three or four members of Parliament, including the Marquis of Lounsbury, who was accompanied by his wife and his stepmother, the Dowager Marchioness of Lounsbury. Jake's mother was a handsome woman of perhaps fifty.

Rachel had spoken with the marquis earlier in the day, having sent him a note asking him to call. He had done so promptly. She informed him of the turn her life had taken, including the truth about her marriage, though she did not dwell on that.

"So, you see, my lord, you need have no further obligation to me, though I am most sincerely grateful you were here at the beginning."

"How fortunate this turn is for you," Robert said. "I am sure Jake will be pleased for you, too."

"I *have* written him. The letter was posted this morning, but of course there is no guarantee he will even receive it."

"Mail to and from the Peninsula has never been very reliable."

"At your convenience, my lord, I should like an accounting of the expenditures you have had on my behalf. Now that I am well able to pay them myself, I should prefer to do so."

"As you wish, madam."

She smiled. "Including, if you please, a full accounting from Madame Celeste."

He looked a bit sheepish, but returned her smile. "I should probably pay that one myself—as an object lesson, if nothing else."

"No. No. I insist. As it turns out, you were absolutely right."

Now, here was the marquis at the Aylesworth party, introducing Rachel to the women in his family—in Jake's family—just as though she were worthy of meeting them.

Well, you ninny. What did you expect? she asked herself. He could hardly announce to them, "Oh, by the way, do say hello to Jake's mistress"—now, could he?

However, when neither of the Lounsbury women accorded her extraordinary attention, Rachel concluded Robert had not shared her story with them. In introducing her, Robert announced, "Mrs. Brady knew Jacob in the Peninsula." He gave Rachel a look that seemed to tell her she could elaborate on that as much or as little as she pleased.

The Duke and Duchess of Aylesworth had earlier consulted Rachel about her name and the three of them agreed she should continue to be called "Mrs. Brady." They dropped hints that she was the *widow* of a Peninsula casualty, though none of them actually lied. They merely indicated that Mrs. Brady had lost her husband in the Peninsula—which was certainly true enough.

Rachel's interest had been piqued when she learned the given name of the current Marchioness of Lounsbury. "Celia" was the name Jake had called in his delirium—what?—a lifetime ago. Lady Lounsbury was a lovely woman. Tall, blonde, and self-assured, she commanded the attention of every man in the room and most of the women as well.

"So you knew our Jacob, did you?" she asked Rachel when the ladies had returned to the drawing room, leaving the men to their port. "I suppose he was breaking Spanish women's hearts just as he did English women's before."

"Celia!" the dowager admonished. "You know very well my son did no such thing."

"Well, you must own, Mama dearest, that he was much sought after when he came home from India—before he left for the Peninsula."

"A presentable young man of good family and comfortable fortune—of course he was!"

Celia shrugged prettily and said to Rachel, "I hope he was well when you saw him last?"

"Yes, he was." Rachel was afraid to reveal more than Jake might want known. She was glad when the Duchess of Aylesworth came to her rescue and changed the subject.

When all the other guests had departed, leaving only Rachel and Luisa, the Aylesworth couple invited them into the library. The duke served the ladies a refreshing mint-flavored nightcap, then poured himself one.

"Well! I think that went very well." The duchess had a note of triumph in her voice.

"I had a lovely time," Rachel said politely.

"As did I," Luisa echoed.

"I think the general here had something more in mind than mere entertainment." Aylesworth gestured toward his wife.

"*And* I achieved it," the duchess said proudly. "Tomorrow it will be all over town that Aylesworth's niece is a prettily behaved lady. Mind you, it will probably be a discreet carrying of the tale, but it *will* get around."

"Oh, dear." Rachel worried about such a turn.

The duchess waved aside Rachel's misgivings and said, "Tomorrow you will find yourself besieged with invitations."

"But—but I have no desire to go into society." Rachel glanced at Luisa and went on, "I have discussed our status at length with Luisa and we agree we would prefer to stay where we are until Sergeant Humphrey returns and they can be married. After that . . ." She shrugged.

"Hmm." The duchess appeared thoughtful, then exchanged a look with her husband. "Well, with Luisa as a companion, I think there will be little of interest in a *widow's* setting up her own residence. When Miss Lopez marries, perhaps you will consider coming to us."

"Yes, your grace."

"Now *that* is another thing, Rachel." The duchess had assumed a stern tone. "You are family. You simply must stop 'your gracing' us at every turn. 'Aunt' and 'Uncle' are a bit off-putting, too. After all, we are not so *very* much your seniors. So—why don't you just call us Charles and Libby; at least within the family? My name is really Olivia, but I have never been called anything but Libby in family."

"Thank you, your g—Libby."

Later, Rachel lay in bed, too keyed up to sleep, considering the whirlwind events of the last few days. She still found it difficult to accept Edwin's deplorable acts. She could not shake the feeling of having been sorely abused, of having the taint of something dirty, something sordid about her. Well, she *had* been sorely used, and it *was* a sordid business—but it was not of her making! So why should *she* feel so much shame and even *guilt?*

In truth, the shame and guilt, ill founded as they were, were rapidly dissolving into anger—anger for which there was no vent. She pounded her pillow in frustration. It was unlikely she would ever see Edwin Brady again. And besides, what would be the use? What good would it do her to see him incarcerated? She wondered if his wife—his *real* wife—knew about all this. Surely not. . . .

She forced herself to move to more pleasant thoughts. She was intensely grateful to a grandmother she had never known. The previous Duchess of Aylesworth had given Rachel an incalculable gift—freedom. Freedom from the constraints of poverty. That freedom brought with it freedom from the constraints of society, to a large degree. She need never again bend her will to another's. This was heady stuff, indeed, for one whose freedom had been curtailed since she was a child.

She was also grateful, though, to Jake and Lord Lounsbury and the Duke of Aylesworth, all three of whom were men of honor and integrity. Most of all was she grateful to Jake. However, it was not gratitude that had finally led her to invite Jake into her bed.

No. It was sheer lust, some inner voice argued.

Not only, another countered. *There was more to it than lust alone.*

Perhaps . . . but was it love?

No! She was not ready to entertain that idea. Love was far too painful.

In early April the newspapers trumpeted news of Napoleon's abdication. The emperor was gone, exiled to the island of Elba. The Bourbon King Louis was restored to the French throne. Hard on the heels of this news came word of the Battle of Toulouse, the last battle of the war in the Peninsula.

Rachel read the account of the battle with a feeling of utter horror. "Oh, Luisa! Napoleon abdicated on the sixth of April. This battle occurred on the tenth! *It need never have happened!*"

"Lord Wellington surely did not know that," Luisa said.

"No, of course not."

Once again they combed the extensive casualty lists, fearing to see two names in particular.

Rachel ran her finger down the list, stopping midway.

She looked up and smiled. "Neither a Forrester nor a Humphrey listed!"

"Thank heaven!"

Rachel continued down the list. "Oh, no. No!" she wailed.

"What? Who?"

Rachel read, "Paxton, Sergeant Joseph."

"Dead? Or wounded?"

"D-dead. Oh, poor, poor Clara." Rachel continued down the list. "Oh, no! Travers, too."

"The lieutenant?" Luisa asked.

Rachel spoke through her tears. "Yes. Why? Why? They made it all that way! Such fine, good men, too."

"Death has no sense of honor." Luisa's voice was infinitely sad.

"I must write Travers' mother," Rachel said. "And Clara. Oh, Luisa, what can I possibly say to Clara?"

Three weeks later she heard the door knocker sound one early afternoon, and then Ellison's footsteps going to answer the summons. There was some commotion, then Jake burst through the drawing room door, followed closely by Sergeant Humphrey. Neither man paid the slightest attention to polite decorum in sweeping his woman into his arms and kissing her soundly.

Jake had gone first to Lounsbury House to find the exact location of the rooms Robert had found for Rachel. He had been detained far longer than he wished. The butler, Jeffers, had been beside himself in welcoming Lord Jacob. Jake had indulged the old man, who had known both Forrester lads in short coats. Humphrey was shown to a small waiting room off the foyer and given refreshments as Robert ushered his brother into the library.

"Just tell me where she is," Jake said impatiently once he had greeted the brother he had not seen in nearly five years.

Robert grinned at him. "That bad, is it?" When Jake

merely glared at him, Robert went on, "There are some things you should know."

Jake frowned. "Rachel wrote me about her volunteering at the hospital."

Robert waved a hand to dismiss this. "Did you not get her letter about Aylesworth, then?"

"Aylesworth? What has he—you don't mean to say there *is* a connection there!"

"That there is. You'd best stop your pacing a hole in the carpet and sit down while I tell you all." Jake sat, and Robert related the tale as Rachel had told him. "Aylesworth confirmed the relationship and her inheritance when I saw him a day or two later. He said nothing of the marriage—but then, he would not do so, would he?"

"That bastard Brady! That dirty, rotten, son-of-a-bitch! To subject a woman like Rachel to such ill treatment. If he is not dead already, I swear I'll track him down and kill him."

"Careful. You'd be committing fratricide," Robert said calmly.

"What—? What did you say?"

"Fratricide. You know—killing one's brother. By all indications, that blackguard is our brother."

"Is this some sort of twisted joke?"

"If it is, 'tis the gods who are laughing. I've had a Runner working on your 'Brady' ever since you said you recognized him in Badajoz. The Runner, too, came up with Brady's marriage to a woman in East Anglia, but he had the information after Rachel had already told me. Woman of honor, that one is."

Jake noted Robert's use of Rachel's name and the genuine warmth with which he spoke of her. "Go on," he prompted.

"Earlier the Runner had found a connection between Brady and Mullens. In tracing that, he came back to an upstairs maid at Lounsbury Manor. She married Mullens a mere four months before the birth of her son—a son our father ensured an extraordinarily proper education for a farmer's son. There is some evidence Father also arranged the marriage and for their removal to Devon."

"That does not mean that snake is related to *us*," Jake argued.

"When I pressed her, Mrs. Kenniston confirmed it," Robert said.

"Mrs. Kenniston? She's still alive?"

"And as alert as ever. Still not much gets beyond her. I think she's eighty-five or so now. Father pensioned her off as the Manor's housekeeper years ago. And I might add that she had a *very* generous stipend."

"Because . . . ?"

"Because she knew so much family business. Did not want to talk to me about this situation either, but she finally did. After all, the principals were mostly dead."

"Well, I'll be—. Brady knew all along. I'm sure he did."

"Very possible. Jeffers thinks he remembers a young man named Mullens visiting here once and demanding to see Father 'about a private matter.' "

"How has Rachel taken all this?" Jake asked.

"Like she was hit with a sledgehammer. But she's a plucky one, your Rachel. She's paying her own way, by the way. Even wanted an accounting of her trip to London and the stay in the hotel. Seemed a matter of pride to her."

"I'm not surprised," Jake said, smiling.

Mindful of Humphrey stoically waiting, and of his own eagerness to see Rachel, Jake had not lingered long at Lounsbury House.

Twenty-three

The two couples eventually found their way to the dining room, where the Ellisons had laid out a lavish luncheon. Rachel admired their having done so on such short notice, but she was sure they were aware of Jake's identity as the man who had, albeit indirectly, been the one who initially hired them. The meal over, neither man wanted the other's company while the ladies languished in the drawing room.

"Get your shawl, my lovely," Humphrey said to Luisa. "I'm taking you for a long walk on this fine May day."

"Be sure to take an umbrella," Rachel warned. "Our fine May days have had a tendency to dissolve into showers of an afternoon."

She was sure Humphrey had come up with this walk idea as a way of giving her and Jake some time alone together. The smiling, conspiratory look Luisa gave her told her Luisa knew this, too. As soon as the other two were out the door, Jake moved to take a seat very close to Rachel on the settee.

"I thought I would never have you to myself," he said, nibbling at her ear.

"I've missed you dreadfully, Jake." She relished the feel of her cheek against the stubble of his beard and the growing sensations generated by his lips trailing kisses down her neck.

His hand cupped her breast as he buried his face in the cleavage showing above her fashionably low neckline. His thumb caressed her nipple and she felt her whole being concentrated in the sensations he was arousing.

"Kiss me," she whispered, and he took her mouth in a fierce kiss, full of infinite yearning. She welcomed his tongue against hers in a dance as old as time, as new as now.

"Rachel?" It was an urgent plea.

"Yes, Jake. Oh, my darling, *yes!*"

She took his hand and led him into the bedroom.

A marvelous blend of familiarity and discovery marked their coming together. Knowing well the needs and preferences of the other, each strove to give the partner exactly what would please most. Long absence added the spice of rediscovering the wonder of their bodies as one.

Fully sated, Jake lay beside her holding her close. "That, my love, was fairly close to absolute perfection," he murmured.

"Um-hmm," she agreed.

He gave her a little shake. "Don't you dare go to sleep on me. We need to talk."

"Now? I really had no intention of *sleeping.*" She feathered light caresses over his body. "I thought we might come even closer to perfection with a second try."

"Yes, now. And do stop distracting me." He caught her mischievous hand in his.

"Very well." She heaved an exaggerated sigh. "So— talk."

"Robert told me everything."

"I . . . I thought he might have done so."

"No. I mean *everything.* Did you know Brady was not 'Brady' at all, but Mullens?"

"What?" She pulled away to look at him in utter surprise, fully distracted—if only temporarily—from her previous intent.

"Ah, I thought you might not know *that.*" He told her of Brady's relationship to his own family.

"Your *brother?*"

"That's what Robert tells me."

"Well, he certainly inherited little of the Forrester goodness."

He pulled her close again. "In some ways, he was probably more of a Forrester than either Robert or I."

"I don't understand."

"Our father was a self-centered man who rarely considered the feelings of others in going after whatever it was he wanted, whenever the urge struck him."

"But neither you nor Robert is like that."

"I hope not. My mother spent a great deal of time in the nursery with us. She is the only mother Robert remembers."

"I met her," Rachel said.

"You did? When?"

She told him of the Aylesworth dinner party. "Do you object to my meeting her?"

"No. Why would I?"

"I do not think it is customary for a man's mother to be introduced to his mistress."

"How about to his prospective wife?"

She lay very still. She was not surprised, for she had expected this to be his reaction on learning the truth about her marriage. His sense of honor would require him to propose again.

"Rachel?" He nuzzled her in that sensitive place just below her ear. "You are free now. We could marry tomorrow."

"Tomorrow?" she squeaked.

"Or the next day—with a special license."

She hedged. "Jake, you must not feel you are obligated to make an honest woman of me."

He rose on one elbow and put his hand against her chin to hold her gaze. "Good God, Rachel. Is that what you think? That I would feel *obliged* to marry you? Is it not enough that I *love* you?"

"Oh, Jake. Really, I am most grateful for that . . . for all that you have done for me . . ."

Releasing her, he sat up and ran his hand through his hair. His voice was soft but firm as he ground out his words slowly. "I do not want gratitude from you, Rachel."

"I'm . . . not sure I can give you what you *do* want." She struggled with her own ambivalent feelings.

"You can't love me? Is that it?" Sounding angry now, he started to pull on his trousers. He stood and looked down at her. "Then what the hell was *this* all about?"

She reached a hand toward him in a supplicating gesture, but he ignored it. He held her gaze until she was forced to look away from the pain and anger she saw in his eyes.

"Well?" he demanded.

"Please, Jake. Try to understand. It . . . it isn't that I cannot love you. It's just . . . well . . . I am not sure I want to be a wife again. Can we . . . can we not continue as we are?" She stifled tears that threatened.

Shaking his head in confusion, he sat again on the edge of the bed. "You'd rather be my mistress than my wife? For God's sake, *why?*"

She sat up, oblivious to her nakedness as the sheet slid down to her lap. "I'm not sure I can make you understand, but a . . . a mistress is more independent—has more control over her life. Don't you see, Jake? I've never, ever been *free.* In my whole life, I have never been the one to direct its course."

"You think marrying me would restrict your *freedom?*"

"It isn't *you,* Jake—it's the idea of being married."

He was silent for a long while, looking at some nothingness above her head. Finally, he brought his gaze back to meet hers. She found it difficult to read the expression there.

His voice was hard, almost toneless. "Be honest with me, Rachel. Have you met someone else?"

"Have I—? Someone *else?*" Anger quickly replaced her surprise. "For heaven's sake, Jake! How could you possibly think—? After . . . after *this?*" She gestured to the crumpled bedding. "You certainly have a fine opinion of me, haven't you?"

"Yes. So fine that I've just ask you to marry me." The bitterness in his tone belied the beauty of his words. He stood and turned away from her as he continued to get dressed.

"Can we not go on as we are, though?" she pleaded.

He was silent as he sat in a nearby chair to pull on his

boots. Finally, fully dressed now, he stood and looked down at her. "I was prepared to do just that when I thought you legally tied to one so undeserving of you. I'm not at all sure that will be enough now."

"Enough for whom?" She was becoming angry at his apparent refusal to understand her position.

"Enough for me," he snapped. "And for you, too, if you'd only think it through."

"I *have* thought it through. I've had several weeks in which to do so. I want to be in control of my life—to be independent."

"Fine. I wish you well of your independence." He turned toward the door.

"Jake! You're leaving—just like that? And just because you cannot dictate the terms of our . . . our being together?"

He paused on the threshold. His voice, calmer now, was laced with both sadness and bitterness. "I'll be back, Rachel. I won't be able to stay away. That is . . . if I will be welcomed?"

"Of course," she said, trying for equal calm. "You are the dearest friend I have ever had."

He grimaced at this, gave her a little bow, and then he was gone.

Rachel buried her head in her pillow—a pillow that still smelled pleasantly of Jake—and dissolved into tears.

As he left her building, Jake encountered Humphrey and Luisa returning from their walk. They were obviously surprised to see him out on the street so soon. Jake murmured something inane about needing to see the rest of his family.

"You have my direction at my mother's house?" he asked Humphrey.

"Yes, sir."

"Good. I shall expect you tomorrow morning and we can at least see to *your* wedding."

"Yes, sir. Thank you, sir."

As he strode away, Jake heard Luisa say, "They've quarreled."

He walked all the way to his mother's house. It was in a more fashionable neighborhood than Rachel's, but not quite so fashionable as that of Lounsbury House. However, Major Lord Jacob Forrester paid little heed to his surroundings. Hurt, confused, and very, very angry, he kept asking himself the same questions over and over. Why was she refusing him? How *could* she respond so eagerly to his lovemaking and remain indifferent to his proposal? And what *was* this nonsense about freedom and independence? He was offering her a name any other woman would be glad to have—and a way of life many would envy.

His mother's butler answered his knock. "We've been expecting you, my lord. Her ladyship is in the drawing room."

Jake took the stairs two at a time. He was determined to put the recent scene with Rachel aside for the time being.

His mother rose from a small writing table and swept him into her arms. Her voice caught as she said, "Jake, darling, I am *so* glad to have you home at last!"

"It's good to be here." He hugged her tightly and whirled her around. "How's my favorite mother?"

"Your favorite *mother?* I used to be your favorite girl. Oh, Jake—have you at last found someone to love?"

Oh, Lord, he thought. Trust his far-too-observant mother to cut right to the core immediately. "Perhaps," he said cautiously.

"But . . . how could you have done so? You've been home a few hours at best. Ah! Someone you met in the Peninsula? Is she English? Will I like her?"

He laughed and drew her to sit with him on a settee. "Yes. Someone I met in the Peninsula. She saved my life and I know I wrote you of her at the time. Yes, she is English. I don't know, but I hope you will like her. Do you? You have met her."

"I have?" She was obviously surprised.

"Rachel Brady. Aylesworth's niece."

"Mrs. Brady? The widow. Yes, I did meet her. Quiet, but

amiable. Well, if she saved your life, my son, I do, indeed, like her prodigiously."

He hugged her again at this, but said nothing.

"Jake? There's something wrong, isn't there?"

He still said nothing, trying to think how much to tell her.

"Jake?" she prompted. "Is Mrs. Brady related to this Edwin Brady—or should I say Mullens?—that Robert has been investigating?"

"He told you?"

"He asked me if I knew of a maid named Brady. Of course I knew. A thing like that cannot remain a secret long in a closed community like that around Lounsbury Manor."

"You knew the whole of it? And it didn't bother you?"

"Of *course* it bothered me, my dear. But I was so young and as it happened before my marriage was contracted, I was able to put it aside." She paused. "It was later . . . other . . . uh . . . situations . . . that I found difficult to accept." She ended on a despairing note, then she brightened. "Now—tell me about your Rachel."

And he did. He told her the whole of it—Rachel's nursing him back to health, her abuse from her "husband," the sale, Morton's attack, her taking a bullet meant for Jake, and his falling in love with her. Finally, he revealed Rachel's refusal to marry him.

Through it all, the Dowager Marchioness of Lounsbury murmured sympathetically now and then, asked several questions, and finally said, "She sounds a remarkable young woman, and I cannot but be grateful to her."

"But she has this maggot in her brain about her freedom and independence—and, frankly, Mother, I simply do not know how to fight this!"

She patted his hand. "Then don't. Don't fight it. Give her time, Jacob. Give her time—and don't crowd her. Time is on your side, for I suspect your Rachel cares for you very deeply."

"Ha! She has a strange way of showing it."

"She put herself between you and a bullet that might have killed you," his mother reminded him.

"Yes, she did, didn't she?"

"I think I understand her desire to be in charge of her own . . . well . . . her *self,* if you will."

"Well, I certainly do not!" he said vehemently.

"Of course not. You're a man. You've never *not* had control of *your* life. When your father died, I mourned him, of course. I loved him despite his . . . his peccadilloes. But then I felt guilty because I was actually *enjoying* my freedom. I had never been free to make my own independent choices. My parents had always told me what to do, when to do it, how to behave. Then I married and Lounsbury had some very rigid ideas on the role his *wife* should fulfill."

"Rachel's husband—that is, Brady—beat her, I think."

"And she was powerless against such abuse. But there are many kinds of abuse, son. She probably bears scars of a different sort, too."

He gave his mother a penetrating look of understanding. "I'm sorry, Mother. I never knew . . ."

Again she patted his hand. "You were not meant to. Besides, you were away at school all those years and then off to India at such an early age . . . but back to my point. Your Rachel needs time—time to relish her independence, and time to realize just what a treasure she has in you."

"Hmm." Jake was not convinced, but what choice had he?

His mother rose to tug on the bellpull. "Now, before I send you off to dress for dinner, tell me—who is that child who arrived on my doorstep with your man Henry this morning?"

Jake slapped the heel of his hand against his forehead. "Juan! I forgot all about him. He's all right, I hope?"

She laughed. "I think he and his dog—from which he seems positively inseparable—have created havoc in the servants' quarters, but Henry seems to have control of the situation."

"Good." He told her a very brief version of Juan's story.

"Ultimately, I shall take him to the abbey with me, but for now . . ."

"For now, he is fine where he is, poor child."

"Thank you, Mother."

To Rachel's surprise and disappointment, Jake did not call on her the next day. Humphrey did call on Luisa and the two of them busied themselves with their wedding plans. When Rachel would have excused herself to leave them to their planning, they begged her to stay.

"The major, he's off to Doctor's Commons for a special license even as we speak," Humphrey announced.

This information eased Rachel's pain at Jake's absence only slightly.

"Oh, Rachel," Luisa begged, "you will stand up with me, will you not?"

"Of course, my dear. I shall be honored to do so."

Luisa bubbled on. "Major Forrester will be Will's witness and Will says Captain Hastings will be there, too."

"Aye. And the Binghams," Humphrey said. "They're staying in town just to see me tie the knot."

Two days later, the wedding took place in a private drawing room in the same hotel, Grillon's, that Luisa and Rachel had stayed in earlier. Because a special license had been procured, Luisa and her sergeant exchanged vows late in the afternoon rather than in the morning hours. The hotel laid out a fine supper, and three musicians had been hired to provide music.

Rachel had wondered only briefly who was paying for such a lavish affair for an enlisted man and his bride. Of course it was Jake.

"You know," Luisa confided, "my Will objected. But the major, he insist. He say Will 'saved his bacon' in India and this was the least he could do. What means 'save his bacon'?"

Rachel laughed and explained the phrase. She was determined to be happy for Luisa and her Will. Hastings and the

Binghams did attend, along with Ferguson and MacLachlan. Rachel was reminded of their Christmas dinner—and saddened by those missing. When the bridal couple toasted "absent friends," she thought of the Paxtons and Travers and Corporal Collins and felt tears spring to her eyes. She looked at Jake, and he smiled his understanding.

His smile melted her nervousness. She spent the rest of the party happily talking with other guests, including Juan and Henry. Juan fairly preened in his new clothing. That he was very glad to see Rachel again was apparent in the way he hovered near her and seemed to lean into her touch if she patted his shoulder or touched his arm. Henry, too, greeted her warmly.

The usually brusque, reserved MacLachlan surprised her by giving her a hug. "I've missed you, lass. I understand you've not given up your hospital work."

"That is true," she said, "but how did you know?"

"I'll be there myself in a couple of weeks. Soon as I can get up north to the lowlands and bring my wife back. Ferguson's already on staff here."

Rachel had known that Mac was married, but she had not before really thought of him as anything but a surgeon. "I hope I will meet the woman who can handle you, Mac!"

"Oh, you will. You will, indeed. I've written her all about you, and she's anxious to meet the only woman who's ever been a serious rival!" He laughed his booming laugh.

Luisa and Will would spend their wedding night in a room above stairs and would depart early the next morning for Wiltshire, where Will would take up duties as an assistant to Jake's steward. When the bride and groom left the party, it broke up, and Rachel gladly accepted Jake's offer to see her home.

Henry and Juan were in the carriage already when Jake handed her in. She fully expected him to send them on when they arrived at her place, but he did not do so. Instead, he walked her to her door and gave her a chaste kiss on the cheek before Ellison opened the door to admit her.

"Good night, Rachel. I'll see you soon."

* * *

She did see him occasionally over the next few weeks. They often attended the same social affairs, though rarely together. He was cordial and friendly, but without the teasing familiarity that had been so much a part of their friendship. He even paid her an occasional morning call, but never stayed longer than propriety dictated, nor discussed any but mundane matters. There were no passionate kisses, nor any lovemaking.

With Luisa's marriage, the Duke and Duchess of Aylesworth had renewed their invitation for Rachel to stay at their house. When she demurred at this, they sent Libby's cousin Dorothea to stay with her, for it would not do—not at all— for a young woman to live alone, widow or no. Herself a widow, Dorothea was a rather colorless, complaisant woman. Rachel did not find her a particularly warm personality, but Dorothea was cordial and polite, so Rachel had no strong objections to her as a companion. She did miss Luisa, though.

Confused and hurt by what she saw as Jake's being standoffish, she assumed he was still angry about her refusal to marry. Now that she saw him so often, she missed their easy camaraderie even more than she had when she had first returned to England and he remained in the Peninsula. And, Lord! how she missed his kisses and his lovemaking!

If he chanced to dance with another woman at some social affair, Rachel found herself fiercely resentful of his partner. On the rare occasions when he sought *her* partnership, she steeled herself against clinging to him. Always the familiar smell of sandalwood and his mere touch would send her senses reeling. Each time, she swore that *next* time she would be able to school herself against such a reaction. She never quite managed to do so.

Her pride forbade her admitting to any but herself that she was lonely, despite an active social life and her work at the hospital. The loneliness was only partly balanced by her sense of independence. She did not want anyone else telling her what to do, but it would be nice to have someone with whom she could discuss the options. It would be nice if that someone were Jake—again.

England was beside herself in celebrating victory over the despised Napoleon Bonaparte. The pace of celebration had picked up during the last two weeks of May. In June, the island kingdom saw the arrival of the Prussian King Frederick William and the Russian Czar Alexander. In addition, the Prussian general, von Blücher, made many public appearances and was a great favorite with England's common people.

"For his prodigious drinking," Dorothea said, "as much as his role in defeating Bonaparte!"

There was also the ongoing tragical farce—or was it a farcical tragedy?—of the Prince Regent's marital problems—all played out in a very public forum. Even in the Peninsula, the Regent's subjects had heard of the royal fiasco—the Prince of Wales and his extramarital affairs overshadowed occasionally by his flamboyant estranged Princess and hers. One afternoon in late June, Rachel called upon the Duchess of Aylesworth to find the hostess's drawing room abuzz with the latest escapade.

A middle-aged matron known to be an inveterate gossip was holding forth. "I tell you, my dears, it was a sight to behold! There was our Prince on one side of the theater—resplendent in his royal box with his royal guests, accepting the accolades of his public, waving grandly to those below."

Another chimed in. "And then *she* arrived in the box opposite—for she is never invited to join him, you know."

"She?" someone asked innocently.

"Caroline, of course. Caroline of Brunswick. Future Queen of England."

"Unless Prinny can find a way to be rid of her."

Well, Rachel thought, the Princess was probably in no danger of being *sold*. Then her attention was pulled back to the story at hand.

"When she entered *her* box—directly across from his, mind you—the theater audience went mad—simply mad—

showing their support for her and, incidentally, turning their backs on him."

"That must have been quite a blow to Prinny's pride."

"Oh, it was. To be sure, it was! And *then*——oh, it was too much—just too much—the Prussian king and Russian czar *bowed* to her! Prinny could not but do the same!"

"I wish I could have seen his expression." This comment put Rachel in mind of vultures picking over a carcass.

"I felt *so* embarrassed for him," said the first speaker, whose tone lacked any semblance of sincerity.

Soon the duchess pointedly changed the subject, but the Prince's private woes continued to fascinate his public throughout the summer. The social season was prolonged this year to allow for a succession of extravagant celebrations. For the first time in a period spanning more than two decades, the nation was not at war with France. The glorious victory over Napoleon was only slightly tarnished by the fiasco in the former colonies. The fighting continued there and many seasoned veterans of the war against Napoleon were being deployed to what was now known as the United States.

"I just hope we will have no need of them on *this* side of the Atlantic any time soon," Jake said at the party following the Humphreys's wedding.

Hastings had provided a glib response. "We should not have such need—so long as Boney is confined to Elba."

"So long as . . ." Jake repeated vaguely. Then he had brightened and proposed yet another wedding toast.

Only recently Rachel had received an answer to the note she had written Clara, who had returned to live with her parents in the midlands. They were spoiling their grandson Benny rather frightfully. Clara was trying to accept Joe's death, but with little success thus far. She ended by saying "Grab your happiness while you can, dear friend. Love is far too precious to allow petty concerns to stand in your way."

In July, when Lord Wellington returned to England, the Prince spared no amount of the public's money in welcom-

ing home the conquering hero. There were parades and fire-
works and a fair was set up in Hyde Park that reduced the
grassy lawns to dusty—or muddy—splotches for months to
come. The most elegant party, though, was one which found
neither Rachel nor the Prince's wife on the guest list.

The Prince spent and spent and spent on a magnificent
dinner and ball at Carlton House, his London residence. The
guests were confined to a mere two thousand and more of
his highness's closest friends. For days, the newspapers oo-
hed and ahhed over the elegance or raged against the expense, depending on their editors' politics.

Rachel had had no illusions about her place in society
and was neither surprised nor disappointed to find her name
omitted from the Prince's guest list. Even before the Prince's
grand soiree came to her attention, she began to feel a distinct cooling of attitudes toward her. As Libby had predicted,
she received a fair number of invitations, though she was
never taken up as a favorite in society. Rachel neither sought
nor welcomed the limelight. However, she *had* enjoyed making the acquaintance of certain people in society's inner circle, and she now missed conversing with them.

With the city full of high-ranking military officers—and
their ladies—being feted at every turn, Rachel noted a dwin-
dling of invitations coming her way. Celia, Marchioness of
Lounsbury, all but gave her the cut direct at a dinner party
Rachel attended in the company of the Duke and Duchess
of Aylesworth. Rachel felt sure it *would* have been the cut
direct had Libby not been at her side.

However, the dowager marchioness—Jake's mother—deliberately sought Rachel's attention and chatted amiably with
her. She even went so far as to invite Rachel to call upon
her. Rachel found the dowager a warm and charming person.
Her own embarrassment over being—or having been—the
mistress of the woman's son, though, prevented her from
responding with anything but polite reserve.

In the Aylesworth carriage on the way home, Rachel
asked, "Was I imagining things, or was there an undercur-

rent of . . . of *something* going on this evening? I was not very comfortable."

Libby sighed. "No, my dear. You were not imagining that. The story of that infamous sale has found its way to *ton* drawing rooms."

"Oh, dear." Rachel, too, sighed. "I suppose it was inevitable someone should recognize me as 'that' Brady woman."

"Probably," the duchess agreed.

"If . . . if you'd rather I . . . that is, if you should wish to lessen your connection to me, I shall understand."

"Certainly not!" The ducal couple spoke in unison and their vehemence sent a flush of warmth into Rachel's heart.

The duchess leaned across from her seat opposite and patted Rachel's hand. "Put that thought out of your head. No. We shall go on just as we have. In fact, I may just give a ball in your honor." She laughed. "After all, you missed having a proper come-out ball."

Rachel, too, laughed at that absurdity. "Oh, please don't."

But Libby went right on with her flight of fancy until the carriage arrived at Rachel's door.

The next day any sense of comfort she had gained from Aylesworth's support came to an abrupt end.

Twenty-four

As Rachel left the hospital the next afternoon, a man rose from where he had been sitting on the steps.

"Ah, at last," he said. "Kept me waiting, you did."

"Edwin! What on earth—?"

Ellison, who had, as usual, been waiting at the entrance to escort her home, started forward at the shock in her tone.

"It's all right, Ellison. Just wait at the gate for me." She turned to Brady, noting he was dressed in worn but clean clothing such as a dockworker might wear. He was also sporting a full beard. "What do you want?"

"Now, is that any way to greet your long lost husband?"

"Husband?" she asked scornfully. "What about your wife and family in East Anglia?"

He paused for only a moment. "Ah, so you know about them, do you?"

"And that your supposed marriage to me was all a hum. How could you—how could any man do such a despicable thing? You ruined my life."

"Oh, I don't know, my pretty." He reached out to touch her, but she backed away with a shudder of disgust which was not lost on him. She saw fury flash across his countenance. He gestured at her attire. "Look at you. Playing the fine lady. You seem to have done right well for someone whose life has been ruined."

"What do you want?" she repeated.

"Just some of what you've got," he said. "As your husband, I'm entitled."

"You might be—*if* you had ever been my husband. Now, if you will excuse me . . ." She turned away.

"Not so damned fast." He grabbed her arm and held it tightly. When Ellison started forward, Brady pulled his coat back to show her a pistol. "Call off your watchdog, or he will get hurt."

"It's all right, Ellison," she said. "Just give me a moment." She looked at the roughened hand clasping her arm far too tightly. "Let go of my arm," she demanded. To her surprise, he did.

"I've been watching you for over a week," he said. "Your comings and goings. Hobnobbing with the swells and all. I figure you can afford to help out a . . . a friend . . . in need."

"Why on earth would I even think of doing so after what you did to me?"

"Maybe to keep the swells from knowing that their Mrs. Brady is no widow at all. In fact, she was never even a wife." His smile was a triumphant leer. "See? I know the story you've put about."

She tried to think, to forestall his demands. "This is brave talk for a man who could still face a firing squad as an army deserter."

"Edwin Brady died in the Peninsula. I'm Mullens now, a respectable worker on London's docks. Not many as would even recognize me now."

"Major Forrester would."

"Ah, yes. Forrester. But he's enjoying my leftovers so much, he'd probably not say anything."

"You despicable toad!"

"Ah, ah. Behave yourself, my lovely."

"How much?"

"I figure—maybe—fifty guineas to start with? You're worth fifty guineas, aren't you?" He laughed crudely.

"I—it will take me a couple of days to raise that kind of money." Although her relationship to the Duke of Aylesworth had been bruited about, she knew her inheritance was not common knowledge. With luck, Edwin would not know of it.

"I know where you live. I'll be in touch with you, my sweet."

With that, he walked off, whistling a jaunty tune and leaving her profoundly shaken. She wondered, though, if his tune was inspired by confidence or bravado.

Instantly, Ellison was at her side. "Did he harm you?"

"No. Not really." *Not physically,* she thought.

Ellison looked at her in concern. "Wait here, ma'am. I'll get a hackney cab to take us home."

Jake was alone in his mother's library when Foster, the butler, knocked on the door. For days—no, weeks—now, he had been trying to force himself to go to Trenton Abbey, his estate in Wiltshire.

The "abbey" had once been a real abbey which Henry VIII, in his fury against the Roman church, had appropriated and turned over to one of his favorites, a certain Baron Trenton. Trenton's descendants had eventually managed to lose the property back to the crown. Jake's maternal grandfather had purchased it from a monarch in need of funds to finance his colonial ventures. Once the abbey was in Jacob Nachman's hands, the old man had been determined it was to stay with *his* bloodlines, hence his stipulation to that effect in his daughter's marriage settlements. In any event, Jake had ever been grateful for his own independence from Lounsbury holdings.

This thought brought him up short. He, Jake, relished his independence. Was this not what Rachel had been talking about, too? Why a woman would need to be independent, though, when she might rely upon a husband was beyond him. Then he reminded himself of two things. He himself refused to rely on his brother and Lounsbury wealth, and Rachel's experience was with a husband who was far from reliable.

"Come in," he called, glad for an interruption to these disturbing thoughts.

"My lord, there's a man named Ellison who wishes to speak with you."

"Ellison? Oh. Ellison. Send him in." Jake stood to welcome the man who, he remembered, worked for Rachel. "What can I do for you, Ellison?"

The man seemed uncomfortable. "My lord, I am not sure I am doing the right thing. What I mean to say is, when Lord Lounsbury hired us—my wife and me—he said as how it was on your account."

"Yes, he did do that."

"And I know Mrs. Brady is paying our salaries now—and generous she is, too, but . . . well . . . something's come up, my lord, and—"

Jake was becoming alarmed. "Come on. Out with it, man. Has Mrs. Brady come to some harm?"

"No, sir. At least not yet."

"Not *yet?* Explain yourself immediately." the former army officer demanded.

"When the marquis hired me, I was to act as a sort of bodyguard for Mrs. Brady as well as butler and general handyman. He wanted me to report any suspicious-appearing folk that might seek her out. I—I assumed he was acting on your order, my lord."

"He was."

"Well, sir, earlier this afternoon was the first time it happened. I know this is not strictly your affair now that *she* pays all the bills, but . . . well . . . my wife and I are worried and . . . we thought you might like to know."

"You thought right. Sit down and tell me."

Ellison did just that, describing the incident outside the hospital and the bearded man who had accosted Rachel. Jake made him describe the man twice.

"Dark hair and blue eyes? Hmm. I wonder. Seems unlikely, but you never know."

"My lord?" Ellison asked.

"Never mind. You heard nothing of the conversation he had with her?"

"No, sir. But it looked to me like he was threatening her. He grabbed her suddenly, too, but then he let loose of her."

"He was dressed as a common laborer?"

"Yes, sir. Dockworker, I'd say."

"Thank you, Ellison. You did the right thing in coming to me. I'll see to it right away."

"Very good, my lord."

When Ellison had gone—with extra coin in his pocket—Jake called in Henry and Thompkins.

"I want you two to go down to the docks," he told them. "Nose around the taverns there and see what you come up with." He described the man as Ellison had described him. "I've a hunch this may be Brady, and since you two might recognize him, beard and all . . ."

"Yes, my lord," they said at once.

He handed Henry a bag of coins. "Here. This might help to loosen a few tongues. Mind you," Jake warned, "you are *not* to accost him. Just find him, and I'll take it from there."

Nearly two hours later—far too early for him to hear yet from Henry and Thompkins—Foster discreetly broke in on a conversation between Jake and his mother.

The butler handed Jake a note. "That man, Ellison, just delivered this, my lord."

Jake recognized Rachel's script immediately. The note was brief.

Jake,
   May I see you at your earliest convenience, please?
                                                       R.

"Excuse me, Mother, this is something I must see to."

"Shall I set dinner back?"

"No. I may not be here."

Ellison was still in the foyer, waiting to carry Jake's reply.

"Did you tell Mrs. Brady of your visit to me?" Jake asked him.

"No, my lord. Should I have done so?"

"No. No need at all." Jake was inordinately pleased that Rachel was apparently turning to him in a crisis.

Rachel had fretted most of the afternoon about what she should do. She knew she could not succumb to Edwin's demand. If one paid such extortion, it would go on and on. Once again, she wondered how on earth she had ever found such a man attractive. But, of course, she had not seen this side of him before the marriage, had she?

Should she inform the Duke of Aylesworth? No, it was not really his problem. Nor was it truly the Forresters' problem. Yet she knew she could not deal with it alone, and Edwin did have ties of a sort to the Forrester brothers. So she sent the note around to Jake. Jake, who had come to her rescue before.

He arrived within minutes of her sending the note.

"Oh! I hadn't expected you quite so soon," she said, flustered.

"I assumed it was an urgent matter," he said.

"It may be. Edwin is back in England."

"Is he now?"

She gave him an account of the meeting, ending with, "He wants money from me. Jake, he *laughed* when he named a sum of fifty guineas! He laughed." She could not hide the pain of this revelation.

Jake quickly closed the distance between them and enfolded her in his arms. "Never mind, love. I'll take care of it. I'll take care of you."

"I . . . I didn't want to trouble you, but . . ."

"I know. Ellison came to me earlier. He and his wife were worried about you. From what he told me, I suspected it was Brady who had accosted you."

"Ellison went to you?" She did not know quite how she felt about this.

"Don't be angry with him. He was worried. And properly, so, I believe."

"Well . . ." She sounded dubious.

"I've sent Henry and Thompkins to the docks to find Brady."

"They won't—?"

"Hurt him? No. They are merely to locate him. *I* may strangle the blackguard later, but they won't."

"I—I do not want to be responsible for his being arrested and . . . perhaps going before a firing squad. Isn't that what happens to deserters?" she asked.

"Usually, but I promise I will do what I can to prevent that. He is the rottenest of fellows, but he *does* have Forrester connections."

"Thank you, Jake. I do so appreciate your help." She would have stepped away, but he would not permit her to do so.

He gave her a gentle shake. "Don't you dare go behind that stiff 'lady of the manor' facade with me," he growled and lifted her chin to settle his lips firmly on hers.

She could not help herself. All her longing of the last few weeks, her fear during this afternoon's meeting, and the essential rightness of having him here went into her response.

"That's better," he murmured at last. Then he put her reluctantly from him. "I must go. I will consult Robert and then wait for Henry and Thompkins to report."

"You will tell me—?"

"As soon as I know anything, I'll be back."

"Thank you." She pulled his head down to hers for another brief kiss before he was gone.

It was several days before Jake and Robert could deal with the problem of Brady—or Mullens, as he was now calling himself. Mullens had caught sight of Henry in one of the dockside pubs and immediately fled. Informed of this entire turn of events, Aylesworth had persuaded his niece to take up residence in Aylesworth House until the situation was fully resolved. She was not to leave the premises without the company of a burly footman.

In the meantime, Jake was faced with another emotionally wrenching problem.

He had called one afternoon to speak with Robert about the Brady-Mullens affair. Robert had engaged the Runners again and could well have new information by now. The marquis was not in, but his wife was. She had apparently been crossing the hall when she heard Jake's voice.

"Send Lord Jacob up to the west drawing room, Jeffers," she called. "And see to some refreshments for us."

"Yes, ma'am." The butler shrugged his shoulders. "You know the way, my lord."

Reluctantly, Jake climbed the stairs. He had not been alone with Celia in well over a decade, though in the early years of his voluntary exile, she had never been far from his thoughts.

"Ah, Jake. How nice to have you all to myself for a change." She was dressed in a pale green muslin with small puffed sleeves that left her arms bare. With an extremely low neckline as well, she was exposing a good deal of flesh.

"Celia." He gave her a slight bow and kissed the air above the hand she thrust at him.

"Do have a seat." She gestured to a large couch upholstered in expensive gold brocade.

Jake chose a wing chair instead, and saw a fleeting look of annoyance cross her face. He stood near the chair, waiting as she arranged herself decoratively on the couch. Jeffers brought in a tray.

"Tea? Or lemonade?" she asked.

"Tea will do nicely. A drop of milk, no sugar."

He watched as she completed this ritual with pretty gestures, but he said nothing.

"You are extraordinarily quiet this afternoon," she said, looking at him flirtatiously over the rim of her cup.

"To own the truth, I have something on my mind I had hoped Robert might help me with."

"Oh, I do hope it's not that tiresome Brady woman again."

Jake was startled at this rather crass statement, but he merely raised an inquisitive brow.

This was all the encouragement Celia needed. "Jake, dear, I know you credit her with saving your life—though, in truth, you must have been far too ill to know quite *how* ill you were or *who* was tending you."

He set his cup down. "I beg your pardon?" he asked in what another listener might have interpreted as a forbidding tone.

Ignoring this, she prattled on. "I'm sure that was the way of it. And then she came here making truly extraordinary demands on poor Robert—in your name, of course—so Robert could hardly refuse. I do dislike encroaching females, don't you?"

He spoke carefully. "I have never thought of Rachel— Mrs. Brady—in those terms."

She had caught his slip with Rachel's name. "Really, Jake, I do hope you have better taste than to allow yourself to be . . . well, fooled by such a one. Though I'll allow she's a pretty face."

"This conversation is most inappropriate," he said. "Have you any idea when Robert will return?"

"There is nothing at all inappropriate in a woman's entertaining her husband's brother. That is one of the advantages to our situation—there can be no untoward gossip about *us*."

" 'Us'? 'Our situation'? I have no idea what you are talking about, Celia." He could feel his neckcloth growing tighter.

"Oh, Jake, darling. Don't you see?" She leaned forward to allow him a full view of the perfect globes of her breasts. "I've known for years I married the wrong brother—indeed, I knew it at the time. But Robert has his heir now, and I may consider myself free to follow my first inclination."

"Celia! For God's sake!" Genuinely shocked, he stood

and picked up the gloves he had laid on a side table earlier. "I will return when Robert is at home."

She stood, too, and moved to place her hand on his arm. "Oh, come now, Jake. 'Tis the way of the *ton*. And I know you loved me."

He merely looked his objection to her hand on his arm. She removed it with a pout. He lifted his gaze to engage hers. *"Loved,* Celia. Past tense. It was a lifetime ago and does not bear remembering now. Whatever may be the habits of the *ton,* neither my brother nor I would dishonor the other in the manner you seem to suggest."

Her pretty face contorted in fury. "You think to reject *me* in favor of some grasping nobody from God knows where? I find her connection to Aylesworth *highly* suspect, and I wonder that the duchess puts up with it beneath her very nose."

"Celia, you go too far." He wanted to slap her. Instead he walked through the door and closed it firmly behind him. He heard a crash of breaking pottery. *Pity,* he thought. *That was a nice teapot.*

Two days later, the rumors finally reached Jake's ears. The gossipmongers painted Rachel as a brazen hussy, a Jezebel whose appetites and experiences knew no bounds. What was more, she had no shame. Had she not engaged in a farce of an auction for her favors in the Peninsula? An *auction,* mind you. And in a public arena. Now she had set her sights on the Duke of Aylesworth, and his duchess—poor thing—was blind to what was going on.

Jake knew precisely where these stories came from, and he was furious. And even more furious because he could not bring himself to confront Robert about his wife's behavior.

His solution was to become more marked in his attentions to Rachel. Surely if the gossips saw him as a serious suitor for Rachel's hand, they would be diverted from those horrible stories. He even spoke with Aylesworth to secure his permission to pay his addresses to the duke's niece.

Aylesworth had given him an amused smile. "You must know, Forrester, that you have little need of *my* permission. My niece is a very independent woman."

"Oh, yes. I am very aware of *that.*"

Aylesworth chuckled. "Strong-minded women make wonderful wives, but sometimes they can be infernally hard to live with."

At first Rachel seemed to welcome his attentions, but then she cooled in her attitude and when he again mentioned marriage to her, she sidestepped the question by saying she was not yet ready to discuss that idea. Still, it had not been an outright refusal.

Rachel had accompanied Charles and Libby to a musicale given by the Countess of Leland. A large affair, it was to show off the talents of several amateur musicians and featured a performance by a soprano who was the current sensation of Italian opera.

Jake arrived with his mother, his brother, and his brother's wife. All four spoke cordially to the Aylesworth party before the audience was seated, though the marchioness seemed constrained in her greeting to Rachel. Rachel gave an inward shrug, but she smiled warmly at the rest of the Lounsbury group.

She was aware of the current bizarre tales. Libby was privy to that mysterious network that included the *ton's* most successful hostesses. In the interest of merely informing Rachel of what she faced—that is, what was going on behind her back—Libby had told Rachel.

"Not to worry, my dear," Libby assured her. "This, too, will pass if we just pretend it is too preposterous to exist— which it is, of course."

"But to accuse me and Charles—!"

"I told you it is preposterous."

Rachel smiled. "Besides, everyone knows Charles is besotted with you."

"Hmm. After fifteen years . . . I'm not so sure," the duchess said, but she was obviously teasing. "However, I *am* sure his Aylesworth pride would *never* allow any scandal to ensue!"

Rachel gave an unladylike snort. "Charles Hendon's pride—notwithstanding that he loves his wife—would never allow him to be in such a position at all!"

Libby laughed. "You wigged to him quickly, my dear!"

Libby's plan for dealing with the tale-bearing, along with Lord Jacob Forrester's continued attentions to Rachel, had dampened the worst of the gossip. Jake was seen as a frequent caller in the Aylesworth drawing room. He also singled Rachel out at other affairs—like this musicale.

"The man makes no secret of *his* intentions," Charles said approvingly and then smiled at Rachel's blush.

During an intermission, Rachel visited the ladies' withdrawing room and found the Marchioness of Lounsbury apparently waiting for her as she emerged.

"Might I have a word with you, Mrs. Brady?"

"But of course," Rachel answered, puzzled.

"In here." The marchioness opened the door of what proved to be a small sitting room. Both women remained standing. Dressed in her favorite green, Lady Lounsbury was the very picture of the lady of fashion. Rachel, in a equally elegant but more conservative gown of dark blue silk, felt dowdy next to her. She again remembered Jake's calling this woman's name as he lay wounded.

"It has come to my notice," Celia said in a condescending tone, "that my husband's brother has been paying you rather marked attentions of late."

Nonplussed, Rachel floundered for a response to what bordered on being an attack. Then the other woman removed the border.

"That simply will not do," Celia went on. "The family has high ambitions for our Jake. He cannot be tainted by association with a woman of your reputation. Not even your somewhat questionable connection to Aylesworth can overshadow the sordidness of that hideous wife sale. Nor do men of any real standing go about *marrying* their mistresses."

"I think the major—Lord Jacob—is capable of handling his own affairs," Rachel finally said in what she hoped was a forbidding tone.

"Men do not always think with the organ between their ears," Celia said. "Certainly Jake is not doing so these days. If you *truly* care for him, you will do the right thing by him."

"And that is . . . ?"

"Why give it up, of course. Send him on his way. He deserves much better."

"So he does," Rachel agreed. "But I think it is not your place to dictate to him—or to me! Now, if you will excuse me—" She turned and left the room before Celia could add to her insidious discussion.

"You mark my words, now," Celia called after her.

Rachel was so furious she was shaking as she returned to her seat. Libby gave her a penetrating look.

"What is wrong? Do you wish to leave?"

"Nothing. I'll tell you later. No, I do not wish to leave." That was a lie. She wished to leave in the worst way. But leave and let that . . . that woman know she had sent her— Rachel, intrepid woman of the Peninsula—off in a panicked retreat? Never! So she sat listening, but unhearing to the rest of the presentations.

Celia was right, of course. She had said nothing that had not already occurred to Rachel. In fact, it was these very considerations that had prompted her to put off giving Jake a straight answer to his renewed offer. If she flatly refused him, she knew she would lose him. She was not yet ready to have him walk out of her life.

As long as she was out of reach as his wife, Jake had accepted the idea of her as his mistress. But she was no longer out of reach. And Jacob Forrester, she knew, would now settle for nothing less than the *wife* he wanted.

Yes. She loved him. She had always loved him, it seemed. But did she have the right to destroy his dream of a seat in Parliament, his ambition to bring about changes that would benefit many? Then it occurred to her that she was doing to Jake what others had done to her—denying him the right to make his own decision, to take his life in the direction *he* chose.

As her thinking developed along these lines, she received an unexpected visitor.

"The Dowager Marchioness of Lounsbury?" Rachel said in surprise, reading from the card the butler had given her.

Rachel and Libby had been sitting in the morning room idly reading mail and the newspapers.

"You may receive her in the blue salon, my dear. That will afford you some privacy," Libby said in a voice meant for the butler as well as Rachel.

Lady Lounsbury had shed her cloak and bonnet when she was shown into the blue salon. Rachel rose to greet her with a slight curtsy.

"Your ladyship. Please. Have a seat."

The dowager took a chair and laid aside her reticule. "I hope you will forgive my calling at this unorthodox hour, Mrs. Brady, but I felt I had to see you." She sounded very businesslike.

"Oh?" Rachel wondered if Jake's mother was here to repeat his sister-in-law's admonishments.

"You are driving my son mad. He loves you to distraction, and I perceive you are not indifferent to him."

Rachel was surprised at this forthright declaration, but she refused to dissemble. "No. I am not."

"Then what earth is the problem? Neither of you is promised to another." She paused. "You are not, are you? I *have* heard that the Viscount Mitchelson was rather earnest in his pursuit . . ."

Rachel laughed. "No, madam. I am not committed elsewhere. The viscount is a very nice—very *young*—man."

The dowager smiled. "Well, then . . . ?" When Rachel hesitated to respond, the older woman went on, "I have been afraid you might be entertaining some misguided sense of honor—what with the *on dits* that flit through so many of London's drawing rooms."

"But there is a grain of truth in some of the stories, as I am sure Jake—Lord Jacob—must have told you."

" 'Jake' is fine. You needn't stand on ceremony with me. If you mean that infamous sale—well, one cannot hold that against you. You were the *victim,* for heaven's sake. As for your working with wounded soldiers—as a mother, I cannot but be grateful to you."

"There is also the small matter of . . . of my . . . uh . . . marriage. Perhaps Jake has not told you—"

The dowager interrupted. "He told me. And I also know of Brady or Mullens—or whatever he calls himself. He is a despicable worm. But that is beside the point."

"The point being . . . ?"

"My son loves you. He is convinced that *you* are essential to his happiness. What is more, I think you love him, too."

"I do, but—"

"Then what else matters?"

Rachel told her, laying out all her own concerns for Jake's future, and ending with, "So far as I know, the gossips have not learned of the fact that the so-called widow Brady was never a wife, but when they do . . ."

"If they do. Very few people know of it. Robert has not even told his wife. Nor will he. No, I think that secret is safe, my dear."

"Hmm."

"As for your other concerns, they are not baseless, but I truly think them less significant than you believe them to be. With the Duchess of Aylesworth on your side, you need have few worries. Also, *my* credit is fairly good in certain quarters."

Suddenly, Rachel felt as though a tremendous weight had been lifted from her. Unable to contain her happiness, she smiled broadly at her visitor. "Thank you, my lady. Thank you, thank you."

" 'My Lady.' Hmm. Well, we'll work out what you should call me once you are my daughter. 'Mama,' perhaps?"

This brought tears to Rachel's eyes.

Twenty-five

"We've found him, my lord," Henry announced late one night.

Jake and his mother had just returned from a theater outing with Rachel and the Aylesworths. Jake was not surprised, but he *was* pleased that Rachel and his mother got on so well together. He had returned to their box during the intermission to find the two of them with their heads together, giggling like a couple of schoolgirls.

"Is this a private joke?" he asked.

They both looked a little guilty. "No," his mother said reluctantly, "but it is a rather catty female thing."

"Perhaps I do no want to know then," he said in a great pretense of pompous righteousness.

"Actually, we were wondering how many footmen it now takes to lace Prinny into his stays," Lady Lounsbury replied, and when she turned her twinkling eyes on Rachel, the two of them were off again.

Jake laughed and shook his head. "Why do you suppose that to be a 'female thing'? Last night two men were wondering the same thing at White's. In fact, I believe they entered a wager in the club's betting book."

This set them off yet again. "Oh, my," Rachel said, wiping her eyes. "You will tell us the result, won't you?"

Just then Aylesworth and his duchess returned and the joke had to be explained to them, too.

"I think," the duke said, totally straight-faced, "you will

find it takes only one—but he's a fellow of six feet, nine inches, weighing about twenty-two stone."

"Charles!" his wife admonished through her laughter. "If the Prince hears of your saying such a thing, he will cut you right out of the inner circle. You *know* what happened to the Beau."

"Ah, but Brummel did not pay enough heed to his audience—and I have," he said smugly.

Jake had been enjoying the memory of a pleasant evening with good entertainment and convivial company. He had even managed to drive Rachel home in his own carriage as his mother rode with the Duke and Duchess. He had, of course, thanked his clever mama for manipulating *that* turn of events. After all, it had meant several *very* satisfying kisses on the way home.

More and more he was coming to feel that the next time he pressed her to marry him, Rachel would say yes.

Now here was Henry with the news he and Robert had been anticipating.

"Brady—or Mullens—is nursing a bottle at the Hole in the Wall tavern down near the docks. Thompkins is keeping an eye on him," Henry explained.

"How long ago?" Jake asked.

"Not yet an hour, my lord, and he seemed pretty well fixed for a while. I don't think he was going anywhere."

"While I change, you ride over and tell Robert the news. I will pick you both up in the carriage. With Thompkins, that will be four of us. Should certainly be enough," Jake said.

"Yes, my lord."

"Foster," Jake called. "Have John Coachman put the grays to the carriage."

"Right away, my lord."

Jake bounded up the stairs and quickly changed into nondescript clothing that would be less conspicuous near the docks than his theater garb. He checked his pistols—three of them—and shoved one into his belt. He also slipped a knife into his boot. Jake hated knives, but just in case . . .

As he came out of his room, his mother met him in the hall. "You will be careful, won't you?"

"Yes, Mother. Don't worry." He gave her a hurried kiss on the cheek.

Robert and Henry were waiting. Henry climbed up to sit with John Coachman and give him directions.

"Needless to say," Robert said, "Celia was extremely curious about my going out at this hour. We had just come home from Holland House."

"What did you tell her?"

"Very little, but she will not leave it alone once I return."

Jake was cautious about asking his next question, but he needed to know. "Do you . . . uh . . . think she connects Rachel's Brady with Mullens and with us?"

"Not yet. But Celia is not stupid, and once we return to the manor and there are all those people who know of that maid and the farmer she married . . ." Robert ran a hand through his hair in a gesture of worry, that, had Jake been thinking about such, would have reminded him of himself.

They were both silent for several minutes as the coach rumbled over cobblestoned streets. Then Robert spoke again.

"By the way, Darby—the Runner—located the first Mrs. Brady in a village not far from Newcastle."

"The *real* Mrs. Brady, eh?"

"She and her children are on a farm with her parents, barely eking out a living. Darby said there were a two or three other half-grown youngsters as well."

"Not hers?"

"No, no. Her brothers and a sister."

"Did Darby propose our plan to her?" Jake asked.

"Yes. She is willing to go along with it. Actually, little as it is, it appears to be her best opportunity for making a life for her children."

"*If* that scoundrel cooperates."

"He will," Robert said. "He'll have no choice."

The capture of one Edwin Michael Brady Mullens proved surprisingly easy. The carriage stopped several doors down from the tavern in question. Jake, Robert, and Henry approached casually. Thompkins was just outside the door.

"He's still here?" Jake asked.

"Yes, sir. On his second bottle, he is."

"Is he alone?"

"More or less. He's sitting alone, but he seems a regular in this tavern an' he knows others."

"Where is he sitting?"

Thompkins gestured at a latticed window. "He's at a table in that corner—on your right just inside the door. Behind the door as you go in."

"Robert, you go first," Jake ordered. "He probably won't recognize you. But for God's sake, be careful. Rachel said he showed her a pistol."

"Yes, little brother," Robert said lightly.

"Henry, you and Thompkins watch our backs. Here." He handed them the two extra pistols. "They're ready. Don't use them unless you have to."

"Yes, my lord."

They went in then, Robert first. Several other patrons in the tavern looked up curiously at this invasion of four men who were dressed better than the others in the room and who moved with such authority. Noting the pistols in the hands of Henry and Thompkins, no one moved, though someone muttered an oath, followed with "What the—?"

"Edwin Mullens?" Robert asked.

"Yeah?" Mullens growled and looked up through what must have been an alcoholic haze. "Whaddya want?" Then he looked beyond Robert and saw Jake. His speech was slightly less slurred as he said, "You! What the hell do *you* want?" Then he looked back at Robert. "Ah, you must be the other one. Well, well, well. Little family gathering, eh?" He laughed bitterly.

"You're coming with us," Jake said.

"Like hell I am."

He tried to rise, moving his hand toward his waist as he did so.

Jake jumped quickly to push him back down to the bench. "Don't even think it, Brady. We've four guns on you."

"What d'ye want with me?" he whined. "You got the woman. She's yours."

With Jake on one side and Robert on the other, they lifted him under his arms to a standing position. Jake removed the pistol at Brady's waist and, knowing well the habits of soldiers, also removed a deadly knife from the man's boot.

"Now, come on," Robert said.

"No. I'm not going anywhere with you two." He tried to jerk away from their grip. "Help!" he shouted to the other patrons. "These bloody damned Forresters are kidnapping me. Don't let 'em do it. Help me!"

With Henry and Thompkins calmly holding their pistols on them, however, no one moved to answer Brady's plea. Later, Jake wondered if they would have done so even if the guns had *not* been trained on them. There was no hue and cry when the captors left the tavern with their charge.

Outside, they tied Brady's hands behind his back, and Jake gave a sharp whistle to call the coachman with the carriage. They bundled Brady into the carriage; then Jake, Robert, and Henry climbed in. Thompkins climbed up with the driver.

"Did you get him?" the dowager asked, having appeared in her own library in her dressing gown as Robert and Jake were topping off the evening with glasses of brandy.

"I'm sorry if we woke you," Robert said.

"You didn't. I could hardly sleep knowing what you two were up to. Did you find him?" She looked from one son to the other and back. Jake knew she had never thought of Robert as a *step*son.

"That we did," Robert said.

"What have you done with him?"

"Right now, he's locked in the tack room in the stable," Jake told her. "Thompkins and Ferris will keep watch and we'll decide what to do with him in the morning." Ferris was one of the young grooms.

"You should probably turn him over to the army." She went to the sideboard and poured herself a very small portion of the brandy.

"Probably," Robert said. "But that might not be in our own best interests. His relationship to us would be bound to come out, and then that supposed marriage. It would just stir up all that talk again. Wouldn't help *any* of our causes."

"Yes, I can see that," she said. "But what *will* you do?"

"That will depend on Brady—or Mullens, as he's calling himself now," Jake said.

Edwin Brady—that is, Mullens—was scared. He could not remember a time when he had been more frightened of what the future might hold. He had sworn vengeance against the Forresters and the Lounsbury title, and now he was totally in their hands. He had not expected mousy, agreeable Rachel to do anything but cooperate with him. Now it seemed she had gone straight to that bastard Forrester. Where had *she* come by enough backbone to defy him, Edwin, anyway?

He had sobered up a great deal on that carriage ride. Then they had untied him and shoved him into the tack room. There was a cot and a blanket. They had also supplied him with two buckets, one containing fresh water and a dipper. Through the cracks in the wall he could see a lantern—and his guard.

The next morning one of the guards brought him a very substantial breakfast, which he wolfed down. Edwin had not allowed himself a decent meal in days, preferring instead to *drink* his meals. Actually, he had had money for food or for drink, but not for both.

Finally, the two guards had come for him. He recognized one of them as having been Major Forrester's flunky in the Peninsula. They tied his hands behind his back again and led him to the house. He was taken to the library where both Forresters—his brothers, he thought bitterly—waited for him.

"You must be the ever-so-noble Robert," he said to the one.

"I am."

Mullens turned to Jake. "Well, *Major.*" He deliberately made the rank a word of contempt. "Are you so afraid of me that you need to keep me trussed up like a pig?"

"It is more a matter of caution than fear," Forrester replied calmly. "Give me your word you will stay put and I'll have the ropes removed. However, I feel I should warn you there will be three armed men in the hallway."

"You really *are* cautious," Edwin said, his voice again dripping contempt. "Very well. You have my word."

"Untie him, Thompkins. Then wait in the hall with Henry and Ferris."

"Yes, my lord."

"Yes, my lord," Edwin sneered as the man untied him. This earned him a wrenching tug as the rope was released. That "my lord" should have been *his* title.

"Sit down," Robert, Marquis of Lounsbury, ordered, pointing to a barrel-shaped chair. He and Forrester took chairs that faced Edwin's.

"Now," Robert began, "we are putting some options in front of you."

Jake outlined the first one. "You *might* be turned over to the nearest army provost marshal—in which case you will surely end up before a firing squad. Even in peacetime, the army hasn't much love for deserters."

"Or," Robert said, "we could turn you over to a press gang and see you shipped off to New South Wales, where it would not be difficult to ensure that you would stay."

"Some choices," Edwin sneered. "You hold all the cards. Did you have to mark the deck as well?"

Jake held up his hand. "Or, the third choice is this—you, along with your wife—your *real* wife—and two children, will be put on a ship bound for Canada."

"Canada? Bloody hell!"

"Canada," Robert affirmed. "The family has a holding there, a fur-trading establishment. Much as it pains me to admit it, you do have our blood running through your veins. You will work for our man there—and receive a fair wage."

"I may as well continue as a London dockworker," Edwin said.

"That is *not* one of your options," Jake growled.

"At the end of ten years," Robert went on, just as though there had been no interruption, "if your performance merits it—and assuming the fur business continues to show a profit—we will make you a full partner in that business—in for a full third of it—*provided* you stay in Canada and never return to England."

Fully taken aback now, Edwin shook his head in confusion. "I—I don't understand."

"We want no more scandal attached to our family name. Nor do we wish to see any connection of ours sent before a firing squad. And we want *you* out of the country."

"What's more," Jake added, "you are to do the right thing by your wife, Anna, and those two children."

"To that end," Robert went on sternly, "Anna will be told that she has only to notify us if you subject *her* to the kind of abuse you directed at another who tried to be a good wife to you. *If* you do, you may be sure local authorities will pick you up and—well, it will probably be New South Wales after all."

"Ten years?" he asked.

"Ten years of competent service," Robert said.

"You leave me little choice, so I will have to do it," Edwin said grudgingly.

"Right," Robert affirmed. "Now, if you will give us your direction, we shall send someone for your things. You will be kept here under house arrest until we actually see you on the ship bound for Canada."

"We shall send for Anna and the children immediately," Jake said. "They should be here in three days' time."

"We'll also see that you are all properly outfitted for the journey," Robert added.

"You've thought of everything, haven't you?" Edwin asked, but some of the sneer was gone from his voice.

A week later, Jake and his brother had seen their other brother on board a ship bound for Canada. Brady—that is, Mullens—Jake had a difficult time thinking of him as anything but Brady—had seemed resigned to his fate. Jake thought he might even be hopeful. And why should he not be? It was a chance to start over on entirely new footing. Brady had maintained his sullen demeanor, but his wife Anna was particularly grateful.

Just as Jake and Robert were congratulating themselves, the rumors about Rachel started again. The dowager returned one evening from a card party incensed over having been asked some rather pointed questions "about that woman calling herself Mrs. Brady."

"Mrs. Herman—we always called her 'Nosy Nora' at school—even asked me if it were true that Brady and Mullens were the same person!"

"Oh, good grief!" Jake responded. "What did you tell her?"

"I laughed and told her that was ridiculous and I wondered at her being taken in by such a humbug tale. I told her again that Brady had died in the Peninsula, but that Mullens had also served there and that the confusion probably arose from their being in the same regiment and having the same first name. I then explained that Mullens had a connection to Lounsbury's Devon estate and that my wonderfully generous sons were doing what they could to help out a brave veteran of the war against Bonaparte."

Jake hugged her. "*You* are a prize. Just enough truth there to make it work."

"Careful, darling. You're rumpling my dress." She sounded more pleased than annoyed, though.

It took little ingenuity to track down the latest rumors. Ferris, it turned out, was keeping company with one of the upstairs maids at Lounsbury House, and this maid was a bosom friend of the personal maid to the current marchioness.

Celia again, Jake thought.

Jake and his mother wracked their brains for some way to curb Celia's tongue without letting Robert know of his wife's jealous pique. However, before they could do so, Robert brought his wife for a very private afternoon call. The four of them met behind the closed door of the drawing room. With two vivid spots of color on her cheeks, Celia did not appear to be happy to be there.

"I really have no idea why we are here," Celia announced. "My dear husband seems to have a bee in his bonnet."

Ignoring her, Robert looked from his mother to Jake. "I suppose you've heard the latest *on dits?*"

Jake nodded and the dowager said, "Yes. Last night."

"And do you know where they originated?" Robert asked.

Again Jake nodded as his mother looked at Celia and answered, "We think so."

"It embarrasses me profoundly to say so, but it appears you are right," Robert said.

Celia's expression was a defiant pout. "I fail to see why you should fly into the boughs over a stupid bit of gossip about a woman who is no better than she should be—and has abused her connections to two fine families besides!"

Jake felt his face grow warm with rage. Once again he wanted to deliver his sister-in-law a sharp slap. But it was his mother who responded.

"This gossip reflects on us, as well. There are a number of issues—issues before Parliament—on which we should like to be taken seriously, and it does not help to have people so distracted. Distrust and contempt carries over from one setting to another."

Celia waved her hand in a dismissive gesture. "Politics! I care nothing for politics."

"Well, the rest of us in this family do," her husband said stonily. "These stories must stop, here and now."

"I am sure there is little to be done about it at this point," Celia said airily. "And I am equally sure that woman will involve herself again in some scandalous affair. In fact, she already has, what with her going off to that filthy hospital and associating with those vulgar sorts there. Ooh!" She exhibited an exaggerated shudder.

Her husband looked at her in disgust.

Furious, Jake rose and shook his finger under her nose. "Now, see here! We lost thousands—thousands!—of good men in the Peninsula—not to mention the other actions. Those men in hospital often left parts of their bodies on battlefields! And all to protect a way of life for the likes of you!"

"Robert!" she squeaked. "Are you going to allow him to talk to me this way?"

Robert gave her a patient look. "So far, my dear, what he has said is merely the truth."

Jake turned away, slightly chagrined by his own vehemence.

"Well!" Celia made a show of being offended, then added in a petulant tone, "Well, I don't care. No woman of any refined feeling would voluntarily subject herself to such . . . such people."

The dowager spoke softly. "I should have said that helping another human being in need is the highest form of Christian charity."

"Oh. Oh-h," Celia wailed. "You are all against me. And taking up for . . . for . . . *her.* And *I* am family!"

"If I have my way," Jake said flatly, "Rachel will become a member of this family, too."

"So you see, dear," her mother-in-law told her, "we simply must put a stop to all this talk."

Celia gave Jake an accusing look. "Can you not find someone else? Someone more . . . more respectable?"

Jake had no idea how to respond to this ridiculous question. He simply flashed his brother a sympathetic look.

"Besides," Celia went on smugly, "I cannot be held responsible for the tales people want to bandy about in their own drawing rooms."

"Perhaps not," the dowager agreed. "But you—especially

you—can do much to scotch those stories that come your way."

"Why should I wish to protect someone I find . . . objectionable?"

Robert had obviously had enough. "How about because you will find it in your own self-interest?"

"My self-interest?"

"Yes. Yours. You enjoy town life a great deal, dear wife. Well, understand this. Henry II locked *his* wife up in a tower for several years. I can certainly confine you to the country and visits with your family. *And* cut back on that very generous allowance you enjoy."

Celia blanched. "Oh, Robert, you couldn't do that to *me*."

"I *can*—and I *will*—if there is one more bit of scurrilous gossip about Rachel traceable to you. Furthermore, you will do what you can to undo the damage that has already been done."

"I still don't see—" She apparently read something in her husband's expression she had rarely seen before. "Oh, very well."

Jake thought it was clear, even to Celia, that Robert meant every word of his ultimatum. She listened to the dowager's approach to curbing the gossip and agreed—albeit reluctantly—to do her part.

Twenty-six

Jake bided his time with Rachel for the next few weeks. He was determined to give her sufficient time in which to make her own choice. To this end, he even absented himself from town for over a week, at the end of which he was dying to get back to the city, where he could at least see her.

And see her he did—at innumerable *ton* affairs. She had not been taken up as society's latest diamond of the first water, but she did enjoy a fair amount of popularity. Her acceptance was facilitated by her close ties to the Dowager Marchioness of Lounsbury and the Duchess of Aylesworth, but soon enough she was appreciated for her own quiet wit and caring personality.

Jake was pleased and proud of her blossoming at social affairs, but his pleasure and pride did not blind him to the quiet fits of jealousy he suffered at seeing her dance with another, or laugh gaily with this man, or go into supper with that one.

He tried to find some comfort in the fact that most people seemed to consider *him* the front-runner in the race—if there were one—for her affections. She always appeared glad to see him, and they had regained the easy camaraderie of those early days in Badajoz and later on the trail from Vitoria to Bayonne.

Nor was his time in town confined to frivolous social affairs. He often visited the hospital—ostensibly to check on his own men still there, but he managed often to be the one to escort Rachel to and from the hospital. While she went about her duties, he visited patients he knew or engaged in long discussions with MacLachlan and Ferguson.

For Rachel, these days brought fulfillment and satisfaction and offered the prospect of a happy future. She experienced a sense of anticipation, of waiting for something to happen.

Jake had told her the full story of what had happened with Edwin. While she knew Jake and his brother had acted from their own family concerns, she also knew Jake, at least, had acted in *her* interests. Then when the gossips were about to indulge in yet another round of whispering behind their fans, the talk had stopped. The dowager had told her enough that she knew that three of the immediate Forrester family—if not the fourth—had her welfare at heart.

For someone who had grown up without a family to speak of—and now to belong to *two* such amiable groups—it was enough to bring tears to her eyes—and occasionally did.

Rachel had become acquainted with the Hendon children, and she spent nearly as much time with them as she did in the hospital.

"I swear, Rachel, every time I wonder where you are, I find you here in the nursery," Libby exclaimed. "Perhaps I should hire you as a nursery maid!"

Rachel laughed. "You do not mind, do you? I do *so* enjoy the children."

"I do not object at all. I must own you are spoiling them dreadfully, but I imagine a mean governess or tutor will one day beat that out of them!"

"You don't mean it—" Then she realized Libby was joking.

"Of course not. Beat *my* children? Not if they hope to remain employed."

The youngest Hendon was a little boy who put Rachel poignantly in mind of Clara's Benny. She hoped his grandfather was enjoying spoiling Benny, too.

Over, beneath, and through everything she did these days

floated thoughts and dreams of Jake. Even when he was not physically present, he dominated her life. She, who had thought herself incapable of ever entrusting her future to any man, now found she could—if that man were Jake. But would he ever bring up the topic of marriage again? Or had she managed to put him off completely?

Then one afternoon he called to take her for a drive. Instead of the curricle she might have expected, he arrived in the carriage driven by his mother's coachman. And instead of going to the park, which would be full of those seeking to see and be seen at this hour, they drove out into the countryside. It was a long drive, and they talked of many things or were silent as the mood struck, but they were companionable silences.

Finally, Jake caught the coachman's attention. "Over there, John." Jake got out and handed Rachel from the carriage. They were under a great elm tree and there was a stream nearby.

"Jake! What a perfectly beautiful spot," she said. "We have such a lovely day, too. Did you *know* about this place?"

"Actually, I scouted it out," he admitted. "I thought it would suit my purposes very well."

"Your purposes?"

"In due time, my love. In due time."

The endearment went right to her heart and heightened her anticipation.

Jake reached up as John Coachman handed him a blanket and a covered basket.

"A picnic?" she asked gleefully.

"Of a sort." Then he said to the driver. "Thank you, John. Come back for us in a couple of hours."

"Yes, my lord."

Rachel blushed at seeing the coachman give Jake what looked like an encouraging smile as he urged the horses forward.

Jake set the basket down and spread the blanket under the tree. "Your couch, my lady." He held her hand as she lowered herself to the blanket, then he sat beside her.

"You *are* full of surprises," she said teasingly.

"Oh, I doubt it comes as *such* a surprise," he said. "After all, we've been here at least twice before."

"I've never been here before in my life," she insisted, spreading her hand in a sweeping gesture.

"Not there. Here." He stopped any further words by kissing her. It was a kiss of tenderness, longing, and promise. Finally, he said, "Now. *Will* you marry me?"

"Oh, Jake." She caressed his cheek and jaw with her hand. "I was beginning to think *I* was going to have to ask *you.*"

"Then you will?" Delight shone in his eyes.

"Yes, oh *yes!*" She pulled his head toward her. This time it was a kiss of fierce, raw hunger.

"Well, at last!" he said and reached for the basket. He produced a bottle of champagne and two glasses.

"You plan to get me tipsy and seduce me?" she asked hopefully.

"Certainly not, my love." He gazed at her intently. "The next time I make love, it will be with my *wife*. And the sooner the better."

She smiled. "Oh, I quite agree."

They touched their glasses and drank, holding each other's gaze over the rims.

"Good. I'm glad you agree." He pulled a paper from his pocket.

"What is this?"

"A special license."

She studied it carefully. "But . . . it is dated—" She looked up at him in dawning wonder.

"I know. I got it when I got that one for Humphrey and Luisa. If we do not use it this week, I shall have to go and get another."

"Oh, well," she said brightly, "we certainly don't want you to go to such trouble, do we?" She kissed him again and they toasted each other again.

"Rachel?" his tone was serious. "You're sure? I want you to be happy. I know you value your independence."

"I'm sure. I think . . . I think one can maintain a degree of self-sufficiency *within* a marriage—don't you? Without you, my independence would be mere loneliness."

He hugged her tightly and his eyes were bright with unshed tears of happiness. And she knew her own were as well.

"I think I'd better tell you the rest of what I have been up to of late," he said.

"Plotting and planning?" she teased.

"I've arranged for a Spanish-speaking tutor to come to the abbey to prepare Juan to go to school."

"That is good news. He is a very bright child and eager to learn. I am glad you are giving him such opportunity."

He merely nodded. "Nor have I wasted *all* my time while waiting for you at the hospital."

"I know you have visited many of the men there. And they do *so* appreciate it. Some of them never even have a visitor."

"I've also talked with Mac at length. Did you know he dreams of establishing a hospital for veterans in the country? He thinks fresh air would be most beneficial to them."

"Yes, I have even arranged to provide him some funding."

"I know."

"You do?" She was surprised, for they had not discussed this before, nor had Mac mentioned talking about his dream with Jake.

He grinned at her. "Yes, I do. And my mother plans to contribute as well. So will Aylesworth. And we are sure there will be others, also."

"How wonderful. Mac will be so happy. But . . . *where?*"

"In Wiltshire on the edge of an estate called Trenton Abbey."

"Jake! *You* are providing the land?"

"Well, I had to find *some* way to allow my wife her independence and still keep her close to me."

"And ever will she be!"

HISTORICAL NOTES

Although the practice was medieval in origin, wife selling existed among the lower classes in England throughout the eighteenth century and well into the nineteenth. It has been called "the poor people's divorce." Perhaps it may be viewed as a prelude to the "no fault" divorce of modern times. A public event, arranged by mutual consent, a wife sale was conducted largely to absolve the husband of financial responsibilities for his spouse as she went off to live with another man.

Illegal in both ecclesiastical and secular courts, wife selling was widely condemned in the public press and members of Parliament sometimes railed against it, but it was recognized and accepted by the working classes. Lawrence Stone suggests the practice was more notorious than actually prevalent. He notes only three hundred recorded sales and says some of those cases are doubtful. The practice reached its peak in the 1820s and 1830s; the last recorded instance occurred in 1887.

The sale was conducted as a cattle sale and often took place at a market fair where animals were sold. Both the price and the buyer were usually prearranged. The wife was led to the "sale" with a symbolic halter around her neck and led away by her new "owner." [See Lawrence Stone: *The Family, Sex, and Marriage in England 1500–1800* (1979); *Road to Divorce* (1990); *Broken Lives* (1993).] Thomas Hardy dealt with wife selling in *The Mayor of Casterbridge*.

I know of no recorded instance of wife selling among Wellington's forces in the Peninsula, but the idea is not inconceivable.

Regarding the Peninsula Campaign: I have taken few liberties with the basic facts and the timeline of Wellington's struggles in Iberia, but I have tried to add credible details of daily living.

Some may quarrel with Rachel's being readily accepted by London society on her return to England. However, she had the backing of a duke and a marquis—and this was the Regency, not Victorian England. The Regent's marital problems were well known, with public and peers alike taking sides. Regency society also accepted Lady Caroline Lamb, overlooking her sometimes bizarre antics. Surely they would have accepted the quietly generous Rachel.

ABOUT THE AUTHOR

WILMA COUNTS, who now lives in Nevada, spent many years in Germany teaching dependents of American military personnel stationed there. Widely traveled, she directed students in the Model United Nations program, and she values the friendship that resulted from an exchange program with a Russian school. She is currently working on her next historical set in the Regency period. Look for it in July, 2003! Wilma loves hearing from readers, and you may write her c/o Zebra Books. Please include a self-addressed stamped envelope if you wish a response, or you may contact her on the internet, wilma@ableweb.net

Embrace the Romances of
Shannon Drake

__Come the Morning $6.99US/$8.99CAN
0-8217-6471-3

__Blue Heaven, Black Night $6.50US/$8.00CAN
0-8217-5982-5

__Conquer the Night $6.99US/$8.99CAN
0-8217-6639-2

__The King's Pleasure $6.50US/$8.00CAN
0-8217-5857-8

__Lie Down in Roses $5.99US/$6.99CAN
0-8217-4749-0

__Tomorrow the Glory $5.99US/$6.99CAN
0-7860-0021-4

Call toll free **1-888-345-BOOK** to order by phone or use this coupon to order by mail.
Name_____
Address_____
City_____ State _____ Zip _____
Please send me the books that I have checked above.
I am enclosing $_____
Plus postage and handling* $_____
Sales tax (in New York and Tennessee) $_____
Total amount enclosed $_____
*Add $2.50 for the first book and $.50 for each additional book. Send check or money order (no cash or CODs) to:
Kensington Publishing Corp., 850 Third Avenue, New York, NY 10022
Prices and numbers subject to change without notice.
All orders subject to availability.
Check out our website at **www.kensingtonbooks.com**.

The Queen of Romance

Cassie Edwards

__Desire's Blossom 0-8217-6405-5	$5.99US/$7.99CAN
__Exclusive Ecstasy 0-8217-6597-3	$5.99US/$7.99CAN
__Passion's Web 0-8217-5726-1	$5.99US/$7.50CAN
__Portrait of Desire 0-8217-5862-4	$5.99US/$7.50CAN
__Savage Obsession 0-8217-5554-4	$5.99US/$7.50CAN
__Silken Rapture 0-8217-5999-X	$5.99US/$7.50CAN
__Rapture's Rendezvous 0-8217-6115-3	$5.99US/$7.50CAN

Call toll free **1-888-345-BOOK** to order by phone or use this coupon to order by mail.

Name_____

Address_____

City_____ State _____ Zip _____

Please send me the books that I have checked above.

I am enclosing	$_____
Plus postage and handling*	$_____
Sales tax (in New York and Tennessee)	$_____
Total amount enclosed	$_____

*Add $2.50 for the first book and $.50 for each additional book. Send check or money order (no cash or CODs) to:

Kensington Publishing Corp., 850 Third Avenue, New York, NY 10022

Prices and numbers subject to change without notice.

All orders subject to availability.

Check out our website at **www.kensingtonbooks.com**.